A FEVERISH PASSION

"When you act like a child, sir, you should expect to be treated like one," snapped Olivia. "You must go home at once. I am certain you have a fever. You cannot be here!"

"Why can I not be here, Olivia?" his husky voice purred.

"Because you are ill and—I will not have you suffer more!" Olivia stamped her dancing slipper with the jewelled heel and then gasped as Abbercombe's arm went about her waist and he tugged her against him. He brought his lips softly down upon hers. Shocked, she struggled and he released her. Her palm flew up to slap his face, but she found herself unwilling to do so. "How dare you?" she cried instead, her hand fluttering across the bodice of her gown.

"I beg your pardon, Olivia," the duke whispered. "I could not help myself. You must be correct. I have savaged my health by coming here, and even now I am delirious."

Olivia scowled, only to see his eyes twinkling in the moonlight and his mouth twitching helplessly into a beguiling grin. "You are shameless," she scolded, coerced into a giggle.

"Yes, I know. I cannot account for it, Miss Weebuttonsmite, but the moment a lovely lady rings a peal over me, my senses go reeling." Once again his arm came about her waist and he drew her to him. His eyes gazing steadily into hers, he pressed his lips gently against her own, and this time she did not pull away. Her arms went about his neck and she kissed him back.

The Bedeviled Duke

Judith A. Lansdowne

ZEBRA BOOKS
KENSINGTON PUBLISHING CORP.

To Al, my much-Bedeviled Husband:
you are my Rogue, my Hero.
I love you.

ZEBRA BOOKS are published by

Kensington Publishing Corp.
850 Third Avenue
New York, NY 10022

Copyright © 1996 by Judith A. Lansdowne

Zebra and the Z logo Reg. U.S. Pat. & TM Off.

First Printing: April, 1996

Printed in the United States of America

10 9 8 7 6 5 4 3 2 1

One

Booming thunder drowned the string of expletives that escaped from Abbercombe's grimly pursed lips as lightning felled the branch of an oak directly before him and the trembling bit of blood he rode reared in fright. He settled the animal; tugged his greatcoat collar tighter about his neck; tipped his head forward to let a stream of chill rain water run from the tip of his wide-brimmed hat onto the half-frozen, half-muddied quagmire of an English road upon which he found himself; and sneezed halfheartedly. The Rose and Crown should be no more than a mile ahead. He guided the quaking chestnut around the fallen branch and they plodded onward, he shivering as much with cold and exhaustion as the horse did with fear.

The truth was that Abbercombe had not recovered from his trip across the channel where a churning, white-capped sea had kept him racked in agony over the rail of the *Peregrine*. Furthermore, he should not have set off from Portsmouth to London so soon. Still, if the weather had held, he might even now have been settled before a comforting fire in the parlor of Fielding House on Great Stanhope Street. But what had promised to be fine weather had turned foul and his speed had decreased.

In his salad days, he mused, adjusting himself in the damp saddle, he would have known every rut in the road and neither storm nor approaching darkness would have slowed him to less than a gallop. But he was no longer a neck-or-nothing stripling, and he was more than willing, at the moment, to settle for the

Rose and Crown and a snifter of brandy and let London wait for tomorrow.

When at last he sighted the inn its size bewildered him. What he had known as a hedge tavern with a few rooms to let had become an edifice three stories high with leaded glass windows and stables large enough to house a hundred horses. Two hostlers appeared immediately as he entered the yard and took his mount in charge. Abbercombe then stomped through gullies of rainwater past three traveling coaches, a phaeton, four curricles and a gig to reach the steps into the public room. That chamber had grown as well and he came to an abrupt standstill inside the entrance. An amused light sprang into his eyes and his lips twitched. His hands on his hips, he looked quickly down at his mud-covered boots to keep from laughing aloud at the absurd contrast he must make to the finely-dressed gentlemen ranged about two blazing hearths, glasses in hands and voices raised in conversation.

"Be there somethin' wi' which I kin help ye, milord?"

Abbercombe looked up and smiled at a rotund personage in a wide white apron.

"Bill Wentworth's me name," stated the man, eyeing Abbercombe oddly. "I be the host o' this here establishment, an' yer more'n welcome ta bide awhile an' warm yerself by the fire. Thing is, we ain't got no rooms, milord. Rooms bin all reserved up like fer weeks. There be a mill termorrow near here." The brandy-faced innkeeper paused, and taking a deep breath, rubbed at the back of his neck. "Ye'll pardon me seemin' forward, milord," he began again, "but I got this feelin' that I be acquainted o' ye. Still, I kinnot quite place ye in me mind. The moment I laid eyes upon ye, I come a thinkin' how I should be havin' yer name upon me tongue."

"I am amazed at your memory," Abbercombe grinned, stripping off his wet gloves and extending a cold, damp hand in the landlord's direction. "You could not have been more than seven the last I saw you and everyone called you Willy then. You were a great deal shorter at the time and much less, ah, round."

Bill Wentworth's eyebrows rose in surprise as he took the proffered hand. He studied the gentleman's face intently. "Why, I'll be swagged," he snorted, releasing the hand. "Lord Warren! I niver thought ta see the day! Come in. Come in, milord, an' I'll fix ye a spot by the fire an' ye'll drink what ye like on the house. Do ye be needin' a room? O' course ye do. Be maggot-headed to travel farther tonight in sich a storm as this. I'll be sendin' Molly ta turn down me own bed an' put a warmin' pan atween the sheets fer ye."

"A glass of brandy wouldn't come amiss or a place by the fire, and I admit a bed would be highly desirable—but I cannot take yours, Willy."

"Ye will, milord. Me father swore as he'd always have a room fer ye. 'In chains er outta 'em', he tole me, 'the Marquis o' Warren be welcome here, an' a pillow be a waitin' fer his head.' "

"Well, I'm honored by the thought, Willy, ah, Bill, but I am not the Marquis of Warren anymore."

"Ye may call me Willy, milord, an' it don't make no niver mind ta me do ye be a marquis er a mouse. Ye've a room here what's bin a waitin' on ye since eighty-nine."

"Thank you," smiled the bemused Abbercombe. "I'm grateful."

"An' ye'd like to be a changin' out o' them wet things, milord. Come wi' me, an' I'll see to gettin' ye settled in."

"I'm afraid I've nothing to change into," Abbercombe sighed. "My trunks lie at Portsmouth and I've nothing in my saddle bags any less damp and scummy than what I'm wearing."

"Bosh," grinned the landlord clapping a hand on Abbercombe's shoulder and tugging him toward the stairs, "we'll find ye somethin' as is warm an' dry, milord. Might not be in the height o' fashion, but ye'll feel a might better fer it."

"If ye don't mind me askin'," Wentworth ventured a while later as he assisted a bathed and dried Abbercombe into one of his own warm woolen coats, "how come ye ain't a marquis no more, milord? I didna know the bullies could strip that title from ye."

"No, they could not," Abbercombe replied, tying a Belcher neckerchief roguishly at his throat. "It is just that my father died five years ago and so I am now Duke of Abbercombe." He laughed aloud at the sight of the landlord's wide eyes. "Do not cease to be my friend because of it, Willy. I have very few friends in England, and I should regret losing even one of them."

"Lord a'mighty," breathed Wentworth, "I'm a standin' here helpin' ta dress a duke in me own duds."

"Indeed. A very obliged duke. I do not believe I have been warm since I boarded *Peregrine* on the other side of the channel, and I know I have not been dry since late this morning. I look a quiz, Willy. Shall we go below and try the brandy? You will drink with me, will you not?"

"Wi' ye an' to ye," Wentworth asserted with a sharp nod. "An' the divil take those as would not!"

Bryan Kettering was not the first to notice Abbercombe's descent into the public room—in stockinged feet, a pair of breeches much too large and too short, a voluminous cambric shirt, and a brown wool jacket with sleeves that extended to his fingertips and which he was attempting to roll back to a decent length—but he was the first to break into laughter at the sight.

The duke glanced across the room and winked broadly at him, then allowed himself to be escorted to a seat before one of the fires and installed there with a glass of brandy in his hand. Wentworth, with a ceremonious bow, toasted Abbercombe with a glass of his own, then hurried off to serve his other patrons. Resting his head against the high back of the chair, the duke stretched his legs out before him and gazed silently into the fire. He sipped the brandy slowly and expertly and relished each drop of it. As always, he was aware of every person, movement, and sound in the chamber, but he shut his mind to them and sank into a world of his own making.

"Who is he?" Kettering asked quietly of his companions. "Some relation of Bill?"

"Doubtful," offered Lord Goddering, sipping at a glass of rack punch. "Perhaps one of the country squires?"

"No, the man's French," protested John Westbury. "Did you not note that greatcoat he wore when he first entered? All the crack on the continent. Expensive as well."

"One of the aristocrats, you think, Westbury? Escaped the guillotine with his fortune intact?" Goddering put his quizzing glass to his eye and studied the figure lounging before the hearth. "Don't look French. Blond for one thing."

"Well, Frogs are blond. Some Frogs."

"Name one," Goddering prompted and laughed as Westbury stuttered and came up empty.

"Old enough to be my father," Kettering observed. "But Westbury's right, he don't look at all the country squire, not even dressed in Bill's clothes."

"Well, I don't much care who he is," came a fourth voice into the conversation. "What I want to know is how he got himself a room in this establishment three minutes after he walked in when Bill's been turning people away all day, saying he was full-up because of the mill tomorrow."

"Right you are, Hastings," agreed Lord Goddering with a nod. "All the rooms have been reserved."

"Maybe he reserved one of them," shrugged Kettering.

"And turned up with only the clothes on his back? I hardly think so," Hastings protested. "Man arrives with no valet, no luggage, and, I'd lay odds, no reservation, and Bill gives him his own clothes and a private room. Got to be somebody important. Why, Bill was stunned to see him, didn't you notice? For a moment or two he looked like he'd seen a ghost."

Abbercombe stirred in the chair, set the empty brandy glass down upon a side table and rose to his feet. Then he thrust his hands into his breeches pockets and strolled back toward the stairs. He had heard the final part of Hastings' comment and, reluctant to excite any further curiosity, chose instead to depart the company and put himself to bed. A multitude of gazes followed him, for more than one group of young bucks had been discussing his identity, and several wagers had already been laid.

"Milord, your grace," Wentworth's voice echoed across the large room as Abbercombe reached the third stair, "will ye not have some dinner? A tray in yer room per'aps?"

Abbercombe declined with a shake of his head and continued up to the small room under the eaves.

"My lord, your grace?" whispered several voices around the room, including Kettering's.

"Here, Bill," Lord Goddering called, once Abbercombe had disappeared into the upper regions, "which of the dukes did he tell you he was?"

The host stared at the eager faces. "Well, now," he replied, assuming a defiantly proud stance, "he's the Duke of Abbercombe, is who he is, though he warn't when first I knowed him. The Marquis o' Warren he was then, an' demme if it ain't time he was a gettin' back home."

"Devil you say," hissed Kettering. "M'father will fall into an apoplexy when he hears this. Abbercombe returned to England!"

In the tidy little room at the rear of the third floor overlooking the garden, which he could not see except when the lightning flashed, Abbercombe was sincerely regretting his decision. He had for years been adamant about remaining in exile and never would have set foot on English soil again if he had not promised Celia, in her last moments, that he would see the girls given every opportunity to contract a desirable marriage. It had not occurred to him then—in fact, had not occurred to him at all until Amaryllis and Bethany had brought up the matter themselves—that they would wish to meet and perhaps marry English gentlemen. What a fool he must have looked when they spoke of travelling to England to experience the elegance and excitement of a London Season.

"You cannot mean it," he had whispered, stunned. "A Season in London? Have you not met enough gentlemen in all the places we have lived? Cannot you like any of them enough to marry? I have been tripping over your beaux for the last year."

Still, he had promised Celia. And so he had sent his agents to ready Fielding House and had even gone so far as to address a letter to his brother announcing his intended return. But he had held out hope through it all that something would happen to prevent the accomplishment of those plans. However nothing had happened and here he was, ill-at-ease, already the subject of unbridled curiosity, ensconced in Bill Wentworth's chamber at the Rose and Crown, and wishing with all his heart to be elsewhere.

Miss Olivia Willburton-Smythe had never dreamed of being elsewhere in her entire life. The daughter of the third son of an earl, the sister of a captain in the First Hussars, and the granddaughter of a countess, her life had been spent upon English soil. She could imagine no reason to leave it. Settled for a coze in Lady Jessica Denbigh's charming rose and gold drawing room, with a cup of tea on the small cricket table beside her, she scowled meaningfully at her hostess.

"I, for one, shall have nothing to do with those young women," she proclaimed, her emerald-green eyes flashing. "It is common knowledge, Jessica, that their father is an abominable rogue and the twigs cannot fall far from the tree."

Lady Jessica sighed, nervously fingering the low neckline of her pretty jonquille gown. She knew she should not have spoken of Abbercombe's letter, but sharing confidences with Olivia had become habitual. "*I* shall have to acknowledge them, you know," she whispered apprehensively. "They are my nieces after all."

"I do not think, my dear, that Sebastian should expect it of you," pronounced Olivia decisively. "No one of Quality will accept them, and you will suffer for it if you do. I would not be surprised if the more influential hostesses were to cut you from their invitation lists. And as for Sebastian, his standing for Parliament must certainly be at stake should he display the least acceptance of Abbercombe."

"But Abbercombe is his half brother, Olivia. Sebastian cannot ignore him. And—and—he does not wish to do so."

Miss Willburton-Smythe shook her dusky curls in consternation and raised the fine china teacup to her lips. She said nothing until she had replaced the cup upon the cherrywood table. "I would not be put in such a position for all the world, Jessica. They say Abbercombe is the devil himself, and to be asked to present his daughters into Polite Society—"

"But he has not asked me to present them," Lady Jessica interrupted hurriedly. "Though how he imagines to give them a Season without a proper *entrée* into the *ton,* I cannot imagine. Celia's family are all deceased and I can think of no one for him to turn to in such a matter other than myself."

"Jessica, to be seen chaperoning Abbercombe's daughters about town will most certainly sink you! It is too much! You must speak to Sebastian. He cannot expect you to acknowledge them!"

The truth was that Lady Jessica had already had a very long discussion with her husband, and Sebastian Denbigh did, indeed, expect her to acknowledge his nieces—and his brother as well. "For you will remember, Jess," he told her adamantly, "that we should have been in bad loaf if Cash had not provided us with his support when father died. Moreover, he is my brother and I have not seen him in twenty-two years, and I have never seen his children. I will not be kept from him for fear of some crotchety old gossip mongers and busybodies."

Olivia noticed the apprehension that spread across her friend's lovely countenance as Lady Jess mused silently over her husband's wishes. The sweet face became so forlorn that Olivia regretted her previous tone. She was not callous and she could see that her first response to the news of Abbercombe's approaching arrival was causing Lady Jessica anxiety. "Come now, Jess, do not put so much stock in what I say," she urged, a becoming dimple appearing in one cheek. "You know I am outspoken and apt to say too much before I stop to think. It is one of the reasons I am on the shelf, I have no doubt."

"You are not on the shelf," protested Lady Jessica quietly, her solemn brown eyes seeking solace from Olivia's bright green ones. "You have just not met the right man, Olivia."

"I am thirty-one and have not met the right man," smiled that lady. "I think that puts me on the shelf, my dear. Lord Sebastian has made you promise to acknowledge the girls, hasn't he?"

"Yes. And he is perfectly correct, you know. They are his family and Abbercombe has been most generous to us. He bought us this house, you know, because I could not bear to live at that dreadful place in Yorkshire, and he gives us free run of his estate in Somerset as well. It would be unforgivable of us to cut him or his children. Olivia," she added plaintively, "do you know why Abbercombe was transported?"

"Do you not?" Miss Willburton-Smythe responded in surprise.

"No, only that it was something dreadful. Even Sebastian does not know. He was only ten at the time and no one would explain to him what had happened. And afterwards his father would not hear Cash spoken of."

"Did he not think simply to ask his brother?"

"I think he feared to mention it. They corresponded only thrice that I know of—when Celia died, when their father died, and this last letter announcing Abbercombe's intention to come to London. We did not even know that he had daughters until this last message. And I have no idea of their ages, though the youngest must be at least seventeen, don't you think? Even Abbercombe would not dare to introduce his daughters into society at a younger age. It would be most exceptionable."

"But *he* is most exceptionable," sighed Olivia. "Perhaps their ages have not even crossed his mind. Now that I come to think of it, Jess, I believe I was wrong. I think you should acknowledge the girls. Not merely because Lord Sebastian asks you to do so, but only think how hard it must be for them to live with such a monster. I have no doubt they are in dreadful need of love and understanding and a woman's hand, for Celia has been dead at least six years, has she not? And they have had to deal with that devil all alone. Yes, I am determined we shall both acknowledge them. It is most unfair to lay their father's sins upon them without at least making their acquaintances."

A grateful smile crept into Lady Jessica's eyes. "You are doing this for me, Olivia," she murmured, "and your reputation shall sink quite as low as mine. No, I will not allow it."

"Nothing shall sink me," proclaimed Miss Willburton-Smythe. "I have been too long upon the town with never a rumor of scandal to my name. I am well-cemented in Polite Society, Jess, and for once, I shall take advantage of it."

"Olivia? You have not told me. What did Abbercombe do? Why did they send him off in chains?"

Miss Willburton-Smythe's emerald eyes glowed fiercely. "He beat a man to death in a gambling den in Seven Dials."

"Oh!" gasped Lady Jessica, the color draining from her face.

The following afternoon, Dawson, newly appointed butler to the Duke of Abbercombe, took a very deep breath, straightened his shoulders, lifted his chin, and lowered his eyelids slightly, hoping to appear both competent and imposing. Below him in the courtyard, the cause of these adjustments handed the reins of his mount into the care of a waiting groom, took the marble steps two at a time, and extended his kidskin-gloved hand. Flustered, Dawson paused in the midst of a bow, extended his own hand in return and found it strongly clasped and shaken. "Anthony Dawson, I presume," the duke said in a soft, low voice. "I regret there is no one present to introduce us. Lowery follows with the carriages. I could not very well leave the children with no one to accompany them."

"No, your grace. Would your grace care to meet the staff?" Dawson's eyebrows had risen slightly at the disheveled state of his grace's riding clothes, but he forced them back into place. Caught in last night's storm, he thought. Some boot boy at an inn did what he could, which wasn't much.

"My apparel misses Fanning's touch, does it not?" the duke

asked, watching Dawson's eyebrows settle. "Fanning did arrive?"

"Yes, your grace. Indeed. Mr. Fanning arrived last Monday night. He is not here at present, having gone to make some purchases on your behalf." Dawson blinked and stared up into a pair of brilliant blue eyes sparkling with mirth.

"Do not look so somber, Dawson. I am not going to eat you, you know—nor murder you in your bed."

Stripping his gloves from his hands, Abbercombe gave them, along with his rain battered hat, into Dawson's care. "I shall meet the staff later, when you have had sufficient leisure to muster them." He nonchalantly shoved his riding crop into a boot top and strode into the hall. His finely-featured face was saved from effeminate beauty by a duelling scar below one eye and a twice broken nose; and his broad shoulders, graceful stance, and trim, well-muscled physique all belied his years, as did the energetic bounce in his step.

"I should like to speak to you and the housekeeper first, if I may. Perhaps you will fetch her and come to the library? But first you must escort me to that chamber, for I have not been in this house in over twenty years and seldom before then, and I do not quite remember where the library is."

Dawson preceded his employer up the wide, curving, carpeted staircase and down the long corridor to the center of the house where he opened the door upon a dark, book-lined room. With a bow, he stood aside and Abbercombe strolled past him into the room. "What, by the way, is my housekeeper's name, Dawson? I fear Lowery neglected to inform me."

"Mrs. Griffin, your grace."

"Thank you. Fetch her please."

A few moments later Dawson reappeared accompanied by a nervous, plump, elderly woman. With an infectious grin Abbercombe welcomed her into his presence and insisted she settle herself into a lyre-backed rosewood chair. He urged Dawson to a seat as well and then pulled up a ladder-backed chair facing them. Swinging the chair around, he straddled it, his long, admirably shaped legs stretching out before him. Dawson's eyebrows rose in disapproval. "I think, Dawson, that you must be most patient with me," Abbercombe chuckled. "If you are going to raise your eyebrows every time I do or say something unbecoming to a duke, you will never get them to settle down."

"Yes, no, yes, your grace."

"I do not mean to tease you, Dawson, but the truth is that I am not in your general run of noblemen and I shall undoubtedly disappoint you if you expect too much of me at first. Mrs. Griffin, I trust Lowery or Holt has informed you that my children will be residing here?"

"Yes, your grace," nodded the housekeeper, her fine grey eyes meeting his expectantly. "Yourself and the children, Mr. Lowery said."

"And did Lowery tell you anything about the children before you agreed to take us on?"

"Your grace?" Mrs. Griffin's eyebrows danced upwards in a good imitation of Dawson's.

"No, I thought not. I knew he had not found it expedient to make a particular point of them to Dawson and I feared he had forgotten to bring them to your attention as well. You do not mind children in the house?"

"Not at all, milord duke. Fond of young ones I am."

"And you, Dawson? Numerous small ones under your feet will not drive you to distraction? They are all well-behaved, I promise you, but not, shall we say, without a vast amount of energy and ingenious ways of expending it."

"I anticipate no problem, your grace."

Abbercombe laughed and the sound seemed to Mrs. Griffin to lighten and brighten the stuffy old room and make it almost cozy. "It will be nice to have children about," she smiled.

"Yes, well, there are eight of them, Mrs. Griffin," grinned the duke, "and they do tend to be about—everywhere."

Mrs. Griffin gasped. "Eight, milord? Good heavens, and I was told to ready only four bedchambers besides your own!"

"Exactly so. They have always shared their chambers and will again. You are certain they will not frighten you away though? I have seen their mere existence lose me housekeepers before."

"I am not so easily intimidated, your grace."

"And you, Dawson? Can I depend upon you to remain as well?"

"Most assuredly, your grace," nodded the butler intrepidly. "I shall find it most stimulating I am sure."

Late the following afternoon four coaches drew up in the forecourt of Fielding House and poured forth a veritable tide of humanity. Urging himself to remain calm, Dawson sent all ten footmen out to aid in the unloading of the travelers' luggage.

"Do not panic, Dawson," the duke whispered as he strode up beside him. "They are somewhat intimidating at first, but you shall rapidly grow accustomed to them."

"Papa!" called a sweetly husky voice as a young lady dressed in the finest of Parisian traveling costumes rushed up the marble steps and flung herself into the duke's arms. This vision of loveliness, with bright golden curls and smiling blue eyes, Abbercombe lifted from the ground and swung in a complete circle. The moment he set her down, he was confronted by an identical young lady in an equally fetching traveling costume who threw herself into his arms with the same abandon. This vision, too, he lifted from the ground and swung around in a violent hug.

Swiftly upon her descent, four bewilderingly similar children tore madly up the steps and shouted at the top of their lungs that their papa had been unfair to ride ahead, that they had barely had a chance to speak with him since they had sailed for England, that they had seen a reg'lar out an' outer graze by the coaches in a curricle with horses in tandem, and that they were exceptionally hungry. The duke, without comment, lifted each of them separately, kissed them soundly, and tossed them, giggling, into the hall behind him. Almost immediately two lean, eager striplings dashed up the steps and were enveloped in a rough bearhug.

"I believe, Dawson, it might be an excellent idea to send for Mrs. Griffin," the duke grinned as he released these two. "The children are quite capable of settling themselves in once they know which rooms are to be theirs."

Abbercombe spent the rest of the afternoon and evening conferring with his solicitors over the qualifications for a governess, a tutor, and two abigails; devouring a six course dinner with four removes in the elegance of the formal dining room with all of his progeny present; and indulging in a cigar and a bottle of Madeira while he read the *Post* in the comfort of his study. He then kissed the four youngest of his brood goodnight, tucked them in, and now stood glaring into the mirror in his dressing room inspecting the fit of a coat his valet had purchased for him.

"It is all the crack, your grace. I assure you," pleaded Fanning, swiping a hand through his hair.

"Perhaps for some buck in his twenties, Robin."

"London is not like Paris, my lord."

"No. Nor is it like Vienna, St. Petersburg, or Boston, but why I must stuff myself into this coat because of it, you will have to explain to me. Gads, Robin, I cannot shrug my way out of the thing alone. Come help me."

"No, your grace, I will not."

Abbercombe turned from the mirror to glare at Fanning.

Fanning crossed his arms and stood firm. Rudolph Casimir Denbigh and he had argued and debated and proclaimed their own positions on fashion through twenty-five years and ten countries and Robin Fanning was not about to give in now. "There is no reason to help you out of it, your grace, unless you have changed your mind and intend to remain at home. You are perfectly attired. Your cravat is excellent, your waistcoat wonderfully understated, your pantaloons exactly as they should be, your boots incredible, and your coat, spectacular. You are the essence of British manhood."

"Well, I do not wish to be the essence of British manhood, Robin. I wish to be comfortable."

"You are comfortable, my lord duke. You wish to be shabby."

"No, not shabby, Robin. But it would be nice if the blood in my shoulders had room to circulate, don't you think?"

"I have seen here, sir, at least a hundred gentlemen who would give everything they own to possess such shoulders and to have them displayed to such perfection, circulation or no!"

"Damnation, Robin, if you are not the stubbornest man alive!"

"Indeed, your grace."

"Indeed, Robin. No, put that hat back. I shall not wear a hat, nor do I want this fool cane. Get rid of it, if you please."

"Yes, your grace." Fanning smiled. Having won the battle of the coat, he was more than willing to concede the hat and cane. "May I know where you are bound?"

"I am bound for hell," muttered the duke, buckling a thin, delicately balanced sabre about his waist. "Which hell is the problem. But I shall find an acceptable one, you may lay odds upon it. Will you ask Dawson to leave a candle for me in the front hall? I do not expect to return before dawn."

"Yes, your grace. I will see he is informed."

Two

Jack Sloan stared at the gentleman with the ash blond curls blowing across his brow. A vague remembrance of the finely-sculpted face nagged at him. White's Club admitted to their hallowed halls only members and their guests, and Jack Sloan, as keeper of the gate, prided himself on knowing every one of the members. "I beg your pardon," he said, as the gentleman's lips tilted in an accepting grin, "but—"

"It's perfectly all right, Jack. I have no intention of invading the place. I merely thought you might know where I could find a game. I do not require it be honest, just open to me."

At the sound of that soft voice, Sloan's expression flickered from doubt to recollection to amazement. "My gawd!" he exclaimed, grasping the gentleman's hand and shaking it enthusiastically. "I never thought to see the day! Welcome home, my lord, only it's your grace now, ain't it? It's pleased as punch I am to see you."

"Likewise, Jack. Can you point me in the right direction?"

"Aye, your grace, through this door, and turn right."

"No, I couldn't go in there."

"Certainly ye could. You're still a member o' this club. I don't recall your name being withdrawn."

"It wasn't?"

"No, sir, and there's those inside'd be pleased to see ye."

The duke retrieved his hand from Sloan's grip. "Another time, Jack, when I am more courageous. What I need now is a hell where no one knows me. But I don't seem able to distinguish the gaming establishments from the bordellos these days."

"Brothels, your grace."

"Pardon?"

"Brothels in England, your grace; bordellos in France."

Sloan attempted again to urge the duke into White's but, finding Abbercombe immovable, set about to explain where several of the more notorious gaming establishments were located.

"That's him," Kettering hissed, tugging at his brother's arm as they approached White's.

"Who?"

"Him! Abbercombe!"

"Can't be," Viscount Harcort mumbled, staring at the gentleman who conversed with Sloan on the landing above them. "Abbercombe is as old as father—older."

"It's him," Kettering insisted. "I swear it, Davey."

The two gentlemen watched as the duke thanked Sloan for his assistance, then turned on his heel and departed the premises. They followed him at a discreet distance as he strolled through the lamplit streets to a haunt in Pickering Place next to Berry Brothers and Rudd, where he spent two hours relieving that establishment of well over twenty thousand pounds.

"I cannot see how he does it," Kettering whispered to his brother as Abbercombe pocketed his winnings and strolled toward the door. "He must be the luckiest man alive."

"Don't believe it has anything to do with luck, Bry. A real dab at the games, he is. Be barred from play here soon." Harcort paid the tab and he and Kettering exited the establishment. They followed the duke down three streets before Abbercombe halted and faced them, one hand falling to the hilt of his sabre. "Clearly you are not footpads," he said quietly, "for I've given you every opportunity to rob me. Now, would one of you care to explain why you have been in my shadow since I left White's?"

The two gentlemen stared at each other apprehensively.

"Come now," urged Abbercombe, "answer, or I shall be forced

to investigate with the point of my sword, and that would be extremely regrettable, don't you think?"

It was Harcort who laughed aloud. "Extremely regrettable, your grace. Shouldn't like it a bit. I beg your pardon," he added, "but my little brother is determined to know you and cannot come upon a reasonable way to go about it, and so I have been humoring him by trailing in your footsteps all evening."

Bryan glared at David and then raised his eyes sheepishly to Abbercombe's bemused countenance.

"Is this true?" Abbercombe asked.

"Yes, sir. I have been determined to make your acquaintance since I saw you at the Rose and Crown, but there don't seem to be a reasonable way to do it."

This time Abbercombe laughed, but his hand remained upon his sword hilt. "Then I believe you must take advantage of this most unreasonable opportunity. Introduce yourself."

"Kettering, sir. Bryan Kettering. And this is my brother, Viscount Harcort."

"David," interjected his brother with a nod.

"What? The Earl of Stamford's boys?"

"Yes, sir," they answered simultaneously.

Abbercombe's hand released the sabre hilt. "You've no business to make my acquaintance. Were your father to learn of it, he'd like as not have you beheaded."

Harcort extended his hand in Abbercombe's direction. "You know my father well, your grace. Will you not take my hand?"

"I do not think so," replied the duke with a twisted smile. "You would likely regret it. Has your father not warned you to stay clear of me? Or has my presence not yet reached his ears?"

"Oh, he knows you've returned," Kettering offered. "I told him myself the minute I got back to town. I never saw the old man in such high dudgeon as when I gave him that news."

"Then you should know better than to seek my acquaintance."

"But that's exactly why I do, sir, and David, too, though he won't admit it. Anyone who could raise father's ire to such a height simply by coming to London must be worth knowing.

Will you join us in a glass of wine? There's a tavern down the way."

Abbercombe gave an abrupt nod and fell into step with them.

"We were wondering," Harcort said, "how you won at The Haunt. Place is crooked. Most of the dice are weighted."

"All of the dice are weighted," Abbercombe corrected quietly, "some more subtly than others. When someone contests the dice, the house substitutes a set more ingeniously done and the flat thinks he has caught them and forced them to be honest."

"Really? But you won despite it, sir," Harcort replied.

"Indeed. I have my own means of evening the odds."

"How?" Kettering asked, unable to contain his curiosity.

Abbercombe looked past the viscount to Kettering and grinned. "Are you sure you're Stamford's boy? I would not have expected any of his children to know what dice were, much less want to know how to separate a hell from its money."

"Bryan's always curious, your grace," offered Harcort, giving his brother a poke in the ribs with his elbow. "Especially about things he ought not be curious about."

They reached the pub and Abbercombe held the door for the younger gentlemen as they entered, which gave both the Ketterings pause. "I do not care to give anyone a chance at my back," he explained, settling behind a table at the far corner of the tap-room. "That's what you are wondering, no? Why age and title held the door for you? Am I paying?" he added with a glance at the approaching waiter.

"Sir?" Harcort asked, dumbfounded that someone considered Bryan and himself capable of homicide.

Abbercombe grinned and ordered a bottle of Canary and three glasses. "I am paying," he stated with a twinkle in his eyes. "You have likely never tasted Canary. Not right to make you pay for wine you may despise."

Abbercombe studied the gentlemen over the rim of his glass as they sipped tentatively. "Delicious," Kettering said, amazed.

Harcort nodded and took a longer draught. "So," he asked, "how do you cheat the cheaters?"

Abbercombe drained his glass and poured himself another. "Many ways. At hazard you slip your own dice in on them."

Miss April Willburton-Smythe shivered in the early dawn. She had donned her best pelisse, the one with the ermine collar, and the matching bonnet with the ermine trim. Her delicate little hands were encased in fine kid gloves, and still she was freezing. A tear crept silently down her face as she gazed up and down the street. Geoffery was not coming. She could not believe it. He was her every hope and dream, and he had abandoned her to freeze to death on this wretched street corner. "Oh, please," she murmured tearfully to herself. "Please, dear God, don't let me be abandoned. Please just let him be late. Please."

The sound of a deep voice muttering curses into the still night reached her ears, and she dodged back against the nearest building hoping to hide herself in the shadows. The gentleman who rounded the corner, hands in his pockets, gaze fastened upon the cobbles, strolled directly past her without once lifting his head. As she gave silent thanks, he turned in mid-stride and came back to pause directly before her.

"Do not be frightened, little one," he drawled a bit thickly. "I have had a bit too much Canary, else I should have realized your presence before I passed. Are you in trouble? May I be of help?"

April knew that it was most unwise to speak to any stranger, much less to a gentleman who cursed aloud to himself while walking the streets of London before dawn. She bit her lower lip, wishing him away, and shrank closer to the building until her back was tight against the rough bricks.

"There," the gentleman sighed, "I have frightened you. I thought I might. But I could not pass by, you see, without offering my assistance. It is most unwise for you to be out here alone." His eyes strayed to the bandbox upon the cobbles close by and then returned to April's face. "I expect he is not coming. Was your heart set upon him, *petite?* Cannot you go home and pretend it never happened?"

The tenderness of his tone made more tears flow down April's frigid cheeks and she could not help but sniff. She heard him chuckle and lifted her eyes to meet his. "It is n-not hu-humorous," she declared. "I have waited here since t-two o'clock and—and—" She burst into sobs and the gentleman put his arms around her. "Do not cry, *ma petite*," he whispered. "Things are not so very bad." He sheltered her against his chest as she succumbed to her despair.

When at last her crying ceased, she stared up into brilliant blue eyes tinged with sympathy. A half-smile of understanding lingered on a face that must once have been beautiful. What she supposed was a duelling scar blemished one cheek. His nose changed directions twice before it came to an end. But his thick ash blond hair swept untamed across his brow and curled recklessly about his ears, and his lips were perfectly lovely. She looked back into his eyes and noted an irrepressible twinkle there.

"Have you completed your survey, my dear?"

Realizing she was in his arms, April gave a little gasp and pulled away. He let her do so without the least resistance.

"If you have waited on this corner since two o'clock, little one, it is more than time for you to go home."

"Wh-what time is it?"

He took a watch from his waistcoat pocket and squinted down at it. "Almost four." April's teeth began to chatter as he replaced the timepiece. "That," he scowled, "is the final straw," and he began unbuttoning his coat. "Help me to shrug out of this thing, my dear. No, do not be afraid, just grab and pull. There! This will warm you up a bit," he murmured. With the expertise of long experience he slipped her into the garment, tugging the sleeves of her pelisse down through the coat sleeves and going down on one knee before her to button the buttons as if she were a toddler. "Now," he said, rising and taking one of her sleeve-enveloped hands in his, "no more nonsense. You will point me in the direction of your home." His other hand scooped the band-box from the cobbles.

"B-but I can n-not go home," April stuttered on an unexpected sob. "I have r-run away, you see."

"You have run away to elope with the man of your dreams but he has met with a mishap," replied the gentleman in quite the most ordinary way. "May I ask the young man's name?"

"Geoffery," April whispered.

"Geoffery," he continued, leading her by the hand up the street, "does not wish for you to remain alone on a street corner freezing to death. He is undoubtedly anxious about you and at point-non-plus wondering what to do."

"Oh, do you think so?" asked April hopefully.

"Indeed. Something has occurred over which he had not the least control and so you must take the matter into your own hands. Do we turn here?"

April nodded meekly, beginning to feel warm at last and surprisingly secure with his large hand protectively over hers. "I live in the third house down. Aunt Olivia will be very angry."

"Then you must not tell her. Surely she will not be up and about at this hour?"

"N-no, but when you knock on the door, she will hear you."

"Did you lock the door behind you then? Have you no key?"

"I did not leave by the door. I climbed out of the window and down over the balcony." She heard him chuckle softly.

"If I help you, do you think you can climb back up the balcony and go in through that same window?"

"I should like to try if you wouldn't mind."

"Oh, no, mademoiselle. I assure you I shall not mind in the least. I will consider it the greatest honor."

He laughed softly and his laughter made her feel just as warm within as his coat did without. "That is our house," April said, pointing. "The balcony is just around to the side. Oh," she breathed, leading him to the spot where she had descended, "it looks so high from down here."

"It is not exceptionally high," the gentleman said, looking up. "I doubt we will even need the vines, *petite.*" He set the bandbox down upon the ground, knelt before her and rolled up the sleeves of his coat so that her hands were free of them. "Now," he whispered, making a stirrup of his hands, "put your foot in here and I will give you a boost."

The gentleman held her foot tightly and with the strength of his arms lifted her to the level of his shoulders. Checking to see that she was safely balanced, he shifted his grip and lifted her farther, until her hands easily grasped the balcony rail. Once he judged her hold secure, he released her half-boot from his grasp. "Try the window before I leave," his voice floated up to her on the breeze.

April struggled over the rail and hurried to the window. She turned the latch and it swung open silently. Rushing back to call down that all was well, she met the gentleman almost face to face. "Oh!" she gasped in surprise as he swung on to the balcony.

"It would be awkward for you if this should be discovered below," he whispered, setting her bandbox before her. "Be very quiet now and slip into bed as quickly as you can. Do not tell anyone what it was you intended to do or there will be a terrible row."

"I won't," April whispered back, noticing how long and thick and dark were his eyelashes in the encroaching light of dawn.

"And do not agree to an elopement again, for not only might you have been harmed, but you and your Geoffery would most certainly have ruined yourselves completely. If this aunt of yours frowns upon him, then you must find a way to make him acceptable to her. Or perhaps," he smiled, running one long, gloved finger tenderly down her wind-reddened cheek, "you must merely wait until you are a bit older and he a bit wiser. *A bientot, ma petite,*" he whispered.

April watched, enchanted, as he vaulted the balcony rail and landed lightly on his feet in the grass below. He waved at her, put his hands into his pockets, and strolled out of sight around the side of the house. April, moving as in a dream, was back in her own bedchamber before she realized that she still wore the gentleman's coat.

* * *

A bright sun flirted through the tiny opening between the damask drapes that covered April's window. It woke her at last and she yawned, stretching lazily beneath the warm feather ticking. It must be very late, she thought, for the sun to be coming in so strongly. She was normally up long before her Aunt Olivia, but today she felt so warm, so cozy, so—and then she remembered. With a sense of urgency she sprang from beneath the covers, rushed to the armoire and jerked open its magnificently carved doors. Frantically she pushed aside gown after gown until at last she found the coat where she had hung it behind her oldest morning dress. She sighed in relief to see it there undisturbed and then another brief moment of panic seized her for she feared the entrance of her aunt or her abigail at any moment. There must be a safer place to hide it. Someplace private. Of course, she thought, chiding herself for being such a gudgeon, the cedar chest. Her father had had it made for her years ago and she possessed the only key.

She hurried to a small kingwood table and lifted from it a Venetian glass vase of a red as bright as fire, removed the paper flowers, turned it over and shook the key into her hand. Then she opened the chest and carried the stylish coat of midnight blue superfine from the armoire to her bed where she folded it carefully, finally laying it to rest inside her chest, tucked completely from sight beneath a knitted coverlet of palest pink and blue yarn. Closing and locking the chest and returning the key to its hiding place, she stopped to sit for a moment on the bed, dangling her bare feet above the colorful Persian carpet. She pondered the identity of the gentleman who had so nobly rescued her and wondered would they ever meet again. And then she began to worry about Geoffery. She must discover what had happened to him and assure him that she, herself, was safe.

* * *

At that very moment Mr. Geoffery Hempstead's eyes were fluttering open to stare up into the haggard face of Viscount Harcort. "At last," sighed Harcort with a good deal of relief. "We thought you'd stuck your spoon in the wall for sure this time, old fellow. How do you feel?"

"David? Where am I? What happened?"

"You're home, Geoff," Kettering mumbled from the chaise longue. "The Watch brought you early this morning. Found you lying senseless in an alley near Lisle Street."

Hempstead put a hand to his brow, felt the bandage there and groaned.

"Not feeling quite the thing, I expect," Harcort commiserated. "Apothecary came, said you'd live." He helped Hempstead to sit up and plopped down beside him on the couch. "Hawkins went to fetch you some medicine. Apothecary said if your head was aching badly to give you some of it."

"Footpads!" Hempstead sputtered sitting up straighter. "Damned if I wasn't set upon by footpads!"

Kettering groaned and turned cautiously to stare at his friend. "Are you sure, Geoff? Course it don't surprise me none in that neighborhood. Lord, Davey, I think I'm going to die."

Harcort sighed. "I have you there, little brother. I am dead at least an hour. Why the devil were you wandering about in Lisle Street, Hempstead?" Harcort asked, massaging his own temples.

"Oh, devil!" Hempstead exclaimed. "April!"

"No, old man, it ain't April. Just coming on March," murmured Kettering.

"No, no, April! I was to meet her!"

"What, in Lisle Street? I hardly think so, dear boy. Young lady has no business to be anywhere near Lisle."

"No, Bry, you don't understand. I was on my way to Donovan's stables to hire a post-chaise. April and I, we, well, devil take it, we were going to elope last night. Oh, gawd! What must she think? You do not suppose she has come to any harm?"

"Settle down, Geoff," Harcort urged, "you'll do yourself more harm than good. Whatever has happened to Miss Willburton-Smythe, you can do nothing about it at the moment."

"But she was left standing on Broad Street all alone at two o'clock in the morning."

"Which is merely a short walk from Park Street," responded Kettering with more confidence than he truly felt. "Miss April is not a fool, Geoff. She will have decided you were not coming and taken herself safely home. I tell you what I shall do. I shall take it upon myself to pay a call at Miss Willburton-Smythe's and speak to Miss April on your behalf. No doubt she will be equally worried about you."

"Unless she thinks I have changed my mind and abandoned her," groaned Hempstead. "Bryan, you cannot let her think such a thing. I could not bear to lose her."

"Never fear, Hempstead," Harcort mumbled. "Bry will plead your case admirably, as soon as he is able to walk."

"It's a good thing for us the duke was able to walk or we would never have gotten home," Kettering sighed.

Hempstead eyed his companions inquiringly.

"We spent the shank of the evening drinking with the Duke of Abbercombe," Harcort explained, "at Hodge's in Pickering Place. He had to carry Bry out over his shoulder while holding me up with his other hand. Stuffed the both of us into a hackney."

"Abbercombe?" Hempstead asked, concerned.

"Abbercombe," confirmed Harcort. "Bryan was determined to make his acquaintance."

"Have you both lost your minds? The man must be dangerous. Do you think they transported the heir to a dukedom for—for boxing a charley?"

"We asked what it was all about," Kettering mumbled, trying to keep his head as still as he possibly could.

"And did he tell you?"

"Well, some of it," Harcort muttered. "He told us why we, in particular, should avoid him."

"He murdered our Uncle Channing," Kettering groaned, his eyebrows coming together in deference to the pain in his head.

* * *

It was after ten that morning when Lord Sebastian and Lady Jessica Denbigh were invited to be seated at the table in the Fielding House dining room while the family breakfasted. The hubbub was considerable as children helped themselves from a sideboard piled high with eggs, toast, bacon, kippers, kidneys, muffins and fresh fruit. "Are you sure you will not join us?" Amaryllis, the eldest, urged. "You will have hot chocolate at least, or tea, or coffee? Papa always has coffee."

Lord Sebastian, a bewildered smile on his pleasantly handsome face, nodded. "Coffee would be just the thing," he replied. Bethany immediately rose and fetched a cup from the urn on the sideboard. "Aunt Jessica," she urged, "you must have something."

"Perhaps some tea," Lady Jess whispered hoarsely.

"Are you really our aunt and uncle?" a boy with hair the color of honey and eyes as blue as a winter sky asked, kneeling on a chair next to Lord Sebastian and stretching across the table to swipe a kidney from his sister's plate.

"Yes, Ethan, of course they are," Amaryllis answered. "No one would pretend to be our aunt and uncle if they were not."

" 'Cause why?"

"Because we are intimidating, just as Papa says, and the sight of us all together would frighten any pretenders away."

"Aunt Jess 'fraid us," piped up a tiny girl in a pretty sprigged muslin dress.

"Uh-uh," protested her twin around a mouthful of runny egg. "Uh-huh!"

One of the older boys shushed them and grinned beguilingly. "Papa was most remiss, I think. You were not expecting to see so many of us, were you?"

"Well, no," replied Lady Jessica.

"Your father wrote he was bringing his daughters, Amaryllis and Bethany, to London for the Season," Lord Sebastian offered with a distinct twinkle in his eyes. "And the truth is, that until that letter, we did not even know that we had two nieces."

"Oh, how shocking!" exclaimed Bethany, looking much more amused than shocked. "To think, Uncle Sebastian, that you have been an uncle for eighteen years and never knew of it."

"Were you pleased to discover we did exist?" asked Amaryllis, buttering a muffin.

"Delighted," smiled Lord Sebastian. "Only I did wish he had told me of it sooner. I should like to have sent you presents, you know, and invited you to come for visits."

"But you were only ten when we were born," Bethany replied with a frown upon her lovely cherub's face, "and grandfather would not have permitted you to do any such thing."

"Oh, dear," sighed Lady Jess, taking Sebastian's hand. "I had hoped that you did not know of your grandfather's feelings."

"Bosh," muttered one of the younger boys, "we all of us knows 'bout gran'father an' Papa."

"Still that is no excuse, Frazier, for Papa not to have written about us to Uncle Sebastian." Amaryllis grinned. "What a surprise to find yourselves in the midst of all this mayhem."

"But you barely cringed at all," beamed one of the older boys, "which anyone might have been expected to do. Be careful, Frazier, or you shall have all of your breakfast on the floor."

"No, I shan't," replied Frazier fiercely. "I jus' dropped some muffin. I shall pick it up presen'ly. There's eight of us," he added with an anxious glance at Lady Jess. "Is that too many?"

"Too many?" Lady Jess stared into the serious child-eyes. "Whatever do you mean, my dear?"

"He means maybe you don' wanna be aunt and uncle to all of us," clarified Ethan, transferring a portion of kippers to one of the little girls' plates. "I 'spect you can have jus' Amy an' Beth if you wish. Or don't you wish for Amy and Beth neither?"

There was a sudden and complete silence as Ethan's words tumbled into the room, and eight sets of varying shades of blue eyes stared apprehensively at Lord Sebastian and Lady Jessica. Lady Jess felt her husband's hand tighten upon her own beneath the table and his blue eyes turned to stare at her as well. Never in her life had she been confronted with such apprehension and longing. All thought of Abbercombe's crime and all fear for her reputation vanished before it. "Indeed we wish to be aunt and uncle to Amy and Beth," she breathed, "and to all of you. You are the best surprise we have ever received, are they not, Sebastian?"

"Indeed! The best surprise anyone could receive. But you must help us, you know, to get all of you straight, for your Aunt Jess and I haven't a clue as to which one of you is which. We have never encountered four sets of twins all at the same time."

"Oh, that's easy, sir," declared one of the older boys. "You need only remember your letters and that the beginning of the alphabet is older."

"What?"

"Well, like this. Amaryllis and Bethany are the eldest. And Amy was born before Beth, just the way A comes before B. And it is child's play to tell them apart, because Amaryllis is always telling people what to do and Bethany is seriously romantical."

"Christian, do not tease," the young lady to his left ordered.

"You see, sir. That is Amaryllis."

"Christian," mused Lord Sebastian, his eyes alight. "Then you are next in age after Bethany. Is that correct?"

"Yes, sir. Amy and Beth are eighteen, and Damian and I are fifteen, but I am Marquis of Warren and shall be duke, Papa says, because I was birthed three minutes before Daymee. Then come Ethan and Frazier. They are eight. And Gracie and Helen are six."

"And you can tell Christian from Damian because Chris always has his mouth open and Daymee always has his nose in a book," provided Amaryllis offhandedly.

"An' you can tell me from Frazier," cried Ethan, " 'cause I am nicer."

"Are not!" protested his twin.

"Am, too."

"Are not!"

"You are both just as nice," offered their father as he entered the room. "What on earth brings on this conversa—?" The duke's voice faltered to a halt as he stared at the two adults seated near the head of the table. His smile wavered and the children, watching his expression, slipped again into silence. Lord Sebastian Denbigh snatched his napkin from his lap and stood. His wife did likewise.

Abbercombe, expecting to meet no one but his children at the breakfast table had come down in his shirtsleeves, buckskin breeches, and slippers. He had not bothered to run a brush through his unruly hair, nor shave, and the dark shadow on his chin and cheeks made him appear much more pirate than nobleman. He stuffed his hands into his pockets and took a step backwards toward the doorway, then caught himself and rocked to a halt.

"It's Uncle 'Bastian an' Aunt Jess, Papa," Gracie squeaked into the tense silence. She climbed awkwardly down from her chair and ran to him. Throwing her arms around both his thighs, she hugged him tightly.

Helen was not far behind, her napkin floating to the floor behind her. "They visitin'," she announced, tugging one of his hands from his pocket and grasping it in both of hers. "I thinks they likes us, Papa," she whispered loudly up at him.

"Cash?" Sebastian murmured. Eight sets of blue eyes turned to stare at him and then turned back to their father.

The duke pried himself free from the little girls and took a hesitant step forward, extending his hand. Denbigh extricated himself from behind the table, hurried forward and took the hand in both of his, then dropped it and pulled the duke roughly into his arms. "Damnable rogue," he growled in Abbercombe's ear. "Jessica," he added as his wife came up beside him, "may I at last present my brother, Cash."

Abbercombe looked at her uncertainly. "I am most pleased to know you, Lady Jessica," he said, barely above a whisper. "You need not know me, however, if you have no wish to do so."

Lady Jess felt a fluttering somewhere near her heart as he

bowed over her hand and raised her fingertips to his lips. When he stared down at her once more, she was touched by the doubt and yearning that manifested itself so clearly in his lined face. "But I do wish to know you, Cash," she heard herself say. And she put her hands upon his shoulders and stood upon her toes, and kissed him gently upon his perfect lips.

"Oh, yuk," groaned Ethan and Frazier loudly, and all the children burst into laughter.

Three

Word of Rudolph Casimir Denbigh's return set the *ton* afire. He took his children on a promised visit to the Tower unnoticed, but was recognized and cut by Lords Worcester and Foley when he accompanied Christian and Damian to Westminster the following day. Ethan and Frazier dragged him off to Week's Mechanical Museum without incident, but Lord Airde and Sir Henry Laughton gave him the cut direct in Curzon Street upon the return trek. He moodily declined to attend Astley's Royal Amphitheatre to view "a new grand Equestrian Burletta Spectacle," but the children at last cajoled him into it and he emerged unscathed. His presence was duly noted, however, and he was pointed out to a number of the Quality who would not otherwise have recognized him. His scandalous past was gleefully presented for their review.

Two days later, in the British Museum at Montague House, Lady Caroline Rothenberg brought her entourage to a halt at an exhibit where he stood with Amaryllis and Bethany. "Abbercombe!" she exclaimed in her most penetrating voice. "To think this building houses such vermin! Will no one preserve us from such filth?"

Miss Willburton-Smythe, her attention, like everyone's, instantly drawn to the piercing tone, cringed at the blatant cruelty of it. Not only were such words uncalled for, but that they should be thrown at him in the presence of his daughters was the outside of enough. Emerald eyes ablaze, her countenance rigid with self-righteousness, her heart aflame with compassion, Olivia seized

April's arm and, ignoring the tittering onlookers, swept down upon the duke like a schooner under full sail with a dinghy in tow.

"Your grace," she cried in a voice equally as penetrating as Lady Caroline's, "I cannot believe our luck in finding you here!" With a show of bravado worthy of Drury Lane, she transferred her grip from April's arm to Abbercombe's. "Come along, my darlings," she tossed over her shoulder at all three young ladies, "we shall escort his grace to the artifact we have been discussing and seek his opinion." Whereupon she propelled Abbercombe from the chamber amidst the scrutiny of myriad astounded gazes, down a short hall and into an anteroom which contained a number of chairs and a small couch. "April, close the door," she instructed over her shoulder in a much less piercing tone. "And lean against it," she added as an afterthought. She then withdrew her hand from Abbercombe's arm and stalked to the window. "I have never been so angry in my entire life," she declared, turning to face him. "I hope that you and your daughters will accept my apologies for such rudeness as you have just received."

"It is I, mademoiselle, must apologize," drawled Abbercombe frigidly, twitching the sleeve of his coat back into order, "for putting you to the inconvenience of effecting our deliverance. Though I do think I might have brought us about on my own."

Olivia scowled at the man. "Perhaps you might have done, your grace," she replied, "but from all appearances, I judged it was not to be counted upon." She did not know what she had expected—a thank you, perhaps, but certainly not the insolent demeanor he now affected.

Abbercombe acknowledged her barb with an elegant bow. "Hoist on my own petard," he muttered.

"And deservedly so, Papa," Amaryllis announced behind him. "May we know the names of our rescuers?" she asked, stepping up beside her father and taking his arm.

"Yes, please, ma'am," added Bethany, looking from Olivia to April and back again.

Abbercombe studied the stubborn set of Olivia's jaw and the

consternation betrayed by the grim line of her lips as well as the indecision in her eyes. "Do not, my dears, request an introduction. The lady, I think, does not wish to make your acquaintances, and I am certain she does not wish to make mine. One may, you know, be thoroughly opposed to ragged treatment of others without desiring to take them up yourself."

"What?" Olivia gasped.

"You heard me, mademoiselle. I thank you for your compassion and I set you free from further involvement. If we meet again, you may cut us with impunity just as do the rest of your circle."

"Papa, stop!" scowled Amy, giving his arm a shake. "You are incorrigible."

"No, I am not," responded the duke somberly. "I have been avoided, ignored, insulted and made the subject of whispers and sniggers and pointing fingers since I came to this city, yet I can do nothing to keep it from humiliating you. And now I must be indebted for your deliverance to the charity of some nob chit—it is the outside of enough, I tell you."

"And I tell you, sir," scowled Olivia with hands on her hips and a stamp of her foot, "I object to being labelled a nob chit, and you do not stand in my debt! I'd have done as much for any stray dog were a cat like Caroline Rothenberg clawing upon it!"

"I am no longer vermin? Now I am a dog? A mongrel, I expect. Probably rabid."

"Papa!" exclaimed Bethany, "do behave!"

Olivia, ready with a cutting response, closed her lips upon it as the second of the young ladies walked up beside him and placed her hand gently upon his arm. For the first time she realized that the daughters were identical in all but costume. Why they are twins, she thought, and breathtakingly beautiful.

"You must pardon Papa," sighed Beth with a pretty pout. "He has been extremely vexatious since we came to London. I think it is the water, though Amy swears it is the night air. Papa *will* sleep with his window open even when it is positively frigid."

"Which is a dreadful habit and ought to be gotten over," added Amaryllis, decisively.

Olivia's annoyance dissipated, and she began to smile in response to a twitching at the corners of Abbercombe's lips which she could see he was fighting hard to control. "Do you sleep with your window open, sir?" she quizzed him.

"I hardly think, mademoiselle," sputtered the duke on a chuckle, "that my sleeping habits are a fit subject for discussion in the midst of the British Museum."

"No, I expect not," replied Olivia gravely. "Where might we discuss them, do you suppose?"

Abbercombe gave up the fight and laughed outright, his heretofore brooding countenance breaking into a grin that Olivia thought lit his face like a blazing fire lit a midnight sky.

"May I present my daughters to you, mademoiselle?"

Olivia nodded.

The girls curtsied as he introduced them, and Olivia thought again how ravishing they were. "And I am Miss Willburton-Smythe," she announced with a dip in Abbercombe's direction. "And the young lady who guards the door is my niece, April."

As the Denbighs turned to acknowledge April, that young lady's face flushed then grew pale, "You!" she gasped. Amy and Beth loosed their father's arms on the instant and he sprang forward, catching April a split second before she hit the floor in a dead faint.

Lady Jessica stopped her pacing and took a seat opposite her friend in Olivia's parlor on Park Street. "Do you mean it, Olivia? But once the others hear that Abbercombe's daughters are invited to your drawing room, will they not refuse to attend?"

"Why, to tell the truth, Jess, I had not planned to tell anyone before hand. I doubt even Lady Carrington will have the nerve to cut them in the midst of my drawing room. No, the girls are charming, and the *ton*'s curiosity is at such a peak that I dare say they will make my little party a huge success. And besides, April

wishes to know them better. She was so embarrassed at having
fainted when first they met. I cannot imagine what made her do
so. I vow, if Abbercombe had not moved so swiftly, the poor
child would have hit her head upon that dreadful Kingsley table
and suffered severe damage. As it was he took her in hand wonderfully. He revived her, and carried her to our carriage and
tucked her in as though he had been trained to it."

"I would expect nothing less of him," grinned Lady Jessica.
"I have not seen you since, Olivia, but Sebastian and I have been
to Fielding House and have discovered the most amazing thing."

"What?"

"Why that we are not only aunt and uncle to two very excellent
young ladies, but to six other children as well. I gather that Cash
has been in sole charge of them all for a number of years."

"Six more of them?" Olivia gasped.

"They are darlings. I am determined you shall meet them. And
I shall certainly chaperon Amy and Beth to your drawing room."

In the end Olivia proved to be correct. Not one of her guests
declined to be introduced to Abbercombe's daughters or dared
to snub them in the midst of her *affaire,* and the beauty and appeal
of the girls plus the fact that everyone could boast of having met
them made her little party a huge success. From that day forward
a sincere relationship developed among Amaryllis and Bethany
and April, and the twins became frequent visitors at Park Street.

"I can barely wait," April proclaimed as the three settled for
a comfortable coze in her sitting room one brisk afternoon.
"Lady Skiffington's will be my very first London ball."

"I doubt we shall be invited," sighed Bethany, "though Papa
says we are not to despair of it."

"Well, he may be right," Amy said. "We have already received
invitations to a number of entertainments. Papa says they are
from people who remember Mama and wish to be kind to us
because of her."

"I am sure there are a great many people who will invite you to their parties and balls," April stated with authority. "Even Aunt Olivia says so."

"It is very silly anyway," Beth decided. "We did not come to London to be belles after all."

"I thought that was precisely why you came."

"No," Amy replied, "we came for Papa's sake. The Season was only our excuse."

"But why would you come here for your Papa's sake? He is a pariah here!"

"Because it is much better for him to be outcast," declared Amy, "than to be dead, which he very well would have been had we remained longer in France."

"D-dead?" asked April.

"Yes," responded Bethany. "It was a very close thing, and though Papa would rather have gone elsewhere, Amy and Chris and Daymee and I decided England would be the safest place for him."

"But, who would wish to—to kill him?" April stuttered.

"Oh, any number of people wish to," Bethany shrugged, "though most have no idea it is Papa they seek. He was seriously betrayed, though, in Paris and only moments from being arrested."

"After which he would undoubtedly have been guillotined," Amy added. "But we are forbidden to discuss it, and he is safe here, surely."

"I knew it," declared April. "I knew the moment we met that he was dangerous and enigmatic!"

Amaryllis and Bethany stared at her with intense interest. "How could you know anything of the sort?" asked Bethany. "You fainted dead away when first we met. I am sure you did not gain any such impression from his conversation with your aunt."

"But that was not the first time we met," April said excitedly. "And I only fainted because—because it was such a shock to know who had rescued me and I feared that he might reveal the whole escapade to my aunt—though he assured me that he would not, you know, when he carried me to our carriage. He said I might repose every confidence in him."

"And so you might," smiled Amy, puzzled. "Is it a secret, about how you first met Papa?"

April, her eyes glistening, shook her chestnut curls. "Not from you," she grinned, "for I know you will not betray me." She related the story of her ill-fated elopement in a hushed voice, and by the end of her tale the sisters were sitting with their mouths open and their eyes wide with disbelief.

"You are making it up," declared Amaryllis finally.

"I am not!" protested April, springing up and stalking off into her bedchamber. Amy and Beth listened to a series of strange sounds and then April reappeared with a gentleman's coat of midnight blue superfine held up before her. "Now you must believe me," she declared, "for this is your father's coat, and if you return it to him, he will tell you exactly what happened. You may say he has my permission to do so. I think," she exclaimed, refolding the garment and helping Bethany to wrap it in a shawl, "that your father must be the kindest, sweetest, bravest gentleman in the world, and if he were not so old, I should fall madly in love with him!"

In the delightful ivory and rose parlor on the first floor, Olivia also entertained a visitor. "Mademoiselle," he murmured, bowing over her hand. "I regret that I arrive unannounced, but I could not your lovely home pass without pausing to discover how you go on."

"Monsieur LeBruin," Olivia acknowledged the exquisitely handsome gentleman, "you are a welcome visitor. Will you be seated? Laslow," she addressed the lingering butler, "Monsieur LeBruin would like a glass of Madeira, would you not, monsieur?"

"Indeed, mademoiselle," smiled LeBruin from beneath delicately arched brows. He was not a tall man, but his aristocratic bearing made him appear so. As a child, he had fled Madame

Guillotine with his family and emigrated to England. Though they had left behind considerable wealth, they had managed to transfer enough money and possessions to the English shore to establish themselves quite creditably. M. LeBruin now moved in the highest circles of the *ton* by virtue of his background, his politic sophistication, and his extreme good looks. The fact that he continued to amass a considerable fortune through various investments and ventures did not detract from his appeal, and he was considered by many ladies to be an extremely acceptable match. "I understand that your niece has arrived," he remarked, his gaze resting admiringly upon Olivia as Laslow set off to fetch the wine.

"Indeed, monsieur. You have been from town of late, I think? I have been promising April she might make your acquaintance."

"Business, mademoiselle," replied LeBruin with a bored wave of his hand. "The little villain, Napoleon, he wreaks havoc upon everyone's investments, *n'est-ce pas?* Do you attend the soiree at the Langdon's tomorrow evening, mademoiselle?" the gentleman added much as an afterthought.

Olivia nodded. "Indeed." She paused as Laslow reappeared with the Madeira. "I shall go as April's chaperon, of course," she continued at Laslow's departure. "Do you attend, monsieur?"

"Oui, mademoiselle. It is expected of me. Perhaps there I have the pleasure to make the acquaintance of your *protégée.* Do you know, Mademoiselle Olivia, that since my return I hear everywhere of this *mauvais sujet,* Abbercombe? This one has become the *on dit,* is it not so? All London buzzes with him."

"So it seems," Olivia replied. "I cannot see what all the fuss is about. His past has been scandalous, but he has done nothing untoward since his arrival."

LeBruin's fine grey eyes narrowed a moment and he studied her over the rim of his wine glass. The intensity of his gaze made her uneasy and reminded her all too well of why she did not prize this gentleman's regard. Beneath his calm, controlled exterior, Olivia sensed a depth of seething passion for which she could not account, no more than she could account for his attempts to establish a relationship with herself involving more than a passing friendship.

"Beware, *ma belle chere*," LeBruin drawled. "The past oft predicts the future. Do not involve yourself with such a one."

"Why on earth would I involve myself with Abbercombe? You are absurd, monsieur."

"Then it is false, what I hear? You do not introduce to the *ton* this rogue's daughters?"

"I did introduce them, monsieur, to those who attended my drawing room, but that is neither here nor there. They are pretty behaved young ladies, and I was pleased to do so. But I have certainly no involvement with their father."

LeBruin's visit lasted only the proscribed fifteen minutes and then he bowed himself from her presence, leaving Olivia to wonder what had brought him to her door at all, and why for the remainder of his visit he had sought to appear disinterested in Abbercombe, even as he attempted to obtain information about him.

The very real possibility that Amy and Beth might suffer complete ostracism because of his transgressions had weighed heavily upon Abbercombe. But now Lady Jess's and Miss Willburton-Smythe's efforts had lifted that burden somewhat, and his sensitivity to the cuts he received almost daily decreased considerably, for it did not annoy him nearly so much to be publicly humiliated once he knew his children were not to suffer a similar punishment. With renewed vigor he set himself to interviewing the candidates for governess and tutor that Lowery and Holt had sent him and at last settled upon Miss Clarissa Greene and Mr. Charles Stanton. They were overjoyed, especially since they were both quite inexperienced.

"But I have hired you for precisely that reason," explained Abbercombe as Miss Greene and Mr. Stanton sat before him in his study. "My children have not been raised in the acceptable British manner. You are young enough to be adaptable and patient. Gracie and Helen, Miss Greene, are extremely curious and want to know everything about everything. And Ethan and Frazier, Mr. Stanton, are equally intent on learning, though much more inclined to wish to know the wrong things. The two of you shall be responsible, of course, for setting them to their lessons, but I have no wish for them to be locked away from me for hours at a time. Miss Greene, Amaryllis and Bethany will do all they can to assist you. You need only ask. And Mr. Stanton, Christian and Damian will assist you if you should find their help necessary."

"I assumed I was also to be responsible for the elder boys," Charles Stanton said. "Have they a tutor of their own then?"

The duke looked at him, puzzled. "No," he responded. "They have already stood for entrance to Oxford and been accepted, though whether they shall consent to attend remains a mystery."

"At fifteen, your grace?" Mr. Stanton asked.

"Yes, though as I say, they have not yet decided whether or not they will attend. Something is amiss?" asked Abbercombe, noting anxiety upon the faces across from him.

"Oh, no sir," answered Miss Greene tentatively. "It is only odd for gentlemen to be accepted at university so young and that their attendance should depend upon their own discretion."

"I see. Well, I have probably spoiled them excessively by dragging them about the world all their lives. Good, they have come to escort you to your chambers," he said with a wink at the faces that peeked around the door frame. "I hope you will both be happy here. Lord knows I am happy to have found you." Thus dismissed, both young people were set upon—Miss Greene by Gracie and Helen, and Mr. Stanton by all of the boys—and loudly escorted to the chambers that had been prepared for them.

Abbercombe leaned back, sighed, and closed his eyes.

"What? Exhausted already? For shame, Cash, it is barely three and the best of us are just now beginning to wander about."

The sound of that voice surged through Abbercombe. His eyes popped open; he sprang from his chair; he started across the room eagerly, intending to embrace the figure that lounged in his study doorway. But then he awkwardly brought himself to a halt and shoved his hands into his pockets.

The tall, elegant gentleman who faced him shook his head slowly from side to side and clucked. "How you have become such a nodcock after all this time, Cash, I cannot conceive. I refused to let your man announce me for fear you would pretend to be out. I was justified to do so, obviously. Come here, you insolent rogue and make me believe you are pleased to see my wretched face!" With those words, the Earl of Worth closed the gap between himself and Abbercombe and clasped that gentleman to his bosom, crushing the duke in a violent hug until Abbercombe laughed aloud and begged for mercy.

"Yes," grinned Worth, "and well you should beg for mercy, too. Sloan told me you had stopped by White's almost two weeks ago, would not enter, and have not returned since. Well, it won't do, Cash, not at all. You cannot so easily avoid your friends. We grow dreadfully weary of waiting for you, so I've come to drag you back into the fold myself. No, do not cock your eyebrow at me," Worth drawled, glancing in the mirror to straighten his cravat. "You will accompany me to White's and dine with me there this evening and the devil take anyone who chooses to comment upon it. We must be off immediately, however, for Richardson and Hurley await our arrival at Tattersall's. Since you have not as yet set up your stables, we have decided to help you do so."

"You have not changed a bit," Abbercombe murmured. "You are as cocksure and officious as always, Edward."

"I am?"

"Yes, and by god, I am glad to see you."

"Well, I knew you would be," offered Worth with a grin, wandering to the mantle and resting his shoulders against it. "I have heard, you know, that your welcome to town has been less than delightful. I kept thinking that you would consign all those stiff-rumped slow-tops to the devil and stroll into White's as maggoty and impertinent as always, but I find I was mistaken. You will forgive me that, Cash. Had Sebastian not told me how devilish timid you've become, I might have gone on expecting you for even longer. As it is I regret having waited a moment. How could you doubt, Cash, that I would welcome your return? Has living in foreign parts for so long turned your mind to mush?"

"No—" Abbercombe sat upon the front edge of his desk and let his boots dangle above the soberly carpeted floor. He stared down at them as they swung. His hands gripped the edge of the desk so tensely that Worth could see his knuckles turning white from across the room. " 'Bastian sent you here?"

"No, Sebastian did not. I chose to come here. Now get your hat, we are going to Tat's. Cannot have a duke of the realm hacking about town. It ain't done, Cash. A duke has got to have a few prime one's in his stables, and a stylish chariot or two as well. I cannot fathom why you sold up your father's beasts, but Richardson, Hurley, and I shall help rectify that situation."

As Worth discovered once he had handed the reins of his chestnuts over to Abbercombe, there still wasn't a man could touch the duke when it came to driving. The matched pair, overly-fresh, fretted and danced through the crowded streets striving to break headlong into a run, but Abbercombe controlled them effortlessly, taking them through a throng of merchant's carts, around a gig and a curricle that had run aground of each other, into a flock of sheep and out of it again without having touched a wisp of wool and past a group of raggamuffins in the midst of an energetic mill from which small bodies came flailing into their path.

"London," sighed Abbercombe, steering the chestnuts gingerly around a tiny fighter, "has become sadly crowded and filthy as well."

"Well, but it never was clean, Cash."

"Perhaps not. But I seem to remember it as clean, and small, and not nearly so noisy. Am I going right for Tat's? They have not changed their location?"

"Same place. Bigger though. Added some outbuildings and more rings. Timmy Bittner's been dished-up. His cattle are on the block this afternoon. There's one or two of 'em you might fancy."

Abbercombe nodded and brought the chestnuts, high-stepping prettily, around a carriage stranded in the middle of the street.

"That's Skiffington," Worth observed. "We'll have to stop."

"Why?"

"Oh, you don't know. The old chap's my father-in-law now. It will not do to pass him by when he finds himself in such a fix."

The duke pulled the chestnuts to the side of the street and tossed the reins to Worth's tiger. Together the gentlemen climbed down and strolled to the stranded carriage. "What's happened?" Worth asked the brandy-faced gentleman who stood looking at the vehicle as if he would like to kick it soundly into oblivion.

"Eh? Oh, Worth, you here? Thing won't move. Rear wheels won't turn. Demned Johnny Coachman ain't a bit of help—crawling around under there, doing lord knows what."

"They just stopped turning?" Abbercombe asked.

"Aye. Going along fine we were and then—"

"Brake rods are stuck," the duke said glancing at Worth.

"What?" Worth asked, his eyes widening innocently.

"You know very well what, Edward, but I can see you are not about to rectify the situation."

"I am not dressed for it, Cash," grinned Worth, brushing an invisible piece of lint from his Manilla brown riding coat.

Abbercombe scowled, brushed a lock of fair hair from his brow, and crawled under the carriage. "What's got her stuck?" he asked, meeting Lord Skiffington's coachman.

"I don't be knowin'," muttered the man. "I ain't nothin' but a driver, by gawd. I don't know 'bout all this 'ere machinery."

"Shove over then. These," he explained, flat on his back beneath the vehicle, "are brake rods. When you pull the brake lever, they pull those wooden blocks against the wheel rims. When you release the lever, the rods move back and release the blocks. But the blocks are still against the rims, see? Means your rods are stuck. What's your name?"

"Ivan Jones, milord."

Abbercombe chuckled. "Ivan! That's a killer!"

The coachman frowned. "I'll thank ye kindly not to be makin' sport o' the name me mother gave me," he grumbled.

"No, no, you take me wrong," laughed Abbercombe, working away at the rods. "You, my dear sir, are Ivan and I am Rudolph Casimir. The two standing out there all prim and proper and clean are Edward and John. What's in a name, Ivan?"

The coachman grinned and stretched out to help Abbercombe jiggle at the rods. "Aye, 'tis the likes o' us what was named ta do the dirty work, an' tha's a fac'."

"Indeed, an Ivan and a Rudolph were intended to muck about in gutters, but never an Edward or a John. There, we've got it. Edward," he called, sticking his head out from below the carriage, "move that brake lever back and forth a bit, will you?"

Worth climbed onto the box and jiggled the lever.

"Good, hold it there." The sound of a gloved fist pounding against wood vibrated into the street. "Jiggle the thing again. No, wait, pull it off, but be ready to throw it back on quickly. There! Excellent!" Abbercombe scuttled out from beneath the vehicle and tugged Ivan out after him. "Try now, Ivan," he instructed. "Get the boy to lead the horses ahead just a bit."

"Well, I'll be hornswaggled," muttered Skiffington as the coach rolled forward. "I am in your debt, m'boy. What's your name? I thought to know all of Worth's comrades."

"My lord," smiled Worth, "may I present His Grace, Rudolph Casimir Denbigh, Duke of Abbercombe. Your grace, my father-in-law, Lord Skiffington."

"Abbercombe?" mumbled the older man with a slight frown. "Abbercombe? Ain't you the scapegallows what raised sich a breeze a few years back over that little gel? Scandalized the nation didn't ye, ye rogue? I bin hearing ye'd come back; the dashed tittle-tattles be forever talking about ye."

"Yes, sir," Abbercombe answered. Worth frowned as he saw his friend step back in anticipation of some insult.

"Well, I thank ye, lad," Skiffington said, thumping Abbercombe's shoulders. "I am in your debt."

Worth assisted the elderly gentleman into the carriage, rolled up the steps, and closed the door after him. "By the way," Skiffington called as the carriage began to move, "I'm of the opinion ye done the thing right, boy. Never you mind what these waggles say. Ye face 'em down, lad. Ye done the necessary."

The coachman tipped his hat at Abbercombe and winked as the carriage pulled away.

"I cannot recall the last time I was called a lad, Edward," the duke chuckled. "Does he find you as much of a stripling as he finds me?"

"He finds me a young thatchgallows and a rapscallion. Puts a bit of a bounce back into your step, does it not?"

"Thought I was eighteen again," Abbercombe agreed, grinning.

"We cannot possibly continue on to Tat's with you looking like you've spent the day in the gutter, old man," Worth stated as they returned to his curricle. "Have to go back to Fielding House and get you cleaned up and it will most likely be too late for Tat's by the time you are presentable. Never mind, we are set to meet Richardson and Hurley at White's no matter what."

The gentlemen arrived at the duke's residence just as Miss Willburton-Smythe's landau delivered Amy and Beth to the door. Worth was introduced to the girls as a proper tulip and they duly curtsied to him.

"But, Papa, whatever happened?" Amy queried. "You look as though you have been lying about in a gutter!"

"I have. Come inside and I shall explain it to you."

"We have something else we would like you to explain, please." Bethany smiled sweetly as she unwrapped the coat April had given them. "It is yours, is it not, Papa? April assured us that it was."

Worth's eyes flashed with an unholy glee as he watched a slow reddish tint rise into Abbercombe's face.

Four

Because of Sir Richard Langdon's association with the diplomatic corps, the Langdons' *soiree* proved interesting as well as enjoyable. Olivia, who thought only to act as April's chaperon, found herself the center of a small group of gentlemen who, having discovered that she held decided opinions upon the present political situation, were entranced to hear a great many practical suggestions fall from a set of thoroughly delectable lips.

"Surely we ought to have you working with us, Miss Willburton-Smythe," declared Captain Lovelace, a sturdy and dependable gentleman dressed in regimentals. "It is likely you would have a good deal more success in communicating with our allies. They could not, you know, refuse to listen when such a beautiful countenance confronted them."

"Indeed," agreed the Honorable James Ratherton, his dark eyes shining. "Wyndham ought to compel you to serve in the Foreign Office, I think. We would gain a good deal more cooperation. By the by, have you had word from your brother, Miss Olivia?"

"No, Jamie, not for over two months," Olivia replied, her smile fading. "I cannot guess what keeps him from writing. He is on Wellesley's staff now, you know. I do hope he is safe."

"Certainement, mademoiselle, he is safe," assured a most familiar voice and M. LeBruin appeared before her, his broad shoulders encased in a coat of black superfine over a white waistcoat embroidered in gold. He looked magnificent and quite out-

shone even Captain Lovelace of the Guards. "I have seen your brother recently, mademoiselle, upon my travels."

At that precise moment, as Olivia's attention became riveted upon M. LeBruin, Geoffery Hempstead, shielded from view by a willing Kettering and Harcort, swept April onto the Langdons' balcony. "My dearest girl," he sighed, taking her into his arms and bestowing a chaste kiss upon her brow. "I thought I should never see you again. To think of you left standing alone on that wretched street corner and I responsible for it! I shall never forgive myself."

"Oh, but it was not your fault, Geoffery. Surely you did not wish to be set upon by footpads. Mr. Kettering informed me of it, you know. But I thought at the time that something unforeseen must have occurred, for you would never have abandoned me."

"Never!" exclaimed Hempstead.

"Perhaps it was for the best that we were prevented from running off, dearest. What a scandal we should have created! My father would have been livid and Aunt Olivia—. It was wrong of me to push you into it, and I will not do so again."

Hempstead, his dark, brooding eyes gleaming in the moonlight, felt a wave of relief wash over him at her words. The cessation of the panic he had been under since that night gave his gaze a fresh tenderness as he studied the sweet, upturned little face he had adored since childhood. "I did not feel it to be exactly the thing myself," he confessed. "But what will we do, April? Neither your father nor your Aunt Olivia approves of me."

April thought back to whispered words upon another balcony, and smiled. "I think Geoffery that we must wait awhile, until I am a bit older and you a bit wiser."

"What does that mean? Do you wish me to go away, then, April? Not to see you? I do not think I could survive it."

"Oh, nothing so drastic as that. But I have been thinking. Aunt Olivia does not approve of our relationship because, she says, you have neither fortune nor ambition."

"Well, she is wrong, the old bat! I do have ambition."

"Geoff, do not call her an old bat," giggled April. "She loves me and has only my best interests at heart. She does not understand, you know, how we feel, and worries that you have no way to provide for a wife and a family. And father frowns upon you because, he says, you are a here-and-thereian, though he likes you well enough and I expect he would accept you if Aunt Olivia did. Somehow," pondered April with a pursing of her very kissable lips, "we must discover a way to set Aunt Olivia's mind to rest."

"I shall cease sporting about town and find employment," declared Hempstead confidently.

"But what sort of employment? You may not involve yourself with the Cits or Aunt Olivia will certainly disdain you."

"I have pleaded with father to buy me a commission in the cavalry. She cannot disdain that. Your own father is a captain of the First Hussars. But m'mother will not hear of it. It is enough, she says, that Lionel and Arthur fight for England, she will not have me on the lists as well, and father will not gainsay her. I expect she would not mind if I entered the Church."

The very tone of Hempstead's voice at those words sent April into giggles again. "I rather think not, Vicar Hempstead. You would be struck down in the midst of your first sermon. Perhaps Mr. Kettering and Viscount Harcort will have some ideas. You must seek their advice, and I will consult with Amy and Beth."

"Who?" Hempstead asked.

"Amy and Beth. They are my newest and best friends. And they are exceptionally intelligent and sophisticated. They have lived all over the world. I am certain they will know exactly what kind of employment you may find that will be acceptable to my aunt."

As Hempstead escorted April back inside, again under cover of Kettering and Harcort, M. LeBruin led Olivia into the Langdons' study. "Your brother is courier for Wellesley, is he not?" the gentleman asked quietly.

"Yes, one of them. What message did he send with you, monsieur? Why did you not mention it to me when you visited?"

LeBruin's fine grey eyes flashed in the fire light and then

smouldered. "Because he sent no message, mademoiselle. Your forgiveness I must beg for speaking that nontruth."

Olivia stared at him fearfully. "But you said only a moment ago that—why, then, have you brought me here? I must return to April immediately."

"No, mademoiselle, you must not. What I must speak to you is of great importance. I have not brought a message from the good captain, but what I tell you concerns him. I did not meet with him upon my travels, Mademoiselle Olivia, but I expected to do so. Your brother, *ma belle,* is missing."

"Missing, sir?"

"Missing—disappeared, and no one able to locate him."

"Oh!" gasped Olivia. LeBruin helped her quickly to a seat.

If Jack Sloan's wide smile was meant to ease Abbercombe's trepidation, it did not. The duke was close to panic as he advanced into the front room of White's. The place was overflowing. "My luck to arrive on a night when everyone has decided to abandon their wives," he mumbled, and Worth's face crinkled into silent laughter.

"Buck up, Cash. It'll be over before you know it. You cannot hide away forever, you know."

"Care to call for the Betting Book and write that down?"

"As a matter of fact," grinned Worth, "I believe there is already a bet laid as to whether you will appear here."

"No," sighed Abbercombe under his breath.

"Yes," nodded Worth. "I believe it was a topic for disagreement between Alvanley and Brummell. We'll discover soon enough; they are both here."

"Where?"

"There," Worth bowed in the direction of the Beau and his cohorts. "Do you know about Brummell?"

"Very little. Heard of him."

"After your time, I think," mused Worth, taking Abbercombe's arm and escorting him across the room toward the private parlor that awaited them. "Man's become the arbiter of fashion. Dandies copy everything he wears, says, and does. Women are wild for his commendation. If Beau Brummell likes you, your social life is guaranteed in London."

"Surely you jest," Abbercombe grinned.

"That's better, Cash. No one's going to bite you, you know."

Conversations dwindled to a halt as the two crossed the colorful Turkish carpeting. All eyes in the room followed their progress. "I say," drawled a voice languidly into the expectant silence, "I believe you have lost your blunt, Alvanley. Ain't that the rogue on Worth's arm?"

Abbercombe tensed, but to all outward appearances the duke was calm and self-possessed and Worth was proud of him.

At a table a few feet to their right, a gentleman of medium height with brown hair and extremely expressive eyes rose from his chair and approached them.

"You will introduce us, I beg of you, Worth," he smiled, standing before Abbercombe in a coat of dark blue superfine and buff pantaloons, a red tea rose in his buttonhole.

Worth nodded. "Your grace, may I present Mr. George Bryan Brummell. Mr. Brummell, Rudolph Denbigh, Duke of Abbercombe."

The Beau bowed. Abbercombe nodded curtly.

"I have wished for your acquaintance, your grace, for the longest time and now I can think of nothing to say." Brummell's eyes twinkled. "Will you do me the honor to shake my hand?"

"Why?" asked Abbercombe softly, slipping his hands into his pockets. "Have you a bet laid on that as well?"

The Beau's eyebrows lifted in surprise. "Sir?"

"If you have, I shall be obliged to claim a share of your winnings—or let you lose the thing. How much are you willing to pay, Mr. George Bryan Brummell, for a handshake?"

Brummell's countenance turned haughty. "Do you realize, your grace," he drawled quietly, "that if I am seen to take you up, you have an excellent chance of being restored to the fold?"

"Indeed?" Abbercombe droned. "You are young, don't you

think, to wield such power? Very young, or it would occur to you that I might have no desire to *be* restored to the fold."

Worth attempted to hold back his laughter at the stunned look on Brummell's face but could not and broke into whoops, starting a buzz of curiosity around the room.

"Edward, control yourself," murmured Abbercombe, bringing one of his hands from his pocket and giving a tug at his friend's arm. "Brummell and I strive for understanding here and I do not want his mind diverted. So, brat," he continued, tucking his hand once again into his pocket, "what price do you put upon my handshake?"

The Beau fought to keep a somber countenance. "I might say your handshake would be priceless, sir."

"Yes, undoubtedly you might, but I am not fool enough to believe it. What's the wager? Out with it or Worth and I continue on."

"Five thousand," Brummell muttered, "though I find I should have bet more, now I come to meet you."

"I will take a thousand," Abbercombe explained quietly. "Worth will take two. He did, after all, win one wager for you already by bringing me here, did he not?"

"Indeed," Brummell agreed giving Worth a quick glance and then lowering his eyes for fear they would both burst into laughter. "Do you wish a part of those winnings as well?"

"No, three thousand will do," smiled Abbercombe taking his hand from his pocket and proffering it to the Beau.

Brummell took it, shook it, and then placed it through his arm, escorting Abbercombe and Worth the rest of the way across the room. "I shall see the money in your hands before you finish your dinner," he said, striving for a businesslike attitude. He bid them goodbye at the private parlor with another bow.

Abbercombe survived the evening in good form. He had not seen Ralph Richardson or Donald Hurley since his ignominious exit from England, and he found the spirit in which they welcomed his return overwhelming. They stuffed him with oysters, roast beef, pheasant and salmon; turned him up sweet with coffee creams, apricot tarts and chocolate-covered cherries; and shared stories with him over bottles of his favourite Canary. He learned that Worth had not married until thirty-one and then chosen a mere chit of a girl; that Richardson had a daughter the same age as Amy and Beth; that Hurley's brother had been in Portugal with Sir John Moore's ill-fated troops and barely made it home alive.

"If it had not been for that chap they call The Rogue who squeaked those troop ships past the Frenchies and managed to ferry the troops safely back to England, Neil would be as dead as Sir John, himself," Hurley sighed. "Never did discover the fellow's true identity. Man saved all those lives and no one has a name to put to him."

"Enough," Worth proclaimed, bringing an end to the stories. "Time we visited the tables, no? Care for a bit of whist, Cash?"

Abbercombe grinned and followed his friends into one of the card rooms. Hurley and Richardson declined to play but sat down to watch as Worth and Abbercombe were challenged by an enthusiastic Brummell and a dubious but willing Alvanley. Several members of the club left the room in protest when Abbercombe entered but most continued their own play with nothing more than pointed glances and a few whispers. Worth gave silent thanks that no one chose to confront the duke, giving considerable credit for it to Brummell's whimsical enchantment with Abbercombe with which not even the most respected of the *ton* gentlemen chose to quarrel. Brummell's whimsical enchantment, however, was severely tested several hours later when Abbercombe threatened to leave the table with ten thousand pounds of Brummell's lining his own pockets.

"You cannot," the Beau stated, his eyes narrowing. "You must give me an opportunity to recoup my losses."

"Must I, brat? Is it a law now in England?"

"Cash," Worth sighed watching the Beau's eyes, "reconsider."

Abbercombe leaned back in his chair and studied Brummell's

pristine waistcoat silently. "Very well," he mumbled at last. "One more game—ten thousand against that waistcoat of yours."

Brummell flinched. "I am not in need of your charity, sir," he replied, nonplussed.

"I am not offering charity. I desire that waistcoat. Those are the stakes. Decide."

Worth shook his head sadly when Brummell cajoled Alvanley into accepting the rematch. "You know not what you do," he whispered to Brummell, taking up his cards.

Abbercombe played silently, his eyes glowing with mirth. At the game's end a snickering Alvanley assisted the Beau to discard his coat. Worth rocked back in his chair with tears of laughter in his eyes as Brummell stripped off his white waistcoat and placed it in Abbercombe's outstretched hand. The duke rolled it up, stuffed it into his boot top, nodded to Alvanley and turned on his heel. Immediately surrounded by a laughing Worth, Hurley and Richardson, he left the room.

Brummell who had managed to keep a sober countenance throughout the whole, collapsed into his chair, rested his forehead on the table and remained there for a full two minutes.

"Beau, are you all right?" Alvanley asked at last.

"Certainly," drawled Brummell, sitting up straight and swiping at his eyes with the back of his hand. "I am not only all right, Alvanley, I am most fortunate. I am most fortunate he did not take a liking to my pantaloons."

"So," Lord Molyneux winked, approaching the table. "I might have warned you, but then you young gentlemen like to discover things for yourselves. Abbercombe was born with a deck of cards in one hand and a set of dice in the other. 'Tis the reason we all called him Cash—ours always ended in his pockets. You should be grateful he did not discover your bet about shaking his hand, Brummell. He'd have walked off with a goodly portion of that blunt as well."

"Do tell," murmured Brummell, a light of unholy glee in his fine eyes. "How lucky I am, Molyneux. How very lucky I am!"

* * *

Olivia stared at M. LeBruin in silence, anxiety clearly written across her face.

"I am distressed, mademoiselle, to be the bearer of such tidings," LeBruin murmured, kneeling beside her chair and holding her white-gloved hands in his own. "I have put them off for as long as possible, for which I now regret. When I called at your home, I had hoped to find Captain Willburton-Smythe present."

"But—but why would you think that? Andrew is at the front with Wellesley, surely."

"Non, mademoiselle. He was to have delivered a despatch to me in the village of Gironde. When at last my waiting began to attract much suspicion, I departed, hoping to receive word of him upon my return home. Unfortunately, it was not to be."

Olivia could think of nothing to say. Visions of her adored elder brother—his broad, winning smile, his fine patrician features, the glinting laughter that seemed always to linger in his gold-flecked hazel eyes, assailed her.

"How—however am I going to tell April," she whispered on the verge of tears.

LeBruin held her hands more firmly. *"Non, mademoiselle,* you must not speak a word to the child. Not yet. It is early to bring her such distress. Perhaps the captain, he will reappear shortly. It is possible he returned to Wellesley when he found I had left Gironde. I only tell you of his disappearance because it is likely you may hear from him and may then assure me of his safety."

"But why, monsieur, would Andrew carry a despatch to you?" Olivia sat up straighter in her chair, tugging her hands free of his. "Are you, are you a spy, monsieur?"

LeBruin looked away and then back again. His dark curls, swept ruthlessly from his brow, gave her a vision of seething eyes that made her physically recoil. *"Oui, mademoiselle,* a spy. It is my most important investment—my life for the downfall of the tyrant, Napoleon! But you must speak of this to no one. You understand? And should you receive word of your brother, you will tell me at once. I cannot rest until I know of his safety."

Olivia nodded. "Continue to call at Park Street, monsieur, and I shall inform you as soon as word of Andrew reaches me."

Abbercombe parted from his friends at the juncture of Abingdon Street and Great Stanhope, assuring them that he was quite capable of negotiating the cobbles the rest of the way on his own. With a yawn he wandered into the shadowed courtyard of Fielding House. At the base of the front steps he halted. "Who's there?" he growled, whirling toward the bushes on the far side of the drive.

He stood in the fading moonlight listening, but heard nothing. He turned and made his way slowly up the steps one hand resting on the hilt of his sabre, the other searching his pockets for his key. A rustling as he bent to insert the key into the lock made him straighten and peer over his shoulder. Shadows. Keeping his eye on the bushes, he turned the key, swung inside, and closed and locked the door immediately behind him.

"Fool," he whispered in the darkness, seeking the candle Dawson had left for him. "You're home. There is no one following you or lying in wait for you. This is England. England is safe. You are safe." Having listened to himself with great solemnity, he made his way quietly up to the second floor, stopped in each of four bedchambers and placed a thankful kiss on each of his children's brows, then stumbled into his own chambers to find Fanning asleep in a chair beside a barely flickering fire.

Olivia left the *soiree* with a bright smile pasted upon her face, and heard, but did not listen to April as the girl prattled on about the evening party during the ride home. In a state of shock she sent April safely off to bed and sought her own. That Andrew should be missing, possibly hunted or even, God forbid, dead somewhere in France! It could not be! And that M. LeBruin, the gentleman who had always made her so uneasy should prove to be a British spy! No matter her opinions, her witty, intellectual debates, never—never until that instant in the Langdons' study when Andrew's name had dropped from LeBruin's lips—had the reality and horror of war come truly home to her. She spent a sleepless night and took her breakfast in her room, hoping to compose herself before meeting April face to face. She could not lay the worry of Andrew's disappearance upon his daughter's fragile shoulders. She would not do so! She must simply carry on as though nothing untoward had happened.

And that was why, early in the following week, Miss Willburton-Smythe, accompanied by her niece, wandered vaguely from stall to stall at the Burlington Arcade. She wished to purchase, she claimed, some pretty gewgaw or other to sit upon her hall table. She was tired of her grandmother's silver epergne which had been banished from the dining room into the hall several years earlier.

"There must be something that will suit," she murmured to April with a great deal of indecision, her elegantly gloved hand flitting from a fine Venetian glass vase to an ornate, but strangely appealing, silver and onyx urn. "Look about, dearest, and see what catches your eye. Perhaps you will discover some frippery you would like to have for yourself. Do not wander far," she added with a quick glance about her. "I know; take Peggy with you. I shall contrive to do without her for a while."

So saying, Olivia returned to her wandering, pleased because April and the abigail would no longer be trailing behind her with expressions of extreme boredom upon their faces. It is bad enough I must pretend to be interested in such nonsense, Olivia thought, without forcing April to do so as well. She and Peggy will doubtless find something to amuse them. Whereupon she lifted a *papier mache* replica of a pheasant and inspected it with some reservation. She set it down with a shake of the dark curls that peeked from beneath her fetching but outmoded conversation bonnet and moved on through the crowd to the next store.

Not far from where Miss Willburton-Smythe shopped, Abbercombe turned completely around, his eyes searching the mall soberly. A golden haired little girl clung to each of his hands. "Where?" he asked finally, kneeling down to confront his daughters face to face. "I cannot make out which shop you mean."

"Over there, Papa," Gracie pointed with notable impatience.

"The one with the statute front of it," nodded Helen.

"But that's a tobacconist's shop, my dears. You certainly do not wish to go in there."

"Uh-huh," Gracie said stubbornly.

"Uh-huh," Helen agreed, clear blue eyes pleading.

"Well, but you cannot," Abbercombe replied, giving them each a hug. "Not alone. I may take you in with me, but they will not let you enter all by yourselves. All they sell, my darlings, are things for gentlemen—pipes, and tobacco, and snuff, and, well, nothing for little girls."

The two curly heads hung down and two sets of innocent blue eyes gazed at two pairs of tiny half boots.

"Villains," Abbercombe groaned. "Do not look so woebegone. People will think I am being unkind. Is that what you wish?"

"No, Papa," Helen replied, lifting her head only a little so that he might hear her. "But you promised mos' faithf'ly we should spen' our 'lowances."

"Yes, I know I did, and so you shall, Helen, but not in that particular shop. Over there is a shop filled with gewgaws. Would you not rather go there?"

"No," mumbled Gracie so low that he had to lean closer to hear. "We wanna spen' it there!" She looked up, tears glistening, and pointed at the tobacconist's. "An' you can't come!"

"Gracie Irene, do not you dare cry," sighed Abbercombe. "I have been your Papa a very long time and I know you can make tears fall whenever you like, so I will not be swayed by them."

"N-No, Papa," Gracie stuttered, two big teardrops trailing slowly down her pink cheeks.

Abbercombe smiled, took his handkerchief from his pocket and patted away the evidence of Grace's particular talent. "Perhaps, if you tell me why you must spend your allowances in that shop—" he suggested. "Did you see something in the window when you came with Miss Greene? I am sure she did not take you inside."

"No, Papa," pouted Helen. "She said abs'lutely not. But she didn' unnerstan'."

"Well, I am afraid I do not understand either. This is the third time in as many weeks that you have come here to spend your allowances, and you have not spent them yet."

" 'Cause no one will take us to where we wanna spen' 'em," replied Gracie with a stamp of her little foot. "Not Greenie or Amy or nobody!"

Olivia, who had paused with curiosity as had a number of the shoppers, giggled at the footstamp. The giggle caught Abbercombe's ear, and he looked up to find himself the center of a good deal of bemused attention. His handsome face suffused with color as he noted the circle of onlookers. Then his great blue eyes discovered Olivia and he rose to his feet, taking a small hand in each of his own. He stepped toward her hesitantly, his ash blond curls tousled and an endearing smile upon his face.

"Miss Olivia," he said, bowing without relinquishing his hold upon the children. His mouth stayed open a moment, but no more words emerged.

"Do not be embarrassed, your grace," Olivia smiled sympathetically. "I comprehend that this time you do wish me to extricate you from the stares. Pretend that we are together and that all has been settled, and the crowd will disperse directly."

"Please, God, let it be so," he prayed, turning his gaze heavenward, which made Olivia chuckle. "I think you have not yet made the acquaintance of my youngest daughters?"

"No, I have not had that pleasure."

"No, well, this is Grace," he said nodding toward the child on his left. "And this is Helen."

Olivia grinned to see both little girls curtsy on determined but wobbly little legs, his strong hands lending them support.

"This is Miss Willburton-Smythe," he informed the girls. "It is her niece, April, whom Amy and Beth go to visit."

"How d'do?" said Helen, her big eyes staring straight up into Olivia's. Grace stared up as well, but said nothing.

"I do very well, thank you, my dear," Olivia replied. "But it appears that the two of you are having a problem."

"No, ma'am," sighed Grace, holding her father's gloved hand with both of hers.

"Uh-huh," contradicted Helen, releasing her grip on Abbercombe's hand and pressing tightly against his leg instead. "Can you help, Miss Weebuttonsmite?"

Abbercombe shrugged. "It is a hard name," he murmured, his arm going, Olivia noticed, protectively around Helen's tiny form.

"Of course I shall help, Lady Helen. You must only tell me what I may do to be of service."

"For some reason," the duke explained, "they are determined to go into the tobacconist's shop, and they wish to do so without me. I have told them it is most exceptional for ladies to enter such an establishment at any time, and that they certainly cannot do so without my escort, but I fear they will not be content with it."

Olivia proffered her hands to the two little girls. "Remain here, your grace," she ordered as Grace and Helen grabbed hold of her. "We ladies wish to have a brief discussion without you." She smiled at him reassuringly and walked both girls to one side of the large mall. "Now, you must tell me why you wish to go into the tobacconist's without your Papa," she said, kneeling and placing her arms around them.

A few moments later Olivia stood, took their hands, and strolled confidently into the shop. When they emerged, each of the girls carried a package very carefully in their tiny hands. Abbercombe went to meet them.

"I cannot believe you did that," he muttered with a look upon his face that Olivia could not decipher.

"I am hardly a schoolroom miss, your grace," she responded

with some asperity. "I have no qualms about entering an establishment when I have business there."

He opened his mouth, closed it again, stared at the floor, then back up at her. "Thank you," he replied faintly, his look unsettling but his tone grateful. "It was most kind of you."

Five

Olivia thought of him all the way home. He even displaced for a time her worry over Andrew. "Are you very tired, Aunt?" asked April, once they had entered the house on Park Street. "You are so quiet. Would you like to lie down for a bit?"

"No, no, I'm fine. I shall have some tea and feel my old self in no time. No, I shall not. I shall take a walk instead. Peggy," she called to the abigail who had just turned away, "we shall take a stroll. Put your pelisse back on."

Olivia's stroll took her to Cumberland Square and into the arms of a concerned Lady Jessica. "What is it, Olivia? Why do you scowl so? Come sit down. I am just about to have tea and you shall share it with me."

Olivia allowed herself to be coddled and cosseted for a good five minutes before she shook off her megrims and apologized for her behaviour. "I cannot think what it is," she sighed. "No, that is not true at all. I know exactly what it is. It is your brother-in-law."

"Abbercombe?" Lady Jessica's cheeks took on a pinker tinge. "What has he done? Olivia, if he has plagued you in some way, you must tell me immediately."

Olivia opened her mouth to protest that the duke had not plagued her at all, but was prevented from doing so by the entrance of the Denbighs' butler with two curly-haired, well-dressed young gentlemen close on his heels.

"Your nephews wish a moment of your time, ma'am," offered Robson with a whimsical smile.

"It is extremely important, Aunt Jess," announced Christian, stepping around Robson into the room. "Excuse me, ma'am, we did not mean to disturb anyone."

"Good afternoon, ma'am," Damian smiled, coming to stand beside his brother and making a very pretty bow to Olivia.

Lady Jessica introduced them and sent for tea for the boys as well. When they were settled, she leaned back in her chair and grinned at Olivia.

"I have met Amaryllis, Bethany, Christian, Damian, Grace, and Helen," smiled Olivia. "Certainly that must be all of you."

"No, ma'am," Daymee chuckled, "but Ethan and Frazier will be here shortly."

"They will?" asked Lady Jess in surprise.

"Yes, Aunt Jess," Christian nodded. "At least we think they will for we all agreed to meet here. Mr. Stanton, he is their tutor, you know, took them to see the cathedral but they should be rid of him soon. That is, I did not mean to say that exactly. Mr. Stanton is nice and we all like him, but—"

"But you wish him out of your way today," supplied Olivia.

"Exactly, ma'am," agreed Damian.

"We have come to invite you to Fielding House next Saturday evening," offered Christian. "You are not already promised to someone, are you, Aunt Jess? We are going to have a party."

Lady Jessica's eyes opened wide and she turned to Olivia with a look of dread upon her face. Christian, correctly assessing her reaction, grinned reassuringly. "You need not be concerned, Aunt Jessica. No one will cut Papa or insult him or anything like that. It is not to be a party for Polite Society. We are just asking people we like. Mrs. Griffin has promised to see to the refreshments. She is even going to send to Gunter's for strawberry tarts. You do like strawberry tarts, don't you, Aunt Jess? And we shall have gingersnaps and lemonade."

"And Dawson is going to help us decorate, and Mr. Stanton and Miss Greene as well. It will be famous. Please say you will come, Aunt Jess," urged Damian. "And you, Miss Willburton-

Smythe, and Miss April. Amy and Beth have just gone to Park Street to invite you. We are celebrating Papa's birthday."

The sound of booted feet running down the hall turned all eyes toward the doorway as Ethan and Frazier burst into the room. "We're here!" shouted Frazier gleefully. "Where's Uncle 'Bastian? Ain't you found him yet? Oh, 'scuse me," he added hurriedly, Christian having directed his attention to the ladies with a glare. "Af'ernoon, Aunt Jess. Af'ernoon, ma'am."

"This is Miss Willburton-Smythe," announced Christian with great sobriety. "She is April's aunt."

The two eight-year-olds, wind-blown and pink-cheeked from a long excursion in the brisk spring air and obviously breathless from a good deal of running, turned immediately serious and bowed together quite elegantly in Olivia's direction.

"Ethan and Frazier," Damian finished the introduction. "Now, ma'am, you have met the whole scurvy lot of us."

"Daymee, don't say scurvy," Christian ordered. "It ain't polite to say in front of ladies."

"Why not?" asked Ethan, tossing the loose end of a vibrantly striped scarf back over his shoulder. "Papa says it."

"It is not polite to call us scurvy in mixed company."

"But I like being scurvy," protested Frazier. "When Papa says it, it sounds like pirates."

Christian shrugged helplessly at the ladies and dropped the subject. "Will you come, please? At eight o'clock?"

"Saturday!" shouted Ethan, jumping up and down on one foot.

"It will be extr'or'nary!" shouted Frazier, spinning around in a circle. "Better even than dinner with the Tzar!"

"Goodness," gasped Olivia teasingly, "I dare not miss it!"

"No, you mus' not," agreed Ethan with an enthusiastic shake of his honey-blond curls. "Ever'one mus' dress like gypsies, an' those puddin' heads who are cruel to Papa will wish they could come, but we shall not let them. They are none of them invited!"

"Not even Prinny," added Frazier, "not even if he begs. We shall close the door slap in his face!"

By the time Lord Sebastian appeared in his riding clothes and hustled four giggling boys toward the stables, both ladies had accepted their invitations.

"I feel like I have been caught in a gale," laughed Olivia.

"It was kind of you to agree to attend their party."

"How could I not agree? It is going to be better than having dinner with the Tzar! But will you see if you can discover why we must all be dressed as gypsies, Jess? My heart pauses at the thought of it."

"At least," Lady Jessica observed with a grin, "you look much less blue-deviled. What was it you wished to say, Olivia, about Abbercombe?"

"Do you know, Jess, that he took little Gracie and Helen to the Burlington Arcade all by himself? I have never seen a gentleman escort his children upon a shopping tour. It made me think how proud I would have been to have gone to Piccadilly with my father, or Pall Mall, or Mayfair." Olivia described the situation in which she had discovered Abbercombe, bringing mirth to Lady Jess's eyes. "But he looked at me so oddly when the girls and I emerged, Jess. I thought I had offended him in some way by taking them into the place. And I could not tell him, you see, why I had done so, or it would have spoiled their surprise."

"He was thinking of Celia, I expect," mused Lady Jess, a slight frown creasing her brow. "I never met her, but I suspect she would have taken the girls directly into the shop just as you did. Amy and Beth say whenever Cash is reminded of her it sinks him on the instant into anguish, though he recovers quickly." Lady Jessica eyed her friend thoughtfully. "Have you relented toward Abbercombe?" she asked quietly.

"Relented?"

"Do you not remember how you called him a devil and said you wished to save Amaryllis and Bethany from his vagaries? Has your opinion of him changed, Olivia?"

Olivia avoided answering that question by noticing the lateness of the hour and taking hurried leave. Her earlier uneasiness had not abated, however, and she could not seem to dismiss thoughts of Abbercombe from her mind as she strolled toward Park Street with Peggy keeping step silently beside her.

The image of the duke as some sort of roguish devil had become insupportable. The more she saw of his children, the more she was convinced that Abbercombe could not be the same man who had beaten someone to death in Seven Dials. The image of him kneeling with his arms lovingly about Gracie and Helen, totally unconscious of the shoppers surrounding them, convinced her even more that there had been, so long ago, some terrible mistake. And the sight of the flush rising to his face! Who would think that anything could make a gentleman of his age and reputation blush? Yet he had done so, so innocently, that her heart had gone immediately out to him. Jessica was probably quite right. Somehow she had reminded him of his late wife. That had been the cause of his sudden chagrin and the odd look in his eyes. How unfair life was! Here was a kind and loving man mistakenly condemned to be outcast forever; and her darling brother, Andrew, missing and endangered; and M. LeBruin, forced to live a double life in the effort to rid the world of a madman.

By the time she and Peggy arrived at Park Street, she had succeeded in working herself up into a pucker and despite all her efforts to the contrary she knew that she proved to be a very oppressive dinner companion for April that evening.

Abbercombe found himself similarly distressed that evening but accustomed to set aside his own feelings, he dined with his children in what anyone would have labelled excellent spirits, and rather than retiring with a glass of wine at the end of the meal, he challenged his progeny to a game of lottery tickets, baiting Mr. Stanton and Miss Greene until they, too, must join in or be thought terribly high in the instep by their charges.

Not satisfied with seducing the governess and tutor back into childhood, he had the audacity to walk off at the end of an hour amidst the shouts and laughter of the other participants with all of the winnings in his possession and to seek out Fanning,

Dawson and Mrs. Griffin. He managed to inveigle them into becoming members of his team in a wild and whimsical diversion he called "capture the wretched waistcoat" which involved the hiding, protecting and swiping of Beau Brummell's prized white garment and a similar blue one of his own and sent children and adults scurrying about the house, dashing up and down the stairs, scooting under beds and generally running about like wild red Indians.

By eleven o'clock Grace and Helen had gone to sleep under the counter in the back pantry with their father's waistcoat hidden safely between them, and the rest of the two teams had collapsed, chuckling, onto various pieces of furniture in the front drawing room, Mr. Brummell's waistcoat entering at the last as the lining of a tray of hot chocolate carried by a beaming Mrs. Griffin. Abbercombe winked at her and went off to tuck his youngest set of twins into bed. By the time he returned to the drawing room most of the cups were empty and a series of hugs and kisses bid him goodnight.

He urged Dawson, Mrs. Griffin, Miss Greene and Mr. Stanton to remain seated before the fire and finish their conversation and took himself off to the privacy of his study where he poured a brandy, added coal to a dwindling fire, lit himself a cigar, and sank down into a brocade chair before the hearth. Stretching his long legs out before him, he stared into the flames and at last allowed thoughts of Miss Willburton-Smythe his full attention.

He could not imagine what about the woman aroused him so! Yes, by gawd, he could! He just did not wish to credit it. Be damned if he did not find her intriguing. He had not found a woman intriguing since Celia, who had strolled down the gangplank of the *Stout Heart* onto the quay in Boston harbor a year after their marriage and barely two months after his exile and sent his heart and soul reeling. Theirs had been an arranged marriage, and he had not known that he truly loved Celia until that very moment. But he had a suspicion that he could love Miss Willburton-Smythe who in her old-fashioned chip bonnet with its green silk bow tied rakishly atop had looked like Gracie and

Helen playing at dress-up and thus wistfully denied the impression of self-sufficiency which her words and actions expressed. He could not understand for the life of him why the woman was left to care for her niece and not busy with children of her own. Certainly all of the gentlemen of the *ton* had not grown blind, deaf, and dumb in his absence. What were they about to let such a beguiling creature escape them?

He puffed at his cigar to keep it from dying then took another sip of brandy. Devil take it, a man of his age and reputation had no business to allow such a proper young lady to arouse his interests. Well, if he could not allow himself to love her, at least he could strive to help her. He would begin by doing as Amy and Beth had asked late that afternoon. He would assist little April in making Geoffery Hempstead an acceptable suitor and thus relieve Olivia's worries on that subject. He would send a message to Wyndham tonight and suggest that Hempstead be considered as a replacement for Harry.

Olivia looked up from her embroidery to see April gazing dispiritedly into the fire, chided herself for letting her own troubles occupy her thoughts to the detriment of her niece and vowed to set her preoccupation aside until she retired for the night. "Do you ride with Lord Goddering in the park tomorrow, April?" she asked, setting her work aside. "He has the most delicious phaeton, you know, and you will quite enjoy it."

April brought herself to attention. "Yes," she replied, "I promised him this morning that I would do so."

"He is quite nice, is he not? Am I mistaken to think that you find him good company, my dear?"

"He is very nice, Aunt Olivia," answered April, wondering what on earth had brought Lord Goddering to the forefront of her aunt's mind. "I expect I shall enjoy his phaeton very much."

"You certainly shall," nodded Olivia. "And now that more families have arrived in town, you are sure to meet a number of other gentlemen anxious to escort you about London. You will see, my dear. Once the Season is in full swing, you will be wishing for a quiet evening at home such as we now spend."

"Yes," April sighed, turning her gaze back to the hearth.

"Darling, you are not moping over Mr. Hempstead, are you? I realize that you think you love him, but you have so little experience in the matter. Neither your father nor I find him a suitable match for you. You will see, April," she said encouragingly, moving from her chair to sit beside her niece on the settee, "you will develop *tendres* for any number of gentlemen before you decide who will be your husband."

"Did you develop *tendres* for any gentlemen, Aunt Olivia?"

"Oh, I certainly did. And I changed my mind again and again. I was fickle, I suppose, and very hard to please, but I had a wonderful time." She smiled broadly, remembering her own Season, and smoothed the soft silk of her apricot gown across her knees.

"But you never did marry."

"I expect I would have done had your grandfather not died so unexpectedly and left me in a most comfortable position. Since there was no entail and Father left his estate equally between your father and me, I found I had no need for a husband. I fear it was quite exceptional of me to think of it, but I could see only that if I married, my husband would be in control of all that I possessed and I should have no say in it, while if I did not marry, I might do with my inheritance what I wished."

April stared wide-eyed at her aunt. "How could you think so? I want nothing more than to be married and protected and loved."

"I know, my dear. And I think I might have married despite myself had I truly loved any gentleman. But I did not. They courted me because I was passably pretty, came from an old, respectable family, and had a significant dowry, but there was not one of them took my opinions seriously or wished for my advice or needed me. And I did think," Olivia added with a wry grin, "that if I let myself love someone they ought at least try to make me feel needed."

* * *

On Wednesday evening Olivia escorted April to the Sinclairs'
musicale and was delighted to discover Lord Sebastian and Lady
Jessica Denbigh, accompanied by Amaryllis and Bethany, in attendance as well. "Sebastian did not wish to come at all," Lady
Jess whispered as they settled into the delicate white chairs. "But
Cash spoke to him and quite suddenly I had a husband as escort.
I cannot guess what was said, but Sebastian has not frowned once
since we came! Though I doubt he will last through the night if
there should chance to be a young lady with a harp."

There happened, in fact, to be a young lady with a harp near
the middle of the program, and true to Lady Jessica's prophecy,
Sebastian Denbigh excused himself with a mumbled reference
to seeking out the card room and strolled into the hall. He waited
there, leaning nonchalantly against the wall, until the young
lady's performance began and the hall was cleared of humanity.
Then he strolled casually toward the staircase, leaned over the
rail to see that the hall below was empty of servants, and quietly
hurried down the stairs.

Looking left and right to see he was not observed, he made
his way to Sinclair's ground floor study, stepped inside and closed
the door softly behind him. The room stood in deep shadow, the
only light a small coal fire flickering in the grate. Sebastian stood
still a moment to get his bearings then made his way to the set
of draperies that he determined to cover the casement windows
at the rear of the house. He drew them aside, opened one of the
windows and flinched as his brother's gloved hand touched his
own on the latch. He moved back, giving Abbercombe room to
climb inside and watched as the duke pulled the casement closed
again. Abbercombe drew the draperies back across the window,
turned and smiled.

"I thank you, 'Bastian. Now go back to the party."

"But, Cash, can I not stay to help?"

"No."

"I could at least stand lookout for you."

"No, you cannot. Are you about to make me regret placing my trust in you? I do not have time to argue."

Sebastian nodded, moved to the study door and exited the room closing the door gently behind him. In another two minutes he was on the first floor and strolling into the card room where a number of musically disinclined gentlemen conversed over various games, his detour to the ground floor gone unnoticed.

Abbercombe lighted a single candle and set it on Sinclair's desk. Methodically he searched through one drawer after another, scanning through mounds of messages and bills. He moved on to an enclosed bookcase, a red despatch-box that rested upon a cricket table in one corner, and then tackled a wall safe he found behind a landscape above the mantle. Realizing that he pressed his luck, he nevertheless took time to probe at the fireplace and discovered a courier's pouch hidden behind a loose brick.

He was in the midst of opening the pouch when the sound of footsteps reached his ears. Quickly he snatched the papers, closed the pouch and returned it to its hiding place. He snuffed the candle and dove for the casement just as the study door swung silently inward. Safely out of sight behind the draperies, he swung the window open, put one booted foot on the sill, then stopped. In amazement he returned his foot to the floor and cautiously tugged the window closed, his heart thudding almost to a stop at the voice that whispered a few feet from him.

"What do we seek, monsieur?" Olivia asked.

"Papers, mademoiselle," answered a deep voice. "Anything which bears the insignia of the War Office, or if not that, General Wellesley's signature. But we must hurry for the party will begin to disperse shortly, *n'est-ce pas?* If you will search those drawers, *ma chere,* I will investigate these."

The sound of desk drawers sliding gently open and hasty fingers scrabbling through papers jolted Abbercombe's heart up into his throat. He remained frozen until at last Miss Willburton-Smythe and her confederate reached the end of their hurried search and he heard them exit the room. Then he launched himself out of the window and into the rear yard of the Sinclairs' house. Keeping to the shadows, he made his way discreetly to the avenue and strolled off in the direction of Great Stanhope.

It was nigh four A.M. when Fanning, a worried frown creasing his brow, scratched at the door of Abbercombe's study. A weary voice bid him enter, which he did with ready words upon his lips about his grace's need, at his age, for a decent night's sleep. The words died a silent death, however, when the deep blue eyes stared up at him, a look of bewildered despair evident in their depths.

"What is it, your grace?" Fanning asked, settling on the edge of a chair opposite the gentleman. He noted the papers that had fallen haphazardly to the carpet at Abbercombe's feet and bent to pick them from the floor.

"Just leave them, Robin."

"But, your grace—"

"Feed them to the fire then. It makes no matter."

"They will not be missed?"

"Certainly they will be missed, Robin, but I stand no chance of replacing them. And they are useless to me."

"You will find Harry," Fanning said with a quiet confidence, "and you will bring him safely home."

Abbercombe stirred in the depths of his chair. "Of course I shall find Harry. It is not that. I should not have come here," he muttered, his eyes searching the flames. "I should have gone to St. Petersburg or Minsk."

"Nonsense," muttered Fanning, offering the last of the despatch to the blaze. "You are weary, your grace, and disappointed. Once you have rested, you will begin again with renewed enthusiasm."

"Will I, Robin?"

"Indeed, your grace."

It was not renewed enthusiasm that set Abbercombe down in the midst of Olivia's parlor the following afternoon, but a confidence in the judgment of his children whom he had consulted that morning at breakfast and who had assured him that Miss Willburton-Smythe was top of the trees and definitely to be trusted in all things.

Olivia welcomed him warmly though with a modicum of surprise. She noticed that he sat uncomfortably on the very edge of the brocade chair and that his eyes darted everywhere but in her own direction. "Do not be nervous, your grace," she smiled reassuringly, "I seldom bite my visitors." Her statement evoked a wisp of a smile. "If you bring a message from the girls, I am afraid April has gone to join the promenade."

"I did not come to speak with April," he said, studying the floral pattern of the carpet. "I wished to speak to you, Olivia."

"Truly? To what do I owe such an unexpected honor?"

Abbercombe raised his eyes to meet hers and cleared his throat softly. "I have come to—to—Why do you insist upon making yourself out to be a little old lady?" he sputtered suddenly, staring at the very becoming spinster's cap she wore upon her dark curls. "Good lord, you are a beautiful young woman! And you ought not to be sitting here with me without a chaperon."

Olivia stared at him, speechless.

"Damn," he muttered, looking back down at the carpet. When he raised his eyes again, he was looking exceptionally sheepish. "I'm sorry," he said soberly. "I have no right to criticize. Your cap is fetching, Olivia, and I am sure your judgment concerning the propriety of our speaking alone is to be depended upon."

It did occur to Olivia that for a person suddenly so concerned with propriety, the Duke of Abbercombe tended to be most free with the use of her Christian name, but she did not wish to bring this breach of etiquette to his attention. "You are forgiven, sir," she said instead. "Please continue."

"There is a young lady," Abbercombe mumbled, "who appears to be—in need of assistance, and I would like to offer mine, but I cannot—cannot simply come out and do so." He paused and took a very deep breath, which brought a grin to Olivia's face.

"Why can you not?" she asked.

"Because she does not know me very well—not at all," he sighed. "And I can scarcely approach her socially so that she might come to know me and thus repose her trust in me. She would be sunk beneath reproach to be seen publicly in my company."

Olivia's eyes widened. "May I ask, your grace, who—"

"No, you may not."

"But how did you come to discover she was in need of assistance? And is there no one else who might help her?"

"I, ah—Blast! I cannot do this!" grumbled Abbercombe, standing and beginning to pace the room. One hand swept through his perfectly combed hair, setting the curls into wild disarray. "Why must you be so, so guileless? I can no more straight out lie to you than to the children."

"Lie to me? But you barely know me, your grace. What on earth could make you wish to lie to me about anything? You need not even speak to me if you do not wish it."

"But I do wish it!" Abbercombe fairly bellowed. "Damnation, Olivia, I do not know what it is, but if you do not divest yourself of that spinster's cap, I shall go stark, raving mad!"

"Your grace!"

"Yes, I know it is none of my business and it is certainly not in my best interests to annoy you by bringing it up again, but if you persist in wearing that dratted thing, I shall never be able to say why I have come."

"Well, I can only imagine that you are a lunatic," responded Olivia somewhere between amusement and anger. "However," with several deft movements she removed the silk and lace confection and set it aside. "There. May we now get on with it?"

"Where was I?"

"You were somewhere in the midst of lying to me, your grace," Olivia smiled sweetly. "Pray continue."

Abbercombe spun back down into the brocade chair, his long legs stretched before him, his face hidden for a moment behind a lean, finely-chiseled hand with long, slender fingers. One of them bore a sapphire surrounded by diamonds, a second, an onyx signet ring, and a third, a thick gold band. His wedding band, Olivia thought, surprised.

"You are the young lady to whom I wish to offer my assistance," the duke murmured, removing his hand from his face and gripping the chair arm instead. "I know, you see, that you were in Lord Sinclair's study last evening rifling through his private papers. I do not know the gentleman accompanying you. But he is French. One may catch the accent quickly enough."

Olivia's mouth opened, shut, opened again. She could feel a warm flush rise to her cheeks. "Oh," she gasped. "Oh!" and she stood and turned away from him, so totally embarrassed that all she wished to do was to sink through the floor. In a moment strong arms wrapped about her from behind, holding her gently but securely, and she felt a soft breath whisper in her ear.

"You must not turn away from me, dear heart, for that will not answer. I am not come to embarrass you nor to accuse you but to offer my help. Can you find it in your heart to trust me enough to tell me what you sought and why you sought it?"

Olivia's heart beat faster with every word he whispered. The tenderness in his voice, the strength of his arms around her, the soft moist feel of his breath against her ear set her mind to whirling and she turned inside his arms and buried her face in his cravat and began to sob. That horrid sign of weakness made her angry and she brought her small fists upward and pounded at his chest. "I hate you," she mumbled into his neckcloth. "You are a cruel beast!"

"Yes, I have been told so often." Abbercombe smoothed her hair back from her hot little face. Then he held her away from him and placed a chaste kiss upon each tear-stained cheek. With one arm firmly about her waist, he led her to a settee and sat beside her on it. He tugged his handkerchief from his pocket and patted away her tears, then held it to her nose. "Blow," he said, grinning.

Olivia looked up through dark wet lashes into his wonderfully smiling eyes and gurgled.

"No, do not gurgle, blow," he chuckled as she took the handkerchief from him. "And when you have finished, you will tell me what I may do to help."

For no reason on earth other than the look on his face and the tenderness in his eyes, Olivia confided in him her brother's disappearance, the fact that M. LeBruin was a French emigre who spied for the British, and that they had been searching Lord Sinclair's study for any information he might have carried home from the War Office revealing the whereabouts of Wellesley's staff, her brother especially. "B-but we could find nothing," she finished at last, her eyes dry and her face at last cooling.

"Your brother was to have met M. LeBruin at Gironde?" Abbercombe asked. "Are you quite certain that was the place?"

"Yes. And Andrew did not appear," she answered on a gasp.

"Olivia, can you trust me, do you think, to discover your brother for you?"

"But how can you?"

Abbercombe smiled rather sadly down at her. "I have lived a great number of places in the world, my dear. And I have a good many acquaintances in some of the strangest localities. They shall discover Captain Willburton-Smythe's whereabouts for us."

Olivia nodded. It seemed reasonable. It sounded possible.

"But you must promise me not to assist M. LeBruin again. You put yourself in a great deal of danger last evening, though you might not have thought it. To search through the papers of an official of the War Office as you did could be thought treason, my dear, and might have got you hung."

"How did you discover I had done so? Who was it saw us?"

"Someone who will never say a word about it, Olivia. I promise you are safe from the tale reaching any ears but my own."

Six

Saturday evening Olivia and April were escorted into the old ballroom at Fielding House. It stretched across the entire back of the first floor. Fires roared in grates at each end of the room and on every flat surface beeswax candles spluttered and flared. Great pieces of brightly colored cloth hung in graceful flounces from the unlit chandelier, stretching across to the far corners of the room, hiding the original ceiling. Cushions and pillows of reds, blues, bright oranges and deep browns littered the floor, and pieces of highly-polished tack had been carried from the stables to adorn the walls in the oddest way.

In the farthest corner of the room someone had erected a small tent, made quite competently from the house's supply of bed linen. Beside it stood a fiercely visaged little rocking horse with a red saddle and red reins tied to a rail balanced upon two round tables. A long backless bench also covered with pillows, an extremely old chair decorated by a covering of golden velvet which had obviously once been draperies, and assorted stools and ottomans were gathered into a semicircle before the hearth opposite the tent. A similarly eclectic semicircle of furniture stood before the other hearth. A harpsichord, all but its keyboard shrouded in an appalling fringed shawl sat near the center of the room with a violin and bow on top. Along two of the walls stood sideboards laden with fruits and foods and urns filled with lemonade.

"It is meant to be a gypsy camp," laughed Amaryllis, taking Olivia's hand. "We are so happy you came."

"You will not regret it," Bethany added. "At the very least it will be an adventure."

When at last April stopped gazing about and her attention centered on her friends, she laughed aloud. "You both look magnificent. Wherever did you find such clothes? Aunt Olivia and I had the hardest time deciding what a gypsy would wear."

Beth and Amy twirled to display their colorful full skirts, the black stockings and button shoes, the white muslin long-sleeved blouses beneath laced, armless jackets. "You have both done a fine job of it, too," offered Amy. "I think the best way to look like a gypsy is to wear clothes that do not appear as if they were ever meant to go together. And your hair, Miss Willburton-Smythe, is gorgeous," she added with a glint of envy in her eye for the dark, thick tresses that flowed about that lady's shoulders, held in place only by a bright purple riband.

"Oh, look at Lord Sebastian and Lady Jess," cried April.

"Lord Sebastian," Olivia chuckled, making him a bobbing curtsy, "you make a particularly dashing gypsy."

"I do, don't I? But I had help from Ethan and Frazier. They raided their father's trunks for me."

"And lest we forget," put in Lady Jess, teasing, "your earring is due to my grandmother's terrible taste in jewelry."

Sebastian tugged at the huge golden hoop that adorned his right earlobe and bowed to her. "Have you seen the little ones yet?" he asked, taking Olivia's arm and helping her to a seat by one of the hearths. "They look the most appealing ragamuffins. They, too, have been in their papa's trunks and found the most audacious kerchiefs to tie about their curls."

"Yes," laughed Lady Jessica, joining them, "and Grace and Helen's dresses are made from Abbercombe's shirts with his colored neckcloths as sashes. And they have each strings of beads and feathers about their necks like little red Indians. They are so excited they cannot stay in one place and are continually dashing off to peer out the windows for their Papa."

"He is not at home?" Olivia asked.

"The whole is to be a surprise," Lady Jess replied. "Did Grace and Helen not tell you when you helped buy their presents?"

"Well, I knew the presents to be a surprise, but I did not think for a moment Abbercombe knew nothing of the party—especially such a party as this," she giggled.

"Chris and Daymee have gotten Worth to draw Cash off for most of the day," offered Eugenia, Lady Worth, who had settled upon a stool across from Olivia. "What a pleasure to see you, my dear. Have you known Cash long? He and Worth were childhood friends, and Worth dotes upon the man."

For a gentleman who was a pariah amongst the *ton,* Olivia thought, Abbercombe was accepted by some very impressive people. One could not look much higher than the Earl and Countess of Worth when it came to respectability. As Sir Ralph Richardson and the Honorable Donald Hurley joined the group, Olivia took the opportunity to wander off in search of April whom she found inside the little tent with Christian and Damian, setting up a small card table and two chairs. She soon found herself assisting by draping the table with a mauve fringed shawl. "Oh," April gasped, and Olivia turned to see Ethan and Frazier in the tent's opening, an odd little stand in Ethan's hand and a crystal ball balanced in both of Frazier's. Carefully the boys set the stand on the table and the crystal ball on the stand.

"Is it real?" April asked, staring down into it.

Christian's great blue eyes lit with mirth. "No von knoz," he said in a low whisper which made his brothers giggle and Olivia grin. "Zee powerz of zee ball reveal themzelfz only to thoz who pozzez zee gypzy vizion."

"None of us possesses it," snickered Damian.

"It might be real," offered Frazier. "Papa says it is real."

"Papa says Gracie's horse is real," Ethan grumbled, "and Helen's invis'ble frien' Mrs. Bumble."

"Well, I can remember, Ethan," Christian grinned, "when Papa agreed that your bear, which you forced him to lug about everywhere we went, was real as well."

"And our mouse," laughed Damian. "Do not forget how much cheese you and I fed that mouse when we lived in Minsk, Chris."

"And was the mouse not real?" asked April.

"Well, we never actually saw it," Christian murmured "but we left tidbits for it every night."

"Yes," Damian nodded, "and every once in a while after we moved, Mama would set a huge plate of cheese on the dinner table before Papa's place and he would go off into whoops."

"He's coming! He's coming!" shouted two little voices, and Gracie and Helen ran excitedly into the room. The occupants of the tent quickly left it.

"Daymee, close the doors. Hurry," ordered Christian, looking around to see that all his brothers and sisters were present. Sebastian excused himself from a conversation with Hurley, and he and Lady Jess and Lady Worth extinguished candles until only the fires in the grates lit the room. "Now, hide in the shadows," Amaryllis urged. Whispers and giggles followed until everyone found a place where they would not be seen from the door.

On the ground floor, Dawson opened the front door and stepped back, staring.

"Well you may stare, Anthony," muttered Abbercombe, stalking into the hall. "Fanning has turned me into a deuced gypsy!"

"And did he do so to Lord Worth as well, sir?" Dawson asked attempting to keep a sober countenance.

"No, I simply thought that if I joined him in this most extraordinary manner of dress, he might calm down," drawled Worth. "He looks more buccaneer than gypsy, don't you think, Dawson?"

"Where is Robin? Has he run mad?" interrupted Abbercombe. "First Worth leads me at the gallop through a cursed marsh, destroys my boots and covers me head to toe with mud, and then Robin comes to my aid by sending me this charming ensemble to change into. My note said that I planned to go to Covent Garden tonight, not that I meant to appear upon the stage there!"

Dawson's lips twitched maddeningly and his face grew red with the effort of maintaining a proper demeanor.

"I am seriously angry," Abbercombe growled, shoving his gloveless hands into the pockets of tight black kidskin breeches and stamping a booted foot upon the parquet. "Seriously!" But he could not resist the terrible agony under which Dawson struggled and a roar of laughter escaped him. "All right, for pity's sake, laugh, Dawson, or you will explode. And I shall not forgive you if you explode, for everyone will blame me and I shall be hanged as your murderer."

As Dawson crumpled with relief into a spurt of chortles and snorts, the sound of feet pounding down the stairs made Abbercombe whip around, his hand jerking immediately to his side where his sabre would have been, had he been wearing it.

"Sir!" cried Fanning skidding to a stop midway down the stairs. "Thank heaven! Come quickly, the children need you!" Without another word Fanning turned and dashed back up the steps. Abbercombe took them two at a time directly on his heels and Worth, with a quick wink at Dawson, followed the duke. Fanning ran down the first floor hallway and came to a halt, gasping for breath, before the ballroom doors. Abbercombe pushed by him and slammed the doors open. The sight of the room deep in shadow with only the fires burning at both ends made him check on the threshold. And then the sound of flints being struck reached his ears and candles flared. Around the room the sound of flint and the flare of tiny lights repeated itself over and over again, and a series of voices called out to him: "Happy birthday, Papa! Happy birthday! Happy birthday!"

Worth placed his hand upon Abbercombe's shoulder. "Happy birthday, *mon ami*," he whispered close to the duke's ear.

"Happy birthday, your grace," sighed Fanning, still gulping air. "And please refrain from extracting vengeance upon us until you have given it grave consideration."

As the candles continued to be lighted, Olivia stared agog at the lean, muscular figure in the doorway. Nothing could have prepared her for this. Abbercombe's ash blond curls tumbled wildly across his brow; his sapphire blue eyes flashed and glowed and darted from place to place and person to person; his finely sculpted face, its beauty made romantic by the duelling scar and the twice broken nose, wore myriad expressions from fear to bewilderment to surprise to warm happiness in a matter of seconds.

He stood with hands on hips and arms akimbo—coatless, his shirt of fine, glossy silk with wide flowing sleeves open at the neck, its ties dangling. It draped his upper torso in a most sensual, seductive manner; his black kidskin breeches clung like a second skin revealing the trim waist, flat stomach and muscular thighs to remarkable advantage; his boots, unlike any she had ever seen, fitted tightly against his legs, rode above his knees, and then turned downward in a wide fold of glistening black leather; a neckerchief of midnight blue silk hung negligently above the collarless shirt and a wide black belt with a silver buckle made him look a regular pirate.

Olivia watched, entranced, as he was set upon and rowdily and emphatically kissed and hugged by a gaggle of excited children. His grin could not have been more appealing; his eyes could not have glowed more warmly; his pleasure and surprise could not have been more genuine. Never had she thought to see a gentleman welcome such an open display of affection, but Abbercombe delighted in it, giving the children back as good as he got. Everything about him at that moment warmed her heart and argued vigourously that she had been correct to place her reliance upon him and her brother's welfare in his hands. And that was not all about him that pleased her. The agility with which he swung his youngsters, giggling, into the air and the tenderness with which he kept the rough-housing safe for even little Grace and Helen brought a wistful sigh and a wish that her own father might have done the same. Never before had she known such a gentleman or felt so much enjoyment in simply watching him. When finally he extricated himself from the boisterous crowd of tow-headed revelers and moved lithely to greet his guests, she stood in silent awe.

"He does possess a certain subtle animal magnetism, does he

not, Miss Willburton-Smythe?" asked Lord Worth, placing himself, amused, between her and sight of the duke.

"How—nice to see you again, Lord Worth," Olivia responded attempting to peer around him.

"Indeed, Miss Willburton-Smythe, the pleasure is all mine. Have you known Abbercombe long?"

"No, we have met only recently. His eldest girls and my niece are become friends, you see."

"He makes a wonderful gypsy, does he not? I can remember when we were young and such styles were begun to fade."

"You dressed like that?"

"Indeed, but we wore long silk or brocade coats with velvet and satin insets and lace at our collars and cuffs, and always a sword at our sides. That fashion he has not yet dispensed with, though Fanning did manage to remove his sabre this evening."

"You make a charming gypsy, Olivia," the duke declared from behind her and she turned. He stood less than an inch away, nearly but not quite touching her.

Lord Worth, the look in Abbercombe's eyes as he surveyed Miss Willburton-Smythe not lost upon him, coughed delicately. "I am off to speak with Sebastian for a moment. I hope you will both excuse me." He bowed, grinning, and moved away.

"Why did he rush off so?" Abbercombe murmured, his startling blue eyes searching her face. "Surely he did not think I was about to ring a peal over him for his part in this subterfuge?"

"I cannot believe you will ring a peal over anyone involved in this, sir," smiled Olivia self-consciously. She had never been approached so in her life, the gentleman so close that she might feel the heat of his body and yet so far they did not touch at all. The tantalizing nature of it took her breath away. She stepped back. Abbercombe did not close the gap but took her hand and led her to a seat before one of the grates. For the longest time he stood staring down at her in silence, as if she were a problem that must be studied and solved. Though the smile did not leave his eyes, a frown creased his brow.

"Do you know, Olivia," he said at last, "I cannot quite conceive of what it is to be forty-five. I have always imagined I should be in my grave by now."

"You are forty-five today, your grace?" Olivia asked, and then condemned herself for sounding a ninny. Had he not just told her that was the case?

His eyes twinkled but the frown lingered and he sat down beside her, careful this time to keep an acceptable distance between them. "I thank you for coming. The children cannot know what they asked of you. They do not exactly understand what a pariah is, though I have tried to explain it to them, and so they do not understand how kind you were to accept their invitation."

Olivia began to protest his words but he placed one finger tenderly against her lips and shook his head. "Do not protest, my dear," he whispered. "I am a pariah and a rogue. That much has been made clear to me for all my life. And now, I am an old man as well. You are an angel to have come."

"Papa!" piped a tiny voice just as Olivia thought she would die from the seductiveness of his innocent finger upon her lips. "Papa, come an' say our forchins! Uncle 'Bastian don' b'lieve you can. Come on, Papa! Tell ever'body's. Miss Weebuttonsmite's too!"

Abbercombe's finger left Olivia's lips and his arms encircled the little urchin who crawled up into his lap. "You must call her Miss Olivia, Helen," he instructed. "For if we keep trying to say her name, you and I and Gracie will muddle it so badly that even she will forget how to say it aright."

Olivia, her senses dreamlike, gave herself the tiniest shake. "How do you know that is Helen?" she asked hoping to regain reality. "You do not know which girl has donned which color, or anything of that sort."

Abbercombe stood. "Why, Miss Olivia," he winked, "a father knows his own children. Come," he laughed, balancing Helen in one arm and offering Olivia his hand, "let me tell your fortune. I promise I will reveal only the best parts."

April could not guess what to expect as one after the other of the duke's guests entered the little tent. Her aunt had left with a wide grin upon her face and Lady Jessica had done likewise. Lady Worth had stayed within the tent for almost five minutes and, when she had emerged, she had gone quickly to Lord Worth and whispered seriously in his ear. Whereupon Lord Worth had entered and come out again with pursed lips and a chuckle. Mr. Hurley had been muttering under his breath when he entered, tugged into the tent by a laughing Damian, and he had been muttering just as much when he made his way across the room to the lemonade a few minutes later. And Lord Sebastian had come from the tent with a great deal of laughter in his eyes and had whistled, turned around in a circle once, and whistled again.

"April, are you going in?" Amy took her friend's hand and led her toward the tent.

"I think, perhaps, I—"

"It is only our papa. You need not be frightened. He has already asked three times why you do not come."

April longed to resist, fearing that he might question her about Geoffery and she would not know how to answer him. And then she was before him, the tent flaps closing behind her.

"Hello, little one." The duke took her hand in his and helped her to a chair. "Why so timid? You have not decided to be afraid of me after all this time?" Abbercombe sat down opposite her, the crystal ball and the little table itself separating them. "Do you wish me to tell your fortune, April?"

"Y-yes, n-no," April stuttered, studying his face.

Abbercombe shook his head. "That will never do."

"What?" squeaked April. "What will never do?"

"It will never do for you to be gazing at gentlemen in such a fashion. You will break a thousand unsuspecting hearts."

"Oh!"

"April?" he asked gently, extending his hands toward hers across the table top. She placed her own within them. "Are you yet so much in love with your Mr. Hempstead?"

April's hands trembled in his grasp. "Oh, yes."

He laughed and made her laugh as well. "Then I shall tell you his fortune."

"Can you really read the future, your grace?"

"Sometimes," he replied, releasing her hands and placing his own upon the crystal. For a long moment his great blue eyes stared down into the glittering sphere. When at last he raised them, April was breathing heavily and biting at her lower lip. He met the longing in her eyes with a visible empathy. "Your Geoffery will come to the notice of a very important gentleman who will wish to employ his services, April."

"Truly?" April gasped.

"Indeed. The next time you meet, Mr. Hempstead will be employed in a position of some importance within the government and your aunt will begin to think him more worthy of your hand."

"Oh, if only it were so!"

"The crystal ball does not lie, my dear. Come," he smiled, moving around the table to help her up. "From the sound of Frazier's voice the gingersnaps have at last arrived, and we had best move quickly if we are to get any at all!"

As the sideboards lightened and a smiling Mrs. Griffin personally refilled the silver urns with lemonade for the fifth time, all of the gypsies, young and old, found themselves on the pillows and cushions that littered the floor, the odd pieces of furniture before the fires abandoned.

"I cannot remember the last time I sat upon the floor," observed Lady Worth in amazement.

"It is the gypsy costumes make us so bold," offered Lady Jessica. "We would not dare to do so otherwise."

"You are out there, my girl," drawled Sebastian. "It is Cash makes us bold not our apparel."

Worth nodded. "Cash has been gone so long I had almost forgot what it was like to be completely comfortable with oneself and one's friends." Worth's eyes sought Eugenia's and she blushed like a schoolroom miss.

"I have never felt so cozy at a party before," sighed Lady Jess wistfully. "The children make charming hosts and hostesses."

"Have you grown used to so many nieces and nephews, Lady Jess?" Worth asked, cocking an eyebrow at her.

"I cannot think how we ever survived without them."

"Do you know what I wish," murmured Sir Ralph settling himself on a pillow beside Olivia. "I wish my Priscilla and I got on as well as Cash does with his girls. I am always at a loss for something to say to her when we are thrown together. She is like a stranger to me these days. I wish Angela and I had kept her with us more when she was a babe."

"But no one does," mused Lady Worth with a shy glance at her husband. "Simply everyone has nurses and governesses to care for the children most of the time. See how he plays with them even now? Worth says he is always playing with them. I wish my mother and father had thought to tease me so. I should have greatly enjoyed it."

"I saw little of my mother or father," sighed Worth. "And I know that Cash saw little of his father either, for he was shuttled off to Harrow when he was six and did not even go home for the holidays."

"He did not?" asked Sebastian in surprise.

Worth shook his head. "Things were a great deal different before you were born, Sebastian. I can remember Cash telling me, amazed, how your father let your mother cosset you every time you sneezed. Your mother was an enigma to your brother, but he used to go home then, despite not being invited, just to play with you."

"Invited?" exclaimed Olivia. "He had to wait to be invited to his own home?"

"Anyone dying of hunger?" Abbercombe asked, lowering himself to the floor beside Worth, a glass of lemonade in one hand and a large platter of gingersnaps in the other. He set the platter in the midst of the group and smiled across at Olivia.

"No one starving now," replied Worth. "I have forgotten how much I liked these things."

"Yes," replied Hurley, also joining the group, "and how much fun it is to be a child. I wish I had a house filled with them."

"You may borrow a few of mine," the duke offered, grinning.

"Oh, you would not loan out your children as if you were a lending library," laughed Lady Jess.

"Most often I would not," Abbercombe mused, "but there are times, Jessica, when I should be glad to be shunt of them."

"Now, for instance?" asked Sebastian innocently, looking to where the young people gathered around the harpsichord.

Abbercombe followed Sebastian's gaze, mumbled under his breath and made a move as if to rise. Before he could, however, Amaryllis's fingers came down upon the instrument's keys and a happy melody tinkled into the room. To her right, Ethan placed the violin beneath his chin, raised the bow, and joined in. Abbercombe sank back on to his pillow and raised his eyes heavenward in silent supplication. But his prayers were not to be answered and, much to the enjoyment of their guests, Bethany and Damian began to sing. The two pleasant voices raced merrily through a not quite respectable sailor's ditty which set everyone in the room to laughing. Christian and Amy then sang a startling duet in Russian that so invigorated Mr. Hurley and Lord Sebastian, they resorted to pounding out the rhythm upon the floor with their fists. This was followed by a rousing rendition of "Yankee Doodle" with Frazier adding a flute to the instruments, Helen marching around the harpsichord with a little wooden gun and Gracie marching beside her beating upon a toy drum. Olivia looked to Abbercombe, her eyes bright with glee, and discovered him nearly convulsed with laughter. Worth was beating him about the shoulders and shouting deprecations about the colonies and revolutionaries in his ear, which only made Abbercombe laugh the harder.

Then Christian stepped forward, his eyes twinkling merrily, and announced that though the performers knew several other songs that were his father's professed favourites, they did not think anyone else wished to hear "Ride a Cock Horse to Banbury Cross" or "Le Marseillaise," much less Ethan's and Frazier's rendition of "Greensleeves" which, due to their papa's teaching, was not quite proper. "So we thought instead, Papa," he grinned, "to just wish you a happy birthday."

Amaryllis and Bethany, laughing, went to where he sat and tugged him from the floor. "We brought you presents," Amy grinned. "These are from Beth and me." She handed him a package wrapped in bright silver paper which he tore off without the least inhibition to reveal volumes of Maria Edgeworth's *Castle Rackrent* and Jane Austen's *Sense and Sensibility*. "Now you will be able to discover what we find so enticing about novels, Papa."

"Happy birthday, Papa," Christian and Damian said together, presenting him with a framed painting covered with muslin. Olivia watched in expectation as Abbercombe drew the muslin off. She heard his breath catch in his throat and rose to her knees to see better what the canvas held. Then the breath he had caught came booming out in a howl of mirth. Before him images of all eight of his children tumbled and twisted and rolled about in various states of rollicking disarray.

"It is us getting ready to move on," grinned Damian. "That is Helen," he added, pointing at a miniature figure seeming to hang from the frame. I would not have done her so, but Christian insisted that she is always hanging from the windows and so she should hang from the frame as well."

Abbercombe carried the painting to the harpsichord, leaned it against a leg, and turning hugged first Chris and then Daymee. "And all this time I thought you two were working on a—portrait—that was not quite the thing, and that I would be called upon to have a very embarrassing talk with the both of you. Thank you, God. I was wrong," he added, staring up at the ceiling. Worth broke into a series of chuckles that were relayed immediately to Lord Sebastian and Sir Ralph and Mr. Hurley. Lady Worth lowered her eyes only to lift them again with a wicked glint in Worth's direction which sent Lady Jess into whoops, and Olivia and April into trills of laughter.

From the doorway to the hall Grace and Helen came into sight, each balancing a small package carefully in two hands. "Happy bir'day, Papa," they squeaked excitedly. Abbercombe, recognizing the parcels from the Burlington Arcade glanced at Olivia and she smiled, nodding. He knelt down before the girls, took the gifts, and unwrapping them, grinned broadly at two extremely fat cigars. "They are the most magnificent smokes I have ever seen," he gasped dramatically. "However do I come to deserve such wonderful gifts? I shall smoke them both at the same time, shall I?"

Two little golden heads nodded gleefully. "An' let us watch," Gracie urged, clapping her hands.

"An' make smokey circles," added Helen, jumping up and down.

"I most assuredly will. And you shall both sit on my lap and poke fingers through the smokey circles whenever you please."

A series of giggles drew Olivia's attention to two madly smiling little boys shuttling a large box into the room.

"Happy birthday, Papa," Ethan and Frazier grinned. Both boys ran to hang their arms about their father's neck and lean over his shoulders as he eyed their present. The box wiggled. Olivia blinked and stared at it. It wiggled again. Abbercombe stood up suddenly, though Olivia could see it was not so sudden that he did not first make sure to get a tight hold on both Ethan and Frazier and carry them up with him.

"If it is what I think it is, scoundrels, you shall suffer for it," he frowned, backing away from the package.

"Oh, but Papa," cried Bethany, hurrying to his side, "are you not even going to open the box?"

"No," he growled, "for I am sure to regret doing so."

Olivia frowned. But even as he grumbled, Abbercombe tipped Ethan and Frazier safely over his shoulders and against his chest, and kissed each one of them soundly. The box wiggled again and began to rock from side to side.

"But, Papa," Amy pleaded prettily, coming to stand beside him as well, "Ethan and Frazier have spent every last bit of their allowances and most of ours. You must at least open it."

Abbercombe shook his head stubbornly. "No," he said. "I do not see any reason that I must. Unless—"

"Unless what, Papa?" squealed Frazier, wiggling mightily in

his father's arms. Olivia realized that Abbercombe was tickling the boy, and she began to smile again.

"Unless what?" chorused the children, gathering around him.

"Unless—it barks," he said with a dramatic sigh.

"Arf," replied the box on cue.

Lady Worth laughed in delight. Abbercombe, setting the boys down, opened the box and lifted a black, brown, and white puppy into his arms. It stared up at him and then lunged for his face with a long, wet tongue.

"Well, it ain't exactly a fox hound," offered Hurley, as Abbercombe lowered the pup to the floor and wiped the sleeve of his shirt across his chin.

"Thing's got no legs," drawled Richardson. "Feet are big enough, but they are connected directly to its body."

"Does too got legs," replied Frazier, lying down to examine the little dog as it plopped itself on its haunches to stare mystified from one person to another. "Gots four of 'em, Sir Ralph; they are very short ones is all."

"Can't say as I have ever seen a pup put together in quite that way," Sebastian murmured. "What kind is it?"

"It's a Corgi," replied Christian, kneeling down and running his hand through wisps of puppy fur. "They are bred in Wales. Papa had one once when he was a boy."

"Yes," drawled Worth, "I seem to recall. We spent many an hour at school trying to keep the wretched thing out of sight. And now it seems he has another, for he'll not abandon it now he's seen those big brown orbs, you know."

"Yes," laughed Damian, "we were counting on that."

Olivia giggled and looked up to see Abbercombe grin down at her and wink.

$\mathcal{S}\textit{even}$

Abbercombe descended the stairs the following afternoon at a startlingly conservative pace; gathered his hat, gloves and whip from Dawson; mounted a most unusual bit of blood by the name of Gadzooks; and took himself off to Lord Worth's establishment where he was greeted by a butler of immense size and sociable disposition named Marley. "I believe, your grace, that Lord Worth is at his club. Would you care to leave a message?"

"No. Marley, might you know where to find the Earl of Stamford's sons? They do not lodge at Stamford House, do they?"

The large man looked thoughtful for a moment and then beamed at Abbercombe. " 'Tis Sunday afternoon, your grace. Most of the young one's'll be down to Fletcher Common watching the race."

"The race?"

"There is to be a horse race, your grace, though 'tis a secret. Lord Goddering's filly, Midnight Folly, against Lord Dashwood's Sundancer. At half past three, I believe."

"I see. And Fletcher Common is?"

"Through Green Park, your grace, across the goat track and turn left at the first hillock."

Tossing the man a cartwheel along with a grin, Abbercombe set out in the specified direction. When at last he reached the Common his eyebrows raised at the number of bucks gathered to view the action. His chances of coming upon Harcort or Kettering in such a crowd were remote and he was not at all inclined to ride among the throng in search of them, an aversion to being cut by a multitude of fashionable cubs rising to the forefront of his mind. With a sigh and a shrug, he decided to remain until the contest had ended and try his luck at spotting one or the other of them as they left the field. He kicked free of his stirrups, swung one leg up across the saddle bow and settled down to watch the race himself.

"What on earth?" Lord Redvers asked in amazement, knocking the Honorable Charlie Sales in the ribs and directing his attention toward Abbercombe.

Sales glanced up, looked away, glanced back again. "Devil if that ain't the ugliest bit of blood 'n bone I've ever seen."

"Who is the gentleman?"

"Well, I cannot tell. His hat shades his face so it is impossible. Odd way o' sittin' a horse, ain't it? Cannot say as I would find it comfortable."

"You do not find anything about horses comfortable, Charles. Never mind; they are about to begin." Redvers redirected his attention to the starting line. Goddering and Dashwood brought the two fillies up and at the sound of a pistol shot were off along the course, Goddering taking the first turn a full length ahead of Dashwood. The cheers startled Abbercombe who found the joys of a match had lessened a good deal since his youth and that all he really wished to do was to go home. However he curbed that idea and set himself to bet which of the finely bred beasts would cross the finish line first. He watched intently as one then the other of the riders took a small stone fence, coming down solidly on the other side, and decided that though Goddering's filly appeared the better of the two animals Dashwood was far and away the best rider. Mentally he laid a pony on Dashwood to take it in the end—which Dashwood did, by a length and a half, sending a number of young bucks to cheering and an equal number into somber reflection.

As the horses and curricles and phaetons and gigs began to trail out of the Common, Abbercombe attempted to view as many faces as possible without them viewing his, though he realized, with a sigh, that Gadzooks tugged a good many curious glances in his direction. "I have not the brains of a two-year-old," he muttered. "If I had, I would not have ridden you here. You were hardly born to be inconspicuous, you dastardly beast."

At that moment a deep brown curricle with yellow wheels passed within six feet of him and he swung his leg down and urged Gadzooks forward. "Harcort," he called, riding up alongside and shoving his hat farther back on his head, "may I have a word with you? 'Twill only take a moment."

Harcort gave Kettering beside him a surprised glance, nodded, and pulled the curricle over beneath a stand of elms. "At your service, your grace."

"And what kind of devilish beast is that you're riding?" Kettering asked. "You did not find that at Tat's, did you?"

Abbercombe grinned. "No, not at Tat's. He is come down from Chembesley Hall last week."

"They do not breed bits of blood like that in Yorkshire, Abbercombe," Harcort replied, looking Gadzooks over rather disdainfully. "It ain't a racehorse, is it?"

"No, not a racehorse. It's called an Appaloosa. Comes from America where there is a tribe of red Indians swears by them."

"Ain't got much taste, do they?" snickered Kettering. "Damned if that ain't the ugliest animal I have ever seen."

"Yes, well, I haven't much taste either," shrugged Abbercombe, "so I sent several of them to Chembesley Hall a few years back. But it is not horses I wish to speak with you about."

"No, of course it ain't," agreed Harcort sociably. "What is it then?"

"I should like to find a gentleman by the name of Geoffery Hempstead. He is near you in age, I gather, and I hoped one or the other of you could put me onto him."

"Geoff? Lord, yes," offered Kettering. "Shares our chambers on Great Russell Street. What do you want with Hempstead?"

"Well, it depends whether he is the Geoffery Hempstead who has formed a lasting attachment to Miss April Willburton-Smythe."

"Yep, that's Geoff," grinned Harcort. "Head over heels in love with her. Enough to make his friends want to strangle him for speaking of her in every other sentence."

"And moping over her constantly," grumbled Kettering.

Abbercombe smiled sympathetically. "As for the moping, my boy, I believe I have devised a cure. But first I must be introduced to the gentleman. Would you, perhaps?"

Hempstead's jaw dropped as Kettering walked into the little parlor on Great Russell Street followed immediately by the Duke of Abbercombe. "Compose yourself, Hempstead," grinned Kettering, introducing the gentlemen properly. "The duke wishes a word with you. Would you care for a drink, Duke?" he added.

"No, thank you." Abbercombe's brilliant blue eyes raked Hempstead from head to toe with such intensity that that gentleman found himself squirming and thanked god that the duke's scrutiny was not aided by the possession of a quizzing glass. "You are incredibly young," Abbercombe sighed at last.

"I am two-and-twenty," Hempstead huffed.

Abbercombe muttered inaudibly, his hand rubbing at his chin.

"Would you care to be seated, sir," Kettering invited, attempting not to chuckle at the manner in which the two confronted one another.

"Not really. I do not plan to stay."

"Do you wish me to leave the two of you alone?"

"Yes."

Hempstead's eyes met Kettering's worriedly. Kettering shrugged. "You are not about to call Geoff out or anything?" he asked on Hempstead's behalf.

"Hardly. Go away, cub. Come back in five minutes."

When the door had closed, the duke, hands clasped behind his back, legs spread wide, rocked from toe to heel to toe a few times. He then shook his head and, stuffing his hands into his pockets, began to pace the room. "I have come to discover why you thought you must elope with Miss April Willburton-Smythe."

"What?"

"Do not deny you intended to do so. I have spoken to the young lady and yours is the name she mentions. Could you not offer for her in the usual manner?"

"I fail to see," growled Hempstead, flopping angrily down into a wing-backed chair, "how any of this concerns you."

Abbercombe stopped pacing and leaned his shoulders against the mantle. "It does, and I require an answer to my question."

Hempstead was noticeably reluctant but the force of the duke's glare and the grimness of his expression elicited the information. "April begged it of me. Miss Willburton-Smythe don't much care for me and April thought our only chance was to elope. Miss Willburton-Smythe thinks that I am undependable and have no prospects or ambition and will make a terrible husband."

"Do you lack ambition?"

Hempstead blanched at the stern gaze in the icy blue eyes. "No, sir, but it is not as if I had a great deal of choice, you know. M'mother will not hear of my joining in the fight so my father will not buy me a commission. And he is merely a baronet and I, his third son, so I do not have a great many prospects or a good deal of the ready."

"How did you think to support April, once you had married?"

"Well, I—I—"

"You what?"

"I thought that we would work it out, you know. That perhaps I would take Holy Orders and find a living."

Abbercombe's lips twitched. "Do you wish to become a parson, Hempstead?"

"Well, no, but I would do so for April."

"I see. Might you accept a position at the Foreign Office for April as well?"

"The Foreign Office?"

"Yes, Hempstead. Would a position at the Foreign Office be enough to impress Miss Willburton-Smythe with your ambition and dependability? I can assure you it will increase your income."

Hempstead's jaw dropped.

"You must give me an answer now. I shan't offer again. The position disappears immediately I leave this room." The duke offered compensation that was more than generous. "If you prove adequate, you may expect a rise in salary."

"But—but—how can you—why would—?"

"I assure you," the duke drawled, "that I can and do offer you this position, though you must tell no one it was I hired you. Do you accept or no?"

Hempstead's eyes glazed slightly. "I should be a fool not to," he mumbled at last.

"Good." Abbercombe straightened and took three steps toward the door. "Present yourself to Lord Wyndham tomorrow afternoon at three o'clock in the forecourt of Whitehall," he ordered over his shoulder. "He will be the elderly gentleman leaning against the bottom stair rail, squinting at his pocket watch and mumbling. You will recognize him immediately."

"Is it Wyndham I shall work for?"

"Indeed."

"Suppose he don't approve of me?"

"He will approve, Hempstead." The duke bowed curtly and left the chambers. Hempstead hurried to the front windows to watch the gentleman mount a disreputable looking horse and ride on down the cobbles in the direction of St. James's.

As it happened the following afternoon outside Whitehall a nervous Mr. Hempstead *did* recognize Lord Wyndham immediately. It was impossible not to do so, for not only was he exactly where Abbercombe had said he would be, squinting at his pocket watch and mumbling to himself, but his mumbling was so audible, yet so unintelligible, that it attracted the attention of most of the passersby. Hempstead started forward, then halted, then cleared his throat and started forward again. "Pardon me, Lord Wyndham?"

The rotund figure in the raspberry colored coat and powder blue inexpressibles looked up from his watch and muttered at Hempstead, his bushy white eyebrows rising and falling with every word. "Three-oh-one, very good, very good," he muttered. "Come along, my boy, join me in a stroll about the grounds."

He put his arm through Hempstead's and leaning upon him a bit, as if his own legs were not quite strong enough to carry all of his round little figure, he steered Hempstead to the north side of the edifice. "Shall we study the architecture? Splendid bit of work she is, Whitehall. Tourists like her. Never fail but to find some young lady or gentleman from the country snooping about. Ah, there," he muttered, pointing to a bench in the shade of a large oak. "That will do. We will sit and have a coze, you and I."

Hempstead helped the elderly lord to a seat and stood nervously before him. "I am Geoffery Hempstead, Lord Wyndham."

"Yes, of course you are. Come, sit. Rudolph told you that you had the position?"

"It was the Duke of Abbercombe sent me."

"Yes, Rudolph is his Christian name, lad. You do not trust your luck, eh? Think it a hoax? I assure you it is not. Sit, lad, and cease fidgeting."

Hempstead sat.

"I have known Rudolph forever, and since 'twas he suggested you, I have no quarrel with it. I suspect, however, that he did not describe to you what the work involves?"

"No, my lord."

"Ha! No! I thought not, the scamp! Why look at that," the old man said suddenly, pointing upwards at the side of the building. "I do believe, Hempstead, that that particular notch did not exist last year. Is it not the most amazing thing?"

Hempstead, suspecting Wyndham to be mad, gazed where the finger pointed and began to seek a way to extricate himself from the gentleman's clutches, the newly born dream of a respectable income upon which to build a married life for himself and April dying within him. He should have known that no one in their right mind would have given the duke authority to hire anyone.

"I am sure I am correct, Hempstead. It is a recent addition to the edifice. It's all right now, boy, you may cease looking," said the little round man, lowering his finger. "Do you see the gentleman in the bottle green coat and buff pantaloons who has just gone down the path? His name is LeBruin, and I do not depend upon his honor. A weasel-faced slyboots is what he is, always wishing to appear the complete innocent when one knows myriad plots and plans are bubbling about in his brain. You must be extremely cautious of your words whenever he is present, even if he appears just to pass you by. If you do not see the back of him from at least ten paces, do not speak openly of any but the most frivolous topics. Ah, you look just as perplexed as you ought, Hempstead. I admire that in a man. When one don't understand a thing, he ought to make it clear he don't, by thunder!"

"Lord Wyndham," Hempstead began softly, "I am afraid that some awkward mistake has been made."

"No, not as yet. I have had my people check you out."

"You have what?"

"Indeed. The moment Rudolph's message reached me."

"What gives you the right—" Hempstead began.

"Nothing, lad, but we cannot afford a mistake. We had got to know that you were trustworthy, honorable, a flower of English manhood so to speak. You see, my boy," explained the old gentleman, his bushy white eyebrows wagging, "you are about to become my special assistant. Hartshorn, who last held that post, has disappeared. He is dead, I believe, though we cannot prove it. Rudolph, of course, will not give him up."

"Dead?"

"Yes, so I believe. Rudolph swears not, that he will find Harry within a month. Still, I must have someone to replace him."

"Dead?" Hempstead repeated a bit more loudly.

"Caught up in a bit of a bumblebath outside Paris. No need for you to worry. Not likely you'll find yourself in a similar situation—not with The Rogue in England. One cannot imagine how thankful I am to have that devil back. He searched down to the last second to recover Harry, but there was no sign of him."

Hempstead was at a complete loss.

Wyndham chuckled. "All shall be clear directly," he smiled.

"But I must tell you what I am positive Rudolph did not think to mention—this particular position involves a bit of, er, danger. Your job will be to look after and maintain communications with The Rogue—communications which involve national security, the safety of British subjects, the furtherance of the war effort and oft-times, the identification of certain persons not entirely devoted to the continued existence of our government."

Hempstead digested each of Lord Wyndham's phrases with a growing sense of shock, awe, and a rising self-esteem. "Do you mean, sir," he asked at last, his heart beating a very strange rhythm within his chest, "that I am to be involved in espionage?"

"In a manner of speaking, Hempstead—what did you say was your Christian name? Geoffery, you said. Yes, of course you did. In a manner of speaking, Geoffery. Your precise job will be as go-between for myself and one particular gentleman. There is not another like him. I did think Harry was coming close at last but, there, now we must not depend upon Harry. You do not regret your decision, lad?" Wyndham asked, his face wreathed in smiles.

"No," Hempstead replied breathlessly. "Indeed, sir, I am honoured no end. You must only tell me how to go on."

"Why, you will go on as do all my assistants, Geoffery, with a desk at the Foreign Office and piles of papers stacked upon it. Come, escort me to my carriage. That's a good fellow. The papers, you understand, are of little consequence, for your work will be done far outside the bounds of usual business hours."

"I fear for your safety, mademoiselle, and the lovely Miss April's," LeBruin murmured. He stood, hands clasped behind his back, before the window in Olivia's morning room. As he looked gravely down at her, a frown tugging his extraordinarily seductive lips downward, the afternoon sunlight shimmered at his back and Olivia felt a chill run through her. "I have learned that you and your niece have visited Fielding House and that Abbercombe has had the audacity to appear upon your doorstep. Do you realize, *ma belle,* the peril in which you stand?"

"No, I do not," Olivia replied, chagrined by the loathing that flashed in the steel-grey eyes as the gentleman pronounced the duke's name. "Why do you hold Abbercombe in such abhorrence? What has he done, monsieur, that you think him such a menace?"

"Why, mademoiselle, nothing." LeBruin's lips twisted into a smirk. "He merely came into my country one month and left it the next. It was perhaps coincidental that in the brief space of his visit the rabble of Paris were roused again to violence, the Bastille was stormed, my uncle, le Comte de Avirgonne and his sweetly innocent bride were murdered and their estates seized."

"But surely," Olivia gasped, "you cannot place blame for an entire revolution upon one man?"

"No, mademoiselle," LeBruin sneered. "But for aiding to whip the citizens of Paris into a frenzy that July and for the death of my uncle and the seizure of his estates, my family does place blame. And now, after all these years, an agent of Napoleon this duke most surely has become. Mademoiselle, Abbercombe's presence in this country may signal the downfall of all our attempts to rid the continent of the Little General."

Olivia inhaled deeply; one hand fluttered to her brow and back again to her lap. "No, I cannot believe it," she gasped finally. "Abbercombe could not be so treacherous."

"Then why did Napoleon this past year bestow upon him my uncle's long confiscated estates? He delighted in the configuration of the duke's face, perhaps? No, the man is a master spy, mademoiselle. His treachery is legendary though few know his true identity. Beware, *ma belle,* for your own sake and for England's as well. Can you tell me what he has done and said? Perhaps to you he has betrayed his reasons for appearing so abruptly upon these shores. Perhaps you have knowledge, mademoiselle, which will save a continent."

Olivia shivered beneath the emigre's gaze. Truly frightened, she told him of the duke's offer to help locate her brother, confessed that she and LeBruin had been seen rifling through the papers in Lord Sinclair's study, and that she had admitted to Abbercombe that LeBruin, himself, was a British spy. "I am devastated, monsieur. I have ruined you, and put our soldiers in jeopardy. But, but he seemed so—"

"I can imagine how he seemed, mademoiselle," growled LeBruin. "Always this one has had such *eclat* with the ladies. You are blameless, *ma chere*. He has deceived a multitude of great minds, the Tzar Alexander among them. Had I known he thought to approach you, I would have warned you more fully of his menace."

"The Tzar?" Olivia asked meekly, remembering the boys' claim that their party would be better than dinner with that gentleman.

"Oui, mademoiselle. He has made this Alexander a worshipper at his feet. The Tzar's trust in Abbercombe is one obstacle we strive even now to overcome."

"Oh, my Lord," groaned Olivia, "what have I done?"

LeBruin moved from the window to kneel before her and took her hands into his own. "Do not, mademoiselle, despair. All is not lost. There is much may be done to counteract this devil's plots and return your brother safely to England."

"But I have told him where to search for Andrew!" Olivia cried. "I told him Andrew was to have met you in Gironde!"

LeBruin's hands tightened upon her own, and he looked up into her eyes with such determination that she was immediately filled with hope. "What?" she gasped. "What may we do?"

"You, *ma chere,* may do much, I think. He has given you *entrée* for which I could not possibly have hoped. He has come to your home, mademoiselle, and received you into his. He thinks to have deceived you into trust and friendship. We may, if you are brave, take great advantage. You must encourage his attentions, draw him into your circle using your brother's return as the price at which he may buy your eternal gratitude. He will pay the price avidly, thinking to learn from you secrets he may send on to Napoleon. But instead, *ma chere,* we will watch him and once your brother is safe, feed this devil lies that will lead to his own downfall and Napoleon's!"

For a long while after LeBruin had departed, Olivia sat, silent, staring into space. Her mind wandered to visions of Abbercombe, his arms around her, assuring her of his help in discovering Andrew's whereabouts, comforting her and teasing her into smiles. She saw him in the doorway to the small ballroom at Fielding House, and surrounded by his children, and heard the chuckling prediction of her future he had laid before her in the privacy of the little tent. How competent he was, she thought, how talented, to appear so loving, so good, while all the while his heart writhed in a morass of evil. But had she not been warned? Had not they all? He had beaten a man to death, had been transported. She had been a fool to think him falsely accused and falsely convicted; and a fool to have fallen into sympathy with him; and a fool to have taken his children to her heart. No, that she would not allow.

She gave herself an angry shake and rising, began to pace the room. Surely his children were innocent of all deceit. She had been correct when first she had spoken to Jessica. He was a devil and his children suffered beneath his rule, though they did not suffer in precisely the way she had imagined. No, he deceived them into believing in his goodness and then used their innocence for his own ends—used them, she saw at last, to gain entrance into the good graces of those whom he would betray! Well, she would put an end to that. She and M. LeBruin would destroy the monster by his own methods. Though she had never once thought herself capable of deceit, she would from this moment begin the study of it. She swore on her brother's name to bring Abbercombe to his knees before her.

Abbercombe's brows knit into a worried frown as he left his curricle in charge of his tiger and mounted the steps to number 5, Park Street. He could not imagine why Olivia had summoned him so abruptly. The front door opened to his knock and the duke followed Laslow up the staircase. Olivia stood as he entered the morning room and smiled oddly up at him. Waiting only long enough for Laslow to turn on his heel, Abbercombe crossed to her. "What is it, my dear? I came as soon as I received your message."

"And did you bring your curricle as I requested?"

"Yes, Olivia, I did, but what—"

"I am so pleased. I had heard, you know, that you had at last set up your stables."

"Yes, dear heart, I now have horses and carriages enough for three dukes," Abbercombe replied, puzzled, "and they are at your disposal. Have you news of your brother?"

Olivia blinked her fine emerald eyes at him. She played her fingers over her brown merino gown and shook invisible wrinkles from it. "I have made up my mind, Abbercombe, and you shall not change it. Did you drive yourself here?"

"Well, yes, but—"

"Good. You will be seated in that chair until I have changed my dress for a more suitable one," she declared, pointing, "and then you and I shall join the promenade in Hyde Park." Seeing his mouth open to protest, Olivia turned and exited the room. When she returned ten minutes later in a carriage dress of willow green silk, a matching bonnet with the bow tied rakishly under her chin and a bright green Kashmere shawl draped elegantly over her shoulders, his mouth opened once again, but she allowed him not a word, simply taking his arm and leading him through the halls to the front door. "Laslow," she said, as the butler provided Abbercombe's hat and gloves, "the duke and I are going for a drive. If Miss April returns before I do, please inform her to expect me by six."

"Yes, miss," murmured Laslow, opening the front door.

"What a charming curricle," Olivia said, smiling at the bright red paint and the gleaming white wheels. "Help me onto the box, please, your grace."

"Really, Olivia, I do not think I should," Abbercombe protested as she put her hand on his and mounted the vehicle.

"You have no choice if you truly mean to be my friend."

"Oh, I have a choice, my dear," the duke drawled as he mounted beside her and took the reins, the little tiger jumping to his seat at the back, "but I am adverse to take it."

"What choice?"

"Why, to lift you up, set your feet upon the cobbles, and race away, but I find I am not gentleman enough to do so."

"Then I am thankful for the first time that I have found a less than perfect gentleman. I am determined to ride with you in the park, Abbercombe. And I will not be gainsayed. You have been outcast long enough and there shall come an end to it! You do wish an end to it, do you not?"

"Possibly," murmured Abbercombe, noticing with humor that this intimidating young lady whose will he was loathe to cross came only to his shoulder as she sat stubbornly beside him.

"You do know how best to reach Hyde Park?" she asked, turning to look up at him from beneath the perky bonnet.

"Olivia, have you thought what it may do to your reputation to be seen in my company?"

"Yes, and I find I do not care. I have been a pattern card of propriety for thirty-one years, and if one ride in the park by your side sinks my reputation, then it was not worth the effort to begin with." She stopped to survey his face and saw he looked a good deal older than ever before. "It is because you are worried, I have no doubt," she murmured without realizing it.

"What is because I am worried?"

"Oh, did I say that?"

"Yes, my dear, you did. What is because I am worried?"

"Well, I was just noticing, you know, that—that you look older, your grace, than you usually do," she sighed. "I am sorry. I did not mean to say anything at all about it."

Abbercombe chuckled and reached out to give her hand a quick squeeze. "Worry always makes the lines stand out more distinctly upon my face. Are you really thirty-one?"

"Yes, so I am quite old enough to be doing as I like."

"Perhaps," Abbercombe smiled warmly down at her, "but you

are also young enough to learn to regret it, and I would not have you regret knowing me for the world."

Olivia's eyes flashed at his words. No, she thought, turning to watch the strollers as they approached the park, you would not wish me to regret knowing you. You simply wish to trick me into betraying my brother and my country and—and myself!

Abbercombe drew his cattle to a halt beside the west gate. He gazed at the young lady beside him, bewildered and suspicious. "Olivia," he asked softly, already feeling the eyes of public disapproval falling upon them as carriages swung past, "are you certain you wish to do this? Something is very wrong, is it not? Can you not bring yourself to tell me of it?"

"Nothing is wrong," Olivia declared from behind an extremely bright smile designed to wrap him about her competent little finger. "I have simply decided to be your friend publicly as well as privately and Polite Society shall have to adjust to it. You will see. I have enough propriety to support the both of us."

Eight

The extraordinary attention caused by Miss Willburton-Smythe's ride in the park with the Duke of Abbercombe was exceeded only by the attention aroused when she appeared in his curricle again the following afternoon and the afternoon following that.

"I cannot like it," Abbercombe sighed as he drove his blacks through the west gate for the fourth afternoon in a row. "Every gossipmonger in London has your name upon his lips. Even Worth has mentioned our—association."

Olivia smiled brightly, determined he should think her without the least care. "Did he really refer to it as our association? What an odd word to choose. You worry needlessly. For years I have been the starchiest miss in the *ton*."

"No, really?"

"Indeed, and I am considered a bluestocking as well."

"Whatever were you thinking, Olivia, to gain such a shocking reputation? No wonder the buffle-headed fools did not offer for you; you frightened them out of their wits."

"Perhaps," Olivia smiled, "but see what a boon it has turned out to be. Not even you, sir, are capable of sinking me."

"Only because I have not put my mind to it," Abbercombe grinned down at her engagingly. Her heart ached to think that such remarkable charm should hide such perfidy.

She laughed aloud at his joke and drew an amazed stare from Mrs. Drummond-Burrell who occupied the landau passing on their left. "Oh," Olivia gasped, "I am in for it now." The landau, occupied by three other patronesses of Almack's as well, came to a halt and an imperiously waving hand signaled Abbercombe to pull up.

"Good afternoon, Miss Willburton-Smythe," Mrs. Drummond-Burrell scowled.

"Good afternoon, ma'am. How pleasant to see you again. Lady Cowper, Lady Jersey, Lady Castlereagh."

"You and your niece have received your vouchers for Almack's I dare say," Mrs. Drummond-Burrell's haughty drawl continued.

"Oh, yes, indeed, ma'am," replied Olivia, "and we are most grateful for them."

"Well, one does wonder, Miss Willburton-Smythe." The disdainful lady glared significantly at Abbercombe. "If they are not considered valuable, we should be most willing to relieve you of them, I am sure."

"Is that a threat, ma'am?" asked Abbercombe softly. "Ow!" he added as an apricot half-boot embroidered with pale green flowers kicked him in the shin. He scowled at Olivia, but the mirth twinkling in his eyes nearly overpowered her. It took every ounce of her self-control not to laugh. "Good afternoon, Emily Anne," he continued, looking back to the landau. "I do not believe that I have met your delightful friends."

Olivia nearly choked; Mrs. Drummond-Burrell, Lady Jersey, and Lady Cowper gasped at his effrontery. Lady Castlereagh gave a shake of her imposingly turbanned head. "I dare say you have not been properly introduced, Cash, but you know very well who they are. This is Mrs. Drummond-Burrell, Lady Jersey, Lady Cowper. My dears, His Grace, Rudolph Denbigh, Duke of Abbercombe."

Abbercombe nodded to each and then ignored them, returning his attention to Lady Castlereagh. "I need a favour, Emily Anne. Must I say how fetching you look before I broach the thing?"

"Yes," replied Lady Castlereagh, looking up at him from beneath dark lashes, "I really think you must."

"Very well. Your gown is exquisite, my dear, and displays the seething fire of your passionate eyes to sheer perfection."

"I like that. The seething fire of my passionate eyes."

"Yes, I thought you might. Do you remember when Barrington took to calling you the unextinguishable flame of his heart?"

Lady Castlereagh broke into gales of laughter. "And after two weeks, you and Castlereagh lured him to Lady Howe's balcony and doused him with buckets of water! What is the favor, Cash?"

"I should like you to meet my children. You need not come to Fielding House. I shall send them to Sebastian's whenever you wish, but Celia spoke of you so often, and they do not understand precisely why you have not—well—"

"Rudolph Casimir Denbigh, you are the most complete hand! Of course I shall meet your children, and I shall come to Fielding House to do so. Tomorrow at one. Drive on now, for we are tying up traffic to an amazing degree."

"Thank you, Emily Anne," the duke murmured, giving that lady a quick glimpse of the boyish grin she remembered well. "I shall see that they expect you."

"You called Lady Castlereagh, Emily Anne," whispered Olivia agog. "How dared you do that? And to ignore the others—they will censure your audacity for weeks to come."

"Her name is Emily Anne," Abbercombe replied, urging his horses to a trot, "and the others did not wish to speak to me, so I was considerate enough not to demand it of them."

At that moment a gentleman on a bay mare approached the curricle.

"Good afternoon, Miss Willburton-Smythe. A pleasant day for a drive, is it not?"

Olivia smiled apprehensively at the gentleman in the perfectly fitted brown riding coat and buff pantaloons and gleaming, white-topped boots. "Mr. Brummell, how very nice to see you." And then she could think of not another word to say.

He doffed his hat and bowed in Abbercombe's direction. "Y'servant, Abbercombe. May I accompany you for a bit?"

"Why?" the duke asked curtly.

"Why?"

"Yes, Brummell, why? Is it another wager?"

"A wager?" asked Olivia, puzzled.

"Mr. Brummell thinks that I shall make him a fortune if he persists in betting upon my actions," explained the duke, "which is likely the case. What he fails to accept is that once the fortune is made, I shall relieve him of it."

The Beau's eyes laughed so openly upon hearing this explanation that Olivia wondered how she could ever have thought him a cold fish. And then he winked at her, which made her lips twitch upward into a startlingly bright smile. Never before in her life had this paragon done more than nod in her direction.

"Go away, brat," Abbercombe growled. "If you think you are helping by giving Olivia your public approval, you are not. She does not stand in need of it."

"Abbercombe," gasped Olivia, "be quiet!"

"Yes, Abbercombe, be quiet," echoed Brummell. "You are the most insolent, overbearing, cocksure old dog I have ever met."

"Obviously you never met my father," muttered the duke, sending Olivia and the Beau into gales of laughter.

"No, really," the Beau gasped, catching his breath, "I am not come to rescue Miss Willburton-Smythe's reputation. I am come to invite you to dine with me, Duke."

"Surely you jest."

"I give you my word there is not one bet laid upon the thing. I thought we might share dinner at Grillon's Hotel."

"Are you determined to send Florizel into a frenzy, brat? Is that your object?"

"I wish you will not call me brat," Brummell sighed. "It makes me feel no more than six. And I should delight to see Prinny taken down a rung or two. He becomes too sure of himself."

Abbercombe laughed. "So do you, halfling. Very well, we shall dine, you and I. When?"

"Tonight? At eleven?"

Abbercombe nodded and set his team back in motion leaving the Beau staring after them in the middle of the path.

"I do believe, your grace," smiled Olivia, "that the Beau is attempting to bring you into fashion."

"Is he?" Abbercombe chuckled and took one of her prettily gloved hands into his own.

"Do you not care to be brought into fashion?" she asked, enjoying the feel of his hand on hers and needing to remind herself that the man was a devil.

"I do not particularly care, Olivia. But I cannot think that Brummell is a bad sort. Mischievous, rather. Much like Frazier."

"Is Frazier mischievous?"

"A regular dry boots, my dear. Nearly as maggoty as his father. And the cub is up to every rig."

A number of respectable persons, having witnessed Brummell's conversation with the duke, nodded to the couple in the red curricle as it proceeded toward the east gate. Margaret Dunleavy, the dowager Countess of Vale, sat forward in her carriage as she passed and waved. Abbercombe, much to Olivia's surprise, waved back. "Do not look so amazed, Olivia," he said, as he lowered his hand back atop her own. "Lady Vale is my godmother. Though what brings her to town, I cannot imagine."

"Perhaps Sebastian and Jessica brought her?" Olivia replied, glancing up at him with a tentative smile. The responding look in his eyes was unreadable and she hesitated to speak further. The more time she spent with this man, the more her heart ached that he was not what he seemed to be. If only he were as honorable and caring as he appeared, she knew she would love him. But he was not! She could not allow herself to succumb to his charms.

"Why would they do that?"

"What?"

"Bring Aunt Margaret to London?"

"To lend Amaryllis and Bethany consequence."

"Come, Olivia," Abbercombe frowned, "truth. Did Sebastian send for the old girl? Do you know it for fact?"

"I know Lady Jess spoke of doing so. She thought that if the girls appeared at some of the entertainments in the Countess of Vale's company, it would raise them in certain eyes. By the by, why have the girls not appeared since the Langdons' musicale? I thought to see them at least at Lady Doering's drawing room."

Abbercombe's frown turned instantly to a disturbing glare. "They cannot go anywhere, my dear, without a proper chaperon, and I have not, as yet, been able to provide them one."

"But surely Jessica—"

"No, I will not inconvenience her any farther with the charge of them."

"Perhaps she does not see it as an inconvenience?"

"I see it as an inconvenience," Abbercombe declared. "She did never bargain to be saddled with myself and a parcel of children when she married Sebastian, and she shall not be. You do not understand, Olivia. You may choose to ride beside me in the park or not, to attend my children's parties or not, but Jessica has no such freedom. If she wishes to keep peace with Sebastian, she must compromise on these issues. Marriage is a complicated arrangement at best. I have no intention of making it more complicated for her."

Olivia watched as he turned the corner on to Broad Street, and then she left the window beside the front door and hurried up the stairs to the library. In a matter of minutes she had dispatched a footman to M. LeBruin's chambers in Leicester Square with the information that Abbercombe was to dine at Grillon's that evening at eleven o'clock with the Beau.

She stood, when the note had been dispatched, and stared moodily down on to Park Street. It was the danger and excitement of trapping the villain in his own lines that sent her heart leaping to her throat each time she was with Abbercombe and left her so empty each time they parted. That had to be it. Her chin raised slightly and she swept a loose wisp of hair from her cheek. She had not worn one of her spinster's caps since that day he had railed so against them. He had been so splendid to her that day, had made her feel so safe, so important, so—loved? No! she told herself. I will not be such a ninny! He is evil. His whole life has been one of treachery and deceit. He pretended to care for my own and Andrew's welfare only to obtain his own ends—which are fiendish and vile—and if Andrew comes to harm because of him, I will see the gentleman hanged for it! But then she remembered how the duke had carried April so gently from the museum and tucked the girl, tenderly, into the carriage, and how he had knelt in such grave discussion in the midst of the Burlington Arcade, his arms lovingly around Gracie and Helen. And the fanciful gypsy party—she saw again not merely his figure and form, but his delight in his children's love.

"How can you!" she exclaimed under her breath, clasping her hands before her and pacing the room with angry little steps. "How can you be a traitor! You were not born a villain. Some part of your heart is not black and scarred. You know how to love or your children would not love you as they do. Whatever happened to make you into such a monster!"

"Aunt Olivia, what is it? What is the matter?" April rushed into the room and took her suddenly sobbing aunt into her arms. "Why you are crying? Can you not confide in me?" With careful steps April led Olivia to a chair before the hearth and settled her into it. "I shall ring for some tea," she declared, and did so immediately. "Laslow," she ordered with an authority Olivia had never before heard in her sweet young tones, "we will have tea now. And you must tell cook to set dinner back an hour. Aunt Olivia is not feeling quite the thing and she shall wish to lie down a bit before we dine."

Olivia could feel tears streaming down her cheeks but she could not seem to stop them. How I hate you, Abbercombe, she thought, wiping at the little trails of wetness with her handkerchief. You are not worth these tears! You are not!

Abbercombe left Grillon's that night well-fed and chirping merry. Brummell had discovered his grace's fondness for nearly extinct Canary and had provided the dinner table with five bottles of that wonderful stuff. "Come," the Beau urged, taking the duke's arm, "my coach shall set you down at Fielding House."

"Why? Do you think I cannot find the place?" Abbercombe asked with a cocked eyebrow. "I am not as disguised as all that."

"No, of course you are not," Brummell chuckled, "but I, my lord, am much too foxed to walk it and I'll not send you into the night alone—not, sir, when you have forced yourself to be pleasant to me all evening and never once called me brat."

"I cannot understand that. I certainly intended to do so."

"To do what?"

"Call you brat. It must have slipped my mind when the oysters appeared. I lust after raw oysters."

"I know," nodded Brummell, stopping to give his driver directions and then joining the duke inside the carriage. "I have never eaten them before. They are bloody awful."

Abbercombe laughed. "It is definitely an acquired taste. Who was it told you I relished them?"

"Prinny. He told me that you and Charles Fox downed an entire barrel of them one night in less than an hour and made everyone else at table devilish ill from just watching you."

"Yes, well, and we meant to do so. What else has Florizel told you about me?"

"Only that his father was fond of you, and that you are an extremely dangerous man."

"Dangerous? Why would he say that?" Abbercombe sank into deep thought in his corner of the coach. "I have it!" he exclaimed finally beneath Brummell's bemused scrutiny. "You will not listen to him on that score, Beau. He holds an altercation with the point of my sabre against me. I did not run him through, however, so I am not near as dangerous as I should like to be."

Leaning comfortably back against the squabs, Brummell studied the figure across from him. "Was it the duel with Prinny got you transported?" he asked at last.

"No, I do not believe anyone even knew of it but Florizel and myself."

"Why do you call him Florizel? No one still calls him that."

"Not here, but on the continent his legend lives on. He was most impressive when he was young—almost as impressive as

I." Abbercombe laughed. "Unfortunately, we have both grown old."

"Older, perhaps, but no less impressive." Brummell's gaze never left the duke's face. "You mentioned your daughters—"

"Did I?"

"Yes, over the second course, I believe. You returned to England because of them?"

"They wish to find husbands, Brummell, and will not be satisfied with Frenchmen or Russians or even Americans, though I cannot understand it."

"I should like to be introduced to them."

"Why? Have you an urge to bring them into fashion?"

"An extremely strong urge to do so."

Abbercombe's brilliantly blue eyes speared through the Beau. "Amaryllis and Bethany do not exist as pawns with which to display your power over the *ton* or as foibles to increase your vanity and conceit, brat. If you must make someone fashionable let it be some pattern-card miss just up from the country. She will be grateful to you; my daughters will not."

Brummell's eyelids lowered slightly and he tugged at his right earlobe with some violence. "I did not mean to insult you, Abbercombe, or your young ladies," he said at last, "but you must admit that they suffer some because of your, ah, reputation. I only meant to offer my services. If I am seen to spend time with them, you know, the *ton* will be eager to do likewise."

"How the world shudders when a rogue has beautiful daughters," mumbled Abbercombe.

"What does that mean?"

"If you live long enough, Brummell, you will discover it."

The coach at that moment pulled to a stop outside Fielding House and the driver's fist knocked on the trap. "Do ye wish me to drive into the yard, sir? 'Tis after three."

"No, do not," Abbercombe called back, opening the door and jumping down into the street. "I thank you for the dinner and the conversation, brat," he said. "Deliver my regards to Florizel. Tell him I have missed him and sincerely regret his father's—indisposition. He will likely not care, but still it is the truth of the matter." With that the duke closed the door and strolled through the gates, and into the courtyard.

"Wait," Brummell called to his driver. "We will see him safely inside before we leave, Jem."

"Aye, sir."

The Beau's gaze followed the duke as he climbed the steps of Fielding House. Prinny, he thought, may have grown less impressive over the years, but you, sir, are the most impressive gentleman I have ever met. And then a pistol shot cracked through the night; Brummell gasped as he watched Abbercombe spin down the steps, sabre leaping to his hand as shadows whipped toward him from the yard.

"Sir!" cried the driver, giving the trap a quick knock.

"Tie the horses, Jem," Brummell yelled, swinging out of the coach and dashing, cane in hand, in Abbercombe's direction. In less than a minute the burly coachman, whip at the ready, was running into the courtyard behind the Beau. Abbercombe's sabre, already bloodied, slashed silently at a band of specters that surrounded him, but he was badly outnumbered. Brummell entered the fray, his cane coming down with a great deal of enthusiasm upon heads, shoulders, arms. The coachman was quick to follow his master's lead and laid into the phantoms with whip and fists both. A small figure slammed out the front door of the house, cudgel in hand, and joined the mill. The ruffians, with amazing singlemindedness, swatted Brummell and Jem and the late arriving Fanning aside like gnats, saving their lethal blows for the duke alone.

The Beau fought in the midst of a nightmare—the only sounds the scuffling of boots upon the cobbles, the gasping of overworked lungs, and now and then a groan. He thrust out at figures in the night, their faces blackened or hidden, the shapes of their bodies cloaked beneath long, oversized box coats. Another pistol shot sounded, exceedingly close, and Jem the coachman cried out as Abbercombe wavered and fell. As if one mind controlled them, Fanning, Jem and the Beau seized upon the ruffians closest to the duke and battered them away, forming a tight circle about the stricken man. They fought determinedly to keep a death blow from ending the duke's struggle. For what seemed an eternity their desperate attempt to save Abbercombe continued in silence, and then the duke was up, his sabre slashing beside them.

"Aim at their faces," he hissed. "You cannot penetrate the coats!" Brummell's cane and Jem's whip cracked across cheeks and eyes; Fanning's cudgel pounded noses and chins; Abbercombe's blade slashed savagely at necks and ears and hands, until at last the attackers broke and ran. Brummell made to go after them but a hand caught his arm. "No, Beau," gasped the duke breathlessly, blood streaming into his eyes. "They'll only re-form and take you down should you catch up with them." Abbercombe dropped his sabre, put his hands on his hips, and bent at the waist, groaning and inhaling at the same time.

Fanning rushed to the duke, retrieving his sabre then cleaning and sheathing it for him.

"Demmed fine mill, warn't it?" Jem grinned, blood trickling from a split lip.

"I would have enjoyed it more were I a bit younger," sighed Abbercombe as he straightened. "Nice of you to join me though."

Brummell rubbed at a badly bruised shoulder. "There're three over here. Dead," he muttered.

Abbercombe wandered wearily over to where the Beau stood, knelt beside the first and removed the muffler which hid the man's face. Then he swept masks from the other two. "Jem," he said to the coachman who peered over his shoulder, "are you badly injured or can you fetch the Watch?"

"I'll git 'em," the coachman replied, and departed at a run.

Abbercombe stood, wavered slightly, and grabbed for Fanning's arm. "I am feeling devilish queer, Robin," he murmured.

"Are you hurt badly, your grace?" Brummell asked.

"I am not like to die," Abbercombe wiped his sleeve across his brow, "and I thank you for it, brat. I expect there is no way to keep my name out of the thing," he sighed, "but you might

avoid the Watch, Beau. Robin can wake John to drive you home
before they turn up. I am sorry," he added in a shaky tone, "your
yellow pantaloons shall probably end in the fire."

"Indeed," smiled Brummell wryly. "This coat shall meet a
similar end. Doubtless my neckcloth as well. And consider what
scrutiny my oft-professed abhorrence of violence shall undergo,
do I persist in my acquaintance with you, Abbercombe."

"Best drop me then." As the duke turned to mount the steps,
he wobbled uncertainly and both Fanning and Brummell seized
at his arms. Together they helped him inside, along the ground
floor hall and into the kitchen where Fanning pressed him into
a chair, lit candles, and renewed the fire.

"Brandy?" Brummell asked.

"Some in his grace's study, sir. Back up the hall, second door
on your right."

Brummell took a branch of candles in hand and set off in
search of it. By the time he returned, Fanning had already set to
work upon the wide graze the pistol ball had left across Abbercombe's temple. "Stunned you a bit is all," Fanning muttered.
"Need only a few stitches to close it up."

It was well after eleven that morning when Abbercombe, feeling as though his ribs were pinned beneath a bell of St. Paul's,
opened bleary eyes and stared up at the canopy of his bed. The
weight on his chest wriggled; from the corner of the room a
giggle, quickly hushed, reached his ears. He closed his eyes
again. The weight on his chest began to rearrange itself. "By
thunder," he roared, "if I open me eyes and spies a creature wif
furs upon me chest, I'll keelhaul the divils what put it there!
Argh!!"

There was a huge intake of breaths and a considerable amount
of noise as small feet scuttered across the room; small bodies
bounded onto the bed; small hands grabbed the puppy from his
chest; and small bodies jumped hurriedly back to the floor. "Halt,
ye lubbers, right where ye're at!" Abbercombe roared again, sit-

ting up in the bed. Three pairs of feet came to a skidding stop, and three innocently beaming faces turned to smile back at him, while the fourth pair of feet disappeared into his dressing room. "Do not one of ye move, ye villains," the duke cried, pointing a long, slim finger at the three he could see.

He jumped from the bed, tied his dressing gown around him, put a finger to his lips, and sneaked to the dressing room doorway. "Aha, I got ye, ye scurvy marmot!" he shouted, reaching around the casing and seizing Frazier and the puppy both. He carried them, squirming, back to the bed and deposited them in the middle of it. Then he scooped up the madly giggling Ethan, a screeching Grace, and a squealing Helen and corralled them upon the feather ticking as well. " 'Tis me captives ye be, me hearties!" he growled, preventing them from climbing off the bed by tickling them back onto it. By the time Robin entered with a cup of coffee for his grace, they were all of them a flailing, bouncing, barking, giggling, laughing mass.

"What is going on here?" Fanning asked imperiously.

"We's bein' keelhauled, Robin!" gurgled Helen from beneath a pillow. "Cap'n Crooked's got us!"

"I see," Fanning replied, his lips twitching, but his voice steadily arrogant. "And may I ask, is the—dog—suffering a similar fate, miss?"

"Ever'body's sufferin' it," cried Frazier, attempting to scuttle, upside down, over the side of the bed.

"Help us, Robin!" Gracie screamed, laughing, from beneath the counterpane. "Cap'n Crooked's got us pris'ners!"

"Arf!" exclaimed the puppy, tugging at first one child and then another and then licking at Abbercombe's face exuberantly. "Woof! Woof! Arf!"

"We put Bear on 'is chest an' woked 'im up!" chortled Ethan in extreme ecstasy as his father trapped him up against the headboard and tickled his ribs. "Help us, Robin! Help!"

"Not I," Fanning announced with a shake of his head. "However, you might use the magic words."

"What magic words," screamed Frazier as his father caught him half way to the floor and tossed him back on to the bed.

"Lady Castlereagh," said Fanning clearly. "One o'clock."

"Lady Kettlecree!" shouted Gracie at the top of her lungs, just as her father tossed a pillow atop her.

"One o'clock!" yelled Helen and Ethan together. Frazier only giggled wildly as his father dangled him by his knees over the flowered carpeting.

"What is going on?" asked Abbercombe, abruptly. "Frazier, why are you dangling in midair? Where did you all come from? And what is that dratted canine doing upon my bed?"

"It was Cap'n Crooked," Helen squealed, jumping up and down upon the mattress. "Cap'n Crooked got us! We magicked 'im away!"

"Well, thank goodness for that! He might have keelhauled the lot of you. Scatter before he returns," the duke urged, shooing them off the bed and out the door. He took the cup of coffee Fanning offered and sank down upon the edge of the bed.

"You're totally mad," Fanning sighed. "You'll ache like the devil soon enough."

"Yes—I do not remember, Robin, did the Watch come?"

"Indeed. While I was in the midst of sewing you up. They recognized the three scoundrels lyin' on the cobbles. Two of 'em footpads, one a bully ruffian name of Diamond Russell."

"A highwayman? Truly?"

"That's what they said. You do not remember any of it?"

"Oh, I remember the fight well enough—it is the part following slips my mind. Did the brat get home? Was he hurt?"

"Bruised, battered, an' bleeding, your grace, but proud of himself. Never been in a mill before, I expect. You could see he was proud to be standing at the end of it. Now get back to bed and let me have a look at your head and the rest of those bruises. You are not nearly in as fine fettle as you think, and in a moment that rough-housing with the children will tell on you."

Mr. Charles Stanton and Miss Clarissa Greene met in the ground floor corridor outside what had come to be known amongst the staff as the Children's Den. "Have you lost yours as well?" queried Stanton with a lift of his eyebrow and a bright smile.

"I cannot conceive of where they have gone," sighed Miss Greene, brushing a wisp of brown hair from her brow. "When I left the nursery the girls were busy drawing a picture of Bear for their papa's study. I was gone only a moment."

"Yes, the boys have disappeared as well. Chris and Daymee are upstairs planning an expedition to Vauxhall, though I doubt his grace will allow them to go, but they have not seen the little scoundrels. The Children's Den was my last hope."

"Mine as well, Mr. Stanton," smiled Miss Greene. "You do not suppose they have gone outside for some reason?"

"I've been to the stables, in the storage room under the stairs, in Dawson's pantry and the attics."

"And I have been to the kitchen, the still room, the gardening shed and checked inside the clock."

"Inside the clock?" Mr. Stanton chuckled loudly.

"You may laugh, Mr. Stanton, but only two days ago I found both Gracie and Helen squeezed inside the grandfather's clock. They wanted to discover if 'that big gold thin' maked breezes when it moved'." She laughed prettily.

"Look out! Look out!" came a shout from the stairway, followed by screams, giggles and myriad woofs, arfs, grrrs and the thunder of stamping, running feet. Mr. Stanton and Miss Greene were seized by a whirlwind composed of sprigged muslin dresses, short blue coats, white stockings, pretty jean half boots, and a ball of fur. "Hurry! Hide!" shouted the whirlwind, spinning them into the Children's Den and slamming the door.

"Safe!" cried Ethan, collapsing breathless across a battered fainting couch.

"Safe!" echoed Frazier, releasing Miss Greene's hand and spinning to a stop against an oak chair with faded puce padding.

"Safe! Safe!" squealed Gracie and Helen ceasing to push at Mr. Stanton's legs and plopping down in the middle of the rug with Bear wriggling wildly between them.

"Well, I certainly am glad of that," grinned Mr. Stanton. "From what, may I ask, have we been saved?"

"Cap'n Crooked," breathed Helen, staring up at him with wide eyes. "We are jus' lucky that Robin knowed the magicked words."

Nine

With great good humor Mr. Stanton and Miss Greene extracted the tale of Cap'n Crooked, who, it seemed, was accustomed to appear in the children's lives at the most unexpected times. At last settling them down, the two set about the task of straightening various articles of clothing, combing back into some semblance of propriety four sets of golden curls, and helping to clean up sweaty hands and faces. With a good many smiles they delivered their charges, almost perfectly in order, into the Red Saloon at a quarter past one to be introduced properly to Lady Castlereagh.

"I am most pleased to meet you," responded that lady, attempting to hide the amusement that assailed her as Ethan and Frazier bowed seriously and Grace and Helen attempted to curtsy properly. "Your brothers and sisters have been telling me all about the four of you."

"Really?" asked Frazier, his glance turning to Christian and Damian. "Did they say anythin' good, ma'am?"

Amaryllis grinned and ordered them to sit down like young ladies and gentlemen and not frighten Lady Castlereagh away. "For she was a very good friend of Mama's, you know, and has been most kind to come and visit us."

"Mama would tell us stories about London and the balls and routs," Bethany explained shyly. "She said you were the belle of every ball. Amy and I thought you a fairy princess."

"Oh, my goodness," murmured Lady Castlereagh, who had never once thought of herself as any such thing. She had become, in fact, one of the most intimidating patronesses of Almack's and a formidable hostess among the *ton*. "I am certain your Mama did not mean for you to think that."

"Papa used to tease that if Lord Castlereagh had not won the fair Emily Anne, he, himself, would have attempted to do so."

"Is your father happy to be back in London?"

"No, ma'am," offered Christian quietly from where he stood beside the fireplace mantle looking every inch the heir of the manor. "It was a mistake to bring him here. We have been discussing whether or not to remain."

"*You* have been discussing?" Lady Castlereagh asked, shocked.

"Yes, ma'am," nodded Amaryllis. "Papa wished to go to St. Petersburg and should have done so had not the lot of us formed a plan to bring him here instead. We did not understand, you know, how abominably he would be treated. However, that is a family matter and does not bear discussing at the moment," she added with a stern glance at the elder boys.

"What is abonimally, Amy?" Grace asked from the depths of the huge arm chair she shared with Helen.

"Shhh, dearest," Amy replied. "I will explain it to you some other time. Do you not think Lady Castlereagh's dress pretty?"

"She is magicked," breathed Helen, agog. "Cap'n Crooked is feared of her."

Damian snickered. Bethany smothered a laugh. Lady Castlereagh looked totally perplexed.

"It is a game they played, ma'am," Amaryllis said with an encouraging smile. "It appears a magic word was needed, and your name came up. Now Helen thinks it is you who are magic."

Lady Castlereagh did not know whether to be offended or honored by such an odd use of her name. She chose the latter. "Your mother was a lovely person and has raised a wonderful family," she said with enthusiasm. "I see a great deal of Celia in all of you."

" 'Cept me," mumbled Frazier, kicking his heel against the leg of the chair in which he sat. "I am like Papa."

"Perhaps, but you are very like your Mama as well. Your hair is just the color of hers, and you have her nose, you know."

"Papa's nose got broke," Ethan offered solemnly. "Twice."

"Yes, I know," laughed Lady Castlereagh. "It was I who broke it the very first time."

"When you pushed open the door to the Gold Saloon in such a hurry and Papa was on the other side," grinned Bethany. "Mama said they had just formed a plot to draw off your Aunt Lydia so that Lord Castlereagh might propose to you, only Papa's nose bled so much and it caused such a commotion that Lord Castlereagh had to take him home instead of asking you to marry him."

"I had no idea! And to think that all this time Castlereagh has never said a word to me about it. I do wish that he were not off in Venice. He would be so happy to see your Papa and to meet all of you. They were good friends, you know, when they were young gentlemen. One rarely saw one of them without the other—or without Worth or Channing Kettering. They were all very close."

"Would he come to see Papa, do you think?" Christian asked with a slight frown. "Uncle Sebastian and Lord Worth are the only gentlemen who actually came when they learned he had arrived, and then later, Sir Ralph and Mr. Hurley."

"Well, of course Castlereagh would come, young man."

"You will pardon me for noticing, Lady Castlereagh, but you did not come, did you? Without being begged to do so, I mean."

"Christian," hissed Amaryllis.

"I know I should not say so, Amy, but I expect that Papa begged her expressly to appear. My Mama," he continued, his cool gaze returning to Lady Castlereagh, "thought you her very best friend. She often wrote to you, but she never received an answer. Sometimes she cried, because she was lonely, you know, though whenever Papa suggested she return to England, she would not because she was loathe to abandon him. She said 'twas likely her letters never reached you for they had to travel so very far. Did any of them ever reach you, ma'am?"

Lady Castlereagh sat quite still with her mouth open just a bit and her hands clenched about the arms of her chair.

"Perhaps she truly did not receive them," Bethany murmured, scowling at her brother. "And besides, it is not our place to be speaking of these things."

"Well, Papa will never speak of them to her or to Lord Castlereagh either if he should ever see him," mumbled Damian. "Did you receive her letters, Lady Castlereagh?"

Lady Castlereagh, who had never once been confronted with her faults by anyone, and especially not by such young ladies and gentlemen, gasped. For a number of years it had been her part to play both inquisitor and judge of myriad young ladies who wished to procure vouchers to Almack's. Because of this she was always courted and flattered. To be questioned so, without any thought given to her societal power, brought her to a most disrupted state.

"I—I—never thought!" she exclaimed in some confusion. "Yes, of course I received some of them. And I meant to answer them, too, but first I was newly married, and everything was so exciting, and then I became so involved with Castlereagh and society," Lady Castlereagh's voice began to tremble. "I never answered one! How could I have been so—cruel!"

"Papa says hardly anyone's cruel," announced Frazier, quite out of his depth but sympathetic because he could see tears standing in Lady Castlereagh's eyes. He crossed the room and gave her his handkerchief. "Papa says mos'ly what looks like cruel is just people bein' thoughtless or frightened or stoopid."

"Y-yes," agreed Lady Castlereagh with a tiny sob, "and I have been all three of those things, child."

"Well, but so has ever'body. Chris an' Daymee, an' Amy is bein' thoughtless right now, I should think. An' me and Ethan was stoopid jus' yes'erday."

"Were you?" chuckled Lady Castlereagh with his handkerchief to her eyes as she smiled and cried at the same time.

"Uh-huh, terrible stoopid, an' we maked Gracie cry, but that is not the same as bein' cruel, an' we were sorry for it af'er."

"Yes," added Bethany coming to stand behind Lady Castlereagh and placing her hands upon that lady's shoulders, "and Gracie still loves them just as much as ever, and I am quite certain that Mama loved you just as much as ever too. If she had not, she would certainly not have made you the heroine of all her tales."

"Please, ma'am, do not cry," Christian pleaded, kneeling before her. "It was devilish rude of me to bring the thing up."

"Yes, it was exceeding rude of all of us," agreed Amaryllis as she and the rest of the children gathered around Lady Castlereagh's chair. "Please forgive us, ma'am. We should all like for you to be our friend and Lord Castlereagh as well."

"Oh, dear, I am being such a watering pot," Lady Castlereagh murmured through her tears. "I am not usually such a goose, believe me. But I always thought your mother happy, child. She loved your father so, in spite of everything."

"She was only lonely sometimes, ma'am. Papa always did his very best to make all of us happy."

"He is vewy funny," added Helen, nodding emphatically and climbing into Lady Castlereagh's lap, followed by Grace.

Lady Castlereagh found the handkerchief taken from her hands, and her cheeks patted tenderly dry. Quite without thought, she found herself with each arm around a tiny girl and a heart filled with longing for babes of her own.

"My goodness, what a delightful portrait," declared Lady Jessica as she entered the room. "Lady Castlereagh, how good to see you again. I believe you remember Lady Vale."

"No, no, stay as you are," muttered the dowager countess, waving a wrinkled hand at Lady Castlereagh. "So, you are Rudolph's children?" she added studying the group around Lady Castlereagh's chair, and with a most amazing sagacity directed her eyes to Christian and declared, "Warren, help me to a chair, please. Jessica, stop fussing and be seated. Do you know who I am?" she asked as Christian escorted her to a high-backed, elegantly upholstered relic from an earlier age.

"No, ma'am," he murmured, "I am afraid not."

"I am your father's godmother, and I have come from Somerset to inspect the lot of you and to lend my consequence to your eldest sisters. Yes, Emily Anne," she laughed at the surprised look upon Lady Castlereagh's face, "Jessica has informed me that Amy and Beth have received invitations which they are unable to accept because they lack a proper chaperon. She and I have quite decided to divide those duties between us. Now," she said, redirecting her attention to the rest of the children, "I will surprise you all. This young man," a wrinkled hand circled Christian's wrist, "is Chris, who is Marquis of Warren, though his Papa never calls him that; and you, my dear, are Beth—" With amazing accuracy and causing a great many giggles by relating what she knew about each of them, the dowager Countess of Vale identified each of the children.

"However did you do that, ma'am?" Bethany asked when she had finished. "Even Aunt Jessica cannot keep us all straight in her mind, and she has known us for over a month."

"But I, my dear, have known your father for over forty years and for eighteen of them he has written to me about each of you."

"Truly?" asked eight voices all at once.

"Indeed."

"But I thought Papa seldom wrote to anyone," Amy responded, puzzled. "He only wrote three times to Uncle Sebastian."

"That is because he had me to tell him how your Uncle Sebastian went on."

"And because grandfather would not have given Uncle Sebastian his letters anyway," added Damian.

"Exactly," agreed Lady Vale. "Now, Emily Anne, are you or are you not sending the girls vouchers for Almack's? I know you do not mean to request them, my dears," she silenced Amaryllis and Bethany before they could protest, "but I think it only reasonable to accept if they are to be forthcoming."

"I assure you, they will be," Lady Castlereagh smiled. "Despite Abbercombe's standing, Celia's friends will not see the girls ignored."

When Lady Castlereagh had taken her leave, kissing Gracie and Helen, and bestowing a hug upon each of the other children, Lady Vale demanded Abbercombe's presence. Christian nodded and left to summon his father as Amy, Beth and Damian bid their aunt and Lady Vale farewell and herded the younger children from the room.

Lady Jessica gasped when her brother-in-law appeared. "Cash, whatever happened?" Her gaze could not get beyond the silk scarf wound 'round his brow to discover the twinkle in his eyes.

"What? Is it that terrible, Jess? It was Robin's idea, you know, to wrap the kerchief 'round over the bandage. He thought it would look more outrageous than serious that way. He is making, I believe, a new fashion statement. Good afternoon, Aunt Margaret, pleasure to see you."

The dowager studied him thoughtfully. "Can you bow," she asked, "or have you destroyed your ribs as well?"

"I could bow this morning, ma'am," Abbercombe grinned, "but I had rather not attempt the thing at the moment."

"No, it is obvious you are stiff. How did this happen? Did you finally lose your patience, my boy, with being cut?"

"No, ma'am. I was set upon in my own courtyard. The blackguards were meant, I think, to kill me. No, do not look so upset, Jess. They did not succeed after all, and luckily they attempted to do the job quietly enough not to wake the children."

"Sit down. There," ordered Lady Vale, pointing to a chair directly before her. She then rose and fetched a pillow from a settee and despite his protestations, adjusted it competently behind his back. "Now, you are more comfortable, are you not?" she declared, regaining her seat beside Lady Jessica.

Abbercombe's eyes caught Lady Jessica's and she smothered

a laugh. "If I were not, madam," he replied, "I should be loathe to say so. You would have me on my back upon the couch."

"Which is most likely where you should be. Now, who is it hates you enough to wish you dead?"

"Countless numbers, Aunt Margaret, though I cannot think what any of them are doing in England. Unless—"

"Who?"

"You do not think, perhaps, that Stamford—"

"He would not dare! He is a worm with no belly."

Abbercombe broke into whoops and groaned, forced to hold his ribs. "What—what does—that mean?" he gasped.

"It means he is beneath contempt and has no stomach to carry through on his threats. I think. It is what Vale always said about him," replied the elderly lady, her eyes brimming with mirth. "You do, by the way, look a bit like a pirate with that silk kerchief 'round your brow. Perhaps Robin thought it would soothe the little ones. Were you hit with a cudgel?"

"A ball from a horse pistol. It is no more than a graze, Aunt Margaret, but Robin says it bled a good deal, and insists it must stay covered. Now, explain to me why you are here."

Lady Vale explained succinctly and Lady Jessica upheld her in the decisions they had made together. "For Jessie wishes to take the girls about and so do I. And we have agreed that between us they will not be at all burdensome. Besides which, Rudolph, I should like to spend time with the children."

"Then you must abandon Sebastian and Lady Jess and move into Fielding House," Abbercombe muttered, much to the amazement of both ladies, "for I do not see how you are to chaperon the girls adequately, Aunt Margaret, and see the children, if you are living with Sebastian and Jess."

"I should be most pleased. Cash, you have not the least grace about you when you know you have lost," Lady Margaret laughed. "Just accept defeat and give me a kiss," she added, rising and bending over his chair. "Jess and I will be off to collect my things, and you must lie down for a while. You are not as young as you used to be, my dear, and you cannot simply carry on as though nothing had occurred."

Olivia paled the next day at Lady Vale's description of Abbercombe's wounds. "He fought tooth and nail to prevent my ministering to him, but I have nursed Vale through much, and Robin was thankful for my experience. Whoever it was," finished Lady Vale, "they were certainly bent upon putting a period to Abbercombe's life. Had the pistol ball come even the tiniest bit closer, we should now be attending his funeral."

"I cannot believe it," gasped Olivia quietly, so as not to be overheard by Amy, Beth and April who entertained a number of young ladies and gentlemen across the drawing room.

"What I do not understand," mused Lady Vale, "is why they should be waiting for him at three o'clock in the morning. How could they know he had gone out at all, much less that he would be so late? Dawson says they could not have been about the place until after eleven, for that is when Gowan and he locked up the house and stables and Gowan did check about the yard as he does every night. And Cash had not even taken his own carriage!"

Olivia's heart, which was beating more rapidly with each word from the dowager's lips, wrenched at this last sally. Someone had known that Abbercombe would be out. She had known, and she had passed that information along to M. LeBruin. But LeBruin would certainly not hire ruffians to take the duke's life. He merely wished to keep an eye upon the gentleman, to obtain from him Andrew's whereabouts and prevent him from gaining information that might be passed across the channel to France.

"Indeed, I was surprised to see you and he tooling about the park together," the dowager interrupted Olivia's thoughts.

"What? Oh, yes. We have become friends, you see."

"Oh? Before or after you met his children, my dear?"

"Ma'am?"

"What I mean to ask, Olivia—may I call you Olivia?—what

I seek to learn is if you thought him worthy of notice immediately, or if, perhaps, the children won you over?"

Olivia felt a blush rise and gave a shake of her head. She studied April's slim little form near the front window as she sat with a group of friends making plans for some sort of outing. "I think, Lady Vale, it was his children won me, seeing how much . . ."

"He loves them? You must not be shy to say so, my dear. Cash did never know if his parents loved him or not, and he wishes his children to have no doubts about his and Celia's feelings."

"Did you know the duchess, my lady?" Olivia queried, hoping to steer the conversation away from the duke, for every mention of him sent her mind to reeling with apprehension and guilt. Had she been responsible for the assault upon the man? Had LeBruin and his superiors in the War Office intended all along to murder that gentleman? But no, that could not be so. Certainly the government did not go about things in such a harum-scarum fashion. If they wished to put an end to the duke's activities, why they would arrest him and bring him to the dock for treason. And then she thought she knew what she would do, she would arrange a meeting with Jamie Ratherton and she would ask him, very discreetly, of course, how such matters as Englishmen known to spy for the French were dealt with. Jamie would know, and he would tell her, too.

"Yes, my dear, I knew Celia well. She was a termagant."

"I cannot believe it, ma'am."

"Oh, yes! I did never meet a more dominating, exacting, demanding young lady. Cash did not wish to marry her at all, but the match had been arranged by their fathers a number of years earlier and Celia never did prefer any other man to Cash, though he tried like a demon to introduce her to every gentleman in town during her Season." The elderly lady laughed, remembering, and smiled brightly as Lady Pomeroy, the mama of one of April's visitors, came to join them.

"Lady Vale," Lady Pomeroy said, "how wonderful to see you. Do you plan to stay in London for a while?"

"For the Season, Pamela," replied the dowager. "I am come to chaperon Cash's girls." Lady Vale studied the various expressions that flitted across Lady Pomeroy's face. "I must say, Pamela," she added, as that lady took a seat upon the chaise beside her and smoothed the wrinkles from her stylishly beribboned muslin gown, "you have raised a remarkably shy daughter, have you not? I cannot conceive how little young ladies have to say for themselves these days. You were never one to remain in the background as I recall."

"I expect not. But Caroline is not at all like me. The gudgeon is frightened by the mere lift of a male eyebrow."

The topic of the late Duchess of Abbercombe was necessarily dismissed as more of the mamas joined the circle about the dowager. Olivia, though pleased to have the young people that this sprinkling of mamas represented, wished the ladies all at Jericho, for her nerves were on edge and nothing would calm them until she spoke with Jamie. The day was a dreary one and none of the young visitors appeared eager to go back out into the chill drizzle. April begged to invite them all to remain for dinner, and Olivia agreed halfheartedly and attempted to set aside her unease and to set about providing for their guests' further comfort and entertainment.

Abbercombe, receiving a note from his daughters announcing that they and the dowager intended to remain at Park Street for the evening, sent word to Mrs. Griffin that there would be three less for dinner and that he wished to be out of the house by eight. That remarkable lady, whose skills would have been envied by every member of the diplomatic corps, first set about calming the little French chef who ruled the kitchen and then arranged for a smaller dinner to be served earlier than usual at his grace's request. "For you know how he is, André," she said, patting the chef's shoulder. "He does not at all realize how having less dinner earlier can be anything but a boon to you."

While Mrs. Griffin tiptoed from the kitchen, Miss Greene was just receiving word that Lady Grace and Lady Helen should don their very best dresses for dinner, and Mr. Stanton was asked to inform all four of the young gentlemen to dress formally, for after dinner they were to accompany their father to the opera.

"The opera?" Damian gasped, laying aside a book on the works of Da Vinci and staring in disbelief at Charles Stanton.

"So I have been told, Lord Damian. He intends to take Lord Ethan and Lord Frazier as well."

"And I expect Gracie and Helen will go, too," groaned Christian, pulling a cloth over his canvas and beginning to clean his paint brushes.

"Well, I am sure you shall have an excellent time," Stanton said cheeringly. "The Royal Opera House is an amazing place, and there are many things other than the opera to keep one entertained. I understand your father has reopened the family box for the rest of the season. It will at least be comfortable."

"Yes, but you do not understand, Mr. Stanton," Damian sighed. "Papa is not well, and if he goes to the opera, he is like to be a bear all night."

Charles Stanton laughed. "I have yet to see your father anything near bear-like. Is such a thing possible?"

"It is not," proclaimed Christian with a glare at his brother. "Daymee only means Papa will be sullen. He is not fond of opera, besides which it always makes him think of Mama."

"Then why does he go?" Mr. Stanton asked, perplexed.

"I think because he wishes us to learn to appreciate it," Damian replied.

"Which we do not," added Christian.

"Perhaps you ought to tell him so," Mr. Stanton smiled, with a shake of his head.

"No," sighed Damian, "we tried that once, but he only said that we should change our minds as we grew older."

"Perhaps you will."

"Never!" exclaimed both of the boys together.

* * *

Mr. Geoffery Hempstead could not believe that he was about to meet the man Lord Wyndham called the finest spy in the history of the world. He fidgeted with his cravat, hoping it had not somehow become limp, and tugged at the sleeves of his coat, which for some reason seemed to be shorter than they ought to be. Nothing, he noticed, fitted him correctly this night. It was his state of mind, of course. His clothes had not changed at all, his nerves, on the other hand, were making him feel distinctly shabby.

He had waited, as Wyndham had told him to do, until the middle of the third act. And then he had made his way unobtrusively from the pit and climbed the elegant marble staircase in the foyer to the hall which serviced the first row of boxes. His senses alive to every sound and movement about him, he strolled down the corridor to the seventh door, turned the knob quietly, and let himself into the box. The stage flared garishly below him and the strains of Verdi rose vibrant and exciting to his ears. He stood motionless, waiting for his eyes to adjust to the semi-darkness. When they did he was appalled to find himself alone. Somewhat shakily he moved toward the front of the box, wondering if he had gotten the wrong time, or the wrong evening, or, lord, the wrong theatre. He ran over the instructions Wyndham had given him in his mind and decided that, no, he had not misunderstood any of them. He was exactly where he should be—but where was The Rogue?

"You are nearly as jittery as was Hartshorn on his first assignment," murmured an exceedingly soft but penetrating voice behind Hempstead. "No, do not turn around as yet. Put your hands upon the back of the chair in front of you and look as though you are watching the performance. Yes, very good. What you have done wrong, Hempstead—you have walked too far forward in the box. You may be seen, you know, from where you stand now."

"I—I did not realize."

"No, of course you did not. But now you do and you will not make the same mistake again. There is no harm done. I have been watching you since first you entered the theater, and you are not being followed nor have you drawn the least suspicion to yourself. But that will change once it becomes common knowledge that you are one of Wyndham's assistants. The oddest people will begin to take an interest in everything you do and everywhere you go and will become exceeding suspicious do you sneeze at an awkward moment. Do you like Wyndham?"

"Yes, certainly, sir," Hempstead whispered, nodding.

"No, that's wrong."

"Wrong?"

"You must remember, Hempstead, that where you stand now other people may see you nod and will realize that you are responding to someone they cannot see. You may turn now, but do it as if you are bored and stroll toward the back of the box."

Hempstead attempted to look bored, turned, and stalked toward the door at the rear. "Where are you?" he asked, pausing as soon as he judged he was out of sight of the audience.

A softly gloved hand grasped his arm from behind a curtain on the right side of the box and he jumped. The grasp tightened and drew him bodily behind the curtain.

"Abbercombe?" Hempstead's eyes grew large in the darkness. "You are—"

"Here with my children enjoying the opera, yes. Listen very carefully, Hempstead. Wyndham must contact Madame Lavoisier, number 14, Rue Julienne, in Paris. Whomever he sends must tell her that M. LeCheval and companion, lately of Gironde, have been detained. Be sure to say it exactly that way. Do not use your own words or Antoinette will receive the wrong message completely."

"M. LeCheval and companion, lately of Gironde, have been detained," Hempstead repeated. "Got it."

"Let me show you one thing and then you must go." Abbercombe directed Hempstead's attention to the wall behind them.

"It's a door."

"It leads to the next box—my box. I have opened it for the Season. It is one of the ways you may always be safe in meeting me. Only send a note that says opera, and the day I receive it I shall become culturally inclined."

"But suppose someone is using this box?"

"No one ever uses this box, Geoff. It belongs to a gentleman named Matthew Warren. He does not exist."

"But suppose it is critical I contact you at once?"

Abbercombe chuckled. "Do you know, Hempstead, you remind me a great deal of Harry. You must discover where I am and send a message, of course, or come and make yourself obvious to me."

"How?"

"Well, if I am in a gaming hell, for instance, you might sit down within my line of sight, call for a bottle of whatever you choose, and sneeze at me. Or if I happen to be tooling about Hyde Park, you might ride up beside me, cough, and continue on. People will think you are in shocking poor health, of course, if there are too many critical moments. But I will then follow you to wherever you think it safe to meet."

"But how shall I find you in the first place?"

"You must ask my valet who always knows. Simply prise the knocker and ask for Fanning. If it is morning, I shall always be at home and you must just send a boy with a message."

"And what, your grace, if you suffer an emergency and must reach me?"

"I will reach you, Hempstead, however I can and I shall not worry about keeping secrets. This," he added, showing Geoffrey a beautiful ebony cane with a silver head in the shape of a hawk, "is for you. Young men no longer wear swords as a regular thing, so you must keep this by you. I do not intend you should use it, but one never knows when it may come in handy." Hempstead stared as Abbercombe slid the head off the cane betraying a three-sided blade attached to it. "Now, take the thing and be off with you. Just as carefully as you came, mind. Oh, and Hempstead, I am delighted you accepted the position."

$\mathcal{T}$εη

It was midnight before the last of the young people departed
Park Street, and Olivia's only thought was to gain the privacy of
her chamber and sort through her emotions and fears concerning
Abbercombe. April, however, had other plans. "May we sit for
awhile, Aunt?" she asked. "There is something I should like to
discuss with you."

"Oh? Come back into the drawing room, then, love, and we
shall have a comfortable coze before the fire." They arranged
themselves upon the couch and each acquired another cup of tea.
"Now, what is it that you wish to speak with me about?"

April glanced into her aunt's worried eyes, then trained her
gaze upon the dwindling fire. "It is—about the Duke of Abbercombe, Aunt Olivia."

"It is?"

"Yes. Amy says he has had an accident. Did you know?"

"Yes, my dear. Lady Vale informed me. Did Amy say what
sort of accident?" Olivia noticed that April fidgeted with the
Versailles lace that edged the long, tight sleeves of her gown.

"She said that he had slipped upon something in the courtyard
as he descended from Mr. Brummell's carriage last evening and
hit his head. Is that what Lady Vale told you?"

"April, do you think Amy has lied to you?"

"Oh, no, Aunt Olivia, but I think, perhaps, her father did not
tell her precisely the truth." April's bright green eyes caught
quickly at her aunt's and then looked just as quickly away. Olivia
watched a red blush creep up her darling girl's neck and wondered

at it. "I know it is not in the least my business, Aunt Olivia, but—but—his grace is certainly not one to slip when descending from a carriage. He is not that old and rickety."

"No," coughed Olivia, attempting to smother a laugh, "I do not think of him as old and rickety either, but one may slip regardless. Perhaps the gentleman was in his cups? Gentlemen do not keep their balance so well when they have been drinking."

"But he is very well-balanced when he has been drinking. Why he walked me all the way from Broad Street without one misstep. Then he climbed the balcony and jumped from it again and did not even fall to his knees or turn his ankle!"

"He what!" exclaimed Olivia as April's hands flew to cover her mouth. "April, look at me! Abbercombe did what?"

April's eyes were sea-green pools of mortification. "I—I did not mean to say—"

"April," declared Olivia with quiet authority, "I appreciate you have a secret that you did not mean to let fall. But you have let it fall and I shall imagine things to be much worse than they are if you do not explain!"

April began in a little squeak of a voice to relate the tale of her doomed elopement. Olivia's heart beat oddly and rapidly as Abbercombe's involvement came to light. "And I was so frightened, Aunt Olivia, and had not the least idea what to do. If the duke had not come along and rescued me, something terrible might have happened. Of course I did not know who he was then."

"Well, I never!"

"Mr. Hempstead and I are quite aware how wrong we were to attempt such foolishness, I assure you, aunt. We behaved like children. We shall not do so again. We shall wait until you and father decide to give us your blessing. The duke has secured Geoffery a position in Lord Wyndham's office so that he might prove to you that he is responsible and ambitious."

"The duke secured him a position? In the Foreign Office?"

"Well, Geoffery did not say it was the duke, but when his grace told my fortune at his party, he said Geoffery would work for the government, and only a short time later that is precisely what happened. And so I think the duke must have been the one to make the fortune come true, do not you?"

Olivia's hands went to her face and she groaned. "What have I done?" she murmured. "Oh, Abbercombe, what have I done?"

"Aunt Olivia, what is it?" April caught at her aunt's hands and took them tenderly in her own. "I am not ruined. Truly I am not. No one knows what happened but Geoffery and I and the duke, and neither Geoffery nor the duke will betray me."

"April, dearest, do you trust his grace so very much?"

"With my life!" exclaimed that young lady seriously. "He has been nothing but kind to me for all that I was in such dire straits when first we met. And he has gone far out of his way, I think, to help Geoffery, whom he does not even know. And he does not wish anything in return, Aunt Olivia, but for us to behave properly and wait until we may marry respectably."

"Yes," muttered Olivia, "he has been extremely kind."

"Indeed," agreed April, rubbing warmth into her aunt's hands, for she could feel how cold they had grown. "But do you not see, that is why I wished to know the truth of his accident. For I am almost certain he could not simply have fallen, and I am just as certain that he would not wish to worry Amy or Beth if he had—had—been in a mill or something of that nature."

"He was attacked and shot," Olivia blurted out, tears starting to her eyes. "In his own courtyard. And he came very near to being killed. And it is all my fault!"

April's eyes grew very round and her face paled at her aunt's words. She took Olivia in her arms and hugged her tightly. "Surely not, Aunt Olivia," she whispered. "Surely you could have had nothing to do with such a thing."

"Oh, but I did! You do not understand, April. I—I allowed someone to convince me that the duke was—a spy for France, and I—passed on the information that made it possible for his grace to be caught unawares." With some sobs and a great many deep breaths, Olivia confessed the tale of Captain Willburton-Smythe's disappearance, LeBruin's conversations with her, and even that Abbercombe had discovered her search through Lord Sinclair's papers. "And—and—even thinking that I could be a spy myself, he c-came here not to accuse me but to ask wh-what he might do to h-help me," she explained, beginning to sob again just a bit.

"And did you tell him, Aunt, about Father?"

"Y-yes. He—he said he would discover your father for us."

"Then he will," April said confidently. "But I do not see what this has to do with the duke being attacked."

"Well, it does not up till there. It is afterward. M. LeBruin convinced me, you see, that Abbercombe was a spy. And I agreed to invite the duke's friendship even more than I had so that we might keep watch over him, convince him to restore your father to us and feed him lies to send to France. And I—I sent M. LeBruin word that the duke was to dine that evening at eleven with Mr. Brummell."

April made an odd little sound in her throat, gave her Aunt another hug, and then stood and began to pace the room. For a long while they were both silent. At last April returned to her seat and again took Olivia's hands in hers. "I know exactly what you must do, Aunt Olivia. You must go to the duke and tell him all about M. LeBruin and how he deceived you."

"Oh, April, I cannot! I am so ashamed! Abbercombe has never been anything but kind—and to have believed such evil of him!"

"I am sure he will not mind that. Most of London believes him guilty of something terrible and Amy and Beth say he does not care so very much that they do. Do not you see, Aunt Olivia, if you but tell him what has happened, then he will know who is his enemy and he will be better able to defend himself."

The gentleman of whom they spoke was at that moment carrying two slumbering little girls in their very best dresses and cloaks through the crowded lobby of the opera house toward the front entrance. The fact that twin bleary-eyed boys clung to each side of his coat and stumbled tiredly along beside him seemed not at all to hamper his progress nor distract him from his destination. He, however, distracted a number of other persons, many of them in elegant gowns and enormous turbans or dampened muslins and ostrich plumes, as well as at least two gentlemen in the lush splendor of formal evening attire.

The Earl of Stamford, his arm adorned by his spectacular eldest daughter, Miranda, came to a halt upon the curving staircase and glared down upon the grouping of blond heads, one of whom's brow was adorned by a black silk scarf tied pirate-like around it. Near the entrance doors, in the midst of a group of gentlemen, LeBruin's steel-grey eyes followed each step Abbercombe took.

Christian and Damian, who had gone ahead to alert John Coachman to bring the vehicle up, had already lowered the coach steps and opened the door and were ready to help Ethan and Frazier into the cozy interior. The little boys crawled across the plush red seats to the far corners and curled into tired little balls. One at a time Chris and Daymee relieved Abbercombe of Grace and Helen so that he might climb into the coach himself. "It occurs to me," the duke whispered, as he took a seat, his ribs aching and his head doing the same, "that I owe the both of you many thanks for all you have done since your mother's death. I wonder how I shall manage when you are off to university and I am left to stumble about with these puppies on my own."

"We have not yet decided, Papa, whether to attend university or not," whispered Christian back.

"You will. If not Oxford, then some other. And I will be pleased to see it, too."

"You will?" Damian asked, with Gracie asleep in his lap.

"Most certainly. Do you think I want you to grow into bedizened little beetle-heads?"

"That we shall not do," grinned Christian. "But perhaps we shall become artists and invent a new style of painting."

"I thought you had already done so," chuckled the duke softly. "There are certainly no other paintings like that which the two of you produced for my birthday, are there?"

"No," grinned Daymee. "That one is truly an original. Papa, do you think Chris and I might go to Vauxhall one day?"

"Yes, when you are thirty-six."

"Papa!" exclaimed Christian.

"You were already married and had four children when you were thirty-six, Papa," accused Damian softly. "All we wish to do is see the sights, not start a family."

"Oh. Well, then, I expect you might go one afternoon, if Mr. Stanton will consent to accompany you."

"But we wish to go at night and see the water display."

"And dine in one of the boxes, and listen to the music," added Christian in a quiet rush. "And watch the dandies."

"Your mother," the duke mused, "loved to watch the dandies. She used to complain that I was quite incapable of reaching such heights of sartorial splendor."

"You are, Papa," grinned Damian. "No matter how hard Robin tries, you never emerge looking anything near splendid."

"I beg your pardon?" growled the duke, cocking his eyebrow at his second eldest son and sending him into a fit of smothered giggles. "I will have you know, I am deeply wounded."

Late the following morning, shortly after Abbercombe had struggled stiffly from his bed, Dawson appeared in his chambers. "There is someone requests an audience, your grace."

"An audience?" Abbercombe's face creased into a smile. "Do I look like a bishop, Dawson?"

Dawson's lips tilted upward. " 'Tis Miss Willburton-Smythe said it, your grace—she requested an audience with you."

"Olivia? Did you take her to Lady Vale, then?"

"No, sir. She wishes to speak with you privately. She awaits you in the library."

"Say I shall join her presently, Dawson, and see she is made comfortable. It is early for tea, I suppose?"

"Quite, your grace, but I shall look after her."

Robin was hard put from that instant forward to get Abbercombe into his clothes fast enough and had to rant and rave with his back securely against a closed door to get the duke to settle down and have the graze upon his brow tended to. Once he was set free Abbercombe dashed down the stairs two at a time and did not slow until he was within four steps of the library where he brought himself to a halt and then walked sedately into Olivia's presence. She turned from the window as he entered and he bowed stiffly and raised her fingertips lightly to his lips. "How kind of you to visit, Olivia," he said.

"Oh!" Olivia's fingers went to the bandage about his brow. Abbercombe intercepted her hand and led her to one of the two wing chairs in the chamber.

"It is a mere scratch," he smiled, moving a straight backed chair across from her. "Tell me, what may I do for you?"

Olivia stared at him, lowered her eyes, then looked up at him again. The pink blush that began to stain her cheeks did not go unnoticed by Abbercombe and he smiled encouragingly. "You wished to speak with me about something," he prompted gently. "Does it concern your brother, perhaps?"

Olivia shook her head slowly from side to side. "It has to do with—with you, your grace."

"With me?"

"Y-yes. Oh, I cannot! April said I ought. That you would not—but I am so ashamed!"

Abbercombe's eyebrow cocked questioningly and he leaned toward her and took her fidgeting hands in his own. "Tell me, dear heart," he murmured. "I am intimately acquainted with most every kind of shame exists—you cannot shock me, you know."

"But I have done something so—so dreadful, Abbercombe!"

"Not possible," he smiled. "You are a pattern-card of propriety. I have it on the best authority."

Olivia took a very deep breath. "I—I have betrayed you."

"You have what? How, Olivia?"

Olivia hung her head and began to tell him of LeBruin so softly that he had to lean very close to catch her words. She could feel the heat of him, hear his heart beating, feel his every breath, but she could not look at him. By the time she had finished her head was bowed low, and she tugged her hands from his to search blindly through her reticule for a handkerchief. His own appeared, thrust before her eyes, and she dropped the reticule and seized it, wiping the tears away angrily and then sobbing again and burying her face in the fine linen that smelled of sunshine and summer breezes. When finally her sobbing ceased and she clutched the mangled handkerchief in a tight little fist, one of his fingers came under her chin and tilted it gently until she could no longer avoid seeing his perfect lips and broken nose and troubled eyes.

"I am so sorry, love," he whispered. "Can you forgive me?"

"F-forgive *you?* But it is I who have—"

"No, do not speak disdainfully of yourself again. I forbid you to do so when the fault is mine. Why should you not believe M. LeBruin when his reputation is beyond reproach and mine is beyond redemption? I wish you had not believed him and had not joined with him against me, but I do not fault you for it, my dear, and I will not have you fault yourself. And besides, Olivia," he smiled, "I did have an estate in France though I am not aware that it was once his, and the Tzar of Russia *is* twisted about my little finger."

"He is?"

"Most assuredly. I am certain my French holdings have all been confiscated by now, but I am equally as certain that should I travel to Russia, I would be welcomed heartily. Olivia? Did you ride with me in the park only to further LeBruin's plans? Did you not—enjoy it just a bit?"

Olivia stared at him, bewildered.

"What I mean to say is, may we continue to be—friends, Olivia? Might we see each other from time to time?"

"But I have nearly got you killed, Abbercombe!"

"Well, but that is not a rarity in my life, love. I have nearly gotten myself killed a number of times, but I have not driven through Hyde Park with a lovely and diverting woman beside me for years and I find I have developed a fondness for it."

Olivia had not the least idea how to respond. How could he treat her treachery so cavalierly? He could not. He was simply putting a calm face upon it to spare her feelings. "I cannot believe," she said quite composedly, "that you can wish to have anything more to do with me."

Abbercombe broke into gales of laughter. "I—I am s-sorry, Olivia," he gasped between hoots. "You must—pardon me." When he had managed to control himself, his eyes glowed into hers.

"I fail to see where I have said the least humorous thing, your grace." Olivia stared at him, mystified.

"It is—it is a private joke. It is the exact thing Celia s-said each time she—she—presented me with another set of t-twins!" And he was off again into uncontrolled laughter.

She tried, but Olivia could not resist him. Her lips tilted upward, her eyes brimmed with mirth, and of a sudden, laughter was bubbling from her.

" 'C-Cash,' she would s-say," Abbercombe gasped, "with the m-most amazed l-look upon her face and a s-squalling brat in each arm, 'I c-cannot believe that you c-can wish to have anything more to d-do with me!' "

Olivia did not know how it could be, but by the time she had left Fielding House behind her she had also left behind her all her feelings of guilt and had agreed with the duke to begin their friendship anew, without reference to the past.

Abbercombe sat huddled in the wing chair Olivia had vacated, his eyes staring into space, his mind sorting through all she had told him. So, the man he had seen in Lord Sinclair's study was LeBruin. And LeBruin had had the gall to enlist Olivia's aid against him. He cursed himself for a fool for telling Robin to burn the stolen despatch. He should have kept it. He might even now have planted the thing in LeBruin's establishment and Wyndham could have had the man brought up upon charges of treason.

He sighed, leaning his chin on his fist. Damn, but he must be getting old not to have thought of that possibility earlier. But he had seen Olivia in Sinclair's study and a terrible disillusionment had washed over him at the mere thought that she—but that was over and done with. Olivia was not a spy, simply a young woman who had been made to fear for her brother's safety. Well, but Harry was safe now, and if he and Madame Lavoisier proved as capable as always, Captain Willburton-Smythe would soon be home in Olivia's and April's arms. Still, LeBruin's usefulness to Napoleon had to be brought to an end. Thank goodness that Wyndham had set Sinclair's mind to rest on the missing despatch at least, and that he, himself, had found the thing rather than LeBruin.

"Your grace?" Fanning's entrance into the library had gone unnoticed. Recognizing the consternation creasing Abbercombe's brow, Fanning had closed the door behind him and gone immediately to the gentleman. "May I be of some assistance?"

Abbercombe came slowly to the realization of Fanning's presence, and motioned the man into the chair which faced his own. "Do you recall, Robin, the name of Maxim LeBruin?"

"Aye, he was responsible for your betrayal in Paris."

"He is here in London. And he has set his heart, it seems, upon eliminating me."

"The hired ruffians in the courtyard, your grace?"

"It appears so. He knew I would be dining with Brummell that evening. Olivia told him so."

"Miss Willburton-Smythe, your grace?"

"Yes. It is a long story, Robin, and Olivia is not to blame, but he knew my plans well-enough in advance to prepare an ambush. Though why he should wish to kill me so soon, when the way he had arranged things he might have collected a good bit of information first—I shall have to negate his interference if I am to get on with things. I could call him out, but then I shall be forced to flee England and I do not wish to do that."

"You do not, your grace? But I thought that was exactly what you wished. I thought you opposed to coming in the first place."

"Well, I was, Robin, but—I find there are certain affairs here—that is, I cannot quite—devil take it, Robin! Wipe that idiotic grin from your face. It is not what you are thinking!"

"No, your grace," Fanning murmured.

One arm stretched along the mantelpiece, one hand resting placidly upon the head of a malacca cane, Brummell tapped his foot in the drawing room of Worth's establishment, waiting for that gentleman to cease his laughter. "I knew how it would be, you know, but I decided to confront you regardless."

"Sorry, Beau, it is simply that I have never once imagined you capable of getting your daylights darkened."

"It is only one eye blackened, Edward, not both. Although I do admit to various other ripening spots conveniently hidden from view. I dare not venture into public, I think."

"No," grinned Worth, "I think not. You will never live it down. You, who shudder at the slightest mention of violence, will lose all credibility if you are seen like this. So, what brings you here? Why face my laughter especially? I take it there is something I may do that no other can?"

"Not exactly, but you are more likely to wish to do it. I dined with Abbercombe two nights ago—"

"And he beat you bloody?" Worth asked, a smile in his eyes.

"No, he was attacked by a gang of brigands."

The smile fled Worth's eyes and they hardened to flint on the instant. "Tell me all," he said. "Every bit of it."

By the time the Beau had finished, Worth was stalking back and forth across the lush red and black carpeting, his hands clasped firmly behind his back, his eyes narrow slits beneath half-lowered lids. "Has Cash the least idea who hired them?"

"I think not. But his brain was fuzzy. Dazed, he was, and passed out in the midst of Fanning's working on him. Did not regain his senses until the following morning. I sent my man around to inquire. What I think, Worth, is that we ought to set up a guard around him, at least until we discover who is at the bottom of this attempt on his life."

"We, Beau? You and I?"

"Well, yes, blast it. You are his best friend, are you not? And I must be in on it. I cannot sever myself from the man."

"Why not?" Worth asked, coming to a halt before him. "He calls you brat; he takes your blunt; he declines to make use of your influence; and he obviously leads you into vile company."

"Exactly, for all those reasons," Brummell smiled. "I do not recall the last time anyone has treated me so shabbily. I have never been so mesmerized by anyone in my entire life."

"I know exactly how you feel. He treated me just as shabbily and could not be made to comprehend the impeccability of my lineage or the extreme importance of my self. Of course, we were seven at the time and most of the bruises I carried were put there by himself. Still the overall feel of it is the same, I expect. I could not bear to be apart from him for fear of missing whatever magic he chose to dispense next. Well, but, that is enough reminiscing. We must do something about Abbercombe—and I have got just the notion!" Worth exclaimed with a snap of his fingers. "Come, Beau, we'll take your coach. You may sit back, out of view, when we go down Bond Street."

"Whatever you say, my lord," Brummell acquiesced with a bow. "My means are at your command."

Elijah Stone, dressed in a coat of rust brown that opened upon a surprisingly elaborate waistcoat of deep puce embroidered with wide yellow roses, welcomed Worth and Brummell to his office which consisted of several nooks and crannies on the upper floor of an ancient building on Newgate Street. "Af'ernoon, milor'," he greeted Worth. "Bin a while, ain't it just?"

"Indeed," grinned Worth. "This is Mr. Brummell, Stone. He and I have need of your services."

The perfectly nondescript man nodded at the Beau and offered them both a seat. "Out wi' it then," he mumbled, sitting himself behind a huge wooden desk defaced by scratches and carvings and covered with sheaves of papers in wild disarray. "What's up, milor'. Ye ain't gone an' got yerself inta a thicket?"

"Into a what?" Brummell asked, his eyes gleaming with mirth.

"A thicket, Brummell," Worth repeated with a quelling glance. "No, Stone, I have not done that. But a friend of ours requires a modicum of attention just at present, and I thought you and your people might be just the ones to assist us."

"Who's the cove?"

"The Duke of Abbercombe."

"St. George!" exclaimed Stone, pulling a crumpled handkerchief from his pocket and blowing his nose heartily into it. "I done heerd a good bit o' that one," he added, stuffing the handkerchief away. "Bless me, but 'e ain't a friend o' yours, milor'? Man's a demon! Gots the coves at the gamin' 'ouses on their ears. They's all 'bout ready ta bar 'im from playin'."

"Have you watched him play, Stone?"

"Aye, milor', I has. Mos' smoothest dab I ever seed. Purty 'e is ta watch—thrillin' even. Like ta melt a cove's brains ta mush jus' wonnerin' 'ow 'e does it."

"Do you think, Stone, that perhaps he has disturbed someone of particular importance at one of the hells?"

"Disturbed 'em? He's got 'em twirlin' about like dervishes."

"Enough to wish him dead?"

"Dead, milor'? Pshaw! They's all a'wishin' to ketch 'ow 'e does it. Wants ta take their lessons from the cove, so ta speak. Dead? Niver! Can't ketch onter wha' 'e be doin' were 'e dead."

"I see. They all want to watch him play, but none of them want him to play in their own establishments."

"Precisely, milor'. Ain't no 'ate, jis mystification."

"Well, someone seems to be nourishing a bit of hate, Stone," Worth frowned. He leaned back in the chair, crossing one knee over the other, the silver spurs on his boots jingling. "Someone hired a band of brigands to lay for the duke a few nights back. Determined to put an end to him, they were."

"Ye don't say," mumbled Stone, leaning back himself and sticking his thumbs into two tiny pockets on his waistcoat.

"I do say, and I have come to secure your services in discovering who that someone is and handing him over to the Runners, as well as keeping his grace safe until you do."

"Well, an' I'd be pleased ta do it, milor'."

"Yes, I knew you would. But I need you to do it very inconspicuously, Elijah. The duke is not to realize that you and your associates are on the job."

"Tush! An' ain't we masters o' deception so ta speak, milor'? Aye, wi' yer 'elp, why we'll build a reg'lar wall about the cove what won't no villain be cap'ble o' breachin'. Ye interdooce me ta the cove's butler, milor', an' 'im an' me be a fixin' it so's the dook be saroundered by me frien's day an' night. Keep ar daylights on 'im, we will. An' be a lookin' inta findin' the blighter what's afer 'im at one'n the same time."

"I knew I could count on you, Elijah. When can you begin?"

"Well, an' we gots ta finish up the bramble we be inbroggled in at the moment, but I senses we be able ta start on the dook by the beginnings o' nex' week. That'll gi' ye time, milor', ta git ta 'is grace's butler, ye know, an' give 'im the word."

Worth stood and placed a roll of notes on Stone's desktop. "That monkey's to start with. You will send me an accounting once the job is done." He shook Stone's hand and left the odd little office with Brummell close on his heels. Once they had reached the coach and climbed inside, Worth leaned back against the squabs and gave the Beau a fierce frown.

"No, Worth, really," Brummell drawled, "you did not expect I should actually say anything to that person?"

Worth's frown gave way to a chuckle. "I had hopes, Brummell. You have acquired a black eye, after all."

"Yes, but I have not as yet acquired the desire for conversations with back alley businessmen."

"Lost you, didn't he? Admit it, Beau, you could not speak because you could not follow the conversation."

"No, I will not admit it. But really, Worth, wherever did you come in contact with such a being?"

"That, dear boy, is a long story and one you are not likely to become privy to. So, we shall need to speak to Dawson."

"Yes, and we shall be obliged to keep an eye on Abbercombe ourselves until the beginning of next week."

"Can we do that?"

Brummell shrugged his fashionably-coated shoulders. "I do not see why not."

Worth nodded, his eyes twinkling. "You will, Brummell, believe me, but we shall give it our best."

Eleven

The news that the dowager Countess of Vale had taken up residence at Fielding House was received with plaudits by a number of young gentlemen, for it made it quite acceptable for them to appear upon that doorstep with a posy in hand to request a visit with one or both of the elder daughters of the family. Society Mamas trembled, fearing their precious sons might come in contact with the infamous duke. But the majority of them ceased to tremble and merely sniffed after the rumors that Lady Amaryllis and Lady Bethany possessed dowries in excess of ten thousand pounds began to filter throughout the *ton*. And even the sniffing disappeared when certain unnamed but reliable sources discovered that all of Abbercombe's estates were unencumbered and in excellent repair, and that the duke intended to settle a portion of the lands that were not entailed upon each of his children.

When speculation on the amount of money Abbercombe held in the funds reached the shell-like ears of the *ton* matrons, even Mamas with precious daughters forgot to worry and escorted their darlings to pay morning visits upon Lady Vale and her charges, for one could quite depend upon it—eligible gentlemen of rank and fortune would be found in the drawing room or the Gold Saloon or the morning room at Fielding House. And not being always occupied with the young ladies who resided there, these gentlemen could be made to appreciate the particular set of a pretty smile, or the particular lift of a fine eyebrow or the very good common sense of a certain young lady who was also in attendance.

Viscount Harcort and the Honorable Bryan Kettering rapidly became frequent visitors. "I vow, they may as well be let to run tame about the place for they are always here," declared Lady Vale one morning over breakfast. "There is not a day goes by but one or the other of them trails after Dawson into our presence."

"No, sweetest, do not stir the jam about with your finger," Abbercombe murmured distractedly, removing the little plate of jam from Helen's reach. "Do you think, Aunt Margaret, that I should warn them off? Stamford is like to come down hard on them if it reaches his ears. Frazier, perhaps you ought to give that kipper to Bear since she has already eaten most of it."

"Oh, no, Papa, please," begged Bethany, refilling his cup with coffee from the urn on the sideboard. "They are not either of them a bother. Truly they are not, are they, Aunt Margaret?"

"I did not mean to imply any such thing, Beth. It is only that—well—"

"What your Aunt Margaret means to say, Bethany, is that Harcort and his brother do not belong at Fielding House."

"Papa, what are you saying?" cried Amaryllis, staring at him from across the table. "Surely they are as welcome here as anyone else? They have never been anything but kind."

Abbercombe thanked Bethany for the coffee, took one sip of it and found a piece of muffin placed into the palm of his left hand. "What's this for? Gracie?"

"Butter please, Papa."

"Grace Irene Denbigh, you are six years old and you have known how to butter a muffin for at least three of them."

"But this ones gots lumps and fluffs, Papa, and the butter pulls out the fluffs and makes the lumps all crumbles."

"Oh," Abbercombe nodded, "I do beg your pardon, my dear. In that case you have entrusted its buttering to exactly the right person. Of course they are welcome here, Amy," he continued as he spread the butter capably about the contentious muffin and handed it back to its little owner. "But there are reasons why they should not come."

"What reasons, Papa?" asked Christian.

"The Earl of Stamford believes your father responsible for his brother's death," declared Lady Vale. "And he will not countenance any sort of acquaintance with this family."

"But do his sons know about it, Papa?" Damian queried, setting aside his own plate and swiping a piece of kidney from Ethan's.

"Yes," sighed Abbercombe. "I told them that I had killed their Uncle Channing, but it does not seem to deter them. Still, I expect they ought not to be underfoot all the time. If Stamford discovers it, they will have the devil to pay. I cannot imagine why they choose to overlook the thing."

"Because they are fairly caught, Papa," laughed Christian.

"I say, old fellow, do you never get a half-day at that place? They are working you too hard, Geoff," Kettering muttered from his bed as Hempstead took a final look in the pier glass.

"I enjoy every moment of it," Hempstead grinned. "Besides I shall have two days off shortly and blunt to spend when I do. Do you ride in the park this afternoon, Bry?"

"Yes, if Lady Amy will consent to accompany me."

"You are becoming a dead bore, Kettering. Everything is Lady Amy this and Lady Amy that. I am growing exceeding tired of hearing about Lady Amy."

"Good, then you have discovered how we all felt when Miss April fell from your lips every time you opened your mouth," teased Harcort, already dressed and sipping at a cup of hot chocolate. "Have you and April settled things, Geoff?"

"Perfectly. She has agreed to wait for me to prove to her father and her aunt that I am ambitious, responsible and dependable and have become a man of substance—well, at least a gentleman with prospects of substance. Wyndham has put me on to some investments, you know, and the little I have saved begins to grow. Tomorrow evening at the Skiffingtons' ball I shall be able to reassure April that things are well underway."

"Well, I am glad of that," yawned Kettering, tugging his night-cap from his head and tossing it onto a chair.

"I'm off," grinned Hempstead, giving his chums a quick salute and hurrying through the parlor and out the door.

"I am off as well, Bry," Harcort muttered, setting his empty cup upon the bedside table. "I expect I shall not get away from father until at least two. He is determined, I think, to make an estate manager out of me, though why he bothers when he has Browning, I cannot guess. Take care, Hawkins," he added, as the valet the three gentlemen shared entered the room with a steaming cup of chocolate for Kettering. "I am off to Stamford House if anyone should come looking for me."

Hawkins nodded.

Kettering, once dressed and breakfasted, set out upon a showy bay for Fielding House. Knowing himself to look all the crack, he ceased all thought of his dress and began instead to dream of Amaryllis, whose sapphire eyes and golden curls and stubborn little chin, attached as they were to the most forthright tongue and engaging sense of humor he had yet to encounter in a young lady, had held him spellbound since their first meeting.

By the time he arrived upon her doorstep he was already presenting himself to her in his mind on bended knee, words of love and marriage upon his lips. And she was nodding at him, the sweet dimple in her cheek emerging for his private delight. He sighed as he prised the door knocker and heard her soft husky voice whispering, "yes, oh, yes, Bryan," in his dreams. The door jerked inward and slammed against a wall startling Kettering violently from his daydream.

"Look out! Look out!" hollered a small boy, running into him, bouncing off one of his legs. " 'Scuse me!" the child shouted, shoving fiercely at Kettering with both hands until he managed to squeak past and flee down the front steps. "Run! Run!" he yelled as he hit the cobbles of the courtyard.

"Move! Move!" yelled another voice, and this time Kettering stepped aside as a second boy came plummeting down the stairs and out the door without so much as a by your leave. This blond-

haired whirlwind was followed by an enthusiastically barking puppy— Surely, Kettering thought, the ugliest dog I have ever seen—which tumbled down the last two steps and charged directly across the toes of Kettering's freshly polished Hessians.

Kettering heard the bellow from the top of the staircase before he saw the toes of the duke's boots hit the first stair. "You are in for it now, scoundrels! I'll slit the both of you in half and use you for fish bait!" Abbercombe came pounding down two stairs at a time not stopping when he reached the parquet but barreling straight at Kettering. The duke's arms reached out, his hands seized Kettering's shoulders and set him aside to keep from knocking him over as he slammed past him. "When I get my hands on the two of you, I'll grind your bones to bake my bread," the duke roared, crashing down the front steps in the wake of the now screeching cubs.

Kettering stared as Abbercombe dashed around the side of the house after Ethan and Frazier. His face, not knowing what expression to hold, flickered between laughter and disbelief. He turned back to be greeted by Chris's laughing blue eyes.

"Amy and Beth are in the morning room, Kettering," provided that young gentleman blithely. "You know the way, do you not?"

Kettering mounted the stairs and wandered down the first floor hallway. He found himself not the only morning caller. He bowed to Lady Vale and then spent the next fifteen minutes attempting to gain a smidgen of private conversation with Lady Amy. This proving impossible, he invited her to drive with him that afternoon, and upon being accepted, departed Fielding House and then remembered that Harcort had taken their curricle to their father's. Well, he thought, I shall have to discover whether or not Redvers will give me the loan of his phaeton to tool Lady Amaryllis about the park. As he reached the gate he thought he heard his name called and halted the bay. The duke, mounted upon a more likely looking steed than the last Kettering had seen, galloped toward him. "Where are you off to, Kettering?"

"To find Redvers, sir. Thought I might borrow his phaeton and cattle for a bit this afternoon."

"To accommodate one of my daughters?" The duke took his mount through the gate at a walk, Kettering beside him, and they started together down Great Stanhope.

"Lady Amy has been gracious enough to agree to accompany me to Hyde Park, your grace."

For only a moment Kettering thought he saw frustration in the sapphire eyes that stared at him from beneath partly lowered lids, but then it was gone and the eyes became unreadable.

"I do not know, Kettering, if you understood me correctly when first we met," the duke said, "or if you are hoping your father will die of an apoplexy before he finds opportunity to murder you."

"Sir?" Kettering stared, puzzled.

"Did I not make myself clear? It is like this, Kettering. Your Uncle Channing and I engaged in a brawl. He died."

"A brawl, sir? You killed my Uncle Channing in a brawl?"

"Yes, boy, that is exactly what I did. It was an unforgivable act and your father has not forgiven me. Should he discover you and your brother chasing about with my girls there will be hell to pay. Do be a good fellow and remove yourself from the lists, won't you? And get Harcort to do so as well? Amy and Beth are dears but your father will not stand for them anywhere near his sons."

"But, sir," Kettering protested.

"Think on it and you will see I am correct, Kettering. Neither of you should be so lacking in respect for Stamford that you would force him into an acquaintanceship repugnant to him. Amaryllis will understand if you do not turn up this afternoon. Send her a note and I will explain what I have said to you."

The duke turned his mount in midstride and rode off, leaving Kettering, a variety of emotions vying for prominence on his countenance, to ponder the suggestion.

In her dressing room at Park Street April excitedly posed before Olivia in every ball gown her aunt had had made for her so that they might judge which would be most flattering to wear for her appearance at the Skiffingtons'. At the moment she stood nervously in the last of the four. "This will be my very first actual ball, Aunt Olivia, and I do so want to look pretty."

"But you are pretty, April," Olivia replied, signalling to that young lady to turn around so that she might see the gown from all sides, "but I think this gown makes you look absolutely beautiful. It is by far the best of the lot."

"Oh, how can you say so?" April asked with a pout of her bow-shaped lips. "It is not at all fancy like the others."

"No, and that is what I like about it. It is simple and elegant and old-fashioned, and it shows you off to perfection. And it is willow green, the very newest shade and so becoming, especially with your coloring. And it makes your eyes incredibly beautiful. They fairly glow."

April blushed, but hesitated in bestowing her own goodwill upon the gown. "I think," she almost whispered, turning about before the mirror, "that it makes me look too much of a child. And I must not look like a child."

Olivia laughed. "Believe me, darling," she said, "you will not look like a child. Here, let me show you." With deft, well-practiced hands she whipped April's hair into a top knot and with tender twirls and twistings, released a series of natural curls and ringlets that softly framed the heart-shaped face.

"And these are perfect," she exclaimed, threading a series of light and dark green ribands through the hastily devised coiffure. "All you need is a necklet of pearls and you will be exquisite. We shall go to Ruben's as soon as you are changed into your walking dress and see can we discover precisely the right thing. Look," Olivia urged, turning April toward the pier glass.

"Oh," gasped April, gazing at her reflection and playing her hands over the smooth, cool, pale green silk confection she wore. Then one hand went to the silken ringlets of her hair. "I cannot believe I am seeing myself!"

"Indeed you are, gudgeon," grinned Olivia. "And once we find the precise pearls, you will be even more dazzling. Hurry now and change and I shall order up the carriage to take us to the jewelers." With a wide smile, Olivia left the chamber and wandered down to the ground floor where she asked Laslow to have the carriage brought 'round. Then she entered the little waiting room at the front of the house and sat down upon the window seat to stare out at the street. April found her there fifteen minutes later deep in her own thoughts, a slight frown creasing her brow.

"Aunt Olivia, what is it?" April asked, joining her on the window seat. "You look so sullen."

"No, not at all, my dear. I was just thinking."

"About something quite serious?"

"About the Duke of Abbercombe."

"But, aunt, did you not tell me that he had forgiven you and not thought it a bother, just as I said?"

"Yes, my dear, but I cannot help but think there must be some way in which I may make up to him for my—my—treachery."

"But it was not treachery, Aunt Olivia. You thought him to be a French spy. Certainly you did what you thought best, and he understood perfectly."

Olivia's hands tightened into fists in the lap of her sprigged muslin walking dress. "I am determined to do more, April, than to accept his forgiveness. I am determined to make everything up to him. And I will do it, too!"

April studied the stubborn tilt of her aunt's chin, the slight flaring of her nostrils, and the fierce glow in her emerald eyes. "What is your plan?" she asked, a glow building behind her own eyes. "What must we do?"

"Oh, my dear, not you."

"Yes, indeed, aunt. I will not be left out. I have reason to be grateful to the duke as well as you and I wish to join in aiding him. Is there a way to protect him from M. LeBruin?"

"I believe," murmured Olivia, "that I shall turn the tables upon that unprincipled French monster. I shall let him go on believing that I seek to aid him in regard to Abbercombe, and then I shall feed him false information or lead him into some trap."

"How, Aunt Olivia?"

"I do not know, precisely. I must think on it more."

"I shall think on it, too," April declared, her own chin tilting at a stubborn angle quite like her aunt's. "After all, it is my own father LeBruin used as bait to lure you to his will. And I shall be most happy to make the beast pay for that."

Olivia looked at the young lady beside her and was very proud. She had spunk, did April, and courage, and what she lacked in experience, she certainly made up for in determination. Olivia held her hand out and April took it firmly in her own, sealing their partnership in the duke's cause.

The two spent the drive to Ruben's discussing plan after plan and when they had reached the jeweler's shop, were still undecided quite how to go about entrapping M. LeBruin and protecting the duke. As they entered the shop they were amazed to find Abbercombe in deep discussion with the senior Mr. Ruben. The duke swung around as he heard one of the clerks address Olivia by name and a boyish grin swept across his face.

"Miss Willburton-Smythe," he drawled, bowing elegantly, "and Miss April. Well met indeed. You are exactly the two people to solve my dilemma." His eyes wandered admiringly over Olivia's sprigged muslin with the willow green ribands and her very jaunty, high-crowned bonnet set at a cocky angle upon her dark curls. It did not escape his attention that no ruffles from a spinster's cap peeked out from beneath the bonnet, or that her entire outfit was not only charming, but at the height of fashion. "I am in great need of your expert advice," he said, winking at April. "Please say you will help me."

"Of course we will, your grace," April grinned, taking Olivia's arm and urging her aunt toward the gentleman. "What is it you wish to know? Good afternoon, Mr. Ruben," she added with a tiny dip of a curtsy. Olivia nodded to the jeweler.

"Mr. Ruben has been good enough to make these pieces for me." Abbercombe stood away from the counter, giving the ladies a view of black velvet on which rested four cameos. "Oh," Olivia sighed and a finger went to caress first one and then another of the finely-carved profiles on delicately braided silver chains.

"They are the most exquisite, ethereal pieces I have ever seen. Are the faces of ivory?"

"Yes, Olivia," Abbercombe smiled. "Two upon sapphire and two upon emerald. But Mr. Ruben informs me that young ladies in their first Season are now expected only to wear pearls."

"Well, it has become the norm, your grace."

"But pearls are the most insipid ornaments ever conceived," the duke grumbled, "and not in the least flattering. April, do you not like these trinkets better than a string of pearls?"

"Oh, yes, your grace," breathed April, her eyes shining. "They are so delicate and beautiful."

"And might you set aside the accepted norm to wear one, say, to the Skiffingtons' Ball? They are not ostentatious, Olivia, after all," he added with a glance at that enthralled lady. "Nor pretentious. And they are so much more attractive."

April's pretty bow lips broke into a wide smile. "I knew it!" she exclaimed in triumph. "Amy and Beth have been invited to the Skiffingtons'! How cruel of them not to tell me immediately."

"They meant to surprise you, I think," Abbercombe grinned, "and I have spoiled it. But they will forgive me. Do you think, Olivia," he asked, his eyes twinkling down at her, "that Amy and Beth might each wear one of these? One of the sapphires?"

"Will they match their gowns, Abbercombe?"

"Yes, and their eyes."

"Well, I know that." Olivia could not take her eyes from the pieces and April glanced mischievously up at the duke. He winked at her and she giggled.

"I cannot see any harm in it," Olivia said decidedly. "They are unique, Abbercombe, but no one can find them inappropriate."

The duke's eyes met Mr. Ruben's above the lady's head. "Thank you, my dear. You have solved our problem."

With great reverence Mr. Ruben senior removed the cameos from the counter and carried them into his back room. Olivia's eyes left the trinkets only when that gentleman disappeared from view. "Tell me, my dear," Abbercombe drawled to April, "have you and your aunt decided upon your gowns as well?"

"Oh, yes. I am to wear a willow green one," April answered, trying hard not to giggle again at the smug look upon the duke's face. "It is just exactly the color of Aunt Olivia's ribands. And she is to wear the most wonderful emerald silk!"

"Gracie and Helen shall be in despair to miss the sight of you. They have never seen even their mother dressed for a ball, and are already ecstatic over the prospect of seeing Amy and Beth. I do not suppose there is any hope that you might stop by—no, that is an exceptional favor to ask."

"I think it is charming of you to wish it," Olivia smiled. "And since we must pass Fielding House on the way to the Skiffingtons', I cannot think why we should not stop for just a moment. I remember how thrilling I thought it to see my mother in her very best."

Mr. Ruben appeared then, grinning widely, and placed a wrapped package into the duke's hand. "Exactly as you wished, your grace."

"My thanks, Ruben," the duke smiled and with a bow to Olivia and April, he left the shop.

Abbercombe reached home just as Worth and Brummell were preparing to take their leave of a very sober-faced Dawson. "What goes on?" he called, stepping down and handing his mount into the care of a waiting stableboy. "Have these scoundrels been giving you a hard time, Anthony?"

"Not at all, your grace," Dawson replied, schooling his countenance into one of obliging pleasantry.

"What earthly reason would we have to give Dawson a hard time?" muttered Worth as the duke joined them on the doorstep.

"I cannot guess," Abbercombe replied with a cocked eyebrow. "Are you coming in?"

"Actually, we came to see if you wished to join us for a ride in the park," drawled Brummell.

"And dinner at White's later," Worth added.

"And perhaps a game or two of whist," Brummell grinned.

"No," Abbercombe answered succinctly.

"No?" Worth's eyebrows arched and made the duke chuckle. "May I ask why not, your grace?"

"I have plans, Edward."

"What sort of plans?"

"None that are any business of yours, *mon ami*. You will hold me excused."

"I do not think so, Cash. Brummell and I were counting upon you. Can you not put off your plans for a day or two?"

"Come inside," the duke ordered looking suspiciously from one to the other of them. "You and the brat, Edward, are engaged in some sort of plot. I can tell from the look of you."

Ensconced comfortably in the back parlor, each with a snifter of brandy in hand, Worth and Brummell strove subtly to engage Abbercombe for the evening, going so far as to offer to accompany him to any or all of the hells, if that was his desire. The longer they talked, the more suspicious the duke became, until at last their object in the exercise dawned upon him. "You are attempting to stand guard over me, Edward!" he exclaimed abruptly, choking on a sip of the brandy. "By gawd, but you are a presumptuous dandy!"

"Perhaps," Worth grinned. "But we did intend to go about it unobtrusively, Cash. Except you will not allow us to do so. You cannot go traipsing about the streets on your own, old boy. Not when there is so obviously someone out for your blood."

"And so you propose to strap on your sword and Brummell to stuff a pistol into his breeches and follow me everywhere I go? I think not. For one thing, Brummell would look most unfashionable and lose all credibility, and I doubt, Worth, that you have used a sword since I left London so inelegantly twenty years ago. No. I appreciate the sentiment, but I cannot accept. Besides, I have agreed to meet with someone tonight who is rather determined to go unrecognized in certain circles and if he sees the two of you near he will not keep his appointment. I stand in great need of his services, so you will excuse me, but I will not have either of you anywhere about."

Brummell and Worth exchanged worried glances. "How deep are you in the brambles, Cash?" Worth asked. "You are not about to make another stay at Newgate?"

Abbercombe grinned beguilingly.

"No, really, sir," Brummell declared. "If there is some misunderstanding with the law, I could approach Prinny."

"You will not do so on my behalf, Brummell. I am quite capable of approaching Florizel myself should I discover need of it." Abbercombe stared at them thoughtfully over the rim of his glass. "What it is," he said softly, "is that a good friend of mine has gotten himself into some trouble. Word has reached me that he finds himself trapped on the French coast and I have agreed to help him cross to England. But I cannot do so without the aid of a certain free-trader."

"Whom you go to meet tonight?" Worth asked.

"Whom I go to meet tonight. And he will recognize Brummell even behind that black eye, and I think you, Edward."

"And he will not deal with you if he sees us."

"Precisely."

"Then I have the answer," Brummell offered, crossing one knee over the other, setting the tassels on his Hessians swinging. "Worth and I shall drive you to the meeting place and wait in the coach until you have completed your—arrangements."

"Where do you meet?" Worth asked.

"Number seventy-seven, Jermyn Street."

"Lord, Jermyn Street?" Brummell scowled. "We shall take my coach, Worth, for yours will draw too much attention."

"And yours will not, brat?" asked Abbercombe. "No, if you must accompany me, we take a hackney."

Worth sighed with relief. "Then you accept our assistance?"

"For tonight at least, Edward. But you must not think to be forever hanging about. If I come to the conclusion that I am in need of body guards, I will not draft my friends for the job. So, will you stay to dine with us instead of running off to White's? I guarantee you will find it an adventure."

"I have been waiting to be invited for a month, Cash. It's about time, I must say," Worth smiled.

"Brummell?"

"Indeed. I should be honored, your grace."

"Which reminds me," Worth stood and searched through his coat pockets. "I have got something. Now where did I—? Oh, yes, here it is. You, too, have been greatly honored, my friend," he announced, presenting Abbercombe with a sealed paper.

The duke stared, puzzled, at the handwriting then broke the seal, silently read the message inside and gave a roar of laughter. "You are hoaxing me, Edward. Where did this come from?"

"From Lady Skiffington, you ninny. What? Do you think I wrote the thing?"

"Yes, as a matter of fact. Why the devil would Lady Skiffington invite me, of all people, to her ball? Does she want everyone to turn their backs upon her?"

"You are invited to the Skiffingtons'?" the Beau asked, standing and going to read the invitation over Abbercombe's shoulder. "Well, I'll be damned. It is exactly the same as mine. Worth could not be that good a forger."

"Recall, Cash, Lady Skiffington is my mother-in-law."

"And you had the cheek to ask her to invite me?"

"Not at all, you corkbrain. John and Eugenia between them had the cheek. John because you fixed his carriage, and Eugenia because—because—she not only likes you but yesterday she discovered that—that—"

"I was correct!" Abbercombe exclaimed, jumping up to shake his friend's hand. "I knew it the moment she came to have her fortune told."

"How did you know?"

"Devil, Edward, I have had Celia present me with eight of the urchins. Only the first two came as a surprise. There is something about women who are increasing. You can see it, if you look closely enough. They—they—glow."

Twelve

Hempstead spent the evening being regaled by a recital of the attributes and virtues of the Denbigh Ladies. Kettering, having considered the duke's advice, had chosen to ignore it and had arrived during Abbercombe's absence to drive Lady Amy to the park. But Harcort had been unable to break from his father before six and thus deprived of escorting Lady Beth, he now felt the need to discuss that young lady extensively over dinner at Grillon's and over port at White's. "I have never met a more delightful young lady, Geoff, than Lady Bethany," he confessed at last. "She is likely the sweetest girl in all London."

"Well, I'll not argue that with you," Hempstead grinned, "for April is many things, but the sweetest girl in all London is not one of them."

"No, nor Lady Amaryllis either," laughed Kettering. "But she is the most beautiful, independent chit I have ever encountered—with a mind like a fine Swiss timepiece. She is exceptional."

Hempstead leaned back in his chair, and sighed.

"I know it is hard on you, Geoff," Kettering murmured, "but you shall see April tomorrow night, and only think what a welcome she will give you."

"Yes, I do hope so, or else I have done it all for nothing."

"Done what for nothing?" Harcort asked.

"Taken the position on Wyndham's staff, of course," Kettering replied with a meaningful glance at his brother. "Hempstead has been working his fingers to the bone. You do work your fingers to the bone, do you not, Geoff?"

"To the bone," sighed Hempstead. "Now what," he muttered, as Jack Sloan's familiar figure crossed the parlor toward them.

"Note for you, Mr. Hempstead, sir. The gentleman did not wait for an answer." With a nod the keeper of White's door departed.

Hempstead untwisted the screw of paper and leaned toward the fire to read the thing better. His stomach lurched and he stood instantly. "I apologize," he stammered, "but I must leave for a while." Without further explanation he grabbed for his greatcoat and hat and the cane Abbercombe had given him—which had brought admiration from every one of his friends the first time they had seen the thing—and pulling on his gloves, started for the door.

"Geoff, wait!" called Kettering. "What is it, some emergency? May Harcort and I be of assistance?"

Hempstead stopped in midstride, looked them up and down, and thought a moment. His thoughts admittedly churned and he might easily misjudge which line to follow, but he could not think why Harcort and Kettering should not accompany him. If trouble was likely, their presence would certainly add to the duke's safety. "Yes," he answered finally. "I should be grateful."

The brothers rushed to don their own greatcoats, hats and gloves. Hempstead signalled a hack and they piled into the sour-smelling vehicle. Harcort nearly gagged at the smell and stuck his head out the window. Kettering grinned. "Should have waited and caught a better smelling one, Geoff. This may be the death of all three of us. Did you tell him number seventy-seven, Jermyn?"

"Yes, I know what the place is, but that's where I'm bound. Do you care to rescind your offer?"

"No, no, Hempstead," Harcort replied, ducking his head back in through the window. "We are definitely accompanying you. Pardon me." He stuck his head back out again.

"Weak stomach, m'brother," Kettering chuckled, "but game, I assure you."

"Got more bottom than brains sometimes," Hempstead nodded. He watched uneasily as the coach swung into Jermyn Street.

His eyes raked the shadows between the buildings. "Here it is," he announced, finally, jumping from the coach and paying the driver. "No need to wait," he told the man as Kettering and Harcort descended onto the cobbles. Close together outside the door to one of the lowest gaming hells in London, Hempstead explained his idea. "We must all pretend to be foxed and looking for a good time. We'll find us a table, call for a bottle and look around a bit. Chances are we won't need to get involved in a game."

"Who are we looking for, Geoff?" Harcort asked promptly.

"I never said we were looking for anyone."

"I am not a buffle-head. You get a note which causes you to run off to this hell, it's 'cause someone's here shouldn't be. Three pairs of eyes are better than one, my friend."

Hempstead thought a moment. "I cannot tell you everything," he muttered finally, "but someone from Wyndham's office has sent word that Abbercombe may be here and in some trouble. The duke being in London at all is problematic to our Office though not many people realize it. I did not at first."

"Because he was transported?" Kettering asked.

"Precisely," lied Hempstead. "And may be transported again if he should cause too much unrest."

"Well, I'll be damned," muttered Harcort. "Does the duke know you people are keeping an eye on him?"

"No, and I shall be obliged if you do not let it slip out—especially to his daughters. You won't, will you?"

"Not a chance," they assured him, and putting their arms about his shoulders, gained entrance to the gaming hell at Number 77, and strolled cheerily to a table. Kettering called raucously for drinks and the three set to playing cup-shot nobs who had wandered inadvertently into a den of thieves.

Abbercombe and about thirty other patrons of the establishment could not help but notice them. The duke took a long look down his nose at the noisy trio then returned his attention to the faro table. He heard a loud sneeze, and something inside of him smiled though his face revealed not the least sign of it.

He centered his attention on the dealer, watched as the man turned the next card, and saw his blunt take up residence in the faro bank. With grim determination Abbercombe remained in the game losing steadily and silently amidst the other, chattering players. Finally he tugged a leather pouch from his pocket and dumped the contents onto the baize table top. The other players, wide-eyed, ceased all speech.

"Yer sure ye want ta do that, milord dook," the dealer asked quietly, his eyes greedily caressing the stack of flimsies.

"There's a hundred thousand. I assume the bank is now large enough to cover it. Ought to be with all I've lost tonight."

"Aye, bank's able ta cover ye, milord—I doubt as any of these other gentlemen'll come in on it."

"Then turn the next card just for me," Abbercombe drawled. "Just for me, Solomon, and one of us will be wiped out. I am tired and wish to quit this business. 'Twill take me the rest of the night otherwise to lose it all."

The dealer looked about him and spied one of the proprietors at the far end of the table. That gentleman nodded. "All right, milord, it's a bet, 'tis. Would ye be wantin' me to open a clean pack o' cards?"

Abbercombe shrugged languidly. "I cannot see any need for it, but if you wish—"

The dealer shook his head, a grin mounting to his eyes. "These be fine far as the bank be concerned. Name yer card."

Abbercombe stood and with admirable grace drew his sabre and thrust its point into the top card of the deck before him. "Knave of Hearts," he murmured, and with a quick flick of his wrist flipped the card, face up, onto the table. The Knave of Hearts stared sightlessly up at him. Abbercombe chuckled as the rest of the players exhaled loudly. Cocking an eyebrow, he accepted his winnings with sabre still drawn, and folded the flimsies in half with one hand. He tucked them into his inside pocket, sheathed his sword and tossed the dealer a guinea. "Much obliged," the duke whispered "We must play again sometime, no?"

The knot in Hempstead's stomach tightened as the duke set a beaver hat rakishly upon his head, pulled on his gloves, and strolled toward the door. The two men who had been sitting one to either side of him rose and took their leave as well, following close on his heels. Hempstead nodded at Kettering and Harcort and they quickly made their own exit.

"There," Hempstead whispered, pointing, as the door to Number 77 closed behind them. Abbercombe was plainly visible ahead. He appeared to await an approaching hack. Hempstead had expected to see the other two men directly upon the duke's heels but there was no sign of either one. Perhaps they walked off in the opposite direction, he thought. The notion gave him some relief, for he had, from the moment Abbercombe had placed the one hundred thousand pounds upon the faro table, expected the duke to be attacked and robbed. Yet Abbercombe seemed singularly alone and undisturbed. The hackney coach pulled up beside him, the door opened, the steps rattled down and the sound of a pistol shot cracked through the night. The duke's foot slipped off the first step and he reeled, slamming against the side of the coach. Hempstead, Harcort and Kettering broke into a run. Worth launched himself from the hack into the street just as another shot ripped through the murky gloom and Abbercombe crumpled to the cobbles.

"There!" shouted Brummell, leaping from the carriage, dueling pistol in hand. "Between the warehouses."

"Stay with the duke," Hempstead yelled, as he, Harcort and Kettering pounded past the hackney and down the narrow alley in pursuit of two specters dashing in and out of the shadows. One veered off to the left at the alley's end, past the front doors of the Benning and Davis warehouse. Harcort rushed after the dark figure, closing the gap between them as the man stumbled, righted himself, and continued his flight. But the stumble had slowed him enough and Harcort, gasping for breath, flung himself at the villain's knees and brought him to the ground. Instantly the viscount was met by wildly flailing fists and the jolt of heavy boots against his ribs.

Farther up the avenue Hempstead and Kettering were fast closing upon the second figure when that phantom swerved to the right and disappeared before their eyes. They searched frantically, tugging upon street doors, peering into nooks and crannies and behind piles of moldering garbage. "Devil!" Hempstead exclaimed breathlessly. "Gone!"

"Completely," Kettering agreed on a gasp. "How? It's like the night swallowed the cur up."

They worked their way slowly back toward the Benning and Davis building, checking carefully around them. By the time they reached the alley Harcort was limping toward them from the opposite direction. "Got away," he muttered, swiping at a gash on his forehead. "Cracked me with the butt of his pistol—at least I expect that's what it was. Damned lucky, I suppose, that he did not pause to finish me off."

"Did you get a look at him?" Hempstead asked, as Kettering offered his brother an arm to lean upon.

"I—I—"

"What, Davey?" queried Kettering. "You what?"

"I thought I recognized the scoundrel, but— I cannot seem to put a name to the face. I am all right, Bry. Just a bit bruised. He did not crack me all that hard, merely enough to get free. Damme, but I know I should have recognized the fellow. There was something about him—"

"Are you all in one piece, gentlemen?" Worth hurried toward them as they reached the exit to the alley. "Bless me if Cash was not correct. He said Hempstead, Kettering and Harcort, though Beau and I could not fathom how it could be you in this precise locality. Blasted rogue has won a pony from each of us!"

"What? He bet you who had gone in chase of the bloody scoundrels?" Kettering thankfully let Worth support Harcort and took a deep breath to ease the pressure on his gasping lungs.

"And won. I wished to get him to a surgeon immediately while Brummell waited for you, but Cash would not hear of leaving until he saw you all safe. You came quite close to at least one of them, eh?" Worth grinned at the viscount. "Not to worry, Harcort, we'll get you tended to shortly."

"It is nothing, sir. Bit of a headache is all."

"Well, we shall get it tended to anyway."

"Is the duke not badly hurt, then?" Hempstead asked, his heart still pummeling his ribs. He wiped at the sweat that cascaded into his eyes.

"The answer to that depends upon whether you ask him or Brummell and I. He says not, but he has lost a deal of blood. Got them," Worth added, helping Harcort into the coach and urging Hempstead and Kettering in behind. "Cash has won again, Beau. We shall both need to pay up. Onward," Worth called with a knock on the trap. "Great Stanhope."

By the time they reached Fielding House the bandage Brummell had fashioned from his and Worth's neckcloths and tied as tightly as possible about Abbercombe's shoulder was saturated with blood.

"Gawd!" Dawson exclaimed as he opened the door to the lot of them. He hurried them into the ground floor parlor and lighted several braces of candles. "Have you sent for a surgeon? No? I'll send Nathan. He'll go without mincing about."

Abbercombe sank thankfully on to the couch and leaned his head back against the cushions. He reached out and caught Dawson by the coatsleeve. "Do not send for a surgeon, Anthony. Tell Robin I need him."

"Immediately," Dawson assured him and raced off through the door and up the stairs.

"You ought to lie down and put your feet up," Brummell suggested standing before him.

Abbercombe eyed the Beau critically. "Once again I have destroyed your apparel, brat. I cannot believe that you do not strangle me."

"We have got to staunch that blood or you will not require strangling," muttered Worth. "Kettering, can you find the kitchen do you think? Take a branch of candles to light your way. Is it down at the end of the hall, Cash?"

The duke nodded. "Beyond the Children's Den, on the right."

"I shall find it," Kettering assured them.

"Oh, my goodness," exclaimed Mrs. Griffin softly as she entered the room carrying a pile of fresh linen. "No, sir, you need not seek the kitchen. I shall fetch whatever is needed." She set the linen upon a table and pulled a pair of scissors from the pocket of her apron, handing them to Lord Worth. "Cut his coat and shirt away, Mr. Fanning says. And you, sir," she added, crossing to where Harcort sat. "You shall let me attend to your brow. Bring the water in as soon as it is warm, Nathan," she told the first footman as he approached the door. "And see this fire lit, lest his grace take chill."

"I have never seen so much blood in all my life," muttered Brummell placing a glass of brandy into the duke's hand. "Everything is soaked with it." He carried glasses of brandy to the rest of the gentlemen as well and then stripped off his coat, rolled up his sleeves and set to lighting the fire himself. The duke sipped the brandy and watched as Worth tossed the scissors aside and ripped the rest of the seams, laying the duke's shoulder bare. Fanning appeared carrying a set of saddle bags. The panic in his eyes fled as Abbercombe smiled up at him. "I am not in excellent stirrups, Robin, but now you are here, I shall do comfortably."

"Indeed. And are these the gentlemen I must thank that you are not dead, your grace?"

"Certainly. Do not frown at me so, Robin. The first pistol shot came from behind, but I did manage to avoid the second."

Fanning set the saddle bags on the floor and took the place Worth offered beside the duke. "Did it go all the way through?"

Abbercombe nodded. "I cannot think why it bleeds so. I do not recall it doing as much the last time."

"You, my lord, were not paying attention the last time," Fanning drawled, inspecting the wound carefully and shaking his head in exasperation.

"Come, Robin, get to it," the duke urged, setting his brandy aside. "The children? They are not like to walk in upon us?"

"The young ladies are come home almost an hour ago, your

grace," Robin murmured. With Mrs. Griffin's, Brummell's, Hempstead's and Kettering's aid, Fanning soon had Abbercombe's wound cleaned, packed and tightly bandaged and Harcort's assorted bruises and gashes attended to as well.

"Do me a great service, Brummell," Abbercombe sighed, as the Beau knelt before him placing blood-soaked linen into a large china bowl. "I must have a private word with Hempstead."

Brummell's eyebrow cocked. "Indeed?" he replied. "Gentlemen, madam," he announced, standing, bowl in hand, "will you all join me in the kitchen for a moment please? Hempstead, you will remain and see that his grace does nothing foolhardy, will you not?"

"Are they out of earshot, Geoff?" Abbercombe quietly asked once the others departed the room.

"Yes, sir, quite."

"Good. You did not tell Kettering and Harcort what was in the note I sent you?"

"No, sir. We were at White's and I did not know how to object to their accompanying me. I told them that you might cause some problems and that the Foreign Office was keeping a secret watch over you because of your having been transported."

Abbercombe chuckled. "Did you get a decent look at the men on either side of me at the faro table as I asked?"

"Yes, sir. Do you think they were the ones shot at you?"

"No, Geoff, not they. It was for their benefit that I won the final bet. The gentleman in the puce coat is called Elias Pendleton and the tall, dark gentleman in the grey, Anthony Saukill. They are free-traders, Geoff. Now you have had a good look at them, will you be able to recognize them again?"

"Yes, sir."

"Then you must do me the favor to take my place tomorrow night. Is my coat on the floor yet? Yes? Pick it up, Geoff, and take the blunt from the inside pocket. You must carry it to the stables at Grillon's shortly after midnight and place it into Pendleton's hands."

"Yes, sir. But I think you must lie down now. Your face is the color of ashes and your eyes look extremely odd."

"Do they? Geoff, you must be sure it is either Pendleton or Saukill to whom you give the blunt. No one else."

"Yes, sir. I shall see it is done properly, but you must let Fanning put you to bed. And we must get Harcort home as well."

"In a moment. You will take a hack to Albemarle Street, descend from it outside the Haverson and Pike warehouse, and stroll from there to Grillon's. One of the hostlers—James, he's called—has two front teeth missing—will send you back to the tack room. Pendleton and Saukill will follow you. Do not let on that you know they are behind you, Geoff. They are nervous and will flee if you turn to look at them. You must tell them to make the rendezvous at Marseilles as we discussed and that the cargo will be fetched from Alderney on the twenty-eighth."

Hempstead repeated the instructions. "Got it," he assured the duke confidently. "You may trust in me, your grace."

"Enough!" declared Fanning, entering the room followed by all of the gentlemen but Worth and putting an end to the conversation. "You must rest now, your grace, and Viscount Harcort likewise. I have sent Mrs. Griffin and Nathan to their beds, and Lord Worth has gone to procure a hack to carry the rest to their lodgings. There, I hear the horses drawing up to the door. Now thank the young gentlemen for coming to your aid and we will get you to bed."

"I can very well get myself to bed—"

"You shall allow Dawson and me to help you," Fanning declared stoically. "Now thank the gentlemen and let us depart."

"Thank you, gentlemen," Abbercombe said with a weary but amused glance at the stubborn set of Fanning's jaw. "I am deeply in your debt." He stood then, with Fanning's help, and walked a bit unsteadily toward the door.

"What was that about, Hempstead?" Worth asked as the five settled into the hired coach. "Do you know anything we do not?"

Hempstead grinned and leaned back against the squabs. "No,

sir. He only wished to be assured that I would not mention any of this at the Foreign Office. I said I would not."

"He is one devil of an old man, don't you think, Brummell?" Kettering drawled. "Did I take a pistol ball clear through my shoulder, you shouldn't see me waiting about for us fellows to come back down that stinking alley, no, nor see me sitting up to watch how the blasted wound was tended to."

"Perhaps," Harcort mused, leaning his aching head against the back of the seat, "we ought to keep watch over him, Bryan, for Beth's and Amy's sakes. Someone is out to kill him."

"I would not let Abbercombe catch me watching over him if I were you," Brummell muttered. "He will chew you up and spit you out for being cheeky, presumptuous, little brats."

"Amaryllis says his bark is much worse than his bite," Kettering offered with a yawn.

"Indeed," chuckled Worth, "but as recipient of both, I beg to inform you that his bite is nevertheless significant."

It was well past eleven o'clock the following morning when Chris and Daymee knocked upon the door of their sisters' sitting room and were quietly admitted. "Aunt Margaret has gone to the still room to fix a tonic for Papa and Fanning is changing the dressing," Christian announced. "We shall not be interrupted."

"Good," sighed Beth. "And Mr. Stanton and Miss Greene have taken the little ones on an outing." The four eldest Denbigh children made themselves comfortable before a lazy fire. The boys lounged on the thick carpet while their sisters settled onto a small couch close to the blaze.

"Daymee and I have been checking about the best we can," Christian began quietly, "but so far we have discovered very little. Papa has been sending messages all over the French countryside and into Spain as well. And Captain Dunleavy has orders to ready the *Peregrine*. He is to be available to catch the tide at Portsmouth anytime within the next week, but there is no word as to where they will be bound."

"Oh, I knew it," cried Bethany softly. "I never did think that Papa had given up at discovering Harry's whereabouts."

"Neither did I," agreed Christian. "But even if Harry is held captive and Papa is attempting to find him, that don't explain who the boys have been seeing moving about below their windows."

"Are you sure they do not simply imagine someone there?" Amaryllis asked hopefully. "After all, they have spent their whole lives amongst secret police and espionage agents and the like, and they expect to see prowlers about as likely as not."

"No, I am sure they saw someone," Daymee sighed. "I did not wish to mention it, but not very long ago Papa was attacked by cutthroats in the courtyard."

"Oh, no! Daymee, why did you not tell us immediately!" cried Beth. "How long ago? He was not harmed, was he?"

"It was the night he said he had tripped on the cobbles, and he had the bandage round his head for a whole week. But that was a clanker, for I saw the battle from the boys' window. Something woke me and I heard Bear scratching and whining in their room so I went to fetch her. She had climbed upon the window sill behind the draperies and was trying to get out, so I looked below, you know, to see what sort of animal she wished to chase—and it was not an animal at all, but a number of people scuttling about in the courtyard. And then I heard a pistol shot, and Robin came bolting from the front door. I could not see who they all were, but I saw Robin and Mr. Brummell help Papa inside, for by then I had gone to the top of the stairs to investigate."

"You did not ask what had happened?" Amaryllis queried.

"Well, no. I grabbed Bear and hurried back to bed and pretended to be asleep. I did not think that Papa would have been terribly happy to know I had seen everything. You know how he is, Amy."

"Yes, indeed. He would have sworn you dreamed the entire affair and then spent the next three days angry with himself for being what he is and putting us so close to danger."

"Yes," sighed Christian, wrapping his arms around his knees and gazing into the fire. "He would have been in agony. You were right not to speak to him, though I wish you had confided in us."

"That is twice Papa has been set upon by villains," mused Beth, the knuckle of her index finger caught between her teeth. "I do not think these last wished to rob him at all then. He has just told us another bouncer to keep us from worrying."

"Devil!" exclaimed Amy. "And to think we brought him to London to keep him safe! Well, there is nothing for it. We must discover what's afoot and then devise a plan. Christian, you and Daymee must learn, if you can, who has taken Harry's place, for I am sure someone has since Papa still appears to be operating. Beth and I will attempt to discover who prowls about the yard. We will do so tonight by getting John Coachman to help us search with the carriage lights when we return from Lady Skiffington's."

"How will you get him to do that without explaining and giving everything away?" Daymee asked.

"We will lose something that will roll across the cobbles," mused Beth, "and since John does not suspect danger, he will help us seek it right away. If we do everything quickly enough, we may obtain a glimpse of the villains. At the very least, we should find evidence of their presence."

"And what will you do if you should find them and they fall upon you?" asked Christian soberly.

"Shout for you and Daymee, of course," declared Amaryllis. "You will be hiding on the roof of the portico."

"Yes!" exclaimed Daymee, grinning. "I knew you would not leave us out of it! And we shall have weapons with us."

"What kind of weapons?" asked Christian skeptically.

"Your slingshots?" mused Beth. "Can you not smuggle some stones out through the window to the top of the portico?"

"Oh, and you could lean the shillelaghs Papa bought you in Londonderry against the outside wall of the portico, so that if you wish to jump down and help us, you will have cudgels readily available," added Amy. "You may get Ethan and Frazier and Grace and Helen to collect the stones and hide them until you have time to place them properly. They will think it a game."

"It sounds feasible," agreed Christian. "But you must be sure to keep out of the way if we are to sling stones at them."

"We will," Bethany promised. "And we will try to light them up for you, so that you do not miss your shots."

"At least his wings are clipped for a while," Brummell offered, accepting hot chocolate from Lady Worth's hands. "He must remain at home until that shoulder begins to heal."

"Yes, and you and I will have an easier time keeping an eye on him," Worth nodded, tugging Eugenia down beside him on the little cream settee that faced the armchair in which Brummell sat. "That is, if you wish to continue in this business, Beau. Abbercombe is correct, you know. He has savaged your wardrobe terribly of late."

Brummell's serious eyes caught at Worth's brown ones, and then at Lady Worth's. "I have been involved from the moment he entered White's and consented to shake my hand for a price, Edward," he drawled. "The rapscallion has caught me up and I cannot drive him from my mind. There is nothing about him that does not intrigue me. And I shall not be counted out."

Lady Worth laughed. "I never would have thought it of you, Mr. Brummell. Intrigue is not your forte."

"It has become my forte."

"Good," Worth nodded. "Do you attend the Skiffingtons' ball tonight?"

"Indeed. Would not miss the thing now that I know Abbercombe's daughters are to be there."

"May I ask what are your intentions toward those girls?" Eugenia asked with a tilt of her chin.

"Why simply to engage them in some conversation. Just enough, you understand, to bring them securely into fashion."

Worth chuckled. "I do believe, Brummell, that having dined

but once with those children you are fairly caught by them. But do not underestimate the rogue's daughters. They are not like any chits you are used to deal with in the *ton*."

"And I doubt not that they would become fashionable even without you," added Lady Worth, "if that were their desire."

"So Abbercombe intimated when we last spoke on the subject."

"He did, did he?" asked Worth, surprised. "I hope you did not take it as a challenge, Beau. I doubt he meant it that way."

"No, I took it as a father's pride in his children," Brummell replied quietly. "And now I have met them, I understand it perfectly. So, what is our plan for this evening?"

"Whatever it is," declared Lady Worth, playing her fingers temptingly along her husband's knee, "you must both be very careful. If someone is out to murder Abbercombe, they may find it perfectly acceptable to murder the both of you as well. And I do think," she added gravely, "that one of you ought to inform Sebastian Denbigh of his brother's danger."

Thirteen

It was almost noon when Olivia welcomed the Honorable James Ratherton into her drawing room with a bright smile. "I do so appreciate your coming, Jamie. You know April, do you not?"

"Indeed, ma'am," he replied, bowing in April's direction. "Your message sounded urgent, Miss Olivia. How may I be of assistance?" The handsome gentleman took a seat and accepted a cup of hot chocolate. "We have as yet no word of Andrew if that is what you wish to know."

"That is not what we wish to know at all, Mr. Ratherton," said April impatiently. "We wish to know about spies."

Ratherton glanced, puzzled, from one to the other of the ladies. He had admired Olivia Willburton-Smythe since he was in short coats, and he was more than appreciative of the innocent allure of her niece. But why such picture-perfect ladies should spend one moment's thought on spies escaped him completely. "Spies? Why would you wish to know about spies?"

"We have developed a curiosity, Jamie, because of a discussion at Lord Sinclair's musicale," Olivia supplied quickly. "We wished to know a bit more and I thought immediately of you. I am sorry my message sounded urgent. It was not intended to do so. But since you are come so promptly, do you not think you might answer some questions for us?"

"I shall do my best," smiled Ratherton condescendingly. "Fire away, ladies."

"How do you tell if someone is a spy?" April asked. "I should think they would attempt to appear the most ordinary people."

"Well, yes, or if not ordinary, then impeccable—above suspicion. That is their strength, you see. They seek to gain *entrée* into society and associate on equal footing with the people they wish to spy upon. Lord Sinclair, for instance, must constantly be on guard because of his position at the War Office. It is odd that the discussion came up at his musicale," Ratherton added with an amused gleam in his dark eyes. "Lord Sinclair's study was raided during that *affaire* and a despatch stolen."

"Oh," gasped Olivia. "How dreadful!"

"Not really, though Sinclair was upset to think his hiding place had been discovered. But the despatch was not vital and Lord Wyndham assured him that one of the Foreign Office people had snatched it. Sent to test Lord Sinclair's security, he was. They often play such games back and forth between the offices."

"Did one of his guests steal it?" asked April eagerly.

"I am certain of it, though I would not consider whoever it was a spy, Miss April. I believe no true spies work for the Foreign Office. They all work for us at the War Office."

Olivia smoothed the wrinkles from the lap of her russet brown round gown. "Then if one suspected a person of being a spy, Mr. Ratherton, one would come to your office to report them?"

"Indeed."

"And what would the people in your office do?"

"Why, look into the matter, Miss Olivia."

"You would not arrest them?" April queried.

"Not without significant evidence, no ma'am." Ratherton chuckled and took another sip of chocolate. "Why, we should be arresting the most extraordinary people. Someone accused Brummell of spying, you know. Envious of his fellowship with the Prince of Wales. Nothing in it, of course."

"But if the government were certain someone was a spy," Olivia asked, her eyes wide with innocence, "they would not, say, arrange for that person to be—killed?"

"Heavens, ma'am!" Ratherton exclaimed. "Whoever gave

you such an idea? We are not savages. The person would be arrested."

"That is exactly what we said," replied April, sticking to the tale of their discussion at Lord Sinclair's. "You see, we were correct, Aunt Olivia. Do you think, Mr. Ratherton, that someone like the Duke of Abbercombe might be a spy?"

"April!" cried Olivia.

Ratherton raised a palm to silence Olivia's protest and grinned at April. "An interesting gentleman, is he not, Miss April? I have not seen anyone raise more of a breeze simply by walking down a street. Everyone has something to say about him. But that is just the thing which makes it unlikely he could be a spy."

"Everyone says he is dangerous."

"Yes, but he is also outcast and always under scrutiny. He would make a dreadful spy, Miss April. Who would confide in him or allow him anywhere near information an enemy might seek when they are already suspicious of him?"

"Oh, I see," April smiled prettily.

Ratherton finished his chocolate and set the cup on the table beside his chair. "I am afraid I must be going, ladies. I hope I have helped to appease some of your curiosity?"

"Indeed, Jamie," Olivia assured him, rising and escorting him from the room. She walked with him all the way to the door and brought chuckles from him three times along the way. "Now I am certain!" she declared as she reentered the drawing room. "LeBruin wished to set me against Abbercombe for his own ends, and he shall regret it, April. I guarantee he shall regret it!"

Lady Vale stood beside the chair into which she and Fanning had forced Abbercombe. A fire blazed in the sitting room grate and a shawl was tucked protectively about his lap. Having achieved his will to be allowed out of bed after dinner, the duke's protests had had no effect at all upon where he *was* allowed to be.

"And you will remain right *here,* do you understand me?"

Lady Vale proclaimed, placing one elegantly gloved hand upon his broad shoulder. "If you are going to be troublesome, I shall not accompany the girls. I shall allow Jessica to do the honors."

"No, you must accompany them, Aunt Margaret. It is the reason you came to London after all."

Dawson announced Lord Sebastian and Lady Jessica, Miss Willburton-Smythe, and Miss April Willburton-Smythe. The visitors swept into the room and came to an abrupt halt. "Cash, what happened!" Sebastian exclaimed, seeing his brother's arm held immobile across his chest in a snow white sling. He crossed hastily to the duke.

"Took a pistol ball through the shoulder, 'Bastian. Strolled alone down Jermyn Street, like a regular green one, and someone chose to try their luck at collecting from my account."

Olivia gasped softly. He turned to her and his eyes lit with admiration. "How exquisite you are, my dear. I am dazzled."

His face was ashen and dark shadows huddled beneath his eyes, but his perfect lips tilted upwards in a desperate smile, and Olivia read clearly his need to keep this evening as special as he had intended it to be. Determined to help him do so, she slipped the velvet mantle from her shoulders and placed it across Dawson's waiting arm. Abbercombe inhaled audibly at the sight of her smooth bare shoulders above the clinging emerald silk and brabant lace of her gown. She grinned and turned in a small circle on her matching pumps with the jewelled heels. "Well, sir, do you think we shall pass muster?" she teased, as April and Jessica uncovered their gowns as well. Sebastian, a hand on his brother's knee, grinned as they twirled one by one.

"Now," said Olivia when the show of fashions ended, "where are your scamps? It is their approval we came to seek, you know."

"We's here, M's Weebuttonsmite!" Gracie squeaked.

Four striking young ladies swept into the room on the arms of four urbane young bucks. The boys displayed Fanning's considerable valeting skills in black knee breeches and matching velvet coats, silk stockings, blue waistcoats and intricately tied cravats. Olivia and April sighed; Lady Jess clapped her hands; Lord Sebastian broke into a chuckle as the young gentlemen bowed to them all while the ladies on their arms curtsied politely. Amy and Beth wore matching floor length gowns of glowing sapphire satin with overgowns of delicate, cream Versailles lace. The low, square-cut necklines displayed to perfection the delicate ivory on sapphire cameos their papa had given them, and the high waists of the dresses with their sweeping folds hinted temptingly at luscious figures beneath. In their hair ribands of sapphire silk spiraled temptingly through golden ringlets.

Grace and Helen stood dimpling proudly in long-sleeved velvet dresses of azure blue with lace collars and cuffs. Kid leather slippers peeked from beneath lace bedecked hems. "We's all of us so perty!" Helen squeaked, shaking her little white-gloved hands in the air. "We looks like fairy princesseses."

"Do you likes us, Papa?" Gracie giggled as his sparkling gaze roved over each of them.

"Entrancing," Abbercombe replied solemnly. "But I thought only Amy and Beth and Aunt Margaret were to go to the ball."

"We're goin' to have our own ball, Papa!" exclaimed Frazier gleefully, trying hard to keep from jumping up and down. "Miss Greene an' Mr. Stanton an' Chris an' Daymee are gonna be our orch'stra. An' me an' Ethan an' Gracie an' Helen are gonna dance for you! An' it will be as much fun as Lady Skifflering's!"

"An' there's gonna be 'freshments!" cried Helen.

"Camel tarts an' choc'late cherries an' lemonade!" Ethan shouted ecstatically.

Abbercombe gave up trying not to laugh. "I adore camel tarts." His eyes met Olivia's and set her to laughing as well. "I shall feel like the Tzar, himself, to have my very own ball. Lady Skifflering's shall not be half as fun as ours. Amy?"

"Yes, Papa," replied that young lady stepping forward with a slim box in her white-gloved hand and presenting it to April. "April, this is from all of us, to thank you for being our friend from the very first."

"And we hope you will accept this, Miss Olivia, for quite the same reason," added Beth as she placed a box in Olivia's hand.

April and Olivia stared in amazement.

"Oh, do open them," urged Beth. "We all want to see!"

The two ivory on emerald cameos appeared simultaneously and April squeaked much like little Gracie and Helen.

"Put 'em on! Put 'em on!" cried Ethan ecstatically. "We have waited forever an' ever!"

"It is the gigantikist secret we ever kept!" shouted Frazier triumphantly. "We din't even tell Aunt Jessie, did we, Papa?"

"No, you did not."

"No, we din't; no, we din't," chanted Gracie and Helen spinning about in circles.

Sebastian laughing, rose to help both ladies undo the clasps of the necklaces they wore and replace them with the cameos.

"Oh, Abbercombe," Olivia murmured, fingering the delicately carved jewel, "you should not have—"

"Do you not care for it, Olivia?" he asked worriedly. "I thought at Ruben's that you rather liked it."

"It is lovely. But I cannot accept—"

"Oh, bosh," Lady Vale declared roundly. "It is not in the least exceptional, my dear. It comes from the entire family."

The corners of Olivia's mouth turned sweetly upward betraying the shy dimple in her cheek. "April and I are most honored. We four shall start a new fashion, shall we not?"

"Everyone will envy us," April grinned. "Thank you so much."

"Now?" Christian asked.

"I should think so," Abbercombe chuckled. "She has waited quite long enough."

Christian reached into the pocket of his coat, produced a slim black case and, smiling, presented it to Lady Jess. Upon a bed of black velvet a necklace of beaten gold wrought into delicate flowers each with a single ruby at center glowed enticingly. Lady Jessica gasped.

"Thank you for being our aunt, Lady Jess," Chris murmured shyly, and replaced her necklace with the rubies and gold.

Olivia noted the wide smile on Abbercombe's face and saw Lady Vale hug him from behind and kiss the top of his curls.

"It never looked more beautiful, not even on your mother, Cash," the dowager sighed.

"It was your mother's?" Lady Jess exclaimed, her hand going to the necklace. "Oh, I cannot take it from you."

"Why is it," the duke asked wistfully of no one, "that ladies always say they cannot when one knows very well that they want to with all their hearts? Jessica, I have never seen my mother or anyone else wear it, but it suits you admirably."

"Indeed," gurgled Amy. "It was made for you, Aunt Jessica. It gives you such a delicate, but wealthy, air!"

Everyone laughed at that. Sebastian and Dawson assisted the ladies to don their mantels as Chris and Daymee assisted their sisters to don pelisses, and Abbercombe submitted willingly to thank you kisses and goodbye kisses. "Look after each other," he instructed his daughters.

"Yes, Papa, indeed we shall," replied Bethany. "Please do not worry about us; we are going to have a wonderful time."

"Yes," he laughed with a glance at the impatiently fidgeting Ethan, Frazier, Grace and Helen, "but it will not be nearly as exuberant a time as we shall have here, I think."

A veritable arbiter of fashion in his blue coat of Bath superfine and matching knee breeches with silk stockings adorned by clocks, an ornately embroidered waistcoat, and shirt collars of moderate size, Mr. Geoffery Hempstead fiddled unconsciously with his cravat as he gazed about the Skiffingtons' ballroom. Two antique chandeliers heavy with candles hung above a glowing oak floor. Myriad candelabras provided twinkling light for a room papered in lush cream and gold stripes. Delicate white chairs, small gold brocade settees, and tiny cricket tables lined the walls, and a profusion of flowers added bright color. Off to the side in a small alcove, a modest group of musicians played a joyously rousing rendition of the "Tewlesbury Romp". Young ladies and gentlemen went delightedly down the line, displaying their competency in the steps of a dance that had recently become all the kick. Hempstead, however, leaned against the wall and frowned. His handsome face could not be coaxed to smile as long as April danced with Lord Goddering.

"Do not frown so, Mr. Hempstead," said a light voice at his elbow. "You cannot dance every dance with April."

"Miss Willburton-Smythe—good—good evening, ma'am."

"Good evening, Geoffery. May I call you Geoffery?"

"Y-yes, ma'am. I should be honored."

"Do you think that we might sit down for a moment?"

"Of course." Hempstead escorted his beloved's aunt to a settee flanked by vases of flowers which offered a modicum of privacy. He sat stiffly beside the lady, fearing he was about to have a peal rung over him for his renewed attentions to April.

"Before I say what I intend, Geoffery," began Olivia solemnly, "I should like to know what you thought you were doing to agree to elope with my niece."

Hempstead started. "I—I—did *not* think, Miss Willburton-Smythe," he stuttered. "I was swept away upon emotion. Had I stopped to think, I should never have agreed."

"Was it April's idea then?"

Hempstead looked everywhere but at Olivia.

"Oh, for goodness sake, Geoffery, I know very well that it was April's idea. But I do wish you had put your foot down at the first suggestion of it."

"I should have done, ma'am," Hempstead muttered. "I am ashamed I did not. But it was just after you had forbidden me to address Miss April—and—I was in such despair."

"And now?" Olivia asked quietly.

"Now I hope to win the captain's and your consent, Miss Willburton-Smythe, by proving to you that I am responsible, and devoted to April, and ambitious. I have a position with the Foreign Office and am determined to make a career for myself."

"So I have heard." Olivia smiled at the tentative hopefulness on the handsome young face. "I am quite impressed."

"Lord Wyndham has assured me that I improve daily." His hesitancy seemed to slip away, and Olivia was amazed to hear him speak enthusiastically and knowledgeably. She had never seen the gentleman so filled with self-confidence and self-esteem.

"Geoffery," she said when he had finished, "I can see that you are in the midst of a great change, and I am pleased with the direction it takes. I think it likely should you renew your suit in a few months it might not be frowned upon."

Hempstead felt his heart leap into his throat. "Do you mean, Miss Willburton-Smythe, that you are no longer opposed to—"

"I mean, Geoffery, that should everything continue as it does, I should have no objection, and I do not think that the captain will either." Olivia could not help but grin at the surprise, relief, and joy that flickered across the young man's countenance. "And now," she said, patting Hempstead's knee, "you must excuse me. M. LeBruin comes to claim his dance."

Maxim LeBruin was indeed approaching, and Olivia, standing, walked off to intercept him, taking his arm and whispering into his ear. LeBruin nodded and escorted her out onto the balcony where she sighed with relief.

"I thank you for not holding me to the quadrille. I have been longing for some fresh air."

"Indeed, mademoiselle, it is your charming companionship I seek. The dance means nothing."

"Abbercombe has sent word, monsieur," Olivia began as she walked to the balcony rail and grasped it lightly, looking out over the Skiffington's garden where paper lanterns twinkled, "word that he has a message from Andrew."

"From *le capitan,* mademoiselle? How can this be?"

" 'Twas brought from a village on the coast along with Andrew's signet ring. He wishes me to verify the ring and thus the message. He fears a trap, I think. Is it a trap, monsieur?"

"I know nothing of it, Mademoiselle Olivia."

"But the government, monsieur. Are they likely to attempt to entrap him by such means?"

"No," murmured LeBruin, his fine grey eyes narrowing. 'Does he bring this message to your lovely home?"

"No, monsieur, he brings it to me here. I am to meet with him n Lord Skiffington's conservatory tonight during supper. It will ›e deserted then, you see, so we shall be quite alone."

"Be most careful, *ma belle*," LeBruin warned softly, putting a hand upon her arm. "It is perhaps some trick of this demon's to bring you to betray *le capitain*."

"I shall be most circumspect, M. LeBruin. If the message is indeed from Andrew, I shall recognize his writing as well as his ring. I must go back inside now, April will be searching for me."

"*Oui, mademoiselle*." LeBruin offered Olivia his arm. In the far corner of the balcony a silent shadow reentered the ballroom through a matching set of French doors.

April had just finished her dance with Hempstead and bid him farewell. She caught sight of her aunt upon LeBruin's arm and went directly to that lady. LeBruin bowed gracefully and took his leave. "Did you tell him? Did he believe you?"

"I rather think he did. I should be most surprised if we do not discover M. LeBruin in the conservatory with his pistol at the ready. Has Mr. Hempstead agreed to help us?"

"I did not ask him," April answered, "for he has an appointment he must keep on behalf of Lord Wyndham. He has just now gone. But I know who will agree to help us."

"Who? Is it someone who can be trusted?"

"Viscount Harcort," April whispered, "and Mr. Kettering. They are devoted to Amy and Beth. And Harcort is just the duke's size and will look much like him in the shadows. Mr. Kettering will hide with me and be able to subdue LeBruin should it become necessary. And they will both make excellent witnesses."

Olivia looked bemusedly at April's sparkling eyes. "What a schemer you are, you minx. I never thought it of you. We must speak to Harcort and Kettering immediately."

Hempstead waited as the Skiffingtons' butler sent a footman off to fetch his hat and cane. When the knocker sounded and Lindner opened the door, Hempstead could not believe his eyes.

"Evening, Hempstead," Abbercombe drawled. "You are just the gentleman I seek. Is there somewhere we might speak privately?"

Lindner waved the footman away again, and with a look of amazement, for he knew very well who this latecomer was, suggested that the gentlemen might find the privacy they required in his lordship's study. Abbercombe agreed and the butler led them up the stairway to the first floor, along the hall and into the cozy room. Both gentlemen declining refreshments, Lindner took himself off, closing the door behind him.

"What are you doing here?" Hempstead frowned.

"I am allowed to come, Hempstead. I have an invitation."

"You also have a hole in your shoulder. I should think you would choose to let it heal."

"Balderdash! If I made a list of all the holes I have had in me, it would take you until next Tuesday to read it. I do not require coddling. I think I may require your assistance at the moment, however."

"What? Tell me."

"Well, I could not quite squeeze into a proper English coat with this shoulder—or without Fanning's help. And so I have had to resort to this old thing. But I have mucked up the buttons."

"Am I to understand, your grace, that you wish me to button your buttons?"

"Just the ones I've mucked up, Hempstead. They are not all wrong. And you might have a go at tying my cravat. It is nearly impossible to do the thing one handed."

Hempstead studied the duke. "Am I to assume, your grace, that you sneaked out of your own home?" He set about tying the cravat and rebuttoning the buttons, being exceedingly careful not to bump the arm that Abbercombe had removed from its sling and held immobile by keeping his hand in his pocket.

"Yes, sneaked."

"Well, you ought not have done. How did you get here?"

"Took a hack. Are you bound for Grillon's? It is near time."

"There," Hempstead sighed. "I expect you will do. I am just ut the door. Do you not trust me and wish to go along?"

"No, Geoff, I only hoped to catch you to give you this." The uke produced from his pocket a thick roll of notes and placed hem in Hempstead's hand. "In the center is a missive giving ou directions how to find my schooner and Captain Dunleavy n Portsmouth. He expects me. You will need to convince him I ave sent you instead. Part of the money you must use to hire a haise-and-four to get you to Portsmouth tomorrow. Be sure you re not followed. One hundred thousand goes to Pendleton and aukill upon delivery. Entrust that sum into Dunleavy's hands. am sorry, Geoff, to make you responsible for all of it, but I oubt I am fit to make the journey myself."

"I doubt you are fit enough to have come here," Hempstead numbled, noting the pain in the duke's eyes and the perspiration eading on his brow. "Let me drop you at Fielding House before go on to Grillon's."

"No, you will be late, Geoff. I shall get home on my own."

Upstairs in the Skiffingtons' ballroom an elegant Beau Brummell made his way straight to the Denbigh girls. A rotund personage in a bright red jacket with epaulettes and blue frogging and dark blue pantaloons matched him step for step. Worth, standing between the young ladies, gravely presented the Beau's companion to Lady Vale, Amaryllis, and Bethany.

"You are Abbercombe's daughters?" the Prince Regent asked quietly. "Indeed, you must be. No one but he and Lady Celia could have produced so much beauty."

"Thank you, your highness," answered Amy. "The duke is certainly our Papa, and he has told us all about you."

"Has he? And did you believe him?"

"Oh, yes," answered Beth, her eyes round with innocence.

"Deuce take it," Prinny sighed.

"You must not sound so gloomy, Florizel. The girls will think you a crusty old fellow and that I never told them."

"Papa!" exclaimed Amaryllis. "What are you doing here?"

"Why, I have been invited, my dear," grinned Abbercombe.

"But Papa, your shoulder," admonished Bethany.

"We will not discuss that now, my love. Florizel, I am obliged to you for acknowledging my daughters."

Prinny, an expression very much like awe upon his florid countenance, extended his hand.

"I would take it, your highness, but I have been shot and it's devilish hard to make my arm work. Will you accept my left?"

"Indeed," replied Prinny, doing so.

"How goes your father? They do not expect he will recover?"

Brummell and Worth tensed. No one spoke of George III to the Prince Regent. It was like to set him raving. This time, however, the Prince's countenance softened to a whimsical smile.

"He would remember you, Abbercombe, should you visit him. One must get past those confounded physicians, of course. He still speaks of you fondly when he is lucid."

"Then I shall attempt to see him soon. It appears, *mon ami,* that you and I have brought an entire ballroom to a standstill."

"Eh?" Prinny looked about him at a sea of soundless, staring faces. Even the musicians had ceased playing and stared.

"Perhaps they expect a duel," murmured Abbercombe. "We shall offer them one. Do you remember the steps of the waltz? It was new when we met last in Vienna."

Prinny's eyes lit. "It has not yet been accepted here. The moralists find it outrageous."

"Good, we will both be blacklisted. Worth, will you ask the orchestra to play a waltz? Amy, you are eldest. Will you partner the Regent and Beth, will you waltz with a one-armed villain?"

"No," replied Bethany, "but I will waltz with you, Papa."

Olivia stared like the other guests as the music began and the two couples took the floor. She could not pry her eyes from them. Even with one arm immobile, Abbercombe's dancing was perfection and Prinny, despite his girth, fairly skimmed the glistening oak beneath his slippers.

Lady Worth smiling wistfully, received a nod from her mother,

nd with a toss of her chestnut ringlets she joined her husband,
vhispered in Worth's ear, and in three quick steps he swept her,
oo, into the waltz. A number of gentlemen who had studied
ecretly with one caper merchant or another sought out young
adies who had also learned the steps, and in moments the ball-
oom was filled with twirling couples who had long wished to
valtz but had never before been brave enough to do so.

Flushed cheeks and sparkling eyes accompanied the dancers
rom the floor once the music ended. Only the duke's face lacked
he distinctive color and glowing eyes induced by the forbidden
rolic. As he escorted Beth back to Lady Vale, Olivia, who sat
oeside her, noted his paleness. She stood, took his arm and led
aim out onto the balcony. "You, sir, are the most unruly creature
have ever met," she hissed. "Have you no thought for your own
welfare? Not only do you leave your sickbed to come to a ball
of all things, but then you have the audacity to waltz? Now you
shall be twice as ill as you were. Have you no common sense?"

An eyebrow cocked; a wry smile twisted the duke's lips. "May
ask what interest it is of yours, ma'am? And what gives you
icense to scold me as if I were a child?"

"When you act like a child, sir, you should expect to be treated
ike one," snapped Olivia. "You must go home at once. I am
certain you have a fever. You cannot be here!"

"Why can I not be here, Olivia?" his husky voice purred.

"Because you are ill and—I will not have you suffer more!"
Olivia stamped her dancing slipper with the jewelled heel and
then gasped as Abbercombe's arm went about her waist and he
tugged her against him. He brought his lips softly down upon
hers. Shocked, she struggled and he released her. Her palm flew
up to slap his face, but she found herself unwilling to do so.
"How dare you?" she cried instead, her hand fluttering across
the bodice of her gown.

"I beg your pardon, Olivia," the duke whispered. "I could not
help myself. You must be correct. I have savaged my health by
coming here, and even now I am delirious."

Olivia scowled, only to see his eyes twinkling in the moonlight

and his mouth twitching helplessly into a beguiling grin. "Yo
are shameless," she scolded, coerced into a giggle.

"Yes, I know. I cannot account for it, Miss Weebuttonsmite
but the moment a lovely lady rings a peal over me, my sense
go reeling." Once again his arm came about her waist and h
drew her to him. His eyes gazing steadily into hers, he presse
his lips gently against her own, and this time she did not pul
away. Her arms went about his neck, and she kissed him back
"Oh," she gasped when he drew away, "I cannot imagine wha
has gotten into me. I have never done such a thing before!"

"You do it very well, Olivia, for all that," teased the duke, hi
fingers playing with the loose dark curls beside her ear. Tha
mere whisper of a touch sent sweet tingling sensations rippling
through her. "Olivia," he whispered finally, "I believe we ough
to go inside. I cannot be responsible for what may happen if 1
study your appealing face longer in this moonlight."

Olivia took his arm and walked him back into the ballroom
The supper dance was almost ended. Prinny had taken his leave
Brummell and Worth and Sebastian Denbigh were deep in dis-
cussion at the far side of the chamber with Lady Vale and Lady
Jess; Amy and Beth danced with two young beaux; and Viscoun
Harcort, April and Mr. Kettering had gone from sight.

Fourteen

The Skiffingtons' conservatory stood separate from the house and was gained by means of a graveled path through the garden. Harcort, Kettering and April progressed as silently as possible toward the predominantly glass building. Once or twice they whispered among themselves as to what was expected of each. The inside of the conservatory lay deep in shadow and a soft breeze from an open window stirred the leaves and blossoms of plants whose silhouettes appeared definitely hostile. Harcort cringed as his sleeve brushed a clay pot from one of the counters, and he lunged to catch it before it could crash to the floor. Kettering discovered a cache of gardening tools in one corner and swiftly chose a long-handled pitchfork for himself and bestowed upon April an iron-pronged rake. Hurriedly they found hiding places—April amongst a group of philodendrons and Kettering behind a potted eucalyptus tree and two Siberian pines. Harcort, seeing them safely armed and stowed, returned to the garden to await Olivia.

Olivia stood upon the staircase arguing with the insufferably stubborn duke. "I do not care," she fumed, knowing that the time for her to cross to the conservatory was come but unwilling to have the duke discover their plan. "You should not have come and you may not stay. Look at you. Your shoulder pains you dreadfully."

"It does no such thing," the duke countered, peering suspiciously down his crooked nose at her and wondering why he was inclined to provoke the lady when he actually did not feel well and should like to have been home in bed. "What are you up to, Olivia, that you wish me so heartily gone?"

"What am I up to?"

"Yes, I believe that was what I asked."

Olivia's hands went to her hips, her brow creased in frustration and her foot stamped upon the landing. "How dare you suggest that I am up to anything! It is you sneaked out of your own home, and then had the audacity to—to—take advantage—on the balcony—what are you up to, sir, is the question!" The peculiar look in his eyes brought Olivia's scolding tones to an abrupt halt. "Abbercombe, what is it? Are you going to faint? Oh, you must sit down!"

The duke thought to tell her at once that he was not going to do any such asinine thing as faint and never had done in his life, but then he caught the value of it. "Will you help me down the stairs, my dear?" he asked in the tones of surrender that had always worked with Celia. "I cannot fold within sight of all these people. I shall never live it down. There is a parlor on the ground floor. If you will support me to it, I promise I shall just sit for a moment and then return to Fielding House."

"Well, you are right on that count," Sebastian Denbigh offered, strolling up beside his brother and putting an arm about his waist. "You will return to Fielding House."

"But he wishes to sit down for a moment first, Sebastian," Olivia interceded as she watched the odd look in the magnificent blue eyes become even odder.

"So I heard." With a great deal of care not to disturb the duke's injured shoulder, Sebastian and Olivia escorted Abbercombe to the parlor and settled him before the fire. Lindner sent a footman running for brandy and Sebastian, seeing his brother's pallor increase and perspiration again form on his brow, began to untie Abbercombe's cravat. Olivia fidgeted. If the plan was to work she must leave now, but how could she when the duke was becoming more ill by the moment?

"Go, Olivia," Abbercombe murmured. "I have no wish for you to see me like this. Go to supper."

"Oh, men! You are all such ninnies—afraid to be thought weak!" Olivia flared, and then covered her mouth with her hands.

"Go away, Olivia," Abbercombe muttered again. "You leave April without a chaperon."

"April! Oh, I must go. You will look after him, my lord?"

"With great care," Sebastian assured her and watched the lady rush from the room just as Lindner entered with a decanter of brandy and two glasses.

"Is there anything else I may do, sir?"

"No, thank you, Lindner. We shall just rest here a moment, if that is all right?"

"Most certainly, my lord."

As Lindner's footsteps faded the duke sighed. "Which way did Olivia go, 'Bastian, did you see?"

"Which way?"

"Yes. Back up the staircase or to the left?"

"Cash, you are delirious."

"No, I am suspicious. Olivia has some plot afoot and she don't want me around."

Sebastian shook his head. "Plot or no, you are going home. I shall get Worth to help me if you resist."

"What, join forces against your brother? 'Bastian, you disappoint me."

"I do not. You merely attempt to maneuver me to your will."

Abbercombe rested his head against the back of the couch. "I know. I am sorry, 'Bastian. I see villains and plots everywhere I turn these days."

The husky voice held a tone of such heartbreaking despair that Sebastian would have taken his brother into his arms if he were not so wary of further injuring the duke's shoulder. "It is only natural, Cash, when you are being shot at every time you turn around. But to suspect Olivia of plotting is outrageous."

"Beastly," Abbercombe agreed with a catch in his voice. "I fear I am falling to pieces, 'Bastian. Can you not reassure me just this one more time. Did Miss Olivia go back up the stairs?"

"Well, no, she continued on down the hallway, but perhaps

she goes to fix a hem upon her gown or arrange her hair. I believe Lady Skiffington has provided chambers for the ladies both on the first floor and on this one." Sebastian noticed his brother's eyes drift shut and tension ease from him. The snifter of brandy in the duke's hand began to tip. Sebastian seized it and set it on a table beside the couch. He had never in his life seen anyone fall asleep so rapidly. "Cash?" he whispered, but he got no response. Well, what do you expect, he told himself. Not only does he take a pistol ball through his shoulder last night and lose a vast amount of blood, but then he comes to this dashed ball and dances. Tenderly Denbigh eased the duke down on the couch and tucked a pillow under his head. He took one last look at the sleeping figure then went in search of Lindner to order the coach brought 'round. That accomplished he looked in on Abbercombe once more and then headed for the supper room to enlist Worth's aid in getting his brother safely to the coach.

When Abbercombe heard Sebastian ascend the staircase at last, he rose, peered into the hall and discovered Lindner and a footman in conversation near the front door. With a low curse, he went to one of the windows, moved the draperies aside, opened the latch and stepped down onto the lawn. He would check the garden first and if he did not find Olivia there, reenter the house through the kitchen door and check the ground floor room by room.

Olivia's heart raced as she entered the silent conservatory. The warm, damp air and the smell of humus brought visions of graveyards to her mind. Moonlight flickered, its fickle illumination dim in spots and vibrant in others and in the far recesses of the building, not visible at all. A breeze from an open window whispered through plant leaves and tickled movement into phantom blossoms. There could be no better place, she thought with some agitation, for M. LeBruin to make his final attempt upon Abbercombe's life. Cautiously she stepped farther into the building, took a deep breath and reminded herself that the duke was safe in his brother's keeping and she, too, was safe—though where Kettering and April and Harcort might be she could not make out. Her hands fidgeted with the cameo at her throat and one slipper tapped nervously against the stone floor. Where was Harcort? He had left the ball before she. "Abbercombe," she whispered, remembering to use the duke's name, "I have come."

A rustling and a sighing like wind through the eaves drew her eyes to the dense gloom at the rear of the building where it seemed to her a shadow stirred. "Abbercombe?" she called softly. "Is it you?" Her heart leaped to her throat at a sudden crash and she swung toward the doorway. A tall, muscular figure stood outlined vaguely in moonglow. In a moment Harcort took her hands in his. "Sorry, Miss Olivia. Danged clay pots are everywhere."

Keeping his voice low and soft, hoping to mimic the duke's own husky but quiet tones, Harcort produced a paper and ring from his coat pocket and placed them into her hands. "Tell me, ma'am, do these come from the captain or not?"

Olivia sought a particularly bright patch of moonlight and pretended to study what she saw was a tailor's bill and the Viscount's own signet ring. "It is Andrew's ring," she gasped. "And his handwriting! You have truly found him, your grace!"

"Pity," a voice drawled from midway down the awkward path between the plants. "Had it been mere pretense, monsieur, we might have played our game a bit longer before I must end your life." LeBruin strolled confidently forward, a duelling pistol levelled at Harcort's heart. "But since you know whereat *le capitain* has gone to ground, *mon ami,* you are much too like to effect his rescue, *non?* We have been searching village by village, *mauvais sujet,* just as we did for you, but *le capitain* shall not have the *bonne chance* as you have had. Come, *Mademoiselle Olivia,* bring to me *le capitain's* message, *oui?* "

Olivia's heart pounded with fear. To imagine LeBruin a spy was one thing, to see him standing in shadow, a pistol pointed at Harcort's heart was another. Where were Kettering and April?

Why did they not spring from their hiding places to overset the man?

A clanging of metal and a glimpse of movement in the dim light sent LeBruin's head jerking toward the place where April hid. On the instant Kettering lunged from his own hiding place, bringing the handle of the pitch fork down with paralyzing force across LeBruin's wrist and sending the pistol skidding across the floor. LeBruin spun toward him, ducked in beneath Kettering's weapon and delivered a violent upper cut to the gentleman's jaw. Kettering crumbled. But April had leaped from the philodendrons behind the Frenchman and she brought the flat side of the iron rake down upon his skull without the least hesitation. LeBruin stood very still and then slumped to the stones. Harcort, who had pushed Olivia behind him was halfway to LeBruin when the emigre fell. But no sooner had LeBruin hit the floor and Harcort paused, than another figure rose from the shadows at the rear of the building, pistol in hand.

The duke dove through the open window at which he had been listening and caught Harcort about the knees, driving him to the floor just as a shot exploded through the gloom. Spinning back to his feet, Abbercombe lunged at April and shoved her behind the potted plants. He careened off a countertop, shattered myriad pots, and hurled himself at Olivia, the sound of another shot shrieking in his ears. Olivia screamed as he crashed into her and sent them both rolling out through the door.

"Here," Brummell hissed. He reached from behind a thick oak near the drive at Fielding House and grasped Worth's sleeve. "What took you so long?"

"Young Denbigh came to get me to help with Cash. He left him in Skiffington's front parlor asleep. But when we got back down there, the maggoty rogue was gone. We searched every room in the house and could not find him. I told Denbigh to remain until the ball ends in case his blasted grace should reappear, but I doubt he will. He is more likely to turn up here. I sincerely hope he does. I should feel a fool were we to spend the rest of the night on guard in this yard and Cash be in deep waters elsewhere."

"I shall feel a fool regardless," sighed Brummell. "If this gets about, the rumors of my supreme apathy, which I have worked so hard to promote, will cease circulation."

"I doubted them anyway, Beau, still, I never thought to see you huddled behind an oak, sword at the ready. That is a sword?"

"Yes, and you are about to witness the ultimate degradation, Worth—Brummell huddled *upon the ground* behind an oak." The Beau slumped wearily to the lawn. "I shall hate myself in the morning when I can actually see the grass stains."

Worth joined him. "Have you seen anyone suspicious as yet?"

"No, only the grooms tending to the cattle. Last time they hid behind that thicket near the drive, I think."

Worth followed the direction of Brummell's pointing finger and nodded. "Buck up, Beau. Shortly Stone and his associates will be on guard, and you will be free to spend the evening comfortably before the fire at Carlton House aggravating Prinny."

"Yes, and what is it, Worth, that goes on between the duke and Prinny? I was amazed to hear Abbercombe speak of the king and Prinny accept it with such civility. And then to suggest that the duke should go to visit the old man!"

"Farmer George always admired Cash. Like to have torn the king's heart out to see him condemned and hauled off in chains. Like to have torn my heart out as well. What's that?"

Both heads turned toward the sound of steps upon the cobbled drive. Amongst the pooling shadows five specters tiptoed toward the thicket. Keeping well out of the flaring torchlights at gates and door, they formed and faded like moonghosts until they struck the cover of the low bushes and disappeared.

On the roof of the portico Christian and Damian, too, followed the phantoms' erratic progress. "That makes seven," Chris murmured.

"Do you not think that we should sound an alarm belowstairs, Chris? Papa has sneaked out and so cannot come to our aid. With so many, the girls may be harmed if we go through with our plan."

"But we cannot warn Amy and Beth we have called it off, and they will never forgive us if we draw the staff into it."

"Not even Robin?"

"I had not thought," mused Christian. "Robin would know just what to do. Can you slip back in without being seen?"

"Yes. I shall be back in a matter of seconds."

Fanning stared at Daymee from the comfort of the wing chair in the duke's sitting room. "You plan to do what, to whom? Your Papa will take you by the ears and hurl you from the parapets."

"There are no parapets here from which to hurl us, Robin, and besides, the plan is already set and we cannot call it off because we cannot tell Amy and Beth we must do so. There are seven that we have seen—two behind the old oak near the stable and five others behind the thicket next to the drive."

Fanning left the confines of the chair and strolled into the duke's bedchamber. He returned with a sword in hand. "I shall take up a station near the west corner of the house. Do not begin any battle if your sisters are not set upon. And if they are, make the most of your shots. John Coachman carries a pistol. The four of us should be able to protect the ladies."

Damian made his way back to the roof. "Robin has taken a sword and waits at the west corner of the house, and John has a pistol with him on the coach. We are not to start a rumpus unless the girls are set upon," he whispered. "Are they still there?"

Christian nodded. "Look, the coach is at the gate."

John Coachman, in the duke's livery of blue and gold brought the heavy vehicle between the granite gate posts and up the drive, halting his team before the front entrance. He swung from his perch and helped the ladies to descend. He was about to raise the steps when he heard something roll across the cobbles and Amy gasped. "Oh, John, my Mama's charm! Will you bring the light and help me to search for it?"

"I shall help as well," offered Beth on cue. "If you will hand me the other coach lantern, John, we may find it quite easily. No, go in Aunt Margaret. We will be but a few moments."

Lady Vale let herself into the house just as Dawson was approaching the door. "I am sorry, my lady," he said. "We did not expect you quite yet."

"And I did not expect you at all. You are off tonight."

"Yes, my lady, but as I had nowhere to go, I have merely been reading in my chambers." He assisted her to doff her cloak. "Are the young ladies not with you?"

"Yes, but Amy has lost a charm and they are looking for it with the coach lights." A loud crack shattered the night, followed by an horrendous howl. "Great heavens, whatever is that?" Lady Vale exclaimed. Even as she and Dawson tugged open the front door, the courtyard was filled with scrambling shadows and the night air with rattled shouts.

"Gawd, I's hit, Jerry! Help me!" a gruff voice cried.

"Look out! Ow! Oh!" a second voice shouted.

Stones whizzed through the air and smacked sharply against moving targets. The coach lamps trembled in slender hands, and Lady Vale cried out as John Coachman threw himself upon a husky figure. Dawson rushed down the steps just as Fanning flashed into view. "Get the girls, Dawson. Take hold of a light and send the girls inside!" Dawson raced toward the coach lamp that a slender hand held aloft, seized it, and with a muffled oath sent Bethany flying to Lady Vale's side. The clash and jangle of engaged swords crossed the courtyard in counterpoint to smacking stones. Shouts and curses brought the entire Fielding House staff into the downstairs hall.

"Not me!" a voice yelled angrily.

"I've got him!"

"No, not me, you ninny, to your left, your left!"

"Hell and damnation! Get to the house, Lady Amy, now!"

Amongst the ruckus no one noticed two ghosts leap from the portico roof, seize shillelaghs, and bound off in pursuit of villains fleeing toward the stables.

Mr. Stanton caught Miss Greene's arm. "Help me to light

whatever candles are about. We will give them to everyone and carry more light out into the courtyard."

Lady Vale grabbed the first of the candelabras and hurried out the door. Behind her Amy, Beth, and the duke's servants did the same, and the courtyard came ablaze with light.

Abbercombe gasped for breath on the damp grass beside a bed of early lilies, holding firmly to a struggling Olivia. "D-do not fight," he gasped. "You—are—safe now."

"Abbercombe? What? How?"

"Wait. I am not—not as young—as I once was." With a low groan he released her and gained his feet. "Stay there," he commanded and stumbled back into the conservatory.

In a matter of moments April came running from the building and fell to her knees throwing her arms about Olivia. "Oh, thank goodness you are safe!"

"April, is—is anyone dead?"

"No, the duke says not even M. LeBruin, though I should not care if he were. To level a pistol at you so! How dare he!"

Olivia thought to point out that the pistol had been levelled at Harcort and not herself but decided the correction was unimportant at the moment. She hugged the girl, but kept her eyes fastened upon the conservatory door. At last Harcort, supporting a groggy Kettering and followed by the duke, stumbled into the garden. "Abbercombe and I have trussed up LeBruin but the other has escaped. Did you know there was a door at the back? I certainly did not."

"Nope," mumbled Kettering, "not a word."

"He don't know what he's saying," Harcort sighed. "Never knew he had a glass jaw. Thought the Frenchie had broken his neck the way he crumbled."

"Yep, grumbled an' grumbled," muttered Kettering.

"There's a pump by the kitchen, Harcort. Go stick the brat's head under it." Abbercombe helped April up and then extended his hand to Olivia. "Up, madam," he ordered. "We shall all repair to the kitchen. You have some explaining to do, I think."

"Is't a war?" Helen asked, kneeling upon the window seat, her nose pressed against the pane.

Gracie nodded. "We never haded one in our own yard."

Ethan and Frazier stared apprehensively at the blazing courtyard filled with people shouting and fighting. "Le's get dressed," Ethan urged anxiously, "an' then we'll help Gracie an' Helen. If it is a war, we will hafta leave quick."

"Where's Bear?" Frazier gasped. "We cannot leave Bear!"

"I want Papa," cried Gracie as she watched her brother tug the puppy out from beneath the bed.

"We can't wait upon Papa," Ethan explained as he crossed to an armoire and fetched breeches for himself and Frazier.

"He is prob'ly right down there, fightin'," Frazier offered, setting Bear atop the bed and pulling on his breeches. "We will fine Robin, an' he will tell us how we are to 'scape."

The boys dressed themselves and their sisters and, Bear held firmly in Frazier's arms, the four raced down the stairs to the ground floor. "Where do you s'pose Robin is?" Ethan queried, peering out the door. "There is men runnin' up the drive!"

"Hide! Hide!" yelled Frazier jumping down the last two steps and grabbing Helen's hand. Ethan spun around and seized hold of Gracie, tugging her down the hall and toward the Children's Den.

Lord Merriville and Lord Bacon, the masters of the mansions to each side of Fielding House, followed by footmen and grooms armed with anything that had come to hand, rushed up the duke's drive and hurled themselves into the fray. Lady Vale, overcome by excitement, urged them on with shouts of encouragement and then her eyes fell upon the duke's intrepid coachman. "Oh! No, John! That is Mr. Brummell! Do not hit him! Do not—oh, my goodness!"

From the direction of the stables a band of grooms and stable-boys, pitchforks, whips and broomsticks held high, poked and prodded two men toward the candle holders. Christian and Damian, shillelaghs on their shoulders, led the way. "We have got two of them, Amy," Christian called. "Are you all right?"

"We're fine. Blackguards," she hissed as the men came toward her. "How dare you try to murder my Papa!"

The burly men gazed amazedly at her. "M-murder, miss? Us?"

A gun exploded and a loud curse sounded directly afterward. "Are you attempting to put a period to my existence, Merriville?" roared Worth's familiar voice. "I am not the enemy!"

"Nor I!" shouted a nondescript man whose arm was just then being twisted up between his shoulder blades. "Hold off, villain. I'm Elijah Stone, an' Worth 'ired me to come an'—"

"Stone? How the devil do you come to be—ow!"

"Worth?" Lord Merriville called. "Hold on, I'm coming!"

Abbercombe had seated the little group of spycatchers around the Skiffingtons' kitchen table, sent one of the maids for Lindner and sent Lindner in search of Lord Sebastian and Lady Jessica. His face a study in forbearance, he glared at the conspirators as they finished their story and then rested his head upon his arm on the smooth, worn table and closed his eyes. Harcort opened his mouth, closed it again. April squirmed. Kettering's wet head rested in much the same position as the duke's. Olivia, unnerved by what had almost been Harcort's early demise and possibly her own, needed to hear someone speak—anyone—so she murmured softly herself. "It is not as though we did not have a plan. And we do have witnesses now who will testify against Le-Bruin."

Abbercombe lifted his head to stare at her.

"Have you nothing at all to say, your grace?"

"You might all have been killed."

"But we are not," April piped up. "Oh! Your coat! There is blood all over it!"

"Abbercombe!" Olivia cried, her senses returning rapidly. "The wound in your shoulder has torn open!"

"Do not fuss. Robin will close it up again."

"Fetch linen, Olivia," Sebastian ordered as he sailed into the kitchen. "Jess, help Cash doff his coat. April, ask Lindner to send my coach 'round at once. We are going home."

The scene as Sebastian Denbigh's coach entered the courtyard at Fielding House was nightmarish but the battle was winding to a close. Mr. Stanton approached the vehicle and stammered out as much of the tale as he knew. The duke's weary head lifted from Sebastian's shoulder; his muddied shoe kicked the carriage door open; he jumped to the cobbles and dashed into the house. Olivia hurried after him. The children, she thought. He fears for the children.

"Abbercombe," she cried, catching his sleeve. "Sit there on the bench. I shall find them." Without awaiting an answer, she dashed up to the second floor. She had seen Amy and Beth and Daymee and Chris close by Lady Vale in the courtyard, though she doubted Abbercombe had. So room by room she searched only for the four youngest, calling their names loudly. Finding none of them on the second floor, she descended to the first. Terror began to dog her heels as first one room and then the next proved empty. If something terrible has happened to his children, what will he do? "Ethan!" she shouted. "Frazier! Gracie! Helen!" Abandoning the first floor she swept again down the stairs, but the hem of her gown caught upon her slipper and sent her tumbling. She might have screamed but no sooner did she realize that she was airborne, than a pair of arms caught her and settled her gently to the floor.

"Are you all right, Olivia?"

She looked fearfully up into the duke's sweet, weary face. "Abbercombe, I cannot find the children!"

"Answer me first," the duke murmured, bringing his lips close to her ear as he pulled her gently against him. "Are you hurt? Is your ankle twisted? Can you move your arm? You hit it against the rail, you know."

"No, no, I did not realize. I am not hurt. But I cannot find the little ones!"

"You have not tried this floor, Olivia. If you are sure you are all right, we shall seek them together."

Olivia nodded and he released her from his embrace, then took her hand in his and led her down the ground floor hallway checking into one room after another until at last he reached the Children's Den. He opened the door. Olivia heard a scuffling and Bear squirmed from beneath closed draperies and bounded barking happily to the duke's feet followed immediately by a scurrying Frazier yelling, "Papa!" who flung himself with abandon into the duke's arms. As Abbercombe knelt to catch him up, Ethan popped from behind the old fainting couch; Helen threw open the doors of a discarded armoire and scrambled down; and Gracie lifted the lid of a badly battered trunk and climbed joyously out. Cries of "Papa! Papa!" filled the chamber and wiggling, ecstatic children clung to the duke and all but knocked him to the floor. Bear danced merrily, attacking heels and ankles and knees, and Olivia, relief plain upon her face, watched Abbercombe kiss one child after the other.

When at last they grew calm in the safety of his arms, he tugged Olivia down beside them. "I am proud of all of you," he said in his quiet voice. "You are all very brave and did exactly the right thing."

"Is't a war, Papa?" Ethan asked. "We din't never have a war right in our own yard afore."

"We couldn't fine Robin," Frazier added.

"Ebrybody wased gone," squeaked Gracie.

"We hided," chirped Helen, "like we does from Cap'n Crooked."

"Indeed, and there are no better hiders in the whole world," Abbercombe grinned. "Can you not say hello to Miss Olivia? She has been searching for you all over the house."

With shy little smiles the intrepid brood of Denbighs tried to bow and curtsy properly, but all of them were much to wiggly to get the things right which made Olivia wish to do nothing more than hug them as hard as she was able. Helen's slippers were on the wrong feet, Gracie's dress backwards, and the boys missing stockings and coats, which only made them more endearing. "Were you asleep," she asked, "when the noise started?"

"Uh-huh," nodded Helen, rubbing her eyes with a tiny fist. "Bear hided unner Frazier's bed."

"She did?"

"Uh-huh, an' me an' Gracie runned as fas' as we could to look out the winnow."

"Papa," Ethan gasped, "you are all bloody!"

Olivia saw that the linen she and Denbigh had bound so tightly about the duke's shoulder had not stopped the bleeding.

The duke grinned, pulling the boy back into his arms. "It is from where the footpads shot me. Remember, I told you all about the footpads? Robin and Aunt Margaret will make it all better."

The little boy nodded gravely. Olivia saw that the other children had grown sober as well and regarded their father with anxious eyes. Of course his shoulder bleeds, she thought. He caught me as I tripped and then he caught up each of these little ones and distressed the injury farther.

"Do not look so solemn, you gudgeons," Abbercombe drawled. "I am not about to die. I am messy is all and Robin will be most upset with me, will he not?"

"Y-yes, Papa," murmured Frazier, easing himself into the circle of his father's arms next to Ethan. "He will be roarin' angry, won' he be?" One very small finger reached out hesitantly to touch the ugly wet stain.

"Enough of these long faces!" Abbercombe stood and scooped Helen and Gracie into his arms. "Time to discover who has been making a battlefield of our very own yard."

Fifteen

The double drawing room on the first floor of Fielding House was the only chamber large enough to hold all the combatants from the battle. The duke, still carrying Helen and Grace, and Olivia, her hands held tightly by Ethan and Frazier, came to a halt in the doorway and gazed about in dismay.

Bear raced between the duke's legs and barreled straight for the blue and gold striped sofa, landing full force upon the gentleman who lay there. "Oof," groaned Brummell as the air was pushed out of him. Then there was the sound of snarling and claws and teeth scrabbled at his waistcoat buttons. "Damnation!" he shouted, obviously unaware of the fact that there were ladies present. He sat part way up and tried to prise the spirited animal from his garments. Bear clung determinedly, loosing one grip and replacing it with another until Brummell fell back laughing uproariously, blood streaming from his nose. "Abbercombe!" he shouted. "If you are anywhere within my reach, run, for I shall pummel the life out of you for this!"

"For what, brat?" Abbercombe asked, sitting upon the long, low, table before the couch, setting Grace upon one knee and Helen upon the other.

"Where the deuce have you been? For teaching this animal to chew my waistcoats! Get it off!"

"But Bear lites you," murmured Helen in a confused little voice, " 'cause you are wearin' her favoritest kine of white thin' with shiny buttonings. Does you know your nose is all bloody?"

"My papa's sholdier is bloody, too." Gracie said in somber tones. "He promised us not to die. You willn't die, will you?"

"Oh, no, my lady," the Beau replied, noting the anxiety on both piquant little faces. "I shall not die. You have my word."

"Good," sighed Abbercombe, Grace, and Helen all together, and that made the girls grin.

"Just how many beautiful daughters do you intend to foist upon society?" Brummell demanded, swiping at his nose with one hand and the puppy with the other. "Are not two enough? And I suppose these are as independent and beguiling as their sisters."

"Well, not yet, brat," Abbercombe smiled, "but they are only six after all." He set Grace and Helen upon the floor and detached Bear from Brummell's waistcoat. "This is Mr. Brummell, my dears, who came to dinner one night when you were fast asleep. And I do believe he took part in our war. Did you not, sir?"

"Yes," grinned Brummell, "I do believe I did."

"Don' be 'fraid," Helen soothed, her soft little hand patting the Beau's brow. Gracie crawled up beside him and planted a wet kiss upon his cheek. "We will maked you all bedder."

"I leave you in capable hands," Abbercombe declared. "You shall rise again. I am convinced of it." He stepped across the table, bent low to whisper in Ethan's and Frazier's ears, then straightened and took Olivia's hand. "I expect we ought to see what we can do to help. I do not recognize half of these people."

At length, after assuring himself that none of the combatants was gravely injured, that his older children were unharmed, and that Ethan and Frazier had gotten the correct bottles of wine and were pouring everyone a glass who desired it, the duke submitted to having his own shoulder tended and allowed himself to be ensconced in a chaise longue near the fire. From there he offered his gratitude to Lord Merriville and Lord Bacon and their men, who confessed they had not had so much excitement in years and wondered why they hadn't thought of pitching a battle in their own courtyards. Once that contingent, a bit bruised and battered but unquestionably rhapsodic, had departed and the majority of the Fielding House staff had gone back to their quarters, the rest of the party proved small enough to gather into the half of the drawing room where the duke sat and Brummell remained reclining upon the sofa, not daring to move for fear of waking the two little girls nestled in his arms.

"Now," said the duke in sober tones, his gaze roaming about the room, "I desire an explanation. Worth?"

"What?" Worth responded, a smile twitching at his lips.

"Why the deuce were you wandering about my yard in the middle of the night?"

"Two attempts on your life, rogue. Brummell and I set ourselves up to catch anyone who trespassed and we did."

"And the gentlemen you caught are—?"

"Well, I grant you they are not the ones we sought, Cash, but it was a damned—excuse me—a regrettable mistake. This is Mr. Elijah Stone," Worth added with a nod at the nondescript, middle-aged gentleman with a black eye and a bandage round his head. "And the others are his associates. I hired them to keep watch over you and discover who—" Worth did not finish the sentence, the presence of Abbercombe's children silencing him. "At any rate, they could not do so until the beginning of the week, so Brummell and I agreed to stand watch tonight."

"Well, an' didn't I tell you as 'ow we'd be doin' our bes' ta draw t'other job ta a close, an' git 'ere as soon as what we could?" grumbled Mr. Stone. "An' that we did. Closed t'other, I mean, an' come straight 'ere."

"Aye," sighed a burly young man with his arm in a hurriedly fashioned sling. "An' look what i' got us."

Abbercombe's solemn scowl began to unravel, but he clung to the look as best he could. "Am I to understand that two groups of people, both concerned for my welfare, attacked each other?"

"Three, Papa," murmured Christian hesitantly from where he and Damian sat on the floor before the fire with Ethan and Frazier and the puppy all asleep in their laps. "We, ah, Daymee and I, I mean. We, ah, were watching for trespassers as well."

"I saw them the night you were attacked—when Mr. Brummell brought you home," Damian offered. "And Ethan and Frazier kept seeing people in the courtyard even after that. They could, you know, from their bedroom windows."

"Yes, so we thought to discover who they were," chimed in Amy to keep her brothers from accepting all the blame.

"We only meant to get a good look at them, Papa, not to start a war," added Beth. "That is why Amy tossed her charm across the cobbles, so John would give us the coach lights to seek it and we might see if anyone were hidden in the bushes."

"They were to shout if anyone came after them, Papa, and Daymee and I were to hurl stones upon the attackers from the portico roof so the girls could safely escape."

"We had our slingshots," added Damian lamely, knowing from the look in his father's eyes that they were all in trouble.

Robin, who also recognized the look, attempted to rescue the crew. "The boys confided in me directly they discovered there were at least seven of them, your grace. They were not so foolish that they thought to protect the girls from so many by themselves. I took your small sword out with me to stand guard."

"None of it would have happened," sighed Amy, "if that gentleman there had not moved so suddenly when my light shone upon him, for John saw him and shot at him with his pistol."

"Yer grace said as I was to keep the thin' with me," stuttered John. "An' this face popped inta the light, an' I was that surprised, ye know, that I shot the thin'."

"Aye, an' 'it me toe," grumbled another of Stone's associates. "An' I lets out a howl coulda waked the dead. An' of a sudden these stones come a whizzin' down at us, and these two nobs come a runnin' wif swords drawn—swords, by gawd!—an' that one, he comes 'roun' the house wif a stubby little sticker!"

"Yes, Cash, and having heard the commotion, Dawson rushed immediately to the girls' aid," Lady Vale continued. "And happily Mr. Stanton thought of carrying more light into the yard so that Robin and Dawson and John should not accidentally kill each other. I did try to warn John that it was Mr.

Brummell whose cork he was about to draw for I recognized him at the last, but I am afraid John did not hear me."

"No, ma'am," John groaned, "or fer sure I'da stopped."

"And then Merriville and Bacon turned up with their men," muttered Worth, "and the whole thing got quite out of hand."

"I am amazed none of you are dead," growled the duke, his exasperated gaze focussing upon Amy, Beth, Chris and Daymee. "Of all the cork-brained plans I have ever heard! You might have killed someone! Do you wish to become murderers? Would you be pleased to see Worth or Brummell or Mr. Stone lying dead at your feet and it all your fault?"

"Stop," interrupted Olivia from her seat beside Lady Jess on the small settee, "you go too far, Abbercombe. Your children only thought to protect you. Lord Worth and Mr. Brummell and all the rest made their own judgements in the matter. It would never have been the children's fault had someone been gravely injured."

"You, madam," scowled the duke, "have little room to speak, having already brought Harcort close to an early grave. I suggest that you keep your opinion to yourself."

"Cash!" cried Lady Jess, seeing a fire light in Olivia's eyes. "That was uncalled for. Olivia only sees that you have gone too far. You are unjust to the boys and to Amy and Beth."

"Justice is not the issue," Abbercombe responded with suppressed anger. "Lives are."

"And it was your life for which they feared," declared Olivia roundly, her hands becoming fists in the confines of her lap. "Just as did Harcort, Kettering, April and I."

"Madam, I am fully cognizant of that. It does not excuse their thoughtlessness nor lessen their responsibility."

"You know," Brummell murmured, hoping not to awaken the babes in his custody, "everything was our fault—Worth's and mine. No one would have been in the yard at all if not for us."

"Exactly so!" declared Olivia, rising, "but his grace is too pigheaded to admit it."

"Do not, Olivia," said Lady Vale coming to stand beside her. "You do not fully understand."

"I understand that he should be on his knees thanking God that he has children and friends who care so much for him!"

Abbercombe rose slowly from the chaise longue and confronted Olivia with eyes smouldering. "If you should ever find yourself mistress of this establishment, Miss Willburton-Smythe," he said very softly and with obvious restraint, "your opinion shall be considered in all things. Until then, I have no longing to be made aware of it. Christian, Damian, take your brothers to bed and yourselves as well. We will discuss this further on the morrow. Amaryllis, Bethany, do likewise with your sisters and yourselves. It is near three o'clock in the morning and not a time for discussing what shall be done with you."

Silently his children did the duke's bidding. "I am exhausted, 'Bastian," Abbercombe growled when they had gone. "Play host for me. I have had quite enough for one night." With a curt bow to no one in particular, he exited the chamber.

"We have done it now," muttered Worth. "I have never seen the rogue so angry. What did he mean, Miss Olivia, about your almost bringing Harcort to an early grave?"

It was the following afternoon that Captain Giles Dunleavy, his weather-creased countenance betraying disbelief, eyed Hempstead in silence. He pushed his chair back from the table they occupied at the rear of the public room of Captain Mason's Inn in High Street and filled his meerschaum pipe. "What's your name, boy?" he asked, setting the tobacco alight.

"Hempstead, sir. Geoffery Hempstead."

"An' you say The Rogue's cargo awaits the tide at Alderney on the twenty-eighth?"

"Yes, sir."

"And did he by chance mention where he expected this cargo to be off-loaded?" The older man puffed on the pipe, his narrow grey eyes fastened suspiciously on Hempstead.

"No, sir," Hempstead responded, wondering why the question of off-loading had not occurred to him. "He did not say, and I did not think to ask. Perhaps he thought you already knew."

Dunleavy crossed one leg over the other and pushed his cap farther back on his head. "You spoke with him when? Last night?"

"Yes, sir."

Captain Dunleavy sighed and puffed thoughtfully. "Come with me," he ordered at last, rising. "There is obviously information I lack. It may lie upon the *Peregrine*." Together they left the inn, crossed the quay and boarded a small skiff in which Dunleavy rowed them out to the schooner.

Hempstead found himself extremely uncomfortable. He had never in his life been upon the water in any sort of boat at all and the skiff seemed slight protection against the cold English Channel. The moment he stood in the rocking skiff to reach out toward the *Peregrine*'s rope ladder his face grew pale and he began to perspire.

Dunleavy chuckled around his pipe stem. "Just grab hold, boy, and step up. She'll not toss ye into the brine, I promise ye. She's a diamond of the first water, *Peregrine* is."

Hempstead only grunted in response and swung himself on to the ladder. It was harder to climb than he had imagined. In the end, the captain tied off the skiff and climbed the ladder behind him, holding him steady most of the way and boosting him over *Peregrine*'s rail. By the time Hempstead's boots touched the deck, Captain Dunleavy was laughing aloud. Hempstead would have requested him to cease his levity, but he was sweating profusely, growing exceedingly dizzy and striving with all his might not to cast up his accounts.

"Ye're turning green, lad," Dunleavy observed merrily. "By gawd, I have not seen such a rapid approach of the seasickness in my life. Tell me, why does The Rogue send me to Alderney? 'Tis no one to overhear us here."

Hempstead groaned and hung his head over the rail. When he straightened again he felt slightly better. "Because he has hired free-traders to carry his cargo—" Hempstead flung himself once more at the rail.

Dunleavy stood puffing upon the pipe, his eyes twinkling.

"Have you no sympathy?" groaned Hempstead.

"None," grinned the Captain. "The Rogue claims it is because I have never suffered the seasickness. Who carries the cargo and where does he load it?"

"Huh?" asked Hempstead clutching the rail.

"Who is to pick up The Rogue's cargo and where?"

"I—I do not think I am supposed to—"

"You may tell me, boy. I have known The Rogue these past fifteen years. It is your face I do not know."

"Yes, but—Marseilles," Hempstead groaned, lurching over the rail once again. "Pendleton and Saukill."

"Come below," growled Dunleavy, a worn hand grasping Hempstead's shoulder. "You'll have a bit of The Rogue's elixir and a lie down, and the dizziness will cease."

"It will?" Hempstead did not believe a bit of it.

"Aye, lad. Works famously it does—for everyone but The Rogue. Never seen a worse sailor than The Rogue."

Several hours later Hempstead woke in the captain's bunk feeling a great deal better to discover Dunleavy comfortably ensconced in a chair, a chart on the table before him. For a few minutes Hempstead was afraid to move, but slowly he tested a bit of movement and found himself only a bit groggy.

"Awake, are ye?" asked Dunleavy. "At least ye are not green anymore, my boy."

"Was I actually green?" Hempstead asked sitting up.

"Aye, but ye're looking as though ye've got yer sea legs at last. Come over here and have a seat. There's words I wish to have with ye before we return to the High Street."

Hempstead stood, wobbled a moment and then found that he was indeed able to cross to a chair by the table without encountering the terrible dizziness. "Whew, that's a deal better!" he exclaimed. "I thought for a moment I was like to die."

"Had you said the free-traders were to load the cargo anywhere but Marseilles, Mr. Hempstead, you very likely would have, but not from the seasickness."

Hempstead's eyebrows rose questioningly. "Was that part of what I should have said at first? No, I am sure he never told me to pass that on to you."

Captain Dunleavy rubbed his hand across a stubbly chin and grinned. "He knew I would ask. It is the only acceptable answer. It is not the correct answer, mind you, but that's what makes it so acceptable. If a man knew The Rogue's business and were guessing at the port, he'd never guess Marseilles. Likely as not The Rogue's right to pay Pendleton to do't. The whole Frog navy knows *Peregrine* since our last little escapade. You're to take The Rogue's place, are ye, lad? And ride along to help us load? Look here, boy, and I'll show ye where we're bound."

April sighed with relief as Amy and Beth entered their Aunt Jess's drawing room the next day. Lady Vale urged all three girls off into a corner the moment she spied Olivia seated beside Lady Jess. "I have something of importance to discuss," she said in a tone that brooked no argument, "and it is not fit for young ears." With that she settled into a chair between Jessica and Olivia, accepted a small glass of wine, and waited for the girls to become engaged in a conversation of their own.

"I am so relieved that you are all right," whispered April as the girls settled upon a couch at the far corner of the room.

"We are fine," grinned Amy. "Why should we not be?"

"Your Papa was so angry with you last night that I thought he would do something dreadful."

"Like what?" asked Beth innocently.

"I thought, perhaps, he might lock you in your rooms and not allow you out for a week!"

"Well, he did something almost as terrible," sighed Amy, fiddling with a pretty lavender bow in her hair. "He made us all eat breakfast in silence while Ethan and Frazier took turns reading from the Reverend Mr. Smithson's *Meditations on the Foibles of*

Youth. And then he sent us to apologize to all of the staff and to Lord Merriville and Lord Bacon and their staffs as well."

"And insisted that we write Lord Worth and Mr. Brummell, thanking them for their kindness and apologizing for our lack of forethought in drawing them into such an outrageous situation," added Beth. "But having to listen to Ethan and Frazier read from that dreadful book was truly the worst."

"No," Amy shook her head, "the worst was seeing Papa so upset. Even this morning he could not hide his anxiety. We shall have to be more discreet next time we do anything of the sort."

"Next time?" April squeaked. "You would never do such a thing again?"

"Well, only if it should become necessary," Beth replied calmly. "But enough—you must tell us what it was you did, for Papa grumbled all morning about the terrible chance that you and Miss Olivia and Kettering and Harcort took last night. And Lord Sinclair of the War Office came to see him this morning."

Across the drawing room Lady Vale's fingers played unconsciously with a fine lawn handkerchief, and Olivia could see that the dowager trembled and her usually sharp, dark eyes seemed clouded. "It was not—not unforgivable," murmured the dowager. "I know you think it was, Olivia, but that is what I wish to explain to you. The children do not hold him accountable. And you must forgive him as well. He did not intend to respond in such a way to your—"

"Interference?" asked Olivia indignantly. "If I were ever to be mistress of his establishment indeed! The gall of the man!"

Lady Vale sighed. "No, I will not see him hurt himself again. I do not care what I promised Wyndham all those years ago." Noting the curious expressions confronting her at those words, the dowager's eyes flashed and she came to a decision. "You must neither of you repeat what I say to you now. Not even to Sebastian, Jessica. I must have your word on it."

Both of the young women agreed immediately.

"Good, then listen closely, for I will not speak of it again." The elderly lady sat up very straight and looked from one to the other of them with a steady gaze. "Have either of you the least idea why Cash was transported?"

"Because he killed a man," Olivia answered quietly, aware that the duke's daughters sat just across the room.

"He killed no one. He was accused of the murder of Channing Kettering, who would have been Earl of Stamford had he lived. But he was innocent of the deed.

"Cash loved Channing. They had been friends for years. But— but something dreadful happened," sighed Lady Vale, twisting the handkerchief into knots. "Cash was never quite respectable, you know, and he often did things that were—dangerous. Well, he had taken to hanging about in Seven Dials, and one night the crowd there invited him to share some opium. He did, thought it intriguing and later gave some to Channing. From that day, Channing craved the drug. The two battled often over it. Once Cash even brought him to our estate in Somerset and with Vale's help kept him from the drug for almost two months, but when they returned to London, Channing returned to the opium.

"And then Cash learned that Channing had lured the daughter of a friend from her home—Miss Wentworth, she was—and he stormed after them, and discovered them in the back room of some disgusting pub. The poor girl was hysterical. Channing was drugged and attempting to ravage her. Well, Cash fought to protect her. But at some point, Channing began to pound Cash's head bloody against the floor and would not stop, and the girl fearing for Cash's life, struck Channing in the head with a brass candlestick. Channing was mortally wounded. He begged Cash to keep the secret of his addiction from his family and to hide the horror of his intentions toward Miss Wentworth as well and Cash gave his word. He swept the girl from the premises and returned her to her father's house.

"Cash was arrested on his return to London, put in chains and tossed into Newgate. Only his godfather, Lord Wyndham, and King George, himself, were allowed to speak with him before he was brought to the docket. They both swore silence and learned the entire story, but neither would repeat it at the trial, because they had pledged their words not to do so."

"But this Miss Wentworth must have come forward," declared Olivia. "She could not have been so heartless as to—"

"Her father came to the trial, so I imagine she told him what had happened," sighed Lady Vale. "But Cash would not allow the man to speak on his behalf. He said that Channing's death belonged on his own head and it would be the sheerest folly to ruin an innocent. Besides, he had promised Channing and how could he explain without betraying his word?"

"There must have been something, some way—" gasped Olivia.

"No, not then. Cash would have hung at Tyburn had he been anything less than the heir to a dukedom. And the truth is, my dears, that Cash felt himself guilty—because he had introduced Channing to the opium and could not separate him from it, and because he chose to brawl with Channing instead of discovering another way to save Miss Wentworth." Lady Vale stared down at the smooth folds of her cream linen dress and at the mangled handkerchief in her lap. She shook her head silently then looked up at Jess and Olivia. "When the children's plan went so awry last night, I am certain all the horror of Channing's death came back to him, and he was overwhelmed with fear that the children might be responsible for a friend's death and suffer as he still does. He cannot see the thing clearly to this day. He only feels his own guilt and will not acknowledge any of Channing's."

Olivia and Jess sat back, stupefied. "And no one knows of this?" Olivia asked finally. "No one but you and Lord Wyndham?"

"And the king. Farmer George was not mad, then, you know, and was extremely fond of Cash. It was the king thought of a way to raise the boy's spirits when he was deported. He made him a special agent for the crown."

"A spy?" Olivia gasped.

"For the crown?" Lady Jessica whispered.

"He has been so now for over twenty years. You remember

you have both given your word that you will not speak to anyone of this?"

"Of course we shall not tell," exclaimed Lady Jess. "Only someone must have confided in his father, at least, or Celia!"

"Not then," replied the dowager with a grim tightening of her lips. "Worth suspected the truth. And I think that several years afterward Cash confided in Celia as he did in me. She followed him, you know. No one who knew her could believe it. But she stood by him through the trial and when he was exiled, booked passage on another vessel as soon as she could do so. But you can see, can you not, how threatened he was by the situation last night and how he could be so terribly upset by it?"

Both of the ladies nodded. Olivia, extremely uncomfortable, rose abruptly and took a turn about the room. "Why have you told us this?" she asked Lady Vale as she returned to her seat. "If it has been a secret so very long and kept from his father and brother and best friends, why do you speak of it now?"

The dowager studied Olivia's face intently. "He lost his mother the day he was born, and his father's love that very moment. He lost his brother and his home and his country. I could not bear to see him lose you, my dear. I thought if I explained at least a bit, you might find it in your heart to forgive him."

"He is in love with you," added Lady Jess. "I have suspected it for a number of weeks."

"Love? He is in love with me? Oh! Both your attics are to let!" declared Olivia in a hoarse whisper, remembering the moonlight and the balcony and the duke's lips pressed passionately against her own and wishing that he did indeed love her. "I can understand now his attitude toward the children last evening, and I will forgive him that, but to address me as madam in that condescending tone and then to invite me to keep my opinions to myself! Well, I might call that a good many things, but certainly not love."

The dowager's lips formed a slow smile. "He is always most ambivalent in the presence of those whose esteem he desires most. It is a provoking mannerism, but the more unsure he becomes, the more stubborn and unreasonable he sounds. I did not realize how very much he valued you and your opinion, Olivia, until he invited you to keep it to yourself. Please try to forgive him, my dear. I assure you he is even now flogging himself for the treachery of his ungovernable tongue."

"Very well, Lady Vale," murmured Olivia. "Though I am positive that I shall never understand the man!"

"Living with Papa is very hard," Amaryllis conceded to April as the conversation at the other end of the room continued. "He is the kindest, gentlest man alive, but when he is in such a state as last night, there is no turning him up sweet."

"He is extremely pigheaded at times," sighed Beth, "just as your aunt said."

"Oh," choked April, "I do not believe I was ever more mortified than to hear her call him so."

"Mama would have said exactly the same," Beth assured her. "At least, she would have had he been raving about anything else but responsibility for other people's lives. Even she would not have confronted him on that. It is better to remain silent and leave immediately he has finished. One cannot deal with him logically once anything has brought the matter to his mind."

"Brought what to mind?"

"Channing Kettering's death," mumbled Bethany, looking across the room to be sure the older ladies were not listening. Seeing them engaged in some deep conversation of their own, she continued. "That was what angered him so last night. He was remembering, you see, how Channing Kettering died in a brangle, though not so big a one as ours."

"It puts him all out of patience with himself to remember even a bit of it," nodded Amy, "and that is why he growled so at us. I do wish he had waited until everyone had gone. I felt so sorry for him. You could see he knew he went too far but could not stop himself. He was more humiliated with each word he said and did not have the least idea how to keep from saying them."

Sixteen

Worth sprawled inelegantly in one of the wing chairs in Abbercombe's study. "Cash," he drawled languidly, "may I ask your intentions regarding that figurine?"

"Why?" Abbercombe mumbled as he paced the room, juggling a little china shepherdess.

"Because I should like to be out of range if you throw it."

"Oh, I am not about to toss the thing at you, Worth."

"No?"

"Not at all, though I may put it through a casement window."

Worth noted with singular trepidation that one of the casements stood directly over his left shoulder. "Ought to sit down," he commented tersely. "Need to rest after last night."

"Do not mention last night," growled the duke. "It is not in your best interests to do so."

Worth shrugged. "Have you had the children annihilated?"

Abbercombe's frown quivered at the edges.

"I mean to say, Cash, no one assaulted me when I came in, not even that wretched puppy. And this door has been closed for over an hour without once being scratched upon."

"Amy and Beth and Aunt Margaret have gone to Sebastian's, and the rest are keeping a low profile. I expect I am the recipient of their pity." He set the figurine back on the mantle. "Is that not the ugliest piece you have ever seen, Edward?"

"Well, the ugliest shepherdess. Did you choose it?"

Abbercombe's frown quivered even more. "I am not the only person sometimes grows attached to ugly things."

"True, but you do grow attached to so many of them."

"It was Celia's. Bought it in a shop in Boston the day she landed. Sauntered down the gang plank, gave me a kiss, tossed a bandbox into my hands, told me I looked a veritable chawbacons, and then walked into a shop and came out with that travesty, and it has travelled with us ever since. Never cracks, never chips, never comes anywhere near disaster."

"Came very near a few moments ago."

"Do you think I have sunk myself with Olivia completely?"

Worth chuckled. "Sit down, you ninny. You are giving me a stiff neck from having to stare up at you."

Abbercombe slouched into the matching chair, almost but not quite banging the arm Fanning had again captured in a sling. "Well, do you?"

"Considering all you have told me, I expect it would take more than your considerable pigheadedness to sink you with her. I think the lady is in love with you, Cash. And ladies in love will forgive a man a great deal. What about LeBruin? He responsible for the two previous attempts on your life, do you think?"

Abbercombe tapped his fingers against the chair arm and sighed. "Dash it all, Edward, I do not think it likely. We have both been hunting Captain Willburton-Smythe, and it was greatly to LeBruin's advantage to keep me alive and doing his work for him. It was only when he thought I had discovered the gentleman's whereabouts that he found me no longer necessary."

Worth's eyebrows rose questioningly. "Then the gentleman at the rear of the conservatory was not in LeBruin's employ?"

"I suspect someone overheard Olivia and LeBruin and expected to find me in the conservatory ripe for the picking. Which brings to mind—must I suffer Stone's associates all over the place? There is a new footman in my employ, Edward, seven foot tall and fifteen stone, I swear; and a tiny fellow in the stables Gracie will know is a leprechaun; and a young woman who pretends to substitute for Beth's abigail, and has the hands of a strangler and a visage to match. Not that they are not all delightful people, but must there be bodyguards everywhere I step?"

"You were not meant to notice them," Worth chuckled.

"Not notice them? Lord, a blind man must notice them!"

"Elijah Stone is excellent at what he does, Cash, and he will discover who has been taking shots at you. But until he does I fear you must suffer the guardianship of his associates. At the very least they will assure the children's safety."

"I suppose I shall grow accustomed. But if they get in my way, Edward, I warn you, I shall lose the lot of them. Do you really think Olivia is in love with me?"

Olivia returned from the Denbighs' unaccountably perplexed. She and April had shared the information they had gathered all the way home, and though April was inclined to forgive the duke his outbreak of the evening before, he had not, after all, thrown his ill-tempered barbs at her. No one had ever before spoken to Olivia so. To Abbercombe, it appeared, she was an interfering busybody whose help and opinions were unappreciated— worse—despised. Had he not told her as much in the museum when first they met? And now he had told her again.

She had doffed her cloak and settled herself in the drawing room with her embroidery, but she had yet to ply her needle even once. Oh, it was well enough for Lady Vale to be supposing that the duke's vitriolic outburst was the result of his previous and admittedly horrifying experiences, and for his children to accept them as such, but why had he chosen to flail her with his caustic tongue? Because he despised her, that was why. Had she been the only one to take the children's part? No, Fanning had done the same as had Brummell, but Abbercombe's wrath had not come down upon them. There was something about her in particular, she concluded, a tear forming at the corner of one eye, that attracted Abbercombe's rage.

Angrily she jabbed the point of her needle into the pretty linen on her frame. And of all the stupid things—for Jessica to say that Abbercombe was in love with her. It was ridiculous. No gentleman had ever been in love with her. Never in her entire life. "Nor do I wish for any gentleman to be," she grumbled, drawing a bright red stitch to an end and beginning another. "And especially not his pigheaded, unfathomable, ungrateful, wretched grace."

April peeked around the door frame. She had changed into a lovely orange carriage dress with a matching deep poke bonnet. "Lord Redvers awaits me downstairs, Aunt Olivia," she announced with a smile. "You have not forgotten that we go to visit the farm at Green Park with Miss Canning and Mr. Anges?"

"No, no, go ahead, darling. You will enjoy it. Mrs. Searle, who is in charge, is Mr. Brummell's aunt. She is most charming in her milkmaid costume and her courtliness most intriguing. You will not wonder that she has always been a favourite of King George."

The thought of King George sent her off again. Abbercombe, a favourite of the King! How appropriate, she told herself, jabbing the needle again into the linen. They are both of them lunatics! It was the memory of Abbercombe's arm about her on the balcony and his lips pressed so gently and then so hungrily against hers that brought another tear to her eye. Oh! That she had been such an imbecile as to kiss him back! Such a man—a spy for the crown—must be in the habit of taking advantage of unwary females. And besides, she told herself with a great deal of asperity, he is an old man, a widower with eight children. What could any lady of Quality find alluring about him? Oh, he was still ruggedly handsome, but he was already forty-five and fairly soon would shrivel into wrinkles and mush!

Olivia set her embroidery upon her lap and tucked her needle safely into it. What was she doing? She had never lied to herself before. Even when it had become clear that her dreams were not to be fulfilled, that there was not to be a marriage and a home and children in her future, she had not lied to herself. She had accepted the fact and gone on, making herself useful to her sister-in-law and her brother and niece. Yet here she sat telling herself lie after lie after lie, all because—because—she cared so deeply for Abbercombe with his silly grin, and his incredible eyes, and his heart which anyone would know overflowed with courage and honor and love if they only took the time to discover it. "Very well," she sniffed, dashing at a tear with the back of her hand, "I have fallen in love. But he does not love me, so I shall just have to get over him."

With a grim little smile she set aside her needlework and took herself to the library to find a book that might distract her from thoughts of the duke. She settled upon *Castle Rackrent* and became so absorbed that she did not notice the darkening sky beyond her window until Laslow appeared.

"Ma'am?"

"Yes, Laslow?"

"There is a messenger belowstairs who wears the Earl of Stamford's livery and begs to deliver a note directly into your hands. Shall I send him to you?"

"I will come down, Laslow. Thank you." She marked her place in the book with a long silver riband and nodded to a young man who stepped in to light the candles and lay the fire. "Do you perchance know the time, Donald?"

"Yes, ma'am, 'tis seven o'clock."

"Already? My goodness." She made her way gracefully down the staircase and stepped into a small antechamber where a swarthy footman dressed in the deep scarlet and black of the Stamfords bowed before her and handed a screw of paper into her hands. Olivia thought it odd that the message should be written so informally. She scanned the writing. When she looked back up into the footman's face, her own countenance had paled. "This comes from the earl, himself?"

"Yes, ma'am. His coach waits to take you to Stamford House."

"Go, wait for me at the coach. I shall be with you directly." Olivia fled into the hall. "Laslow, my cloak, please. Miss April has had an accident and Lord Stamford was kind enough to carry her to his own home. You must tell Camber to set back dinner. I do not know when I shall return."

"Yes, ma'am," replied the butler. "Shall I send to the stable for the carriage?"

"No, no, Stamford's coach awaits me. I shall send you word, Laslow, as soon as I know how badly my darling is injured. Perhaps we will require Dr. Howard—"

"I shall send Donald if necessary, ma'am. You must go," urged Laslow, and he escorted her all the way to the waiting vehicle and helped her inside. He noted with some consternation that the earl's coachman was the same Clive Peesby whom he had himself discharged from Miss Willburton-Smythe's employ three years before, nodded awkwardly to the man, and watched the horses step out onto the avenue.

Alone in the comfortably upholstered vehicle, Olivia fidgeted. With the earl's burly coachman up top and his footman behind, the coach should have flown through the dusk, but instead it stuttered and stumbled through the crowded streets coming to long stops in the traffic three times before they reached the Stamford manor on Green Street. The footman lowered the steps and helped her down. The earl's butler stood with the door wide, and fearfully Olivia hurried up the front steps.

"Wh-where is my niece? Is she badly injured? Has a physician been summoned?"

"If you will follow me, madam," murmured the butler, and preceded Olivia slowly up the staircase and down the first floor hallway. With great show, the man slid a set of double doors aside and announced "Miss Willburton-Smythe, my lord."

Olivia swept hastily into the brightly lit room as the double doors slid closed behind her.

Laslow answered the knocker at Park Street and stared open-mouthed at April who was saying a very proper goodbye to Lord Redvers. "Miss—Miss April. You are all right?"

"Well, of course I am all right, Laslow. I have only been to Green Park after all. Is Aunt Olivia upset? Has she had to set dinner back? It was Miss Canning, you see. She grew faint outside the little house and Mrs. Searle took her inside to sit a while. We did not like to leave her and Mr. Anges there alone, you know, so we waited until she felt more the thing. Laslow? Why do you stare at me so? Is Aunt Olivia in the drawing room?"

"No, miss. Your aunt is not at home."

"Not at home?"

"No, miss. She has gone to visit the Earl of Stamford."

"But Aunt Olivia barely knows the Earl of Stamford. Why would she go to pay him a call?"

"I am sure I do not know, miss," Laslow informed her flatly.

"I shall go up and dress for dinner so I do not keep her waiting. Will you send me word as soon as she arrives?"

"Indeed, miss," Laslow nodded.

Olivia stared at the gentleman, nonplussed. Never before had she actually studied the Earl of Stamford and she was shocked at what she saw. His fine brown hair was touched at the temples with grey and, in opposition to the times, was kept long and tied at the back of his neck with a black velvet riband. His countenance was florid and puffy, and in places seemed to sag as if the skin had simply gone limp. Lines of dissipation creased his face and great dark hollows lay beneath his eyes. And his eyes, as he returned her stare, shone with a cold, dead light.

"Do not be distraught, dear lady," he drawled in a voice so unctuous that it made her wish to scrub herself clean. "You will join me for dinner and if all goes well, you will be most royally entertained."

"You cannot hold me here against my will."

"Oh, but I can, my dear. And I do. Only look," he murmured, indicating with a graceful sweep of his hand the small, intimate dinner that lay on the table before him. "We shall indulge ourselves in a small but elegant feast and drink to the devil's health, and when we have finished, why we shall prepare for old Nick's appearance. That you will certainly enjoy!"

Olivia turned her back upon the man and stalked again to the double doors. They were still locked. She pounded upon them until her fists ached, but the household was deaf to her summons.

"You are mad!" she exclaimed, spinning around to face him where he lounged at the head of the table. "I do not know why you speak of the devil. Are you a witch, sir, that you wish to make his acquaintance? And what has old Nick to do with me? You are quite 'round the bend and I must find help for you. Does no one care, my lord, that you have lost your mind?"

"Sit down!" Stamford roared, rising, and revealing to Olivia's revulsion a form much like a giant spider with a great bloated middle and stick thin legs.

"I shall be seated, sir, when I am ready," she hissed. "I am not your servant!"

"No," sneered Stamford, "you are his. But I shall make you mine, and he shall watch me do so, and then he shall die."

Olivia shuddered at the poison in his tone, but she was not some little miss just up from the country, and she would not be cowed by disgusting words and vague threats. "You shall make no use of me whatsoever," she declared roundly, her eyes burning into his. "Obviously you are demented and are to be pitied. What stupidity to set a trap for such a modest little mouse as I."

"You, my dear, are merely the bait," drawled Stamford.

"I do not understand a word of this!" said Olivia abruptly, with a stamp of her foot upon the ancient grey carpet. "Who is't you wish to catch with such bait as me?"

Stamford laughed and picked at his teeth with a fingernail. "Abbercombe," he whispered as he took the fingernail away. "Abbercombe, my dear. That devil will come for you. I am certain of it. I have left him a clear trail to follow."

It was almost nine o'clock when Abbercombe finished telling one of the more nefarious adventures of Cap'n Crooked to an enthralled audience, then with the help of Amaryllis and Bethany tucked the tiniest members of his household safely into bed. Gracie giggled as he kissed her goodnight and patting his cheek informed him authoritatively that his face was tickly. Helen threw her arms around his neck and whispered in his ear that he was the bestest papa in the whole entire world even if he was fuzzy.

Ethan and Frazier, with Bear close on their heels, dashed into their own room and settled into bed with smiling faces. "Oh, no," Abbercombe drawled as he trailed in behind them. "May I suggest that one of you belongs under the bed and not upon it?" Sniggering, Frazier climbed from between the sheets and crawled under the big four poster. "No!" laughed his Papa, "Not you, scoundrel. I was referring to that puppy, and well you know it." With a good deal of giggling Amy and Beth tugged Frazier from beneath the bed and swept Bear from the counterpane. "Better," grinned Abbercombe. "I do not know how it is, but I cannot quite accustom myself to kissing Bear goodnight."

"Will you be all right, Papa?" Ethan asked, as Beth snuffed out the candles.

"I shall be fine, sir," replied the duke, making his way to the door, "and so shall all of you."

"Your grace," Dawson said, as the duke came into the hall.

"Yes, Dawson?"

"There is a man wishes to speak with you. I have asked him to wait in the front parlor."

"Who is it?" Abbercombe asked, strolling with the butler toward the stairs. "And why so grim, Anthony?"

"There is trouble, I think, your grace. It is Mr. Laslow, Miss Willburton-Smythe's butler."

"What, old sober-sides?"

They reached the ground floor and the duke swung into the front parlor to find Laslow with hands clasped behind his back, staring down into the fire. "Laslow? What can I do for you?"

"Your grace," Laslow turned to face the duke, and Abbercombe noticed that the stern face appeared older than last he'd seen it. The duke wandered across the room to a sidetable and poured three glasses of brandy from the decanter that rested there.

"You do not mind if Anthony joins us, do you, Laslow?"

"No, your grace. Thank you, your grace," Laslow nodded, taking the brandy from the duke's hand.

"Now, sit down, man, and tell me what it is I may do. Miss April has not run off—no, Hempstead is from town."

Laslow took a long sip of the golden liquid and met the duke's eyes over the rim of his glass. "It is most likely nothing at all, sir, but I do think it most odd, and I did not like to tell Miss April so I thought—I thought—"

"Perhaps if you were to start at the beginning, Victor," prompted Dawson quietly.

"Yes, well, I shall try." With a grim determination to leave nothing out, including the appearance of Clive Peesby upon the coach, Laslow related the tale in a tense voice. "And though I would not say so to Miss April, your grace," he finished, "I fear there is something very wrong, for Miss Olivia has not yet returned, nor sent word."

"Where is Miss April, Laslow?" Abbercombe asked calmly.

"At home, your grace."

"And how did you come here?"

"I walked, your grace."

"Dawson," Abbercombe drawled, leaning back in his chair and crossing one knee over the other quite as if he were not in the least concerned by the matter. "Have John bring the coach around from the stables, will you? You and Laslow must go to Park Street and fetch Miss April and her abigail. They will spend the night with us. I shall ask Mrs. Griffin to have rooms prepared for them. You should, I think, Laslow, remain at Park Street in case we worry for nothing and Miss Olivia returns shortly."

"Do you think she may, your grace?"

"Do you think not, Laslow?"

"I do not know what to think. She must be safe with Lord Stamford—and I am positive it was his coach fetched her."

"Then I expect the note was a mistake, and something has merely occurred to detain her, but I will look into the matter."

It was not thirty seconds after the two butlers had climbed into his coach that Abbercombe was in the stables pacing impatiently as Jemmy saddled Gadzooks. "But ye kinnae ride wif yer arm all slunged up like tha', yer grace," the little stableboy protested.

"Right you are, Jemmy." The duke divested himself of Fanning's handiwork. "By the way, my man, where has the leprechaun gone?"

"Why 'e's at 'is dinner, 'e is. Ye be a needin' of 'im, yer grace? I kin runan'fetch 'em fer ye."

"No, Jemmy, but you may take this confounded sling and bestow it upon Fanning if you like."

"What? Go inta the 'ouse, yer grace? An' speak ta the splendid cove what keeps yer clothes?"

"Aye, Jemmy," growled Abbercombe with a squinty glower that sent the boy into giggles, "and tell him that I have gone to visit his lordship, the Earl of Stamford, and if I am not returned by midnight, he must deploy the forces."

Hempstead peered steadily ahead into the starlit darkness as waves rushed across *Peregrine*'s hull and her crew worked silently to lower her sails. "There," Dunleavy murmured, pointing. "Do ye see 'er lying still in the water, just off the island?"

Hempstead sighted an oblong shape amongst the shadows. "But I thought we were to meet on Alderney?"

"No, lad, not this night. Too dangerous for the likes of Pendleton and Saukill. Signals all speak of excise men about."

"What signals?"

"Did ye not keep yer eyes upon the shoreline as I said?"

"Yes, sir, but I did not see any sort of signal."

Dunleavy took a moment to light his pipe. "Ye did not see Mrs. Blakely's old corset blowin' alone upon the line as we passed close to the shore at Bideawee? Or the young man in the skiff fishin' off the buoy as we come past the first o' the islands? They be signals, lad. If our way had been clear, ye would not have seen them."

"But if it is a secret, our picking up The Rogue's cargo, how are people aware to send us signals?"

"Bless ye, lad, the signals ain't for us. They be for the free-trade boys. People along o' these shores send signals day an' night. They've family in the trade, lad. Old Mrs. Blakely's husband an' three boys be engaged in't. She'll not signal falsely, nor the brat in the skiff—he's Pendleton's nevvy."

"Are there different signals if the coast is clear?" Hempstead asked, intrigued.

"Aye. Fremont, drop the anchor. We await 'em here. Job, Tufor, flash the runnin' light an' see do we get an answer."

Hempstead watched as one of the sailors hurried starboard and leaked a bit of light from a darkened lantern over the water. His eyes focussed once again on the oblong shape in the channel ahead of them. Two brief flashes shivered and disappeared. These were followed by two more of equally short duration.

"Be very still now," Dunleavy murmured, "and listen close."

At first Hempstead could hear only the creaking of *Peregrine*'s masts and the slapping of the waves against her strakes, and the squeak of the line as she swung about the anchor. He held his breath and listened more intently, and then he heard a vague, muffled, rhythmic sound. He looked toward Dunleavy and the captain nodded. "Scullin' our cargo over, they are. Do ye got a pistol, lad?"

"Ah—no."

"Here, ye take this. When ye see 'em come up beside o' us, ye train that popper on the man what's plyin' them oars, an' ye don't be gettin' distracted by nothin' what's said nor done." Dunleavy strolled toward the place where the rope ladder dangled over *Peregrine*'s side. "An' should ye see any light whatever movin' toward us across the waters, lad," he hissed back over his shoulder, "sing out which direction it be a comin' from."

Hempstead braced himself against the rail at *Peregrine*'s bow and upon catching his first glimpse of the small, flat-bottomed skiff that flowed toward them in the darkness, trained the pistol Dunleavy had handed him upon the oarsman and kept it there. Four people appeared to occupy the tiny boat, their combined weight making it ride very low. As it came expertly up beside

Peregrine, one of Dunleavy's crew opened a lantern door to provide enough light for the captain to make out the skiff's occupants.

"I'm hopin' ye got the rest of our payment in your possession, Dunleavy," growled a voice from the skiff. "This is not a time for bargaining. The shore's crawlin' with toads this night an' the *Mary Beth* be carryin' other cargo."

"Aye," muttered Dunleavy, reaching slowly inside his coat. " 'Tis one hundred thousand we be owin' ye."

Hempstead heard a grunt as Dunleavy tossed Abbercombe's roll of notes to the shadowman in the bow of the skiff. A small stream of light bounced across the bottom of the little boat and then disappeared. "Give us some help, then," growled the voice that had demanded payment. "They're both of 'em hurt."

Two of Dunleavy's men floated quickly over *Peregrine*'s rails and down the ship's flank and then back up again with a man held between them. They made the trip a second time. Hempstead kept his pistol trained on the oarsman.

"Damnation!" roared a voice from *Peregrine*'s stern. "There's lights aft! Runnin' lights closin' on us, Captain!"

"Off wi' ye, Pendleton! We'll draw 'em after us. Weigh anchor," Dunleavy shouted, "and git them sails set! Hempstead, ye see that our passengers git safely below. Hop to it, lad."

Hempstead stuffed the pistol into the waistband of his breeches and rushed across the deck to where the newly acquired passengers stood, urging them hurriedly below. He discovered he was required to help both of them negotiate the companionway. "I can get to a chair by myself," drawled the younger of the two once they were safely inside the cabin. "Can you help Andrew?"

Hempstead, with an abrupt nod, proceeded to divest Captain Willburton-Smythe of the soggy tunic in which he stood shivering. The gentleman's raggedly torn shirt sleeve and the fact that no right arm emerged from it came as a sudden shock, but he covered his reaction by muttering about the gentleman's need to get warm and urged him down upon the bunk, covering him with

a woolen blanket. He searched rapidly about the cabin for something more to tuck about the man and discovered another blanket
folded neatly inside an old sea chest.

"Here," Hartshorn mumbled, standing and stripping off his
greatcoat. "Put this over him, too. It's not as wet as his and it'll
not soak through the blankets. He's had a rough time of it. The
last thing he needs is an inflammation of the lungs."

Hempstead added the coat to the blankets.

"May I ask your name?" Hartshorn requested hoarsely.

"Hempstead, Geoffery Hempstead."

"Hired to replace me, were you?" Hartshorn chuckled. "Harry
Hartshorn," he extended his hand without rising. "You will excuse me if I don't do the thing proper, but I am exhausted."

Hempstead shook the proffered hand.

"See can you find some wine, Hempstead. As soon as I am
rested, you and I will look to Andrew. We came under fire shortly
before we reached the coast and had to muck our way across
some ungodly country dodging all the way. Andrew was not in
fine fettle to begin with."

"And you?" asked Hempstead.

"Oh, I simply dodged the wrong way once and ended with
this." Hartshorn sighed, presenting his hastily bandaged knee to
Hempstead's view. "Ball's still in it, but it don't hurt much."

Hempstead discovered a decanter of port at the back of the
lowest shelf of Captain Dunleavy's glass-enclosed bookcase together with a set of fine crystal glasses. He carried them to the
table upon which Hartshorn rested his elbows, and filled two
glasses. One of these he pushed across at Hartshorn, and the
other he took into his own hand.

"Where's The Rogue?"

"He could not come. He was attacked on a street in London
and wounded. He thought he would be of little use."

"Where are we bound, Hempstead, do you know?"

"Not actually."

"Gravesend, I should think. His nibs will expect Andrew to
be in queer stirrups and will not wish him to travel farther by

coach than need be. And we have no need to keep our arrival secret."

"I never thought of that," Hempstead replied a bit stunned. "You may have had to dodge the Frenchies, but why on earth are we attempting to evade the excise officers?"

"Dunleavy is having his bit of fun, drawing the cutter off from Pendleton and Saukill—they carry different cargo aboard the *Mary Beth* and could not well stand to be taken."

"And will not be taken," provided Dunleavy as he descended into his cabin. "We have distracted the government lads long enough for the *Mary Beth* to reach the cove."

"Does the cutter still follow?" Hartshorn queried. "They do not fire upon us."

"No, nor they won't neither. Gave 'em a start at the first, I should think, seein' a little beauty like *Peregrine* before 'em. Lit 'er up we did as pretty as a palace, which gave 'em some hesitation about unloadin' a ball across our bow. Doubt they'll come within range at all now. We're flyin', we are, under full sail. Should they overtake us, however, we shall simply come about and allow them to board. *Peregrine* is empty of contraband."

Seventeen

The Earl of Stamford finished the last of a trifle, wiped his fingers on his napkin and rose from the table. "If you will not eat, my dear," he muttered, "then you must travel upon an empty stomach. Put this on," he ordered, tossing Olivia her cloak. "I should not wish you to take a chill."

"Travel?" Olivia looked at the man with genuine surprise.

"Do you think I am so mad as to kill Abbercombe in my own home? Never, my dear. By this time you are sorely missed at Park Street and your butler will have sought the duke's advice."

Olivia remained seated at the foot of the table, the green velvet cloak upon her lap. Her fingers stroked the fur trim uneasily. "What makes you think, my lord, that Laslow would go to Abbercombe? They are not upon such terms."

"The man cannot be blind, my dear. If he suspects you to be in danger, he will rush to inform the gentleman most concerned for your welfare. Even now Abbercombe is on his way here. When he arrives he will find our trail quite easy to follow."

Olivia, struggling to keep her mounting fear from becoming obvious, shrugged and rose, donning her cloak. "You mistake, my lord. If word is carried to anyone it will be to Lady Jessica."

Stamford chuckled obscenely. "Who will consult her husband—Abbercombe's brother, no? And he, I assure you, will contact the duke. Come, we have no more time to waste." The earl crossed the room, seized Olivia's arm and escorted her forcibly to the double doors which opened before them as if a signal had been sounded. Within minutes Olivia was installed in the closed coach, Stamford directly across from her, and Peesby and another man on the box. Olivia noted that they were accompanied by four armed guards as well, two to each side of the coach. "Does it take seven grown men, then, to subdue one feeble duke?"

"Come, Miss Willburton-Smythe," snickered Stamford. "I should not call a man who has survived two attacks on his life, killed three ruffians and veritably flew through a conservatory window to your aid, feeble."

"You!" Olivia gasped.

"In the conservatory? Yes, indeed. I did think, you know, that the fellow you spoke with was actually Abbercombe. Had the duke not succeeded in tackling the man as he did—well, but I knew then that the fellow was an impostor."

"Oh, my goodness," cried Olivia, her hands fluttering to her breast. "But that fellow was Harcort! And the other Kettering! You have narrowly missed killing your own sons, sir!"

Stamford stared at her through the flickering darkness of the coach as they passed beneath the street lamps. "That shall add to the devil's suffering, I assure you. Not only does he murder my brother and seduce my sons to his will, but then does not balk at sacrificing them to protect his own life! Vile creature! I do the world a favor to rid it of him!"

Olivia's mind boggled at the earl's words. Any hope she had held that he would come to his senses through argument and illumination deserted her. To find his sons' peril Abbercombe's responsibility when he alone had held the gun, he had fired the shots. She could not comprehend it. The man was truly beyond reason. Her eyes strayed to the coach window and she discovered to her amazement that they were tooling at a sedate pace down St. James's Street. Her fingers flexed in her lap as she urged herself to reach for the door handle and fling herself from the moving vehicle into the midst of the gentlemen who even now strolled into White's Club and Boodle's and The Guard's.

With a pretended languor she leaned back against the squabs and watched from beneath half-lidded eyes as the earl crossed his legs and leaned back himself. She waited for what seemed an eternity. They were nearly outside White's when she judged him at ease and jerked forward, grabbing for the latch as she flung herself at the door. Stamford's arm came between her and her objective and hurled her back against the seat. His brash laughter rang out.

He seized Olivia's wrist in an iron grip and tugged her forward on the seat until his face was only inches from her own. "You will ride sedately and without protest, my dear, like the lady you are," he hissed, "or I shall have you bound and gagged. Do not think I am unprepared to do so."

"Unhand me," Olivia muttered angrily. "You are hurting me!"

"I shall hurt you much more, madam, if you mistake me for someone whose wishes are easily disregarded." He flung her back against the squabs.

At that precise moment the front door of Stamford House was opened to Abbercombe's knock. The elegantly garbed butler, his face a mask of indifference, answered the duke's queries in a surly drone that set the duke's teeth on edge. But his answers also set Abbercombe's mind to calculating. "Where were they bound? Did Stamford mention his destination?"

"No, your grace."

"Which direction did they take?"

"Through Green Park, your grace."

Abbercombe nodded, spun on his heel, and departed the place. Olivia would not have gone willingly. Stamford had abducted her. His heart lurched at the thought. Not only abducted her, but wished it known he had done so. The duke cursed loudly and rowdily in French, sending Gadzook's ears into quivers and snaps in an attempt to recognize the commands. "No, bucko," the duke mumbled when at last he noticed and gave the beast's neck a pat, " 'tis not your concern." He exited the park near St. James's and made his way past Boodles and The Guard's Club and White's at a trot, his mind whirling. Abruptly he pulled the horse to a halt, leaped down, and ran back toward White's.

"Jack? Jack Sloan? Have you been standing out here long?"

"Indeed, your grace. Do you know you have left your anima alone in the middle of the street?"

"What? Oh, never mind, Jack. He will not stray."

"No, your grace, but the traffic—"

"No, Jack, listen. Have you seen a traveling coach pass in the past hour or so? A black one?"

"They are most of them black, your grace."

"Of course they are. I'm sorry. This one belongs to the Earl of Stamford. I do not know if it carries a crest."

"Aye, Stamford passed barely ten minutes ago, your grace. Two men on the box and four outriders."

"Which way was he bound, Jack?"

"South, your grace, toward the toll road."

Abbercombe hesitated. "I say, Jack, is Worth inside?"

"No, but he desires to be," answered a voice below the duke on the steps. "Is that beast holding stubbornly to the middle of the street yours, Cash? He has just sent Byng into an apoplexy."

"Edward! Thank you, Jack," Abbercombe nodded, slipping a cartwheel into Sloan's palm as he turned and dragged Worth back down the steps.

"May I ask what's afoot?" Worth growled. "Why are you riding alone? One of Stone's people ought to be with you, you maniac. You are a target, lest you forget."

"Be quiet, Edward, do," Abbercombe urged, shoving him up against the front wall of the club. "I need your help, badly."

"What is it?"

"I know who seeks to kill me, and he is well on his way to accomplishing it tonight. You must take a message to Fanning."

"The devil I will!" exclaimed Worth. "If you contemplate that I shall leave you when you are in such bad loaf, your wits have gone a'begging."

"No but, Worth, you do not understand."

"Tell me then."

Abbercombe's hurried words brought deep creases to Worth's brow. He shoved the duke aside when he had caught the gist of it and, grabbing a link boy by the arm, sent the lad running in search of his groom. "Harley shall ride to Fielding House. I shall accompany you. Go remove that ugly nag from the middle of the street before someone shoots it."

The Earl of Stamford snickered as his entourage halted to purchase a pass that would allow them a clear run along the southern turnpike to Gravesend. From beneath the folds of his greatcoat the tip of a horse pistol glinted ominously at Olivia. "I should not alert the gatekeeper, my dear. It would be unfortunate were I forced to kill you *and* an innocent man."

Olivia sniffed haughtily and turned to stare from the coach window. Within minutes they were tooling through the darkness on a riband of moonlight. Her heart pounded in time with the beating of the horses's hooves as her mind searched for some means of escape from this wretched excuse for a man. She had no doubt that Abbercombe would follow the well-laid trail, nor that he would ride directly into whatever trap the lunatic had planned. Though she doubted the duke loved her, she did not doubt that his valor and sense of honor would bring him to her aid. She must save herself before the trap could be sprung.

The coach slowed, departed the turnpike at the Gravesend toll-gate and proceeded in the direction of the Thames. All around them the fog was beginning to roll in. The dampness was visible and streamed through open coach windows to wrap its chilling tentacles around Olivia's shivering form. Though she stared as intently as she could at the landscape, she could make out little of it, merely a tree here or a bush there. She had thought they must, of necessity, head toward the town itself, but they had turned away from the small port and traveled along the riverside. Olivia endeavored to recollect all she could about the area which she had visited only twice in her life. Where were they bound? Certainly Stamford did not think to surround the duke with himself and six men in the open countryside? No one could be so mad as that. And then a stone wall loomed out of the darkness and the fog and was caught in the glare of the coach lights. Olivia gasped. "Evelsisor!"

"Yes, my dear," hissed Stamford through the gloom. "The ruins of Evelsisor Abbey. Abbercombe will be delighted. It is one of his favourite haunts, you know."

Olivia's gaze flew to the earl.

"But of course, you do not know, do you? I doubt you know anything about the villain's childhood. Hid here, he did, whenever he fled Harrow. The fool schoolmasters had not the wit to discover him. He'd be flogged one day and missing the next. Ah, yes," he sighed with distinct pleasure, "I am certain our intrepid duke will be ecstatic I have chosen it for his demise."

Evelsisor Abbey lay several miles to the southwest of the toll road and south of Gravesend in the midst of a thick stand of beeches along the Thames. Like a great grey slug, low, long remnants of buildings undulated amongst the trees, rising in great chunks here and there to catch a glimmer of moonlight and then twisting back into the cover of the increasingly dense fog. Among the weathered stones, invisible now, ivy and grape vines twined high between fallen roof timbers and medieval arches and down into wells and pits and cellars lined with sharp rocks, leafing green among the grey, and in the daylight, striping the grotesque architectural worm with gaudy color.

The coach stopped and Stamford tugged Olivia out into a decrepit courtyard before the remains of the principal hall. "Shall we go inside, my dear?" he chuckled, grasping her elbow and shoving her forward. "There is no need to await his stinking grace amidst this dank, abominable fog."

Olivia struggled against his grip. "I do not require your assistance, sir," she muttered, and with an audaciousness that surprised herself, she swung about and kicked the earl soundly in the shin. He released her in astonishment, but she was instantly seized by one of his henchmen who leered at her in the moonlight and yanked her into the keep. Within moments a fire flared amidst the ruins, and wisps of fog and shadow skittered from its light. Olivia was pushed down upon a rotted wooden bench and across from her, pistol in hand, the earl lounged in a huge chair of carved English oak that had survived within the ruin for at least a century. The ruffians disappeared into the night; Olivia shifted upon the bench; and Stamford levelled the pistol at her heart.

"Do not think it, my dear," he hissed, his eyes cold and dead. "You remain through my partiality for feminine company. Should you attempt to escape, you will find yourself in the pit behind you." The earl cackled as Olivia jerked to her feet and peered over the rotted bench. "Be careful, madam. Should you fall I have no way to retrieve you. You shall remain there and rot."

Gadzooks kept pace with Worth's chestnut to just beyond the turnoff at Gravesend but then began to fall back. Worth's first thought was that the game—but ugly—beast had come up lame. He slowed his mount and turned in the saddle to see the duke pull Gadzooks to a standstill and dismount. Worth swung the chestnut around and galloped back. "What is it, Cash?"

"I know," mumbled the duke, gloved hands on hips, head bowed in a semblance of despair. "I know where he has taken her."

Worth dismounted and put an arm around his friend's shoulders, leaning closer to make out his words. "Where?" he asked softly. "Why have we stopped?"

"He has gone to Evelsisor."

"Never. He is bound for Gravesend, Cash. We will find them at the Ships Inn."

Abbercombe's head shook. He would not look up and Worth's grip around his shoulders tightened. "You shall wait here for Fanning and the others, then, and I shall ride to Evelsisor and see how the land lies. If they are not there, I shall return and we go on to Gravesend. It will be all right, Cash, I promise."

"No, I am acting the fool. I cannot conceive why I still dread the place so. We shall both go to Evelsisor."

"Are you certain, *mon ami?*"

"Yes." They remounted and rode more slowly through the thickening fog. At the crossroads, the duke stopped to strip off his neckcloth and tie it tightly around a limb of a small apple tree to point Fanning along the correct path.

"Will he see the thing in this wretched murk, Cash?"

"He will stop and search for it. Our whole life together has been like hare and hounds, Robin and I. One of us runs and one of us chases. Someday he will tire of it and leave me."

Worth's eyebrows rose in surprise. "Have you been in the brambles all these years, then? Why did you never let me know? Surely I could have helped somehow, Cash."

"I abandoned you, Edward. I determined never again to cause you such pain and humiliation as you suffered for standing by me through that hideous trial." For the first time that night the duke's soft chuckle reached Worth's ears. "And here you are, despite all my good intentions. I doubt we shall be humiliated, Edward, but we will both likely be shot at."

"Life with you is never drab, *mon ami*—baffling, to be sure, but not tedious. Do we intend to shoot back? If we do, I feel I ought to point out that we have no pistols."

"No, nor I ain't got my sabre, either. Seemed immensely stupid to wear the thing when I could not use it."

"Blast," Worth muttered. "I had forgotten your shoulder."

"I haven't—makes itself known to me with every movement."

In deference to the fog, the darkness, and the ill-remembered track, the two men slowed their cattle to a walk. Even so, the first great outcroppings of Evelsisor took them unaware and brought them to a startled halt. Abbercombe cringed as the crumbling walls loomed out at him. A vision of cold, dead black and the sound of gasping lungs brought him a shortness of breath.

"Steady, old man," Worth whispered.

Abbercombe inhaled deeply, and forced himself to replace the vision with one of Olivia—her strong, stubborn little chin tilted in defiance, her green eyes blazing, her sweet, highly kissable lips forming the word 'pigheaded'. He grinned and dismounted. "Best leave the horses. Place is full of pitfalls."

Worth, who had already tied his chestnut to a low branch, grunted. "They brought a coach in here, they must have used the original drive. Do we follow?"

"You to one side of it and I to the other. I hope you are correct, Edward. I hope we waste our time here and they intend to take us at Gravesend."

Olivia gasped as Peesby's disgusting countenance emerged from the fog. "They come, milord," the gruff voice whispered.

"They, Peesby? How many?"

"Only two, milord."

Stamford smirked in Olivia's direction. "Your lover's intellect has grown, my dear. He has acquired enough sense to bring at least one other person with him. Take them both, Peesby. Bring the duke to me alive. The other—I care not."

"Yes, milord," grinned Peesby exposing broken, yellowed teeth in the firelight, "with pleasure."

Olivia's heart wobbled. Abbercombe had come. Her breath caught in her throat. She had to warn him, to let him know he had been seen and was close to capture. From beneath lowered lashes she eyed the earl. His attention was no longer focussed upon her. Expectantly he searched the fog beyond their shelter. She did not know how close Abbercombe might be, if her voice would carry to him, but the earl's inattention would not last and she would be fool not to take advantage of it.

Cautiously she leaned forward, attempting to seize one of the branches destined to renew the fire. She managed to grasp it without her movements alerting Stamford and straightened very slowly, hiding the large stick in the folds of her skirt. She took a deep breath and then launched herself at the man, bringing the branch down with all her strength across the hand that held the pistol and screaming in a voice she did not recognize as her own: "They know you're here! It's a trap, Cash!" Her scream was punctuated by the explosion of the earl's pistol as it cracked against the cobbles and fired.

Stamford, furious, seized the branch and twisted it from her grasp. He hurled it aside and, lifting Olivia from the ground, flung her back with such force that the wooden bench crumbled beneath her and Olivia skidded into the pit beyond. Desperately she flailed for something to stop her fall, expecting at each moment to land, impaled, upon sharp rocks and split timbers in the darkness below. Which was why she was so thoroughly amazed when she landed with an "oof!" as the wind was knocked out of her, and discovered that she was otherwise perfectly sound. She could see nothing around her, not even the hand she held up before her eyes, but she felt carefully and, stupefied, deduced she had landed upon a pile of compressed twigs and leaves—a very thick pile of them. Then she felt an arm snake 'round her and a gloved hand cover her mouth.

"Do not scream, Miss Olivia," whispered Worth hastily in her ear. "You will soon be safe, I promise you." He removed his hand from her mouth and she turned to him, but could not make out his form in the solid darkness.

"L-lord Worth, is it you?"

"Yes. Shhh!" He put his arms protectively about her and held her shivering form against him. Above them Olivia heard the scraping and clacking of boots upon the broken cobbles and quick, heavy breathing. There was a great thud and a cry cut short, then a clatter and scraping and gasping for breath. The sound of bare knuckles striking thick flesh chunked into the pit, and then a flat, dull whack followed by a huge thud and a clattering and clacking and scuffing of broken stone.

"Worth?" Abbercombe's gentle whisper roared like welcome thunder in her ears. He was above her and alive!

"Here, Cash, hurry."

"Is Olivia safe?"

"Safe as houses. Hurry."

"Stand clear; I'm dropping Stamford."

Worth tugged Olivia gently to the far side of the pit. With each step she discovered that the floor beneath her was level and un-obstructed by stones or fallen timbers. "Clear!" hissed Worth, and with a shuddering and a great whoosh of air, the Earl of Stamford's unconscious body rushed down at them, unseen, but obvious to all their other senses. "Do not move," Worth whispered again. She heard him step hesitantly toward the place where she, herself, had fallen. "Damnation," she heard him mutter, "the man weighs a ton." It was only then that the shock from her fall and Worth's sudden appearance left her completely and she realized that Worth was attempting to drag Stamford's body from the well-packed pile of debris and why. She went like a blind woman in his direction, stumbling into him at last. Hurriedly she felt for one of Stamford's arms or legs and was rewarded by the feel of his coat sleeve beneath her fingers. She took a solid hold and heard Worth beside her. "Good girl. At the count of three. One, two, three." Olivia threw every ounce of energy into pulling and the earl's body slid part-way off the pile, dragging bits and pieces of brush and leaves with it. "Again," Worth muttered hurriedly. "One, two, three." Olivia flung herself back toward the far wall with all her might. Worth had done the same. She heard him crash to the floor just as she sat down very hard herself.

Above them the air whooshed again and the sound of Abbercombe landing in the place from which they had just dragged Stamford brought a sigh of relief from both. "Took you the devil of a long time," came the duke's soft, low voice. "I thought to have to fight off the rest of them before bailing out. Olivia?"

Olivia heard herself whimper and in a moment felt Abbercombe's strong hands upon her, lifting her from the floor and into a tight embrace. "Are you all right, my dearest girl? He did not harm you? You did not break anything when you fell?" His lips were pressed so close to her ear that she shivered with each word. From above them came the sound of booted feet running upon the cobbles and a confusion of frightened and exasperated voices.

"What the devil goes on?"

" 'ere, Barney, where's t'boss?"

"I don' know, but I ain't a stayin' ta look. There's ghosts an' spirits all about this place, I'm tellin' ye."

"But where's them coves we was after?"

"They's gone, Jed. Dead an' gone. Swallered up, I bets, by t'specters, jus' like t'earl an' tha' flash mort."

"Clive ain't 'ere nither. Where's Clive?"

"I doan care! Let 'im git 'is own way out! Come on!"

Within a matter of minutes the sound of horses's hooves retreating reached the attentive listeners in the pit. Still held tightly in Abbercombe's arms Olivia let a sigh of relief escape her and felt one finger of the duke's gloved hand barely touch her lips. Once again his face buried itself in her dusky curls and his perfect lips moved against her ear. "We must be very quiet, love. One of them has not yet gone."

Olivia felt the duke shudder and her arms found their way 'round his neck, her fingers entwined themselves in his thick curls. "You shiver," she whispered. "Abbercombe, are you hurt?"

"No," he assured her and his lips touched the tip of her upturned nose which he could not see but kissed anyway. Then he found her lips and tentatively touched them with his own. Olivia's embrace tightened and she kissed him back hungrily.

"If you are doing what I suspect you are, Cash," Worth's voice sighed through the darkness, "I wish you will assert some self-control until we have all gotten out of here."

The duke's lips parted from Olivia's. Somewhere on the floor of the pit Stamford moaned and Olivia stifled a gasp.

"May I?" Worth asked quietly.

"Be my guest, Edward," Abbercombe answered. Olivia heard a quick, whacking sound, and Stamford's voice died in midgroan. "Now, little love," the duke murmured, giving her a quick kiss upon a cheek, "you must help us yet again." She felt his arms release her and he walk cautiously away. "Do you have it, Worth?"

"Here."

In a matter of moments the duke had struck the piece of flint and a thin stick flared, barely bright enough to illuminate the two men who had lit it. The twig and several more like it were given over to Olivia's care as the men shouldered Stamford's body between them. "You must walk ahead of us, love," Abbercombe told her.

"Walk where?"

"To your right, my dear," explained Worth. "There is a tunnel of sorts. Keep one hand on the wall and be very careful."

Olivia had passed the flame on to a sixth twig, and the men behind her were breathing heavily under Stamford's weight when she reached what seemed to be a solid wall. Abbercombe and Worth lowered Stamford to the floor and the duke took the burning stick from her hand. She heard stones moving about and could see his hands groping along the bottom of a huge pile of rocks. And then there was a bit more light, and a bit more, and she stared wide-eyed as she saw Abbercombe rise, an elaborate candelabra, the candles already burned low, in his hand. He raised it high enough so that she could discern that they stood before a huge pile of stone and timber where the floor above had crashed down to block the passage at some long ago time. Near the very top of the pile was a rift, large enough, Olivia thought, for a mouse, but not nearly large enough for any of them. It amazed her to see Worth cautiously climb the debris and disappear through the crevice.

"Now you, my dear," Abbercombe said with a grim smile, and in the candlelight Olivia saw that his face was stark white beneath a layer of dust and grime. Tiny rivulets of sweat streaked through the dirt at odd and sundry angles. "Worth will help you to climb down on the other side." Olivia doubted she could do the thing in her long skirts and half-boots, but Abbercombe supported her up the pile and Worth grabbed her and pulled her through and helped her down to the opposite floor. It took nearly ten minutes, the candles burning lower and lower, for the duke to get Stamford's limp form up into the hole, and Olivia was shocked to see that even the earl's great lump of a figure fit through the thing. She helped Worth to tug the unresisting man down the other side. When she looked back up into the crevice, she could see candle light flickering, but the crevice was empty. Abbercombe was not slipping through it as she had expected. Worth, anxious, climbed back to the rift.

"Cash, hurry," he urged.

"I cannot."

Olivia heard a tremor in the duke's tone.

"You must, Cash. You cannot climb out through that blasted pit. You must come to this side."

"Go on," Abbercombe's voice answered. "Take Olivia. Leave Stamford. He will find his own way out when he revives."

"Cash!" The desperation in Worth's hoarse whisper startled Olivia. Then she heard him strive to change the tone to one of unyielding authority. "You will do as I say, damn you! If you do not, I shall come back and pull you through myself."

There was no answer and Worth groaned.

Olivia, her heart pounding, scrambled up to where Lord Worth balanced precariously. "What is it? What is wrong?"

Worth looked down at her and she was surprised, for she only now realized that she could see the worry on his face quite clearly even though the candles were not in evidence. There was light, then, coming from somewhere at this end of the tunnel. Moonlight? Then they were close now to the surface? But why did Abbercombe not come? Was he injured as she had suspected? Olivia's eyes bored deeply and beseechingly into Worth's.

"He is terrified," Worth said flatly. "He has stood it as long as he can and come as far as he is able."

"But, but—"

Worth looked at her anxiously and turned back to the hole. "If you do not come," he hissed, "I shall tell your father!"

Olivia's mouth dropped open.

"M'father's dead, ninny," muttered Abbercombe. "I am not lost to *all* reason, Worth. Deuced good try though."

Olivia tugged at Worth's sleeve. "Why will he not come?" she demanded as softly as she could.

In hurried whispers Worth told her how as a boy Cash had

been trapped in this tunnel when the great ceiling had come roaring down. Alone and injured, unable to find his candles and with barely air enough to survive an hour, the child had had to dig his own way out. Olivia's heart constricted. She shoved Worth away from the crevice. Through the opening she could see the duke at the base of the pile watching the candles gutter one by one.

"Cash," she called softly, "it is only a few more steps, my darling, and we will all of us be outside. You do want to be outside, do you not?"

"Yes." The sound of unshed tears behind the word tore at Olivia's heart.

"Then you must be brave this one more time and come with us, my dear, and we will all be safe." Olivia's heart sank as she waited silently for a reply that did not come and beyond the crevice the last of the candles guttered.

"Sure, an' I knew ye were not ghosties," laughed Peesby's gruff voice. Olivia gasped and turned immediately toward the sound. The tall, lean coachman stood, sneering, a horse pistol levelled directly at Worth's heart. "Come down from there, madam, if ye please, or I shall kill this cove on t'instant."

Olivia's hand fluttered for a moment in the air as if waving the surly ruffian away. She took a deep breath and climbed perilously down the shifting stones, coming to a stop where the earl lay, once again groaning.

"Come away from t'master," Peesby ordered, "both of ye."

Worth moved cautiously toward Olivia, offered her his arm and escorted her to the place the coachman indicated.

"It took me some time, it did, to find these 'ere tunnels, Mr. Flash Cove," Peesby laughed. "But I knowed they must be 'round. Ye scared t'others good, ye did, a poppin' up an' disappearin' an' pesterin' 'em inta panickin'. I seed 'em ridin' off like old Nick 'imself be after 'em." The coachman walked cautiously as he spoke, keeping the pistol pointed directly at Worth. When he reached the earl, he stooped down to the man. "Do ye be alive then, milord? Hit ye wi' somethin' I 'ave no doubt."

"Peesby?"

"Aye, milord. A bit dizzy are ye? But I got t'remedy fer that. I got me two pris'ners an' I be jist a waitin' on yer word ta do away wif the gen'leman."

The word 'gentleman' provided an extra stimulus to the earl and Stamford gained his knees. "Abbercombe?" he growled, turning toward the place where Worth and Olivia stood. "Abbercombe?"

"Here, Stamford!" snarled the duke, diving from the crevice at their backs. Stamford and Peesby spun around; Abbercombe crashed down onto them; the flash and stink of gunpowder filled the tunnel and the horse pistol exploded and exploded and exploded, its echo refusing to die. Olivia screamed and fainted.

Eighteen

Olivia woke to find herself bundled in heavy blankets inside Stamford's moving coach, her head cradled upon a broad shoulder, a strong arm around her waist. "C-cash?" she murmured.

"No, ma'am, 'is grace ain't 'ere."

Startled by a voice she did not recognize, Olivia sat up quickly. "W-who are you? Where is Abbercombe?" And then the scene within the tunnel came back to her and Olivia trembled. "H-he is dead," she cried on a tiny breath. "They have k-killed him."

"Oh, no, ma'am." Esther Dowling's large, broad hands took Olivia's small ones in her own and squeezed them reassuringly. " 'e's gone on in 'is own coach to Gravesend. 'ad 'im some obligations there, 'e said. Took Mr. Fannin' wid 'im."

"To Gravesend?"

"Yes, ma'am."

"With—with Fanning?"

"Aye, ma'am. We all thought never ta fine ye. But then we heered the blinkin' pistol beneath us, an' Mr. Fannin' he find the way inta them tunnels like a hound wif 'is beak afire."

"You—you were searching for us?"

"Oh, yes, ma'am. Lord Worth's groom, he come wi' a message an' we set out 'mediate-like. Weren't no great job ta be a followin' o' ye, on accounta the trail was so blazin' clear an' all. 'Twas only jus' in that maze o'stones 'n rot, we couldn't seem ta come upon ye. Still in all, when we heerd t'pistol a echoin' right below us like, we finded ye good enuf."

"And—and Abbercombe is not injured?"

"Well, I would not be sayin' tha' exac'ly, ma'am, on accounta 'e's probable got bruises from 'is 'ead ta the bottoms o' 'is feet. An' Lord Worth, 'e's got 'imself a eye gonna be black as midnight by mornin' an' a sight more bumps an' bangs aside. But I figgers ye all comed off like t'blinkin' angels was a watchin' over ye."

"Who are you?" Olivia asked, mystified.

"Me name's Esther, ma'am. Esther Dowlin'. I works fer Mr. Stone, what was 'ired ta perteck 'is grace an' the chillren. Ye don't be worryin' none, no more, now. Mr. Stone's as sure as kin be that 'twas tha' earl all along what bin worritin' the dook, an' tha' earl ain't a goin' ta be doin' so no more."

"Was it Stamford who was shot then?"

" 'Tweren't nobody shot, bless ye, ma'am. Ball missed ever'one o' ye. On accounta the dook, he come down on 'em so fas' an' so 'ard like an' sent stones an' ever'thin' a flyin'. Like to a seed 'im do tha', I would."

Olivia smiled despite herself. "It was not so wonderful, Esther. I thought surely he would be killed. I never wish to see him in such straits again."

Olivia only noticed then that the coach had come to a halt. In a moment the door was opened and the steps let down and a strong hand offered to help her descend. She smiled at the sight of Lord Worth. He was covered in dirt and dust from head to toe. As her feet touched the cobbles, she noticed that instead of Park Street, she was standing in the courtyard of Fielding House. Above her, in the open entranceway, stood Dawson, a relieved smile brightening his countenance. He bowed her graciously into the house, helped her to remove her mantle and she was immediately engulfed by Lady Vale's welcoming arms.

"April is upstairs asleep, my love. She thinks that you and Abbercombe have gone to the opera with Lord and Lady Worth and that we kindly invited her to spend the night with us so that she would not be lonely. I could not think it proper to say you had been abducted when I knew that Cash would bring you safely home. Where is that rogue? Did he not return with you?"

"He has gone on to Gravesend, Lady Vale," Worth provided, allowing Dawson to relieve him of his hat and gloves. "Something about unloading a cargo from the *Peregrine*. If you will forgive all my dirt, madam, I will beg a glass of Abbercombe's cognac and a seat by the fire for a few moments before I ride home. I think perhaps I have taken a chill."

"Oh, my dear," gasped Lady Vale, seeing Worth properly for the first time, "you must sit down immediately and let me look to your eye. It will be horrendous in the morning."

Worth assured her that the fire and the cognac would do well enough and was escorted into Abbercombe's study without delay. Olivia refused to retire to the chambers that had been prepared for her, explaining that she must discover what had happened after she had been such a peagoose as to faint dead away, and Lady Vale with an understanding nod accompanied her in Worth's wake. Esther Dowling, with a grin at Dawson, hurried up the back stairs.

Sprawled in a wing chair, a glass of the duke's best brandy in his hand, Worth answered Olivia's questions with a tired smile. "And Stone's associates crashed into the tunnel behind Fanning, subdued Stamford and Peesby, trussed them up and toted them off, both on Cash's spotty horse, who did not seem a bit disturbed at such a load."

"They have taken them to Newgate, surely," Olivia murmured, sipping at the tea Lady Vale had readily provided.

"Well, Peesby at any rate. Cash would not allow them to deliver up Stamford."

"What?" Olivia stared at Worth wide-eyed.

"You must not worry, my dear. Stamford will not disturb you again. Stone and his associates stand guard over him."

"Cash believes it to be his fault that Kevin has run mad, is that not so?" sighed Lady Vale.

Worth nodded wearily.

"Oh, I cannot believe this!" Olivia exclaimed, one tiny fist striking the chair arm. "Now he blames himself for the man's attempts to murder him? He is quite as mad as Stamford!"

"Well, actually, he ain't," Worth sighed. "Kevin fairly wor-

shipped Channing, and I can see where Cash's return might tip
Kevin's mind a bit, and then to discover his boys were fairly
caught by the rogue's daughters—"

"Cash was quite worried about it," agreed Lady Vale. "He
tried to warn Harcort and Kettering off. But they like him, you
know, and are charmed with Amy and Beth."

"None of which has anything to say to the matter," sputtered
Olivia. "Abbercombe has already been punished outrageously
for something in which he played but a minor role!"

"In which he played a minor role, Miss Olivia?" Worth came
suddenly to attention.

"Oh, I should not have said that."

"No, my dear, you should not," droned Lady Vale. "Worth,
go home. Eugenia likely wonders if you have been killed yourself
by now. And Olivia, you shall come upstairs and bathe then slip
between the sheets. Whatever else needs to be discussed can wait
until morning." With that the dowager rose, compelling Worth
and Olivia to do likewise. "Dawson will see you out, Edward,"
she smiled graciously. "Thank you, for all you have done." And
she put her arm through Olivia's and escorted her from the room.

Olivia's first glimpse of herself in the pier glass brought laughter and an exasperated sigh. I am quite as disreputable as Worth,
she thought, surveying the ruins of her dress, the lamentable state
of her hair and the dirt and grime that stained her face and hands.
Before she could utter a word a hip bath appeared accompanied
by gallons of hot water, fluffy towels, and scented bath soaps.
Esther Dowling reappeared as well and in a more than adequate
imitation of a lady's maid soon helped a clean Olivia slip into
one of Lady Vale's nightgowns.

"My, but yer pretty, if ye'll 'scuse me sayin' o' it," Esther
murmured. "The dook, 'e did say that there were a fine-lookin'
young lady unner all that muck when 'e carried ye ta the coach,
an' tha's a fac'."

Olivia smiled at Esther's peculiarly oblong face with its thick
jaw and heavy lidded eyes and a nose that was particularly imposing. She noticed for the first time how broad were the shoul-

ders and muscular the arms. Esther grinned back at her as her wide, strong hands turned back the counterpane upon the four poster. " 'e says I've the 'ands o' a strangler, and the face to match, though 'e don't knows I know o' it."

"Who says? That is most unkind, and not in the least true."

" 'Tis 'is grace says it," laughed Esther, "and 'tis true enough. 'e don't mean it ta be unkine, milady. 'e says as 'ow Alfie stan's seven foot tall an' weighs fifteen stone, an' Mic Crawley be a lepercan. 'Tis fey 'e is, yer dook. An' a joy fer ta be 'sociated wif. Makes ye feel like ye is livin' in a fairy story. I'd be wishin' we weren't finished o' workin' fer 'im, an' tha's a fac'. 'Cep' I wouldn't be a wantin' 'im shot at no more."

Esther tucked Olivia safely between the sheets and with a stern order to fall fast asleep, snuffed out the candles, leaving her with only the glow of a dying fire to keep her company. Certain that sleep would be a long time in coming, Olivia sighed and closed her eyes, preparing to toss and turn the rest of the night away. In the darkness she felt Abbercombe's arms come around her and his lips press gently against her own and she heard him whisper, "my dearest girl, my love," in his soft husky voice. She was asleep in moments.

The Duke of Abbercombe's plush traveling coach rolled slowly along a narrow track beside the Thames. Ghostlike, appearing and dissolving in the early morning fog, the gleaming black vehicle drawn by a quartet of equally black and gleaming cattle prowled the lanes around Gravesend restlessly, the two gentlemen upon the box searching the river for a glimpse of sails in the dim light of the predawn.

"You will excuse my asking, your grace," Robin Fanning mumbled, huddled in a greatcoat against the damp chill, "but now that Mr. Hartshorn has been recovered, do you intend to resign from your activities permanently?"

"Well, I said I would Robin."

"Yes, your grace, but did you mean it?"

Abbercombe, his shoulder and other acquired injuries aching, held the team in check, grew silent and stared across the water.

When the pensive silence grew too heavy to bear, Fanning grunted and pulled his greatcoat closer about himself. "Have you told Miss Olivia that her brother arrives shortly?"

"No. I thought it better to wait and see him safe first. Are you freezing, Robin?" He reached into the box at his feet and withdrew a silver flask. "Here, this will warm you a bit. I expect I should have told her, but I could not be positive that the captain would stand the nonsense and cross the channel alive. I am not yet sure of it." Abbercombe took a long draught from the flask himself, then sealed it and returned it. "There," he said, pointing up the river. "*Peregrine*." He turned the team with authority in a space too small for such a maneuver and took them back toward the landing.

By the time the *Peregrine* had tied up, the quays were quietly becoming populated and the smell of fresh bread baking in the kitchen of the small inn beside the water was beginning to cover the stink of the catch from the night before. Dunleavy jumped from the boat and rambled toward the coach just as Abbercombe swung from the box and strolled toward the schooner. They met midway and shook hands. Then they turned back toward *Peregrine* while Fanning remained behind in charge of the team.

Abbercombe no sooner descended into the cabin than his glance fell upon Hartshorn. His smile beamed and he took the gentleman in his arms. "Harry, thank God! Wyndham was convinced you were killed. Are you injured?"

"Merely a ball in the knee, sir," Hartshorn grinned. "Madame Lavoisier sends her love. She says to tell you she is a great-grand-mother at last and goes to care for Angelique and *le comte Antoine Christophe*."

Abbercombe's grin could have lighted the entire cabin. "None of our people have been compromised then, Harry. Our lines remain open. She has saved our bacon again!"

"Devil if I will ever understand the codes," Hartshorn replied on a chuckle. "And here I thought she merely wished you to know that Angelique had had a son."

"But Angelique had Antoine, Harry, three months before I left Paris. And since she gave birth in the middle of my drawing room, I could not avoid knowing of it."

Abbercombe, abruptly recalled to thoughts of Willburton-Smythe, turned to find the man sitting precariously on the edge of Dunleavy's bunk looking dazed and wobbly. He crossed to the gentleman and seized Hartshorn's greatcoat from the bunk. "Put this on, Harry." Abbercombe tossed the coat across the room and shed his own, helping the captain to don it. Speedily buttoning the buttons and pulling the collar tightly around the man's neck, his eyes sought Hempstead's. "Help Harry get to the coach, Geoff. Robin has it drawn up at the end of the quay. Captain Willburton-Smythe and I will follow."

Hempstead found himself upon the box next to the duke for their return to town while Fanning attended as best he could to Willburton-Smythe and Hartshorn inside. "I must thank you, Geoff," Abbercombe drawled, turning the horses onto the London road. "You managed admirably."

"You're welcome, but I did nothing. I simply delivered your message and then went along for the ride."

"Yes, and put yourself in the way of smugglers and excise men, followed orders without raising a breeze about them and tended Hartshorn and the captain all the way back which could not have been easy. Dunleavy says you'll do. He is correct."

"Do, sir?"

"Yes, Geoff. He means you've courage, you're trustworthy, intelligent, and you have gained his respect."

"Oh, I say!" grinned Hempstead. "And all along I thought he was merely putting up with me."

"Well, he'll be honoured to put up with you again should there be need for it. It's high praise, Geoff, from Dunleavy. Ask Hartshorn if it isn't." Abbercombe raised the trap and called down into the coach. "What say you, Robin? Is it safe to spring 'em? Or must we keep to this confounded trot?"

"Spring 'em, your grace," Fanning's voice called up. A smile covered the duke's begrimed face in the rising light and he sent the four magnificent horses into a mad run. Hempstead watched with a great deal of admiration the duke's impressive driving and concluded that the gentleman was a veritable Nonesuch. He feathered the swaying coach around turns, skirting other vehicles without hesitation. They did not slow until they entered London, when the duke brought the four blacks back into a sedate trot and took them at length down the center of Bond Street, over to St. James's and from there to Charles and into Great Stanhope. He leaped from the box before the cattle stopped and tossed the reins to one of the grooms who had come running into the drive at the first sound of carriage wheels.

Fanning helped Hartshorn in through the front door which Dawson held wide. Hempstead followed with Willburton-Smythe. "The Children's Den," the duke called from behind them. "Dawson, send to the kitchen—no, never mind, I will get Gerard to see to our breakfast. You ask Mrs. Griffin to have a chamber made up for Harry. Are Miss Olivia and April here, Dawson?" he added in a quick whisper that did not reach the captain's ears.

Dawson nodded.

"Do not mention we've arrived yet."

Between them, Hempstead and Fanning established Hartshorn comfortably in a chaise longue and Willburton-Smythe upon the faded fainting couch while the duke himself laid and lit a fire in the grate. He paused to look speculatively from one tired face to another, then mumbled to himself. Stripping off his gloves, he tossed them onto the mantelpiece and then went about the room collecting greatcoats, stopped to whisper a few words in the captain's ear, and strolled off in the direction of the kitchen.

"I never thought to see England again," Hartshorn drawled, "until word came that The Rogue had discovered my whereabouts."

"He is The Rogue?" Andrew Willburton-Smythe asked weakly, attempting to sit up.

"Indeed," grunted Fanning, pushing the man back down. "Now lie still until the tea comes. You are not fit to be sitting up even then, but the warmth of it will do you good."

The tea came on a silver tray in the hands of a tall, lean footman who set small tables near each of the weary travellers and served them silently. No sooner had he departed than four more footmen entered carrying two washstands and basins and pitchers of hot water, followed by several maids with fresh towels, and one with a warm blanket which she placed carefully around the captain. Fanning washed the grime from his own hands and face and the captain's as well while Hempstead and Hartshorn gratefully took advantage of a chance to get somewhat cleaner. The washstands were removed and covered dishes streamed into the Children's Den. By the time Abbercombe returned, all the gentlemen were well-fed and attempting conversation, though one or the other would nod off in the midst of it.

The duke sank into a chair near the fire. "So, tell me, Fanning, when do we remove the ball from Hartshorn's knee?"

Robin grinned at the gleam in the duke's eyes and shrugged. "Whenever you wish, your grace."

"Oh, no," Hartshorn protested. "Not on your life. If you are to be anywhere about, Abbercombe, no one touches my knee."

"Why not?" Hempstead asked, curious. "Fanning did a remarkably fine job on the duke's shoulder."

"Yes," sighed Fanning, "and it is most likely all to do over again, what with fighting and climbing about those tunnels and jumping from piles of rocks, and then driving those cattle."

"It is not Robin I don't trust," chuckled Hartshorn. "It's the duke. And well he knows it, too. Sadistic devil, he is. If you had a hangnail, he'd cut off your whole finger."

"Nooo," droned Abbercombe softly. "Not I, Harry. You will have Geoff thinking badly of me."

"Who was it sat laughing when I was stabbed and suggested Robin should push the knife the rest of the way through?"

"Me," grinned Abbercombe.

"Yes. And who was it when I fell and cracked my head suggested Robin crack it on the other side as well so it would ache equally everywhere?"

"Me."

"Indeed. And who was it, when I sprained my ankle, proposed to break it because then he could practice splinting something?"

"You do have an unfortunate number of accidents, do you not Harry? But I won't suggest Robin break your leg to get the ball from your knee. I simply wish to dig about with the knife a bit."

"Argh!" groaned Hartshorn. Captain Willburton-Smythe's face broke into a weary grin and Fanning burst into laughter.

Abbercombe saw Harry safely taken off in Fanning's custody with Hempstead steadfastly beside him, and then straddled a ladder backed chair beside the fainting couch and resting his arms along the top of it, studied Willburton-Smythe. "Your daughter and sister are upstairs. I expect they are still asleep. Do you wish me to have them awakened?"

"No," Willburton-Smythe answered immediately.

"No, I thought not. It will not matter, you know, that your arm did not accompany you home. They will be overjoyed to have the rest of you back."

Captain Willburton-Smythe's eyes widened. "What a thing to say," he murmured.

"What?"

"That my arm did not accompany me home."

"Well, but it did not. I know Jean-Claude did his best to save it. I have never known him to give up easily in such a matter."

"I—I believe he tried quite hard—but—" Willburton-Smythe stuttered to a stop at the realization that Abbercombe already knew exactly what had happened. "You actually do know everything that occurs everywhere!" he exclaimed dumbfounded.

Abbercombe laughed. "No, but I am as close to it as anyone can be. We must thank God, you know, that Jean-Claude was called to attend you or I might never have received the information needed to get you home. There were a good number of people involved in that accomplishment. You are not truly afraid that the loss of your arm will make a major difference in your life, are you, Andrew? May I call you Andrew?"

"You, sir, may call me anything you like. I owe you both my life and my freedom."

"Yes, well, but you do not answer my question."

"I feel like a—a freak. I c-cannot ac-accept—I do not know how—how I will f-face April and Olivia and my friends."

"What you mean is, you do not know how you will deal with their pity, or with the way they will attempt to ignore it and turn their eyes away, or with how they will avoid certain words."

"What kind of words?" asked the captain, awestruck that this gentleman could speak so simply of the dread that had plagued his own mind for the past month.

"Oh, like saying that things have gotten 'out of hand', or that they are 'up in arms'. Ridiculous, but people will utter those perfectly normal phrases and then die of embarrassment. It will make you crazy for awhile. What you must learn to do is to be patient with them and put them at their ease. It is they who are most afraid, Andrew—afraid to cause you more pain. Lie back and close your eyes for awhile. You are exhausted and working toward a fever as well, I think. And do not waste any more time worrying. In a few hours you will be safe in your own bed surrounded by people who love you and nothing will seem nearly as bad as it has in the recent past." Abbercombe helped the captain lie back upon the couch, covered him with the blanket, and laid more coal upon the fire. Then he left the room, closing the door quietly behind him.

Once Hartshorn had survived Fanning's ministrations and was tucked warmly into bed and Hempstead was despatched to Lord Wyndham with messages of Harry's and the Captain's arrival, Abbercombe made his way to his study where he indulged, while pacing, in a glass of port and a cigar. The scratch on the door, when it came, brought a gruff order to enter. "Miss Willburton-Smythe has breakfasted, your grace, and awaits your pleasure in the Gold Saloon," Dawson announced quietly.

Abbercombe stubbed out the cigar, set the wine aside, and strolled impatiently past Dawson into the corridor. It was not until he entered the Gold Saloon and saw the look on Olivia's face that he recalled he still wore the clothes he had left home in the evening before.

"Oh, Abbercombe!" Olivia exclaimed, rising and crossing the Turkish carpet to stand before him, a vision of loveliness in a jonquil merino morning dress fetched for her from home, her dusky hair swept up into a chignon, tendrils of curls escaping at the most alluring intervals. "Have you just gotten home from Gravesend this moment then? Your poor face—" One delicate hand went to caress a dark bruise upon his cheek and made him aware that though he had washed up a bit, he did not look at all the thing. His lower lip was split, he'd gained a cut over one eyebrow and his jaw ached and was likely turning blue-green. "Come, sit beside me," Olivia urged him gently, taking his hand in hers and leading him toward the striped settee. "Dawson said that you especially wished to speak to me." Her wonderfully expressive eyes surveyed him from head to toe with obvious pity. "I cannot thank you enough for coming so promptly to my rescue. You were—wonderful."

"I, ah, came to ask your forgiveness, Olivia," said the duke gravely, "for—for involving you in such a—an—uncomfortable situation last night, and—and for my behaviour."

Olivia found herself paying great attention to the design of the Turkish carpet and fought to keep her lips from quivering upward into a smile. "For your behaviour, sir?"

"Yes, in that blasted pit when I—and for my remarkable rudeness, too, in speaking to you as I did after that silly war in the courtyard." He collapsed against the back of the couch, stretched his long legs out in front of him, stuffed his hands into his pockets and sighed. "I *am* pigheaded, you know *and* a wretched, unprincipled boor."

Olivia laughed. "Yes, I know."

"Yes, well," Abbercombe continued above her giggles, "I assure you I am quite sorry to have—offended you, and I hope you will forgive me. You will forgive me, will you not, Olivia, when you have overcome your hilarity?"

Olivia took a very deep breath, snickered, and nodded.

"Thank you, I shall attempt to behave properly from now on."

"Oh, Abbercombe, I do not believe for one moment that you know how to behave properly." Olivia smiled up at him from beneath her long lashes. "Look at yourself. Not even when you were young did gentlemen take it upon themselves to attend a lady in such a state of disarray. Why you have not even shaved."

"Well, but everything was going so splendidly, you know, that I did not stop to think how I must look. I simply wanted to see you. To make things all right between us. I do not wish to lose you—to lose your friendship, Olivia."

"You have not lost my friendship, nor are you likely to do so. I do not know what it is, but I find I cannot seem to dislike you for any extended length of time."

"Good," sighed Abbercombe. "That is a piece of luck."

"What is?"

"That you cannot seem to dislike me for very long. I have something to tell you, Olivia."

Olivia looked at him, puzzled. "Yes?"

"I have located Andrew."

"Oh!" Olivia gasped, her hands fluttering to her lips. "Is he—is he—alive?"

"Very much so—only, he is not exactly in prime twig." Abbercombe straightened and moved to the edge of the seat, his arms resting across his knees, his blue eyes glancing sideways at her. "Your brother has lost an arm, my dear." He raised a hand to silence her before she could speak. "I tell you now, for I do not wish you to appear shocked when you greet him. He needs you to welcome him and not make a great to-do about his injury. He is downstairs in the Children's Den."

Olivia jumped up immediately and ran into the hall toward the staircase. The duke rose slowly and stood in the doorway, staring after her. Then with long strides he made his way to the breakfast room and amidst the chaos chose a seat next to April and whispered in that young lady's ear. Across from them, Lady Vale watched the expressions on the girl's face change from wonder to horror to excitement to all out joy. With a little squeak, April sprang from her seat and rushed out of the room.

"Papa, what did you say to April?" Amaryllis asked, amazed.

"That her father was downstairs in the Children's Den."

"Oh, Cash! You have brought him home!" cried Lady Vale. "I knew you would, only I could not think how."

"Did you find Harry, too, Papa?" asked Christian.

"Yes, Harry is upstairs in bed, but you must none of you disturb him until much later. He is asleep."

"Harry's home! Harry's home!" chanted Ethan and Frazier in unison as Gracie and Helen stood up on the seats of their chairs and clapped. Amy and Beth came 'round the table to hug their father, and Christian and Damian came to shake his hand.

"We knew you would do it, Papa," Damian grinned.

When at last Captain Willburton-Smythe had been tucked safely into the duke's coach in Olivia's and April's tender care, and John Coachman had rolled through the gates on the way to Park Street, Abbercombe, pulsing with repressed energy from the success of his morning, strolled to his stables, saddled Gadzooks and rode off toward the west gate of Hyde Park.

Once inside, to the amazement of the few who populated that haven at such an early hour, he gave the oddly marked horse its head and the two of them sailed across the green, soaring over fences and ditches and hedges with such remarkable grace and speed that everyone who witnessed their glorious flight felt bound to comment upon it. At last he drew Gadzooks into a canter and then into a trot and turned toward home, a puzzled frown upon his face and looking as if he had just fought off an army of wild red Indians.

Nineteen

Olivia waited impatiently outside the bedroom door as Dr. Howard examined Andrew. The physician emerged with a smile and taking her arm, escorted her to a small sitting room down the hall. "He will do nicely, Miss Olivia. Whoever the surgeon was had charge of him, he has done a bang-up job of it."

"But he seems so ill."

"A bit feverish, my dear, and weak. But he has made a long and perilous journey and is greatly fatigued. I should never have let him up from his bed, much less expected him to be capable of such an hectic pace as he has managed in the past few weeks. You must keep him in bed, and I will drop by the apothecary and have a potion delivered for him." Noting the worry in Olivia's fine green eyes, he assured her that he would call again the following afternoon and giving her hand a pat, departed.

Olivia repeated to April all that Howard had said. "May I go in, do you think, and just sit beside him? I will not tax him, I promise, Aunt Olivia."

Olivia smiled and nodded. Once the girl had gone, she settled into a chair in her own sitting room and gazed at the gathering clouds beyond her window. Of all the things in her life that she had not expected, to be indebted to a rogue such as Abbercombe for her brother's life was the most unexpected of all. No, that was not exactly true. The love she felt for Abbercombe was the most unexpected of all.

She could see him even now, unshaven, dirty, a proper mess on the settee beside her. Esther Dowling had mentioned that morning how Abbercombe had asked in particular that she accompany her associates, lest Miss Olivia be compromised. But she had not been compromised. Yet, imagine if she had. Imagine if Abbercombe had offered for her because of it. Would she have accepted him? Oh, how could she even think of such a thing—to accept a proposal of marriage from a man simply to rescue her reputation? Olivia stood and began to pace the floor restlessly. Certainly she was and always had been thoroughly independent and capable. Certainly she required neither the duke's sizable fortune nor his protection for propriety's sake. And most certainly she would never marry a gentleman who considered himself forced to offer for her because he imagined her compromised. But, oh, how much she wanted him, wanted to share his life, to be with him and care for him and feel his arms about her and his lips on hers forever. She gave herself a shake and took herself off to look in upon Andrew.

For the next week Olivia's days and nights were spent caring for and worrying about her brother. Each day Dr. Howard came to change the dressing and be sure that Andrew improved and did not overtax himself. Sometimes, as she sat beside his bed at night, Andrew would mutter in his sleep and once he screamed, but when he woke he would not tell her what his dreams had been.

"The war, my dear," was all he would say, as if it were something to which she should pay little heed. "I shall survive, you know, Livvy. Do not worry so." She knew he was depressed though he would not admit it and she and April thought to take turns reading to him and sharing with him bits of gossip about people he knew well. Still, whenever he thought they were not looking, his eyes would dull, his smile fade, and a little sigh escape his lips.

On Thursday, Lord Sebastian and Lady Jessica stopped by and Lord Sebastian spent a good hour deep in conversation with Andrew while Lady Jess attempted to ease away some of Olivia's and April's worries. On Friday, much to Olivia's amazement, Lord Worth and Mr. Brummell appeared on her doorstep to try their hands at entertaining her brother for an hour or two. On Saturday, Laslow opened the front door to Geoffery Hempstead, who spent merely fifteen minutes with April and then asked to be taken to the captain.

"I do not think, Mr. Hempstead, that this is quite the time for you to—" Olivia began with some consternation.

"You mistake my intentions, ma'am," Hempstead interrupted. "I do not wish to ask him for permission to address Miss April."

"You do not?"

"No, ma'am, only to say hello and see how he comes along."

Olivia was dumbfounded when she escorted Hempstead into Andrew's room and her brother welcomed the gentleman like a long lost friend, and even more dumbfounded when Andrew informed her that Hempstead had been the young man who attended him upon the *Peregrine* from Alderney to Gravesend. With Hempstead's subtle prodding, Andrew began for the first time to tell his sister and daughter how he had been rescued from a cell at Sarvignon Castle, been transported across enemy lines with Harry Hartshorn to the French coast, smuggled aboard the *Mary Beth* to Anderley, and then transferred to *Peregrine* and carried safely home.

"I cannot say," he murmured quietly toward the end of his tale, "how many people came to our aid. It seemed to me there were millions, and all of them risking their lives. I asked some of them, you know, why they helped, and all they would say was that The Rogue had asked it of them. I had heard of The Rogue before," he added with a glance at Hempstead, "though I held a low opinion of spies at the time and thought them all greedy cowards, selling secrets for their own profit. I was mistaken."

Elated that at last Andrew had been able to speak of his ordeal, Olivia gave secret thanks for Geoffery Hempstead and for the other gentlemen who had taken the time to make her brother feel more secure and less fearful of the effects of his injury. On Sunday afternoon Andrew demanded to come down to the drawing room and was settled snugly before the grate with a blanket across his knees. Outside the sun shone brightly and Olivia had opened all the draperies, hoping the fineness of the day would help to cheer him. April, in her prettiest garden frock had seated herself at the pianoforte and was about to entertain her father with several new pieces when Laslow appeared in the doorway, his usually stern countenance wavering toward a grin. "Some ladies and gentlemen to see Captain Andrew," he announced, "but only if he is not too done up and don't mind bears."

"Don't mind bears?!?" exclaimed the captain, his head turned toward the door and his eyebrows rising. "Who is it, Laslow?"

"Miss Olivia's mad duke, sir," declared the butler with an almost perfectly straight face, "and family."

"Miss Olivia's—? Well, show them in by all means," the captain commanded and glanced inquiringly at April, who giggled.

There was a good deal of scuffling in the downstairs hall as pelisses and gloves and hats and canes were left in Laslow's charge, the sound of giggles and whispers and tip-tapping feet climbing the stairs, a shuffling and squeak or two in the hall and then they appeared in the drawing room doorway, looking, Olivia thought, like perfect angels. Gracie and Helen stood at the front in red velvet dresses with lace at the collars and cuffs, and white sashes around their tiny waists and long white stockings and white kid slippers, each of them with a bright red bow set amongst her curls. Both of the girls held to a very long leather leash at the end of which Bear bounced, looking distinctly gratified at the size of the room she expected to disrupt. Behind them stood Ethan and Frazier sporting new riding coats of blue superfine with big brass buttons, and bright red waistcoats. Behind them Amy and Beth and Christian and Damian grinned in their best Sunday clothes.

"Come in, my dears," urged Olivia, happily observing the bemused smile upon her brother's face.

April had left the piano stool and gone to stand behind her father's chair. "Come here, and I will introduce you to my papa."

The Denbighs walked very properly to where the captain waited and curtsied and bowed politely as each of them was introduced. But then Bear grrred and pounced upon the captain's slippers, and Helen squeaked, "No, no, Bear!" and sat down atop the captain's feet. Thwarted, Bear gave an abrupt yarf and charged under the captain's chair from where she scrabbled at the captain's heels. Gracie squealed, "Stop, Bear, stop," and crawled under the chair after the puppy. Ethan groaned loudly and collapsed to hands and knees to unwind the leash from around the chair legs and Helen and Gracie, and Frazier crawled to the other side of the chair to lure Bear from the attack by dangling a tassel from his papa's Hessians before her eyes and then tossing it across the carpeting. The puppy bounded after the toy and entangled Frazier, Christian, and Damian in the leash as well. "Help! Help!" giggled Frazier infectiously, rolling onto his back, "we are all catched in Bear's handle!" Amy and Beth and April, all laughing, went to the rescue just a split second before Chris and Daymee lost their balance as the leash pulled tight behind their knees. Olivia heard Andrew whoop with laughter and laughed so hard herself that tears streamed down her cheeks. She looked up to see Abbercombe grinning at her from the doorway.

"I see the scurvy lot are making their customary well-bred impression," he said above the uproar. "May we come in as well?"

Olivia nodded, unable to catch her breath for a moment. The duke strolled into the drawing room followed by an extremely handsome young gentleman with hair the color of autumn leaves and hazel eyes flecked with gold who walked with the help of an ebony cane. "Oh, I say," chuckled Harry at the children, "you are none of you safe to take anywhere, barbarians."

"Olivia," said the duke, coming to a stop beside her, "may I present Mr. Harry Hartshorn. Harry, Miss Willburton-Smythe."

"You are the gentleman who escaped with Andrew," Olivia said, suddenly serious. "I am very pleased to meet you. Will you not sit down? Abbercombe?"

"In a moment, Olivia, I had best rescue Andrew from the crew first." With an experienced hand Abbercombe loosed the leash from Bear's collar and unwound Daymee and Chris and a giggling April and Amy and Beth, whose attempts at rescue had

somehow ended in their getting tied up as well. He scooped Helen
from Andrew's feet, tugged Grace from beneath Andrew's chair
and deposited both of them in Andrew's lap. Ethan and Frazier
he untangled, tickled, lifted one under each arm and deposited
in the middle of the floor next to the puppy. "Now no one move
for at least thirty seconds." He collapsed into a chair with a sigh
and a chuckle.

"You are as competent as ever, sir," acknowledged Mr. Hartshorn with a twinkle in his eyes.

"Ain't he just, Harry?" Christian grinned, settling beside Mr.
Hartshorn on a long, mauve silk couch. Damian took the space
on Harry's other side, while Amy, Beth and April divided two
footstools and the piano stool among them.

"I don't believe," said Andrew, nervously balancing Helen and
Grace, "that I have ever seen this room so well-filled."

"Do not panic, Andrew," Abbercombe drawled. "Grace and
Helen are already six and so will not fall off nor break if you
move, will you, my dears?"

"Uh-uh, Papa," Helen smiled shyly up at the captain.

"Of course not. Now, how are you feeling, Andrew? Is there
anything we can do—except leave—to make you feel better?"

Captain Willburton-Smythe guffawed and Olivia's heart filled
with joy to hear him. The afternoon surged into early evening
amidst the babble of children, the barking of Bear, loud games
of lottery tickets and jackstraws, and musical entertainment in
which even Mr. Hartshorn took part. April's father was variously
addressed as Cap'n Weebuttonsmite, Mr. Cap'n, Cap'n Button,
and Captain Willburton-Smythe, sir! which Christian and
Damian tossed in off-handedly from time to time to make up for
the way the younger children and their papa murdered the poor
man's name. Olivia held her breath when Helen asked where Mr.
Cap'n had put his arm and Ethan wanted to know how it had
come off in the first place. Then Gracie wondered how come you
couldn't make flour paste and stick it back on and Frazier thought
it would have been a very good idea to put it in a box and have
a funeral. Olivia could not believe her ears when Andrew laugh-

ingly agreed that a funeral would have been great fun and that he wished he had felt well enough to think of it at the time.

"I hope you do not mind, Olivia, that I have brought all this chaos into your drawing room," Abbercombe grinned, stooping before her to attach Bear's lead. "I should not have done, but I thought it would be good for Andrew. It is difficult to wallow in self-pity and despair when confronted with a horde of curious children. Will you walk with Bear and me in the garden?"

Olivia nodded and took the arm he offered. "We shall be back directly," she told Andrew, who winked at her in reply.

"Did Hempstead come earlier in the week?" Abbercombe asked as they descended the staircase.

"Yes. I was never more surprised than to learn that he had taken part in Andrew's rescue." Olivia accepted the wrap Laslow offered her, allowing Abbercombe to place the merino cape about her shoulders. She led him through the house to the side door, and they stepped out into the kitchen garden.

"Hurley and Sir Ralph Richardson intend to drop by tomorrow, I believe," the duke murmured, watching Bear dash into a patch of early lettuce and bounce back out again. "And several of Andrew's fellow Hussars plan a visit later in the week. You must decide if he is well enough to see them. But do not underestimate him, my dear, he has a great deal of bottom and will hurdle every obstacle. You wait and see if he does not."

Olivia stared at the duke with lips slightly parted and eyes awash. "What is it, Olivia?" he asked gently, coming to a halt. "Please do not cry. Are you so exhausted from nursing Andrew? Or have you been so frightened for him and now you are relieved? It cannot be anything I've said—can it?"

Olivia gave a wet little gurgle and sniffed. "N-no, I am just being a silly wet goose."

"You are?"

"Indeed. You have been so good to April and me ever since we met you, and now—now you are everything wonderful to my brother as well. It is you who send the gentlemen to divert him. Even Worth and Brummell have come. And now, his fellow soldiers. I should not have—I should have made a dreadful baby of Andrew if you had not—" Overcome by tears, she buried her face in his neckcloth and sobbed. His arms came around her and held her, one hand rubbing her back gently as the other held to Bear's lead.

"Sweet girl," he said when her sobbing ceased and her head was cushioned on his chest. "I would do most anything for you."

"You would?"

"Yes." He rested his chin on the very top of her head and clasped her to him so tightly that she thought her body might well dissolve into his.

"If you do not move soon, that puppy will have you tied permanently together," a gruff voice announced after an eternity.

Olivia jumped; Abbercombe released her.

"Better," nodded the elderly gentleman with the bushy white eyebrows who took Bear's lead from Abbercombe's hand and began to unwind it from around the two of them. "I expect neither of you even noticed you were being joined."

"Uncle Sully!" Abbercombe cried delightedly.

"Yes, and you should be most grateful it is I and not your Aunt Margaret. At this moment she is in the drawing room wondering what has become of you."

"Miss Willburton-Smythe," Abbercombe grinned down at her, "may I present my godfather, Lord Wyndham. Uncle Sully, Olivia."

"How do you do, my dear," drawled the beaming gentleman in the puce coat and dark blue breeches. "May I escort you inside?" He stuck the puppy's lead into Abbercombe's hand and offered Olivia his arm. She took it sheepishly. "Do not be embarrassed, my dear. I am certain any impropriety was on Rudolph's part."

"Oh, no!"

Wyndham broke into chuckles. "Oh, no? Do you hope to preserve his reputation then? Better to preserve your own, I say, for Rudolph's is far beyond redemption."

"Why are you here?" Abbercombe asked.

"I met your Aunt Margaret in the park and she wished to introduce me to Captain and Miss Willburton-Smythe."

Abbercombe sighed. "You won't tell her, Uncle Sully, that you discovered us doing anything but walking Bear, will you?"

"You must hope she does not ask me what you were doing, Rudolph. I have never been able to lie to that lady."

The Earl of Stamford stood quite still, the only visible movement a slight quivering of his nostrils. His face grew first pink, then red, then a virulent shade of purple. Every muscle in his body clenched and his eyes bulged from their sockets.

"Father, sit down," urged Kettering, attempting to lead the older man to a chair. "It cannot be so terrible as to send you into an apoplexy."

"Do not, ever, say that name in my presence again!" exploded the earl, his muscles suddenly unclenching and his eyes sinking back to where they belonged. "Never, do you hear me!"

"The entire town heard you," drawled Kettering with a glance at Harcort. "Please sit down, sir."

With great passion the earl hurled himself into his favourite chair and pounded loudly upon its great oaken arms.

"Really, Father," murmured Harcort, pouring some of his father's best Madeira, "you are coming it too strong, sir."

"You, Harcort, know nothing," declared the earl, accepting the wine and downing it in two large gulps. "More, boy."

Harcort handed a glass to his brother and with a shrug turned back to refill his father's glass. "We did not come to persecute you, Father, only to discover how to help you. Miranda and Thomas come Tuesday to take you with them to Hollow Hills."

"I shall not be sent to rusticate in my son-in-law's care as if I were a naughty schoolboy!"

"Yes, you shall, sir, and be thankful for it!" Harcort shouted so loudly that Kettering's jaw dropped. "I cannot conceive how you have come to such a pass! Has your mind truly gone? To abduct Miss Willburton-Smythe at gunpoint, to attempt to kill the duke, when neither has harmed you in any way."

"Not harmed me? Not harmed me?" growled Stamford, slurping at his wine. "Hah! Shows your ignorance! He murdered Channing! Murdered him! Hit him over the head with a candlestick, from behind, like the coward he is! And did he hang? No! Should have danced the jig at Tyburn, but not him! Son of a duke! Favourite of the king! Damn bloody murderer! And then he has the gall to come back here. Flaunting himself! Using his daughters to lure my sons to their dooms just as he lured my brother!" Stamford smashed the hand with the wine glass down upon the chair arm sending shards of glass and dark purple wine flying everywhere.

Elijah Stone rushed into the parlor followed by two of his associates and a Bow Street Runner. It took all six of the men to subdue the earl enough to remove the slivers of glass from his hand and clean and bandage it. Kettering, after his father had calmed a bit, sent to the apothecary for laudanum. By the time it arrived, the earl was back in his chair, and Stone, his associates, and the Runner back in their places guarding the doors to the house.

Harcort paced the room, mumbling to himself. "You know, Father," he said, coming to a halt before the scowling man, "you could very well be dead now, or in Newgate if the duke had not had pity upon you."

"I do not wish that villain's pity!"

"No, but, Father," Kettering offered, setting the bottle of laudanum drops down upon a small, cherrywood buffet, "you do not understand the whole of the thing. He did not set his daughters to lure us into his household, or whatever you are thinking. In fact, he warned Harcort and me to have nothing to do with him or the girls. He even told me flat out to stop dangling after Amy. He said that if you discovered I had formed a *tendré* for his daughter, you would lose your mind."

Harcort stared at his brother. "When did he say that?"

"Oh, some time ago. I forgot to tell you. Slipped my mind."

"Wonderful!"

"Well, it would not have mattered, Davey. You would not have stopped seeing Beth, even if I had remembered to tell you."

"True," muttered Harcort, glaring back at his father. "Though how I am to face her now, after my own father has tried at least three times to kill hers, I cannot think."

The Earl of Stamford sank down in his chair, his legs sprawling out before him. He mumbled to himself, scowled at his sons, and mumbled again.

"What, Father?" Kettering asked, stooping down before the chair. "We did not understand you."

"I said that I wish to meet the rogue's daughters."

"By Jove, I don't think so!" exclaimed Harcort.

Kettering stood and took his brother's arm, leading him to the other side of the room. "I think Abbercombe had the right of it, Davey. I think we ought to call in a physician—you know, like the ones caring for Farmer George."

"Well, but they don't seem to be doing the king any good, Bry. What makes you think they could help Father?"

"They could attempt to do something. One never knows."

"All right," nodded Harcort. "We shall discuss the thing with Miranda and Tom, and if they agree, I shall find one will be willing to accompany them into the country. But I confess, I don't hold out much hope."

When they turned back to take leave of their father, they blinked rather stupidly at his empty chair. Harcort, fuming, raced to the parlor door and jerked it open. "Stone!" he called, "has the earl gone up to his dinner, then?"

Elijah Stone, who had been leaning his shoulders against the front door deep in discussion with Alfie Battson, straightened immediately. "Gone where, yer lordship?"

"Upstairs, Stone."

"No, sir, he ain't set one foot inta this 'all. 'e's in that there parlor wi' ye."

"No, he is not. He was, but—" Harcort stared at his brother

and both of them rushed back into the room with Stone and Alfie on their heels. There was no sign of the earl.

"Dash it all, he cannot have vanished into thin air," Kettering groaned. "Father! Answer me, sir!"

When no answer was forthcoming, Stone sent Alfie off to spread the alarm and set out himself to search the grounds. It took only moments for Mic Crawley and Alfie to join him in the yard while Esther Dowling and the Runner, with Kettering and Harcort beside them, began to search the house with the help of those servants who had not been involved in the abduction nor the earlier attempts on the duke's life and had therefore been allowed to remain. At the end of a quarter hour they had all to admit that Stamford was not to be found. Apparently, he *had* vanished into thin air. With great consternation the Bow Street Runner set off to discover if anyone at all in the neighborhood had seen the man, while Stone gave terse orders to his associates to "git yer selfs back over ta the dook's an' don' be lettin' 'im er the chillren outta yer sights 'til we finds the barmy devil."

Harcort and Kettering, unable to decide the best action to take themselves, decided to go back to their own chambers and enlist Hempstead's aid in checking out their father's clubs and cronies. "Did he climb out the window, do you think?" Kettering asked, as he mounted his brother's curricle.

"I ain't got the faintest notion," grumbled Harcort, irate, "but when I get my hands upon him, I shall carry him off to Bedlam myself. You may place your blunt upon it!"

"I say, Davey, you don't suppose he has gone off to kill Abbercombe again, do you?"

"That is exactly what I suppose, and what the Runner and Stone think as well. Why, Bry? Don't you think it?"

"No. I cannot quite conceive of the old villain being so stupid as that. He had a jolly plan the last time, and I expect he has probably been sitting around thinking up another for the past eight days. How else could he have slipped away from all of us so quickly? He has been plotting again."

* * *

The Earl of Stamford stood very still inside the small closet hidden behind the parlor panelling. It sounded to him as if everyone had gone off, but he considered that a few more moments in hiding would do him no harm. Luckily, neither of his sons knew about the closet that had been set into the wall directly behind his chair. Miranda knew, of course, for she had helped her mother badger him into it years ago. Had to have it. Had to have a place to store the grandfather clock when they left town. It was too damned precious to be left under holland covers for the winter. Luckily he had had the workman build it high enough and wide enough so that two men could fit in it beside the clock. Made it easy to carry it in and out that way. He began to giggle to himself but stopped immediately he heard it. Still it amused him to think how angry he had been about the nonsense, and now here he was, putting the thing to excellent use.

When he thought he could stand the cramped space no longer, he eased open the panel and peered cautiously out into the room. No one remained. With quiet steps he made his way into the hall, gathered up his hat, gloves, and cane, and then sneaked silently out the front door. He would have to walk, of course, because he could not chance going 'round to the stables. One of the stablehands would be sure to see him and raise a cry. He adjusted his tall beaver hat jauntily on his head, tugged his coat into just the right position, and rambled off nonchalantly in the direction of Fielding House.

When an hour later the duke's coach drew into the courtyard of Fielding House, Viscount Harcort's curricle was pulled off to one side and the front door of the residence stood wide with Dawson nowhere to be seen. Admonishing his brood and Hartshorn to remain inside the coach, Abbercombe rushed into the house. Just behind him, Lord Wyndham exited the landau that carried Lady Vale, leaving that lady with a similar warning to remain behind. As the elderly gentleman entered the residence, he came to a complete halt beside Abbercombe, both of them listening to sounds of shouting and cursing and a good deal of scuffling.

"First floor, I think, Uncle Sully," Abbercombe muttered and dashed off again, taking the staircase two steps at a time. Wyndham followed less vigorously, but with no less trepidation. The noise emanated from the library and the duke burst into that chamber expecting to find himself confronted by some huge mill. What did confront him was no less astounding. The Earl of Stamford stood amidst several fallen bookshelves, holding Dawson, Harcort, Kettering, Hempstead, and several of Stone's associates at bay with the aid of one of Abbercombe's duelling pistols and a jewelled dagger which the duke kept to slit open the pages of new volumes. Lord Wyndham, puffing, mumbled significantly under his breath words which brought a hoot of laughter from Abbercombe. "No, really, Uncle Sully," he chuckled, "it is not another typical evening at the Denbighs'. May I ask," he continued with a lift of his eyebrows, "what is going on?"

Several voices raised in response and Abbercombe hushed them all with a frown. "Kevin," he commanded, "you tell me."

Stamford's cold, dark eyes met Abbercombe's bright blue ones straight on and the duelling pistol switched position and pointed directly at Abbercombe's heart. There was a quick inhaling of breath among the duke's protectors, but though the pistol was ready cocked, Stamford's finger did not yet touch the trigger.

"Tell me, Kevin," Abbercombe said again, his voice softened.

"I have come to speak with you," drawled Stamford, "but it seems I am begrudged even that dubious pleasure."

"Not at all. What was it you wished to speak with me about?"

"Send them all away," Stamford ordered.

"No, Kevin, I shan't do that. But I shall warn them all not to put a hand to you. Will that do?"

"Aye, nicely." With a flourish the Earl of Stamford set the pistol and dagger upon a shelf behind him, stepped over the fallen volumes which littered the carpeting and, removing one of his gloves, brought it stinging across Abbercombe's cheek. "Harcort and Kettering shall stand my seconds," growled the man, "do they wish to do so or not."

Abbercombe bowed. "I believe the choice of weapons is mine?"

"You know very well it is."

"Pistols. My seconds will arrange the matter promptly."

With his chin high Stamford tugged the glove back on and stepped by the duke and into the hallway. Wide-eyed, Harcort and Kettering stared helplessly at Abbercombe. "Go with him," the duke murmured. "My seconds will contact you, assuming I can find Worth. Geoff, Harry is indisposed; will you do me the honor?"

"I—but—y-yes, sir," stuttered Hempstead.

"Good. Well, go drive your father home, you puppies. And send in my children and Harry and Lady Vale while you're at it." His words sent Kettering and Harcort hurrying from the room. "And the rest of you disappear. Dawson, some brandy for Wyndham and Hempstead and me and probably Harry—in my study."

Twenty

Kettering and Harcort discovered the earl motionless in the courtyard, his eyes fastened on the duke's coach. As they halted beside him, the door of the vehicle opened, the steps clattered down and Christian emerged. He held out his hand to assist both of his elder sisters. Immediately behind them, Damian exited and then Harry. With a good deal of formality they approached the Earl of Stamford and his sons. "Viscount Harcort," Bethany purred, "will you introduce us to this gentleman?"

Hesitantly, ready to pounce upon their father should he begin to act the least bit odd, Harcort and Kettering made the introductions. The girls curtsied prettily and the boys bowed, while Hartshorn shook the earl's hand and excused himself to escort Lady Vale from the landau.

"We are truly pleased to make your acquaintance, my lord," smiled Amy. "Your sons do you great honor by their conduct and bearing whenever we meet and have made us long to know you."

"Though I expect you are not dreadfully pleased to meet us," Bethany sighed.

Stamford could not decide how to look any more than he could decide how to respond. At last he stuttered that of course he was pleased to meet such fine young ladies and gentlemen, which came near to sending Harcort and Kettering reeling from shock.

"You are most kind, my lord," offered Christian, "after all the misery our father has caused you."

"Indeed, sir, and ourselves as well," continued Daymee, "for it was our idea to come to London. We did not understand the consequences of our decision."

"We are very sorry, Lord Stamford," finished Bethany in her most devastatingly ingenuous voice.

Lady Vale then approached the earl on Harry's arm and demanded to be reintroduced lest Kevin had forgotten her after all the years she had been absent from London. Hartshorn left them and went inside to search out the duke.

"Kin we come out, now?" called Ethan from the coach window through which Helen was already hanging, Gracie sticking part way out of the other. "Bear's climbin' all over ever'thin'!"

"Grrr-arf!" agreed the puppy, unseen.

Stamford, mesmerized, moved through the crowd surrounding him to the coach itself. "Come out, then," he said, and watched as Ethan and Frazier scrambled down into the courtyard and helped Gracie and Helen to the cobbles. Bear leaped from the coach with no help at all and bounced happily about the children's legs. Then, tentatively, she went to sniff at the earl's boots, and sitting down, looked inquiringly up at him.

Stamford squatted down and patted the puppy's head. "And who are you?" he asked, eyeing one after the other of the children. When he had learned all of their names and introduced himself and been told excitedly about Cap'n Weebuttonsmite and his lost arm; and how they had none of them had their dinners yet and were starvin'; and asked if him and why-count Hardcut and Mr. Kettlering were gonna' stay an' eat, 'cause then they could prob'ly all have extra tarts if only Lord Stampherd would ask; he told them all that he was very sorry, but he and Harcort and Kettering must go home. "But I am most pleased," he added, standing, "to have made your acquaintances." He shook Ethan's and Frazier's hands, found that Gracie and Helen held theirs out to be shaken as well, and very soberly did so. Then he strolled to Harcort's curricle, climbed to the box and waited patiently as his sons took their leave and joined him.

* * *

As Harry entered the duke's study Lord Wyndham was railing at Abbercombe. "Because, you young puppy, you have never fired a pistol in your life, and Stamford is a demmed fine shot, that's why. Whatever maggot creeps about in that beetle box of yours has chawed upon your brain for much too long. You have not a spot of intelligence left. How you could elect to duel the man when such an enormous amount of evidence exists to implicate him in your attempted murder is a wonder to me—but to elect to duel him with pistols! I despair of you, Cash. I really do."

Flabbergasted at Wyndham's words, Hartshorn sank down beside Hempstead on the window seat.

"Well, but," the duke responded much too casually, acknowledging Hartshorn's entrance by taking him a brandy, "I have no intention of shooting Kevin, Uncle Sully, so what does it matter that I am not a crack shot?"

"Do you even know how to load a pistol?" Wyndham growled.

"No, sir, he don't," offered Hartshorn, quietly.

"No, I don't," agreed Abbercombe, "but I assume Worth does—or Hempstead. You do know how, do you not, Geoff?"

Hempstead looked up to find Abbercombe's eyes staring at him beseechingly and the younger gentleman shuddered. "Y-yes," he answered, "but—"

"So, you see, Wyndham, I shall not make a total ass of myself. At least the thing will be loaded."

"Do you mean the pistol Stamford held in the library was not loaded?" Hempstead queried.

"Of course it was not loaded!" exploded Wyndham. "This pixilated cork-brain has never owned any gunpowder much less any balls for the demmed things!"

"Well, you would not either, Uncle Sully, if you had a constant parade of children prying into everything. D'you think I wished to see one of the cubs pointing a loaded pistol at the other? No, thank you very much. I care a good deal more for them than that. It is not as easy as you think to be a spy when you have eight chicks running about the house. I have had all

I can do to keep them from skewering each other on my swords."

* * *

Only moments after Olivia had bid her brother a fond good-night and seen him safely to his room, she found herself confronted by April in tears and a panicked Hempstead.

"Tell me, again, Geoffery," she murmured. "I think perhaps I have not understood correctly."

"I cannot say it much plainer, ma'am. The Earl of Stamford has challenged the duke to a duel and the duke has accepted. Abbercombe has chosen pistols, which he don't know the first thing about. He declares it don't matter because he has not the least intention of shooting the earl anyway. Worth and Hartshorn are at Fielding House attempting to dissuade him, but I do not see how they will when even Wyndham could not carry the point."

"He will die, Aunt Olivia!" cried April. "I know it! Amy and Beth have told me their papa cannot forgive himself for Channing Kettering's death, and now he has chosen to stand up before the earl and make a target of himself because of it! Oh, Geoffery," she sobbed, clinging to that gentleman's lapels and burying her face in the folds of his neckcloth, "you must stop him."

"Yes, you must," Olivia agreed. "You are one of his seconds. You must bring the thing to a halt."

"I cannot, ma'am. We have all attempted to defuse the situation. Harcort and Kettering have protested and implored, but Stamford will not be satisfied until he faces the duke across fifteen paces of green and the duke is determined to let him."

"When?" Olivia asked, her face gone very pale.

"Tomorrow, ma'am, at dawn. I am even now on my way to accompany Abbercombe to the Rose and Crown, for the duel occurs at St. Charles's Glen which is only a mile or so from the inn. Abbercombe don't care to make such a long journey, he says, so early as he must if he waits until morning."

"And—and Stamford?" Olivia queried fearfully.

"I believe he also lies at the Rose and Crown tonight. We thought, Miss Olivia, if you were to speak to the duke, perhaps he might listen to you."

"Have not Lady Vale or the girls—"

"No, ma'am. The duke has strictly forbidden all of us to broach the matter in their presence. I should be horsewhipped, I expect, were he to discover I had come to you. But Harry, Mr. Hartshorn, that is, and I thought that—"

"You were absolutely correct to come to me, Mr. Hempstead," Olivia declared lifting her chin bravely and tugging April from Hempstead's embrace. "You must go now and give Abbercombe your support. April and I will consider what is best to be done."

Feeling rather much of a traitor, but a bit less panicked, Hempstead left Park Street and returned to Fielding House where Worth informed him that the duke was in the midst of kissing his cubs goodnight and that they were to leave for the Rose and Crown directly he finished that project.

Olivia, in the wake of Hempstead's exit, rang for Laslow and ordered the coach brought 'round. Hurriedly she packed some overnight clothes into a bandbox. "I do not know exactly what I shall be able to do, April," she said on a little gasp, "but I must do something. If needs be, I shall throw myself between the two of them. I vow, I will."

"Oh, Aunt Olivia, no! You will be killed!"

"Well, I will not do so, unless I can find no other means," Olivia assured the girl. "You must remain here and watch over your father. I wonder if—" She was interrupted by a scratching upon her bedchamber door. "Come in," she called.

"There is a young woman, ma'am, wishes a word with you," Laslow announced. "I have asked her to wait in the drawing room."

Olivia rushed down the stairs, hoping perhaps one of Abbercombe's daughters had come to say the duel had been called off. The figure that met her worried gaze as she entered the drawing room was not one of the Denbighs, however.

"Esther! Miss Dowling!" Olivia cried, crossing to give the young woman a quick hug. "You are just the person I require."

"Aye, ma'am, an' I thought ye might. I knowed ye wouldn't be a lettin' the dook go ta 'is death wi'out a struggle. I comed ta see could I he'p ye."

"You certainly may. You may accompany me to the Rose and Crown where I intend to confront him with the senselessness of such an engagement. Have you brought anything with you? No? Then I shall pack you one of my gowns to sleep in, in case that should become necessary. I shall not be long."

The journey to the Rose and Crown seemed interminable. Even in Esther Dowling's kind and reassuring company, Olivia found it hard to still her heart and calm her breathing. Abbercombe could not do this thing. He could not. And yet, it seemed so like him. She knew he would see it as apropos—an end fitting to the beginning of all his troubles. She worried and fidgeted the time away. He might have killed the Earl of Stamford at Evelsisor, but he had not. Nor had he allowed the law to be set upon the man. He blamed himself for Stamford's state of mind, for the earl's murderous attempts upon him. But he could not, *could not* be allowed to offer himself up as a sacrifice on the altar of his misguided guilt. Really, it was too much! The man ought to have a deal more sense. And what about the children? What did he think hearing of their papa's unnatural death upon a duelling ground would do to those sweet, innocent children? The man ought to be flogged!

Harcort and Kettering could find no more words to share between them. They sat, despairing, in the public room of the Rose and Crown, staring into the fire and saying nothing. Their father had retired with a bottle of port to his chamber and requested that they, as his seconds, deal with any and all problems concerning the appropriateness of the ground, the time, and the means of arrival. They had already arranged for a surgeon to meet them at the inn before dawn, and that had given them even

less heart to see the dawn come. "He will kill Abbercombe, you
know," Harcort sighed at last, not looking at his brother. "Father
is the finest shot in all of England despite his age."

"Perhaps the duke is equally as fine, Davey."

"What will that help? Then father will be dead—or perhaps
both of them. There is no question of honor involved. The duke
could have laughed in father's face and sent him home in custody
of Stone or the Runners. What does he gain by duelling a madman?"

Kettering sighed and leaned forward, his elbows on his knees,
his head in his hands. "Do you know what I think, Davey? I think
Abbercombe is as much a lunatic as father."

"Quite possibly," a familiar voice declared over his shoulder.
"But I know that Abbercombe plans to delope, so you need not
worry about your father's safety."

"What?" Kettering turned to stare up into Brummell's somber
face. "You cannot mean it. What are you doing here?"

"I was with Worth when Hempstead turned up to ask him to
be one of Abbercombe's seconds. Word of the thing is probably
all over town by this time. May I join you?"

"Surely, Beau, sit," muttered Harcort. "Brandy?"

"Have some," Brummell grinned, holding his glass up for
Harcort's inspection. "So what is the plan? St. Charles's Glen at
dawn is it? You could call the law."

"No, we cannot. There are certain codes of honor involved,
Brummell," Kettering grumbled, "at least in our cases."

"And not in mine, I take it?"

"Well, you ain't one of the seconds."

"Do you wish me to call in the law?"

Harcort and Kettering glanced at each other, sighed, and both
shook their heads. "Not a good idea," muttered Harcort. "Abbercombe's already been transported once—no telling what
would happen did he get arrested for duelling."

"Bosh!" Brummell exclaimed, "Cumberland duels every time
he turns around."

"Yes, but he is Prinny's brother and a royal duke. I hardly think Abbercombe will be likely to rate the same consideration."

Brummell straddled a chair and rested his arms across the chair back, brandy glass in one hand. "I have reached the conclusion recently that Prinny is fonder of Abbercombe than Cumberland, but you could be correct. Even he might not be able to overcome the duke's reputation. So, what about your father? No chance of his backing down?"

"None," answered Harcort and Kettering simultaneously.

Bill Wentworth stood casually at the corner of the bar, listening, and polishing the same glass he had been polishing for the last fifteen minutes. At last coming to a decision, he set down glass and towel, called for his wife, and placed her in charge of the establishment until he should return, whereupon he saddled a hack from his stables and turned the horse's head in a northwesterly direction. "Dashed fine mess he has gotten himself into this time," grumbled the man, jouncing uncomfortably upon the creature's back. " 'Tis 'bout time Janie knowed of it."

Olivia and Esther burst into the inn and finding Mrs. Wentworth behind the desk, requested the use of a private parlor and beseeched her to deliver a note to the Duke of Abbercombe.

"Oh, but he ain't here, ma'am," responded Mrs. Wentworth. "It's sure I am there ben't no dukes about the place a'tall. We got us a earl though. Stamford, I believe. Will he do?"

"No, no," murmured Olivia, fearing ever to see that evil visage again. "He will not do at all."

"We've beat 'im 'ere, ma'am," Esther breathed quietly in Olivia's ear.

"I expect," Olivia began again, "that the duke will arrive quite soon. If I were to write a note, would you be kind enough to deliver it to him upon his arrival?"

"Indeed, ma'am," smiled Mrs. Wentworth. "An' if you'll foller me, I'll settle ye with pen an' ink in me finest parlor."

Just as they began to cross the hall, the door to the inn swung

open and Abbercombe, followed by Worth and Hempstead,
strolled in. The duke came to a halt at the sight of Olivia. Olivia's
heart wrenched as she saw a tender longing leap to his eyes then
disappear. He turned away toward the desk without so much as
an acknowledgment of her or Esther. Esther's elbow poked Olivia
and she looked up to see a martial light in Miss Dowling's eyes.
"Ye kinnot give 'im t'upper han', miss," she whispered. "Ye got
ta face 'im down, or 'e'll not lis'en ta ye."

Olivia swallowed and nodded. "Your grace," she called across
the small lobby, "a word with you, if you please."

Abbercombe, stuffing his hands into the pockets of his buckskin breeches, stalked back across the hardwood floor. "Yes,
Miss Willburton-Smythe?"

"I have procured a private parlor, your grace. Will you join
me there for a moment or two?"

Abbercombe glared down at her. "I beg your pardon, ma'am,
but I must arrange rooms for Worth, Hempstead and myself."

Worth coming up beside him put a hand upon the duke's shoulder and nodded at the women. "Evening, Miss Willburton-
Smythe, Miss Dowling, Mrs. Wentworth. Bill around?"

" 'E's gone off fer a moment, milord. If ye'll wait 'til I show
the ladies to a parlor, I'll be pleased ta help ye."

"Gladly, Mrs. Wentworth. Abbercombe, go with Miss Olivia,
man. Hempstead and Mrs. Wentworth and I shall deal with the
rooms."

Abbercombe's blue eyes, cold as ice, glared at him. "I think
not," he murmured.

"Ah, worried about the protocol of it, are you, Cash?" drawled
Worth with the lift of an eyebrow. "But Miss Dowling will doubtless be pleased to stand propriety for the two of you, will you
not, Miss Dowling?"

"Aye, milord. More'n 'appy to," responded Miss Dowling
with a dip. "Allas were one fer propriety, meself."

"And when you have finished your conversation, Hempstead
and I will meet you in the public room for a glass or two, no?"

"Right this way, ladies, your grace," urged Mrs. Wentworth.

not giving the duke time to refuse, and she led them down the corridor to her best parlor where a fire already blazed in the grate, and dozens of candles provided sufficient light for most evening activities. Olivia crossed to the far side of the room and stared down at the flowers in the dark carpeting. Abbercombe, with stubborn steps, stalked to the fireplace on the opposite wall and rested his arm along the mantlepiece. Mrs. Wentworth asked if she might bring them some refreshment and receiving a negative response, withdrew.

Esther Dowling stood in the center of the room looking from Olivia to Abbercombe and back again. "I b'lieves," she said quietly, "that I needs me a bit o' fresh air like. Ye won't be a mindin' milady, if I were ta walk out through them loverly Frenchie doors fer jist a bit. I shall be within reach o'course." And without waiting for an answer, she absented herself from the room, not quite closing the French doors behind her.

Olivia shrugged back her shoulders, lifted her chin and turned to see where Abbercombe might be. He stood, glaring straight at her in silence. With determined little steps, she crossed the room to him. "Will you not be seated, your grace?" she asked quietly, indicating an armchair before the fire.

"No, thank you. But please feel free yourself, ma'am."

"Do not call me ma'am," Olivia protested haughtily. "You have called me Olivia from almost the day we met. Why now am I ma'am? Because you are angry with me?"

Abbercombe took a deep breath, stared down at his boots, looked up again into the burning green eyes. "Why should I be angry with you, Olivia? Have you done something to warrant it?"

"No, I have not."

"Why have you come here?"

"Why?"

"Yes, Olivia, why? Are you visiting a friend in the neighborhood, perhaps? Or come to gather Mrs. Wentworth's recipe for souffle? Or were you driving to Portsmouth and one of your team tossed a shoe? There are myriad reasons you might have landed in this place at this time. But there, you did not expect to run smack into me and have not prepared yourself as yet."

Olivia assumed her most imposing stature, which brought her only as high as the stickpin in his neckcloth. "If you are suggesting, your grace, that I have need to—to—provide myself with prevarications . . ."

Abbercombe's heart wrenched at the sight of her in her Kelly green cloak, with her finely gloved hands balled into little fists on her hips, and one jean half-boot poking slightly out from beneath the flounce of her striped walking dress. The stubborn, upward tilt of her chin, and the apprehension in her eyes brought a groan to his throat that he fought to stifle. The way her lower lip pouted out so righteously made him wish to kiss it. He was not even listening to her words, and when she sputtered questioningly to a halt, he had to jerk himself to attention.

"Pardon me? My mind was wandering, I fear."

"I said, your grace, that I have no need to prevaricate. I have come here to stop you from committing suicide, and I am not ashamed to tell you so."

"Suicide? Me? Are you run mad, Olivia?"

"You do not call it suicide when you duel Stamford with a weapon with which he is expert and of which you know nothing?"

"No, Olivia, I do not."

"What do you call it then, sir?"

"Faith."

"Faith?"

"Yes, Olivia, faith. And I might suggest that you strive to have a bit of it in me."

"Oh!" Olivia stamped her foot, but it made absolutely no noise on the carpet. "I know what you are about to do, Abbercombe, and it is totally senseless and has nothing to do with faith. You intend to offer yourself up to Stamford because you feel guilty for his brother's death. But you are a total beetle-brain to think so. How you can have carried such unwarranted guilt around

with you for all these years, I cannot understand. And now, to—
to—make a target of yourself for no reason but that—"

"For no reason but that I helped to kill Stamford's brother and
now have lured his sons away from him as well? Was that what
you were about to say, my dear?"

"You did not kill Channing Kettering!" Olivia's eyes were
fairly scalding him and had he been less stubborn or the argument
about anything else at all, Abbercombe might well have grabbed
her up into his arms and tasted that searing passion. But visions
of Channing soared to his brain and he could not stand down.

"I will tell you what I did, Olivia," he growled. "I discovered
a back room in Seven Dials where for a mere cartwheel one could
ride the raging heavens on the back of a frenzied Pegasus. I
climbed aboard and then dragged Channing into the saddle after
me. I am a contemptible libertine, a heartless villain, and a cold-
blooded murderer. I brought Chan disgrace and dishonor. I trans-
formed an admirable gentleman into a savage. I killed Channing
long before that blasted candlestick ever struck him!"

Olivia's hand cracked across his cheek. "How dare you!" she
shouted. "How dare you speak of yourself so!"

The side of Abbercombe's face held the red outline of her
gloved fingers plainly as he stood motionless and silent before
her, his head high, his expression haughty, and his eyes frigid.
Olivia grasped the hand that had hit him in her other and held it
close against her breast. She stared up at him wide-eyed.

He gave her an insolent smile, bowed curtly and left the room.
Olivia sank hopelessly into the chair before the fire.

"Oh, don't be a givin' in ta 'im, now, mum," Esther Dowling
whispered as she entered the chamber and went to sit on the arm
of Olivia's chair. "Why ye've almos' won."

"You—you heard, Esther?"

"Ever'thin', miss."

"He—he hates himself. He—he thinks—"

" 'Tis wha' ye think, miss, matters ta 'im."

"No," Olivia sighed. "You are out there, Esther. What I think
matters not at all. And I have been such a fool. I have made

everything worse than before. I have brought all of it blazing back full-blown into his memory!"

Abbercombe stalked into the public room, seized the glass of brandy from Worth's hand and downed it in one gulp. He then threw the thing with incredible force between Harcort's and Kettering's heads and over Brummell's shoulder where it smashed into the back of the fireplace. "I have a chamber at my disposal, I expect," he said in a restrained whisper, tossing a cartwheel at an astounded waiter. "Bring a bottle of port to it."

"Cash," Worth started.

"Never mind, Edward. Just tell me which room—and don't join me, will you, for at least an hour?"

Janie Coltrain left the pleasant fire before which her husband dozed and the youngest of her children sat roasting potatoes, tucked the long hem of her gown up between her legs and climbed onto the hack behind her brother, riding astride for the first time in fifteen years. "Are you sure of it, Willy?" she asked, wisps of soft brown hair escaping from her bun and flying haphazardly about her cheeks.

"Positive, my girl. 'Tis all they bin talkin' of since they come. An' it's t'Earl o' Stamford what is upstairs in one o' me bedchambers. I 'spect sooner nor later we'll be a seein' 'is grace, lessen 'e figgers ta drive out from town in t'mornin'."

"Well, ye set yer spurs ta this nag o' yourn, Willy. Fer it ain't a'goin' ta be a easy thin' I gotta be doin' of. An' I reckon the sooner I sets to it, the better." Her arms tightly about her brother's waist, they galloped through the darkness toward the Rose and Crown, and with a deep sigh, Janie pressed her forehead against Willy's back and practiced in her mind what she would say and how she would say it.

The first light of dawn blossomed amidst a tarnished mist that crept fitfully across St. Charles's Glen. Tatters and tangles of low-lying fog shredded about the feet and ankles of duellers and seconds alike. On the road a line of three coaches and a curricle stood one behind the other, empty and silent, the teams still in the early morning, only their ears twitching.

Hempstead and Kettering paced off the distance, checking the ground for rabbit holes, stumps, anything which might trip one of the gentlemen unexpectedly. Harcort and Worth debated between two sets of duelling pistols, deciding at last upon the earl's, and then went about loading them. Brummell, his face a mask of apathy, spoke quietly with the little surgeon who shivered in the chill breeze and confessed that he had rather gentlemen duelled, if they must, with swords, for he was more capable of saving a man from a sabre cut than a pistol ball. Off to one side of the ground, the Earl of Stamford stood attended by a tall, middle-aged woman in country dress whose glistening red-brown hair and clear, hazel eyes drew the Duke of Abbercombe's uncertain glances from where he leaned, hands in his breeches pockets, one knee bent nonchalantly against an oak several yards away.

"Who is the woman with your father?" Worth whispered.

Harcort looked toward the place where the couple stood. "Bill Wentworth's sister."

"What? The innkeeper's sister?"

"Yes. She was in father's room last night. They conversed until very late. I cannot conceive how they should even know each other, but father was adamant she accompany him this morning. Here come Bryan and Geoff, I expect we are ready."

Worth nodded and strolled to where the duke waited alone. "Are you sure, Cash, you will not call the thing off?" he asked quietly. He knew what the answer would be, but it was mandatory he ask the question, just as it was mandatory that Harcort ask it of Stamford. Abbercombe shook his head slowly and straightened. With long strides he accompanied Worth to the center of the ground and weighing the pistols in his hand, chose one. Stamford took the other and without a word they waited back to back as the seconds moved out of range. When everyone had cleared,

Brummell, who had requested the honor, began to count off their paces. He was on ten when Miss Willburton-Smythe's coach came to a halt behind the other coaches, and on twelve when Olivia sprang from the vehicle and rushed, unnoticed, across the verge with Esther Dowling close on her heels. Brummell, his mask of apathy slipping badly and his voice beginning to crack, had reached "fifteen, turn and fi—" when Olivia hurled herself between the two men, the duke's pistol exploded, and Esther Dowling shrieked.

Olivia crashed into Abbercombe knocking him backward a step or two. The smoking pistol fell from his hand and his arms encompassed her and jerked her against him so roughly that every bit of breath was forced from her lungs. "Olivia," he shouted. "Olivia, answer me! Are you shot? Are you hit, Olivia?" His voice roared in her ears. Like the sound of the sea to a drowning man, it was all she heard—not his words, not his fear, only the roar of him. Her arms around him, she hid herself against his chest and clung fiercely.

When at last she found her breath and the sound of his roar had faded, she looked up into the handsome face that had gone ashen in a matter of seconds. Her lips moved, but no words came. She shuddered and he swept her up into his arms and carried her to where Esther Dowling stood with her mouth open and eyes wide. Motioning the others to stay back, he set her feet back upon the ground and, his hands gripping her shoulders, he held her from him and shook her violently. "You might have been killed!" he raged. "Do you understand? You could be dead!" And then he tugged her back into his arms and hugged her passionately.

"I do not care," Olivia sobbed at last, her face buried in his neckcloth. "If you wish to die then I do too. I l-love you. I have never l-loved any man before. And—and if you are k-killed, if you are k-killed—"

The tension in Abbercombe's grip eased, and she felt his cheek press tenderly against her own and his breath tickle at her ear.

"My darling girl," he whispered. "My heart and soul ache with love for you."

"Oh, Abbercombe!"

"I cannot go on as I am, Olivia. I have spent a lifetime attempting to redeem myself, only to discover that 'tis Channing's brother must judge whether I have done so. It is nonsensical—but—but I cannot—Kevin and I are both tormented and will continue to be tormented if I have not faith enough to stand before him and accept his judgement."

He kissed Olivia's brow and then her eyes and then her nose and then at last her lips, passionately and with a yearning he made no attempt to disguise. Then he pulled away from her and admonished Esther to keep her from the duelling ground, and with solid, confident steps, strode back and picked up his pistol. Empty, it dangled at his side as he faced Stamford.

"If you wish to reload, Abbercombe," Stamford said soberly, "I shall allow you the privilege."

Abbercombe stuffed the hand without the pistol into his pocket and shrugged his shoulders. "I could not hit an elephant at this distance, Kevin. Why waste another ball?"

Stamford nodded, raised his own weapon, aimed and fired.

Twenty-one

The company assembled in the Gold Saloon of Fielding House late the following afternoon were all vaguely out of kilter. Lord Wyndham and Captain Willburton-Smythe paced the room. Lady Jessica and Lord Sebastian shared the blue and ivory settee, their hands touching, but their eyes glancing anxiously from painting to mantle to vase to carpet, unable to settle on any one object. Worth sat at the pianoforte, his long, lean fingers flicking across the keys, playing first one melody and then another, never finishing any of them. Lady Worth stood behind him, her hands on his shoulders, her gaze drifting across the side yard beyond the window. Brummell, dressed to the nines as always, stood before a corner china cabinet, his quizzing glass to his eye, examining a multitude of curios in none of which he had the least interest.

In a corner of the room, Harcort, Kettering, Hempstead and April gathered in silence, each thinking their own thoughts, but voicing none of them. In a wing chair Olivia sat and stared into an empty grate, her hands fidgeting nervously in her lap. Harry Hartshorn sat beside her, his leg propped upon a footstool, tossing a pair of dice from one hand to the other. They were all of them so preoccupied with vague bits of thought that when the first roar reached their ears, each and every one of them jumped.

"Argghh, me hearties! An' it be a precious high price ye'll be payin', I vow! Seize 'em, Curmudgeon! Don't be lettin' 'em git by ye! I niver heerd sich insubordination!"

This roar was followed immediately by the scampering of feet

upon the stairway, a goodly number of terrified squeals, an in-
ordinate amount of giggling, erratic but emphatic arfs and grrrs,
and a bellow of "Keelhaul the lot o' 'em, I say! Squelch the
blasted mutiny! Away wi' the whole scurvy crew!"

"Help! Help!" shrieked Ethan rushing into the Gold Saloon
and diving behind his Uncle Sebastian and Aunt Jess.

"Run! Hide!" screeched a madly giggling Frazier dashing toward Lord and Lady Worth, then falling to the carpet and crawling under the pianoforte with Bear bouncing all over him.

"They's affer us, Miss Weebuttonsmite," squeaked Gracie
climbing hurriedly onto that lady's lap. "Don' let 'em git us!
Don' let 'em git us!"

"Lif' me up! Lif' me up!" pleaded Helen, tugging excitedly
on Brummell's pantaloons. "They won' fine me up high!"

The Beau, a grin spreading across his countenance complied
with the request immediately.

More running feet and screams and cries of distress echoed
in the hall, and suddenly Christian staggered backward into the
room, his hands covering his heart. "They got me!" he groaned,
falling into Lord Wyndham's surprised but ready arms.

"Beasts! Villains!" wailed a sweet, husky voice.

"Oh, woe is me!" wailed a second much like it. And with a
great amount of struggling, Amy and Beth dragged Daymee into
the Saloon by his boot heels.

"Close the door! Close the door!" yelled Ethan, and he dashed
across the room, slammed the door shut and ran back behind his
aunt and uncle.

A great tattoo of pounding fists landed upon the closed door
accompanied by a double voiced bray of "It's soup fer whales
ye be me buccaneers!" and with a great whump of a boot against
the door latch, the door sprang open and amidst screams and
screeches two dishevelled looking gentlemen burst into the
room.

"It's Cap'n Crooked an' Cap'n Curmudgeon!" screamed the
four littlest Denbighs at the top of their lungs, while Daymee
and Christian rolled on the floor in gales of laughter and Amy

and Beth scampered, shrieking and laughing, to hide behind Kettering and Harcort who stood stunned, staring at the men in the doorway.

"We needs a magicked word!" squeaked Helen, tugging at Brummell's coat collar excitedly and bouncing in his arms. "We needs a magicked word quick!"

"Snigglehaus," grinned the Beau.

"Sniggle sauce!" shouted Helen.

"Sniggle sauce!" cried Gracie, peering over the wing chair.

"Sniggle sauce!" screamed Ethan and Frazier.

"Sniggle sauce!" yelled Amy, Beth, Chris and Daymee, and Harry, Hempstead, April, Kettering and Harcort in unison while everyone else held their ears and laughed.

"I say, Stamford, what a row we've walked into. Care for a glass of sniggle sauce, old fellow?"

"Don't mind if I do, Abbercombe," nodded the earl amiably. "Noisy lot you have here. Are they generally so berserk?"

"No, no," answered Abbercombe stepping nonchalantly over Chris and Daymee and giving the bellpull a tug. "Only on the last Friday of every third week of every other month. Dawson," he added as the butler answered his ring, "sniggle sauce for everyone if you please."

"S-sniggle sauce, your grace?"

"Indeed. And hop to it, Dawson. Hop to it."

Robin Fanning, beaming happily, entered behind Dawson, whispered in his ear, and the two linking arms, strolled regally out into the hall.

"I have not the least idea what we shall be served," Abbercombe grinned, "but it will, I think, be interesting. Andrew, might I speak to you privately for a moment?"

Captain Willburton-Smythe, delightedly confused, nodded.

"And, Miss Willburton-Smythe, may I have a word with you, if I promise, in front of everyone, not to be the least bit uncivil?" requested the Earl of Stamford, a warmth Olivia had not seen before glowing in the hawk-like eyes.

"I expect so," Olivia complied after a moment, for she could see no danger when the house was so filled with people she loved and trusted. The earl offered her his arm and escorted her from the room and down the hall into the library. Her brother and Abbercombe set off in the opposite direction, leaving the sound of curious buzzing whispers behind them.

Once Stamford had seen Olivia comfortably settled, he began to pace the small room. Then, as if coming to some decision, he pulled a ladder-backed chair up before her and sat down himself. "I owe you a huge apology, Miss Willburton-Smythe," he began quietly. "I cannot expect you to understand, after all I have put you through, how deeply contrite I am, but I am, nonetheless. Not only did I abduct you and threaten you, but I then put you into danger again by duelling Abbercombe. You should not have run between us, my dear. You might well have been killed."

Olivia eyed the gentleman questioningly. "You did not intend to shoot the duke at all, did you?"

"Oh, yes, Miss Willburton-Smythe. I intended to put a period to his existence from the moment he had the gall to return to London. But I had no business to involve you and I regret it sincerely. I spent twenty-two years nurturing my hatred for Cash. It is no excuse, I realize, for terrorizing you so, but it is, nevertheless, the truth. I thought my brother's life bought very cheaply, you know. I expected Abbercombe to hang, not simply to be humiliated and transported, to continue his life in a place where no one even knew of his villainy. And then, to see him return and begin to be accepted—well, I pray you will never understand the agony of such hatred. The thing is that when I met his children and discovered they were aware of my suffering—of their father's infamy—I began to think that he had not escaped so easily as I had supposed. To know he confessed to his own children—that he must have been sorely tormented over it—it gave me pause."

Olivia stared at her lap, smoothing the creases from her apricot silk with nervous fingers. "He was never without guilt, sir, since first it happened, I think. But it was misplaced."

"Indeed," murmured Stamford, and Olivia looked up at him surprised. "But I had no idea how misplaced, Miss Willburton-

Smythe, until I was privileged to speak with a Mrs. Coltrain. She was Janie Wentworth when I knew her. A pretty thing, she was, forever helping her parents around that inn."

"And it was she who—"

"It was she whom Channing lured to Seven Dials, and she whom he attacked, and she who brought the candlestick down across the back of my poor brother's skull. Yes, she told me everything about that night, and more besides. I never did know that Channing had become addicted to opium—" The earl stuttered to a stop, and Olivia could read the grief and bewilderment in his eyes. She reached out to him, taking his hands in her own.

"You were not meant to know, my lord," she whispered.

"No, obviously I was not. I was meant to think that Channing had died a saint at the hands of that rogue, Abbercombe!"

"He felt himself responsible—"

"I know all that, Miss Willburton-Smythe. We have had it out, Cash and I. The unmitigated pride of the man—to assume responsibility for Channing as if he were a total innocent—as if he could not have declined, as if he were dependent upon the judgement of others without will and reason of his own! Channing knew more about opium than Cash ever did. My father was wont to light a pipe from time to time. Even I knew what dangers lay within it—yet Cash assumed that Channing did not. I am relieved I did not hear those damned righteous sentiments from his lips until after the duel, or I should have shot his earlobe off just to remind him of his audacity!" Stamford caught the apprehensive look in Olivia's eyes and smiled drolly at her. "I could have done it, you know. I am the best shot in England, fusty old man or not. As it is, I shot a perfectly good ball into a perfectly good tree and sooner or later it shall make a perfectly good knothole. You have not said, Miss Willburton-Smythe, am I forgiven my recent misdeeds?"

"Yes, my lord," Olivia answered softly, "I believe you are."

"Then I thank you with all my heart." He rose and escorted her back to the Gold Saloon where things had quieted down a good deal and everyone was drinking a most atrocious looking beverage.

Abbercombe and Andrew had returned before them and both looked at Olivia inquiringly as she entered the room on the earl's arm. "Everything all right, my dear?" Andrew asked, walking forward to take her hand and lead her to a chair.

"Now, Papa?" asked Gracie in a very loud whisper.

"No, not now," giggled Bethany, scooping her sister up, little china cup and all and depositing her in Lord Sebastian's lap. "Would you care for some—sniggle sauce—Miss Olivia?"

"Oh, dear," laughed Olivia as Beth poured some of the strange liquid from a teapot into a waiting cup, "I doubt I have had sniggle sauce ever in my life." She lifted the cup and sipped at the liquid, grinned and sipped again.

"It's good, ain't it?" offered Frazier, who sat cross-legged on the floor at Lord Worth's feet. Olivia nodded at the boy and grinned even wider to see that Bear had a cup and saucer of her own right beside him and was busily licking the sweet liquid.

"Aunt Olivia," April began, coming to sit on the arm of her aunt's chair. "Geoffery and I have something to tell you."

"You do?" asked Olivia with a lift of her eyebrows.

"Yes, ma'am," murmured Hempstead nervously, his hands resting upon April's shoulders. "The captain and I have spoken, and I have, ah, offered for April, and she has accepted me."

"Goodness, Andrew, but you have been busy while the earl and I have been away! I am pleased for you, darling," she added giving the girl a squeeze, "and for you as well, Geoffery."

"Now, Papa?" asked Helen, seated happily in Brummell's lap.

"No, not yet, sweetness," whispered the Beau, kissing the top of her head. "Lady Amy, may we have some more sniggle sauce?"

Amy picked up a teapot and refilled their cups. "Would you care for some, my lord?" she queried, carrying the pot to the couch where the earl sat and taking a place beside him. He nodded and she filled his cup, then set the teapot on the table and clasped her hands in her lap. In a moment Christian came to sit beside her and Damian to the earl's other side. "We wish to thank you for not killing Papa," Amaryllis said to the earl with a quick smile.

"Yes, and now we hope you will not kill Viscount Harcort," snickered Christian.

Harcort, with a grin, offered Bethany his arm and escorted her to his father. "I have the pleasure to tell you, sir, that the duke has given me permission to seriously court Lady Beth, though I may not offer for her until the Season ends and only if I have your permission to do so. I hope you are not angry, Father."

Stamford laughed. "Seriously court? Whose phrase was that?"

"Papa's," Amaryllis giggled.

Stamford's gaze sought Abbercombe across the room, then he turned to Bethany. "I am amazed you wish to have anything at all to do with Harcort when his father did such evil things," he sighed. "Are you not afraid I shall lose my mind again?"

"Oh, no, sir," smiled Bethany, bending to kiss his cheek. "Papa promised not to do anything else to set you off, ever. And besides, he is much more maggoty than you and more pigheaded, and David does not hold that against him."

Amaryllis's laughter trilled through the room, and Kettering winked at Hempstead and then crossed to where she sat. "And I have received like permission to court Lady Amy," he said softly, "if she will agree to let me do so."

"What! Mr. Kettering, you never said a word!" Amy cried in surprise.

"How odd," smiled Christian. "Daymee and I and Harry knew."

"Yes, and you had better agree to it, Amy," proclaimed Damian, "for you know how it will be if Beth has a serious suitor and you do not. Everything will be all topsy-turvy around here."

"Oh, I would be honored," exclaimed Amaryllis blushing.

"Well, Hartshorn," Lord Wyndham drawled amiably, "have you nothing to announce?"

"No, sir," Harry answered, blushing almost as red as Amy. "I am afraid I do not have a—a young lady."

"No," agreed Wyndham with a nod, "and a good thing too, I dare say. For how will you take over for The Rogue if you must busy yourself with courting a young lady?"

"Harry's gonna be a spy!" shouted Ethan, wiggling joyously on the settee between Lord Sebastian and Lady Jess.

" 'Bout time!" exclaimed Frazier.

Hartshorn's eyes sought Abbercombe's, and the duke shrugged. "You needn't if you don't care to, Harry. But I am getting too old and tired, and Wyndham and I thought you eminently qualified, with Hempstead's support, of course."

"I am honored," grinned Harry as Hempstead came to shake his hand. "Though how I shall go about it without so much as one child to lend a hand, I must contemplate gravely."

"Well, if everyone is determined to announce everything at one and the same time," Lord Sebastian said with a glint in his sky-blue eyes, "then I suppose I ought to tell you, Jess, that I am abandoning my campaign for M.P."

"You are? But why, Sebastian?"

"It is because of me," Abbercombe muttered, his shoulders resting against the mantlepiece. "He has sunk himself."

"It is because of Cash," Sebastian Denbigh agreed with a grin. "I have received a better offer."

"I would consider it a much better offer," murmured Brummell, watching Helen blow bubbles in her sniggle sauce.

"Do you know everything about everyone, brat?" queried Abbercombe. "What offer, 'Bastian?"

"To become personal envoy for the Prince Regent in St. Petersburg. I am expected to make use of your friendship with Tzar Alexander, of course. You would not mind, would you, Cash?"

Lady Jessica's eyes grew wide with wonder. "Russia?" she said. "We are going to Russia, Sebastian?"

"Well, I have only agreed to it tentatively. We shall not go if it does not appeal to you or if Cash is opposed to it."

"St. Petersburg is wonderful, Aunt Jess!" Damian exclaimed.

"Yes, and then there is Minsk," added Christian with a face that made Ethan and Frazier giggle.

"I should be delighted to introduce you to Alexander," grinned the duke. "You have no obstacle to hurdle there. You and Jess must only decide and let me know. And you, Aunt Margaret? Have you not one single announcement?"

"None," said the dowager with a sad shake of her head but a gleam in her eyes. "Old ladies seldom have announcements to make, unless you consider the fact that Wyndham and I have agreed to make a match of it worth an announcement."

"What? You and Uncle Sully? After all these years?" asked Abbercombe, astonished.

"Well, we had to speak of something while you were off at the Rose and Crown and we were here keeping an eye upon the children as you requested," mumbled Wyndham. "And somehow, the subject of second marriages arose."

"You old dry boots!" exclaimed the duke. "I told Harry to stay and watch the children. I never asked you to do so."

"You didn't?" Lady Margaret gasped. "Oh! And Sylvester stayed the entire night!"

"Well, you rarely come to London, my dear," Wyndham soothed, his eyes twinkling. "And I seldom get to the provinces. I thought to seize my opportunity when it came. You cannot back out now, Margaret. I will not let you. We belong together."

"Eugenia?" urged Worth quietly.

"Do you think I should, Edward?"

"How can you be shy of the subject in a house littered with children, my dear? Besides, I have told Cash and Beau already."

"Told what?" asked Frazier, leaning back to stare up at the lady through Worth's knees.

"That we are going to have a baby," said Eugenia shyly.

"Oh, how wonderful!" cried Lady Jess, Olivia, April, Amy and Beth, which set the gentlemen all to laughing.

When the laughter died away, Brummell cocked an eyebrow at Sebastian, whispered in Helen's ear, took her tea cup from her and lifted her to the floor. Sebastian Denbigh did the same with

Grace. Both little girls rushed to their father, each tugging a hand from his pocket, and led him out into the center of the room. "Now, Papa," Brummell and Sebastian ordered together.

"Yes, now, Papa," Amy and Beth urged, going to stand beside him. Christian and Damian and Ethan and Frazier raced to the center of the room as well, and after a bit of whispering, giggling, poking and rearranging, which brought Bear dodging between legs to jump at the tassels on the boys' boots, they all stood remarkably quiet around their father, smiling angelically in Olivia's direction.

"Now, Papa," hissed all eight of them again.

Olivia chuckled. She could not imagine what was going on, but she could not resist the sight of them all so innocently assembled, especially when Abbercombe's face began to flush.

"Papa! Now!" Christian urged again.

"Well, but, it is not p-precisely how I pictured it," stuttered the duke. "I mean, I know I said—but—I thought first, perhaps, Miss Willburton-Smythe might like to accompany me for a walk in the garden or—or—something."

"We don'ts got a garden, Papa," squeaked Gracie impatiently.

"Whatever is going on?" giggled Olivia.

"Yes, explain yourself, Abbercombe," teased the captain with a wide grin. "I, for one, am interested to hear how you do it."

"Well, the thing is, Olivia, that we have—the children and I—No, I—I have soon to make a decision regarding what is to be done with—Chembesley Hall—my estate in—in—"

"Yorkshire," provided Sebastian, chuckling.

"Yorkshire," echoed Abbercombe. "And I would—would like to have your opin—opinion in the matter."

Lady Jess almost shrieked, but her hands flew to cover her mouth and it sounded only like a little gasp.

Olivia looked up at him, confused. "You what?"

"I would appreciate your opinion, Olivia."

"But, I don't—oh!" cried Olivia, her hands flying to her instantly reddening cheeks. She could not believe that he meant what she thought he meant. Her fine green eyes searched his hopefully. "I thought," she whispered dazedly, "that you did not care to consider my opinion unless I were to become mistress of this establishment."

"I did say that," the duke acknowledged, an unholy mirth lighting his eyes, "when I was being pigheaded. Now I am asking for your opinion. I mean to consider it in all things."

"Papa wants to know, Miss Weebuttonsmite," announced Frazier, jiggling up and down, "if you will be our mistress."

"No, he doesn't!" cried Christian, bursting into laughter along with everyone else in the room.

"Papa wants to know will you marries us!" squealed Helen and Gracie above the hilarity, running to Olivia and climbing into her lap, followed closely by Ethan and Frazier who snuggled against the sides of her chair.

"Will you be our mama? Please?" asked Frazier plaintively.

"Gracie an' Helen ain't never had a mama," murmured Ethan beseechingly, "an' me an' Frazier only for a little."

Olivia felt tears begin to sting the back of her eyes, and her vision blurred. She did not see the adults in the room rise and leave, but she saw very well how Chris and Daymee came and lifted Ethan and Frazier and carried them away, and how Amy and Beth took the girls from her lap as well. And then Abbercombe was on one knee before her, handkerchief in hand, his eyes bright with the oddest combination of mischief and anxiety.

"You are becoming a regular watering pot, you know," he whispered, dabbing tenderly at her tears. "My darling, sweet, adorable, fearless, Olivia. I love you with all my heart. I am not young and not socially acceptable—I am, however, frightfully rich," he chuckled. And he chuckled even more when Olivia laughed back at him, her green eyes alight. "That's much better. You are almost as good a giggler as Frazier. Olivia, dear heart, will you marry me? I have asked your brother, you know, and he did not protest."

"Y-you did?" Olivia hiccuped. "You actually asked Andrew?"

"Yes, and it was like asking Ethan if I might stay up late. But the good captain was most civil and only laughed for two or three

inutes. Will you marry me, Olivia? Please? Blow," he added
nexpectedly, holding his handkerchief to her nose.

Olivia took it from his hands, blew her nose heartily and, smil-
ng, stuffed the handkerchief into his coat pocket. "Yes," she said
oftly, and before she had a chance to say another word, he stood
nd swept her up into his arms. His lips pressed hers tenderly
nd then more roughly, and finally with a passion so strong she
ould feel it set fire to her soul.

When at last their lips parted, she felt a tiny tug upon her dress,
nd then another, and Abbercombe's amazingly blue eyes
aughed. "Are you, perchance, my dear, being tugged at?"

"Yes, my dear," she whispered.

"I expect you shall have to accustom yourself to it," he
rinned, and loosening his hold, but not releasing her, he looked
own at four sets of wishful blue eyes.

"Does she gonna, Papa?" asked Gracie wistfully.

"Forever af'er?" asked Helen, hopefully.

"Is she gonna marry us?" Ethan queried, jiggling nervously.

"All of us?" added Frazier, Bear held tightly in his arms.

"Sorry, Papa, they got away," Christian laughed, sliding to a
top so abruptly that Damian, still running, bumped into him
rom behind and sent him toppling over Frazier and Bear, who
nocked Ethan into Gracie and Helen.

Olivia burst into laughter just as Amy and Beth came running
p to sort out the pile of giggling children. "We're sorry, Papa,"
Amy grinned, tugging Frazier to his feet and tickling him. "The
rchins could not wait any longer."

"Did you say everything you should, Papa?" Beth asked,
cooping Gracie up into her arms. "Just as you ought?"

"Yes," laughed Olivia, "he said everything he should exactly
s he ought, and I am determined to marry him, and we shall all
o to St. Petersburg on our wedding trip, shall we not?"

"What? All of them? On our wedding trip?" moaned Abber-
ombe with a touch of drama equal to Kimble's best perform-
nces.

"Indeed!" proclaimed Olivia, her eyes alight with mirth.

A rowdy cheer went up from ecstatic children who scrambled to kiss and hug her as Abbercombe held her prisoner in his arms and whispered in her ear. "You are a rogue, Olivia Willburton-Smythe, and I am going to make you pay for it!"

About the Author

Judith A. Lansdowne grew up in Kenosha, Wisconsin. Following graduation from high school she moved to New York City where she attended the American Academy of Dramatic Arts and spent several years acting and puppeteering. She returned to the midwest to continue her education, and after receiving her BA from the University of Wisconsin-Parkside worked as a scriptwriter, videographer, journalist and editor before turning to fiction writing full time. She and her husband recently retired to the shores of Lake Guntersville, Alabama where they are pursuing careers in fishing. They write when the weather is bad.

ZEBRA REGENCIES ARE THE TALK OF THE TON!

A REFORMED RAKE (4499, $3.99)
by Jeanne Savery

After governess Harriet Cole helped her young charge flee to France—and the designs of a despicable suitor, more trouble soon arrived in the person of a London rake. Sir Frederick Carrington insisted on providing safe escort back to England. Harriet deemed Carrington more dangerous than any band of brigands, but secretly relished matching wits with him. But after being taken in his arms for a tender kiss, she found herself wondering— *could* a lady find love with an irresistible rogue?

A SCANDALOUS PROPOSAL (4504, $4.99)
by Teresa DesJardien

After only two weeks into the London season, Lady Pamela Premington has already received her first offer of marriage. If only it hadn't come from the *ton's* most notorious rake, Lord Marchmont. Pamela had already set her sights on the distinguished Lieutenant Penford, who had the heroism and honor that made him the ideal match. Now she had to keep from falling under the spell of the seductive Lord so she could pursue the man more worthy of her love. Or was he?

A LADY'S CHAMPION (4535, $3.99)
by Janice Bennett

Miss Daphne, art mistress of the Selwood Academy for Young Ladies, greeted the notion of ghosts haunting the academy with skepticism. However, to avoid rumors frightening off students, she found herself turning to Mr. Adrian Carstairs, sent by her uncle to be her "protector" against the "ghosts." Although, Daphne would accept no interference in her life, she *would* accept aid in exposing any spectral spirits. What she never expected was for Adrian to expose the secret wishes of her hidden heart . . .

CHARITY'S GAMBIT (4537, $3.99)
by Marcy Stewart

Charity Abercrombie reluctantly embarks on a London season in hopes of making a suitable match. However she cannot forget the mysterious Dominic Castille—and the kiss they shared—when he fell from a tree as she strolled through the woods. Charity does not know that the dark and dashing captain harbors a dangerous secret that will ensnare them both in its web—leaving Charity to risk certain ruin and losing the man she so passionately loves . . .

Available wherever paperbacks are sold, or order direct from the Publisher. Send cover price plus 50¢ per copy for mailing and handling to Penguin USA, P.O. Box 999, c/o Dept. 17109, Bergenfield, NJ 07621. Residents of New York and Tennessee must include sales tax. DO NOT SEND CASH.